THOMAS KENEALLY

The author was born in 1935 in New South Wales, Australia. Although originally destined for the Church, he became a teacher and began writing in 1962. His first novel, THE PLACE AT WHITTON was published the following year. He became a full-time writer in 1965 and since then has won many prizes and received great acclaim for his work. His novels THE CHANT OF JIMMIE BLACKSMITH, GOSSIP FROM THE FOREST and CONFEDERATES were all shortlisted for the Booker Prize and in 1982 SCHINDLER'S ARK won the Booker.

Thomas Keneally now lives in Sydney with his wife and two teenage daughters.

sceptre

Thomas Keneally

A FAMILY MADNESS

Copyright © 1985 by Serpentine Publishing Pty Ltd

First published in Great Britain in 1985 by Hodder and Stoughton Ltd

Sceptre edition 1986
Third impression 1990

Sceptre Books is an imprint of Hodder and Stoughton Paperbacks, a division of Hodder and Stoughton Ltd

British Library C.I.P.

Keneally, Thomas
  A family madness.
  I. Title
  823[F]   PR9619.3.K46

  ISBN 0-340-39459-5

Printed and bound in Great Britain for Hodder and Stoughton Paperbacks, a division of Hodder and Stoughton Ltd., Mill Road, Dunton Green, Sevenoaks, Kent (Editorial Office: 47 Bedford Square, London, WC1 3DP) by Richard Clay (The Chaucer Press) Ltd., Bungay, Suffolk. Photoset by Rowland Phototypesetting Ltd., Bury St Edmunds, Suffolk.

To Judith,
who bore the weight
of this book

PART ONE

ONE

Terry Delaney's father often remarked on the state of Main Street, Penrith, in the hard times of the '80s. 'The shops that sell real things close down,' he said, 'and in their place you get the bloody juju medicine stalls.'

By juju medicine stalls Delaney the elder meant the agencies of anxious governments, local, state, Commonwealth; the nine-to-five havens for those to whom heroin, spouses or employers had been cruel; the shopfronts behind which the bewildered were counselled. Off Main Street, on the western edge of the park, stood the house which offered financial advice to those who no longer had finances. This was municipal mercy. If you wanted the mercy of the state you went to Youth and Community Services, and the grace of the Commonwealth was incarnated in Social Services. They all, according to observation and the opinion of Delaney senior, did more business than the barber. At any of them you could meet the same tousled and bruised wives, and men who had once worked at the abattoirs at Homebush or Riverstone or at the forklift factory at Flemington or the heavy engineering at Clyde. As workers they had been loudly discontented and whimsically bought Lotto tickets each week, prepared to wait a lifetime for the gods of the numbers to do them a favour. Now they were reflective and awesomely docile, half-shaven, a sort of fluff of ennui caught in the crevices of their faces. They tried to turn out the world's thinnest roll-your-owns while they waited for the bureaucrats of small bounties to get around to them.

They were the men Terry Delaney had always presumed he'd never sit amongst. Yet when he did give up a day's work to sit amidst these men and their women and wait for a counsellor to speak to him, he no longer had the pride left to make it clear that he was there because of love and not for want. And now, being desperate, he knew why people came to these places. You couldn't help but expect that one of those public servants could produce from behind his desk the glittering answer.

Delaney was there for that very answer. He explained how Danielle Kabbel was a hostage, her child a hostage too, all to old Rudi Kabbel's madness.

'You claim to be the child's father?' the counsellor asked him, used to claims that other parties were lunatics. She was a small dark girl who looked Greek.

'I registered her birth, April 2, 1984,' said Delaney, finding the birth certificate and putting it on the desk in front of the girl. A child social worker. I place my daughter in the hands of this seminar attender.

The girl's arms were stick thin. Delaney feared she was probably one of those inner city vegetarians; her body inadequate for rescuing his child.

He produced his driving licence. 'See that. The same signature as on the registration. I want someone to please go and look at the place. No electricity, no heating. For all I know the water's been cut off. How can they warm a bottle for the child? Without electricity?'

'If I find the conditions you describe,' the girl said, 'there would be grounds for removing the infant from the mother's custody. That wouldn't mean your daughter would be automatically given to you. You would have to apply for custody separately. It may in any case be necessary to house the mother with the child if it is still breastfeeding.' The idea of Alexandra at Danielle's breast made him dizzy with hope.

'Get my baby out of that house,' he pleaded. 'I can't, because Warwick Kabbel threatened me with both barrels of his shotgun when I went round there. But they wouldn't do anything like that to you, because you're in authority.'

'Oh,' she said, laughing bitterly, 'you want me to face firearms, Mr Delaney.'

'I don't mind facing them myself, I'm desperate. But it doesn't do any good.' He could not explain to her how safe she'd be, how law-abiding and polite the Kabbel boys would be. They would have been polite to the man from Prospect Council who came to cut their water supply. Despite the armoury they kept in the house, they understood precisely who held the power in this pre-wave world. Hence he was certain this girl's beansprout authority could bring the Kabbels down.

'Are you able to get the cops to go with you?' he asked.

'I certainly can. And will.'

She made him ecstatic.

'Might not be until this afternoon, Mr Delaney,' she told him. The weariness of attending to a hundred misused children was apparent in her voice.

He drove three miles down the highway to Kabbel's and parked in the triangle of gum trees between the railway line and the cluster of little townhouses. They had architectural pretensions. Delaney imagined they had been designed by the sort of young architect who lived at Kirribili, wore open-neck shirts, drove a BMW. He knew too that whatever the pretensions of the design, there were no pretensions in Kabbel's place, no wall hangings, no light fittings, no light.

By edging twenty paces down the verge of this small clump of trees Delaney could see Warwick Kabbel sitting on a patch of lawn, a baby basket beside him. In it must lie the disputed child, the daughter Delaney had registered as Alexandra. He was grateful to the Kabbels for knowing that a child needs sunlight, for taking account of her amongst their berserk schemes. There must have been a sound from the basket, for Uncle Warwick smiled obliquely at it. Uncle Warwick, booby-trap expert, wielder of Magnums and shotguns.

For some reason, Warwick's smile caused Delaney to suffer a momentary loss of faith in the girl at Youth and Community Services he'd spent the morning persuading. I ought to kidnap the baby, seize Danielle. I shouldn't have spent the morning talking to vegetarian social workers.

Warwick picked up a stalk of grass and placed it as a gift in the basket. Delaney imagined the child's supine hands lying on the baby blanket, the stalk of grass between them, a sceptre.

*   *   *

At noon Warwick hoisted the baby basket and took it inside as
if the time had come for the child to feed and sleep, as if the
good order of electricity still ran into the house on a line, as if
the water of social sanity were still surging in the pipes.

Two further hours passed. From the Blue Mountains to Parramatta, from Richmond to Penrith was a great parish of unhappy
and endangered children, so the counsellor implied. His unhappy
and endangered child had to join the queue. He spent the time, he
kept moisture in his mouth, by sucking – as on a stone – on the
courses open to him. For the child's sake he could offer to pay
Kabbel's bills, but with the Kabbels cut electricity didn't seem to
be an issue; they would let Warwick, who was to be the enforcer
in their paradise, drive him from the door with one of their
weapons. He could pay his friend Brian Stanton to help him kidnap
the child, but Stanton was out on bail awaiting trial for man-
slaughter and Delaney was his surety. And he could wait in the
shade of the gums, in the pleasant autumn air, in the thin murmur
of dying insects, for the vegetarian to arrive, a skinny woman
maybe, but with the fibre of the law in her.

It was nearly two in the afternoon when he saw not the
counsellor but a man in a suit drive up to Kabbel's door. Behind
the man's Commodore came a patrol car with two wallopers.
One of the police Delaney saw emerge was Steve Rammage, a
fullback from the local club. There's leverage I hadn't thought
of. Now I'm notorious. I've broken a jaw, been suspended for
six months – more visible now, under suspension, than I ever
was as just another promising five-eighth. The wallopers in the
club would do anything for me.

The man in the suit knocked on the door. It was answered
by Warwick. Delaney expected that: Warwick was the Kabbels'
delegate to the outside world. Warwick answered all enquiries.
There seemed to be a polite and reasonable conversation
between Warwick and the man in the suit and Delaney could hear
no raised voices. The man handed Warwick a folded document.
Delaney understood at once. This was an eviction. He was sure
Warwick would be explaining that the child was asleep and that
certain things would need to be packed – his manual of explosives, for example.

For two or three seconds Danielle appeared at the upstairs window, a neat blonde woman in a floral dress, a cardigan worn over her shoulders like a cape. She looked down tranquilly on the large young policemen who had escorted the estate agent with the eviction notice to her door. In the edge of the patch of scrub Delaney flinched and raised his wrist to his mouth.

'Oh, you berserk poor bitch,' he murmured against the beat of his pulse. He could feel the darkness of the house bulking and stirring behind her. She turned quietly from the window as if someone behind her had spoken.

You're coming out of that dark bloody hole. That cave without water and power. He could rush down the road and promise the estate agent a month's rent if that was the point. The Kabbels, however, had lost interest in rent, just the same as in water and power. Kabbel himself still owned firearms worth thousands of dollars to enthusiasts; the house was furnished with weaponry. He could sell off half of Uncle Security's arsenal and still have an armoury adequate for starting a new company or a small revolution.

At the door Warwick excused himself and went inside the house. The door itself remained ajar. Waiting, the estate agent turned back to the constables and they spoke softly between themselves, old and – it seemed to Delaney – *sad* hands at evictions. As his father, old Greg, would have said, watching the young coppers, 'Use the working class to piss the working class off.' If only the Kabbel case was just another instance in the class war.

It was not impossible that Danielle would emerge carrying Alexandra in her arms and look around for Delaney. In his daydream, the eviction would shake her loose from her father by mere cumulative effect. First no light, then no water, now no roof. It had to have an impact on a bright girl, it had to cause a bit of doubt in her. There had been no wave, no great ice-melt. The desert was still the desert. They still got bugger-all rain at Ayers Rock. The map was still the map. Rudi Kabbel had delivered her nothing except a dark hutch where she couldn't even warm her baby's milk or give her the breast in any comfort.

From the shade of the gums Delaney believed he now could

hear the Kabbel family moving things – the chest perhaps, the arms cabinet. The young wallopers would open their eyes when they saw Rudi's firearms, but Rudi would smile and show them his business card which said Uncle Security. His pose – an honest professional whose company had in a bad time itself gone bad – would only partially satisfy them. It came to Delaney with a sense of unfamiliar joy that there was no way that Rudi Kabbel could bring his property out into the sunshine on the pavement and not instantly attract the attention of a number of instruments of government, including the New South Wales police and the Department of Youth and Community Services for whom the skinny Greek worked. Rudi would be forced into new directions. The family would disintegrate under scrutiny, and Delaney would pick up the two fragments which were all he wanted of life.

Again he believed he could hear the hard bark of furniture runners against the upstairs floor of Kabbel's townhouse, but no one came to the door to explain the delay to the estate agent and the police. Delaney saw the agent approach the not fully closed door, call towards the kitchen, open the door wider, make a trumpet of his hands and yell up the stairs. He turned for a moment to the police and then the three went indoors. No more than ninety seconds later the estate agent burst out of the door, fell on to the lawn where Alexandra had this morning been placed in her basket, and rolled writhing there. Delaney wondered if Rudi or more likely Warwick had shot the man, if the revolution had begun. Both police ran upright out of the house and one of them bent over the agent, giving aid. The other, the handy fullback, went to the patrol car and reached in for the mouthpiece of the two-way radio.

Delaney raced from his cover amongst the gums and sprinted over vacant land and into the townhouse road. Constable Rammage turned to him a face almost transparent, so drained of substance that it was no more than a filament.

'Oh holy Jesus, Delaney!' Rammage cried, beginning to weep. 'Who are those people?'

TWO

Delaney had first met Rudi Kabbel by the park one humid 3 a.m.
in January 1983. The southerly for which Sydneysiders always
wait on humid nights had not arrived, but weathermen were
assuring a desperate population that it would turn up late the
following morning, flush the humidity away, and restore everyone to well-being. Delaney and his partner Stanton, though they
worked separately, always met up in the small hours to share
coffee from a thermos they took turns in providing.

Delaney and Stanton were responsible as officers of Castle
Security for a range of properties, including a Subaru dealership
and a Rural Bank. At least Stanton persisted in calling it a Rural
Bank, the way he continued to call Westpac the Bank of New
South Wales. You can bank on the Wales, said the old slogan of
the New South Wales. You can wank on the bales, Stanton liked
to say of the Rural, now renamed the State.

The Sun Ya Restaurant was also in the care of Delaney and
Stanton, as was a caravan and trailer dealership and a yard full
of swimming-pool liners. These last lay bluely on their sides like
gigantic children's bathtubs, like – as Brian Stanton said –
bedpans for bloody Gulliver. Within Castle's mandate there fell
as well the premises of a licensed club. During his patrols,
Delaney saw many a late-night inebriate enter his Commodore
and drive away in perfect safety, at least until he reached the
highway, where carnage was always a possibility.

On the night of their meeting with Kabbel, Delaney and
Stanton emerged from the back lane behind Franklin's supermarket and saw Kabbel sitting in the park by the bandstand, his
nightwatch lunch spread before him, a picnicker in the abandoned
shopping centre. He looked so strange in his blue uniform – it
was not the blue most security men wore, it was what Delaney

thought of as a foreign blue. Delaney could tell too – by a sort
of musk of hostility given off by his friend – that the man's
tranquil mastication annoyed Stanton.

As they got closer, Delaney noticed that the top button of the
man's collar was done up and that this added to his foreignness.
On his collars were two brass badges of four circles arranged
rather like the Olympic rings, though there were only two rings
in the top row as in the bottom. Stanton approached the man in
that jovially hostile manner he had picked up in the New South
Wales police force.

'Enjoying our tucker?' Stanton asked.

The man was tall, Germanic-looking, bullet-headed, with spiky
blond hair turning in places to a grey poll.

'Would you like some?' the man asked, pushing the packet of
sandwiches towards Stanton, whimsically reducing him to the
status of a beggar. Stanton said no thanks and moved his
shoulders threateningly inside his blue shirt. But his authority
seemed to Delaney to be debased by this muscle flexing. It may
have meant more had he still been a walloper. It would then
have conveyed to the citizen, even to this foreigner, that Stanton
was thinking of a range of possible provocations, and such
charges as – resisting arrest, using obscene and indecent
language, malicious damage to a police shirt.

'You work for Castle,' said the man reading the label on
their shirts. 'I used to work for Ramparts. Such references to
medieval fortifications! Now I'm in business for myself.'

The man took from his breast pocket a wad of business cards
and peeled off one for Delaney and then one for Stanton. The
business cards displayed the four rings. Below them was the
name Uncle Security, and below the name of the business, in
larger lettering still, *Rudi Kabbel, Managing Director*. The card
conveyed that if not quite a prince of the industry Kabbel was
at least local nobility. His office, he said, was in Parramatta and
he employed a staff of four. In Penrith he had a number of motor
dealerships, a ship's chandler who supplied boaters using the
Nepean river on weekends, and a timber yard.

'My real name is RADISLAW,' said Kabbel, spelling it. 'But
Australians can't handle that.'

Stanton mellowed enough to try half a cup of coffee from Kabbel's thermos. 'My sons, Warwick and Scott, work for me,' the man conceded in return. A family business did not have the same credibility as one which employed total strangers.

'Warwick and Scott,' Stanton murmured. 'Long way from Rudi, isn't it?'

'My wife wanted them to be given Australian names. We're divorced now, but the names linger on. My daughter, though – she runs the control room – I dug in over that name. She's Danielle, after my mother. Danielle is a French name.'

'And this Kabbel, it's French, eh?' Stanton didn't entirely dislike the idea of the French. The people who had once knifed him belonged to a more southerly and swarthy race than that.

'It's Belorussian.'

'Come again?'

'Belorussia. Belorussia. Bela Rus. White Ruthenia.'

'Where's that when it's there?' Stanton asked.

'That is a land of milk and honey which has never been allowed to go its way,' Rudi Kabbel explained. 'A land of plains and forests and gentle hills. You know Lithuania, you know the Baltic?'

Both Stanton and Delaney nodded, though their geography was not exact and the man knew it.

'It's east of Poland. If you want to invade Russia, as has sometimes been tried, you'll have to go through Minsk. Minsk is the capital.'

'Oh,' said Stanton, whose sense of where everything in Eastern Europe was had been improved by an admiration for Lech Walesa. 'You come from Russia?'

'The Soviets would say I do. I do not say I do. I am a Belorussian. We are different in language and religion. Some of us, anyhow. If there was any international justice, we would be our own nation.'

'Like Queenslanders,' Delaney suggested. He could see Kabbel frown but then decide to yield to this small joke about Australian regional feeling. Whenever later he was debating the nature of Kabbel with himself, the question of whether Kabbel was a fanatic, Delaney would remember how in the humid night

Kabbel had given in with a smile and allowed Bela Rus to be compared whimsically with a northern Australian state.

'You could say like Queensland,' Kabbel admitted at last. But, he said, at least the Queenslanders could make their own mistakes. They had the Barrier Reef, which they were ruining for themselves. They had the rain forests which they were decimating and profaning. All the Belorussian treasures had been destroyed by other people, by the Poles, the Litvaks, above all by the Russians. For example, the Belorussians had and treasured a race of buffalo, of bison, like the American bison which Buffalo Bill had hunted. 'Now you didn't know that, did you, boys?' he asked Stanton and Delaney, winking once at them, a heavy comic-opera wink. Though Delaney confessed he didn't, Stanton wouldn't admit to any ignorance of Belorussian wildlife.

These bison were called *zubr*. Kabbel wrote it down for them on the back of one of his Uncle Security cards. You found them in the Forest of Belovezh. The Russians and the Germans, their two great armies, had hunted them out in world war one and world war two. 'What they know they don't own,' said Kabbel, 'the Russians shit on. And what they did to the *zubr* they have done to all the Belorussian treasures.'

'The Americans are bastards too,' said Stanton, not so much to back up Kabbel's argument but to balance the ideological scales. Stanton was in fact very pro-American but didn't want this clever alien to get away with being so expressive.

'They are both unjust kingdoms,' Kabbel conceded. He looked wryly at Delaney. 'But if you were, say, a cosmic force and had to choose a side, which one would you?'

'America,' said Delaney, smiling as he played a divinity. 'For a while, at least. Give them a burl, I reckon.'

'Exactly, my intelligent friend,' said Kabbel – Delaney thought the man's tone patronising. 'For a time! No power gets eternal chances, chances that go on for ever.'

He excused himself then. He had a casual working nearby in the Mount Druitt area and had to look in on him.

'Do they all wear that turquoise bloody uniform of yours?' asked Stanton.

'It's the company uniform,' murmured Kabbel, firm but not being doctrinaire about it. Delaney would remember that as well at a later date. 'A looser cut of shirt. All very well for you blokes' (he pronounced it 'blouks') '. . . your shirts hug the body and remind criminals of Robert Redford or some such. But our shirts allow a layer of air between the fabric and the body, and on such a night as this a layer of air is to be welcomed.'

Delaney sweated all the more at this talk of cool spaces beneath garments, and his shirt seemed to cramp his damp shoulders.

Terry Delaney was the husband of Gina Terracetti, herself the child of a sturdy Italian couple from Palermo. Aldo Terracetti was a market gardener, had left a tribal history of centuries of labour behind him in Sicily to labour just as hard, though to better profit, fifteen miles south of Penrith in a shallow farming depression called Bringelly, one of the few places in Sydney where in winter water left overnight in a bucket or a dog's dish would grow a crust of ice, and which in summer, day after day in the dogdays of January and February, led the metropolitan maximum temperatures. Delaney loved the Terracettis because they had a composure that triumphed over temperature and because they had bred for him Gina, a good wife but not in the bruised, subdued manner of Stanton's wife, Denise. Gina was a robust person, a woman of opinions. Old Mrs Terracetti – not so old in fact – said it was the Australian high school education. It turned women into harpies who challenged their husbands' authority.

Delaney sensed in old Terracetti an honest and ancient connection with the earth, something he had passed on to his larger-boned daughter Gina. Her skin was olive, sometimes reddish like terracotta – Delaney might call her a squaw as a joke, but he never said it without a tremor of desire. Her features represented symbolically to him the Sicily she and he had never visited – strong, with a tendency towards the craggy. In middle age, he supposed, they would be especially craggy, like her mother's. All of history, Delaney thought, from the Romans onwards, looked calmly out of those features. The

Delaneys made love in the mornings, after Delaney had got back from his night patrols, before Gina went off to her work at a discount clothing store in St Mary's. As often as not they ended with Delaney entering Gina from behind, from those well-made flanks which somehow to Delaney signified the geography of the world. As they both cried, Delaney had a sense of remaking and honouring the earth. He was sure that he would not get that sense from anyone else.

He'd been unfaithful to her once, a public infidelity he could not find the words to convey to Gina, but which other men (and perhaps some of their women) you were likely to meet in Main Street knew about. It had occurred the previous October when the third grade team – third grade being the lowest form of professional play – had for the first time in its history reached the grand final at the Sydney Cricket Ground, playing a bloody, defensive game which it lost 12–8 to South Sydney. After the grieving, the Leagues Club had offered the team a trip to Hawaii instead of a grand-final match payment. You had to pay your own accommodation, that was all, but it would be at discount rates. Gina insisted that he should go, even though she knew some of the wild buggers like Steve Mansfield, a second-rower who had an evil reputation for twisting the testicles of the opposing hooker, would play the sort of merry hell for which he was notorious from Parramatta to the mountains.

One night at the Ilikai there had been a party in the adjoining rooms of Steve Mansfield and Chicka Hays. The Maui Wow-ie the team had been smoking for the whole week suffused the air, an acrid sweetness which enlarged the brain. Chicka had filled his bath with ice in which sat dozens of cans of Primo, the Hawaiian beer of which none of the team approved but on which, in the absence of Australian beer, they were willing to incapacitate themselves. As each of the guests arrived – various American girls and a few vacationing Australians – Chicka would hand them a freezing can of the stuff. 'Crook beer, love, but the best we can do!'

Delaney sat in a chair in Mansfield's room, by the window, watching Diamond Head, which he had never thought he would see; a majestic slope and inside it a fort. The idea appealed to

him. It was an example of American extravagance. Only the
Americans would stick their forts inside ancient volcanoes. He
was smoking the stuff like everyone else. Such a thing was
possible to confide to Gina. It would be a delight to see her
scandalised. Delaney holidaying on the silvery fringes of nar-
cotics. Delaney who watched large green headlands. At the far
end of Waikiki! Imagine.

He could afterwards not clearly remember the face of the girl
who came up to him. She was slighter than Gina. Her hair was
brown, cut short for the heat. Her skin was fine-grained. She
was what Delaney thought of as 'un-ethnic' and showed no traces
of any specific origins. Compared to Diamond Head she was not
a primary object of notice. Nor was Mansfield's bed, on which
the two wingers were rubbing gin from the refrigerator bar on
the breasts of a Chinese-American girl and licking them clean.
That sort of thing was to be expected. A Rugby League team
on a celebratory journey had to create a store of outrageous
events to take home. These tales – in the tradition of Rugby
League clubs – should cover four aspects: sexual excess; excess
of alcohol; jovial damage to such property as lobby fountains or
alterations of the clocks behind the reception desk which told
what time it was in Copenhagen and Tokyo; and peripheral
encounters with local police. As arousing as some of the scenes
might be, Delaney, inhaling the smoke, saw himself by temperament and marriage as a witness.

'Charlene,' the slight girl told Delaney now as introduction.

'I'm Terry Delaney,' said Delaney.

'Birth sign?' she said, closing her eyes and seeming to grasp
in the air for the images of the Zodiac.

'Libra. But that's all bloody nonsense, love.'

She opened her eyes so quickly that Delaney thought that his
pot-enlarged senses could hear them click apart.

'You say so, Delaney?'

He stood up. 'Mind my pew and look at Diamond Head, and
I'll get us one of those crook beers each.'

'Crook,' she said. 'Crook?' She chuckled.

When he returned with the two cans from Chicka's brimming
bathtub, the girl was still sitting by the window, was obediently

watching Diamond Head though he'd supposed that to her, since
she was a native, the sight was ordinary. Before he went she'd
seemed to him such a drifty presence that he expected her to
have washed away by now into the other room.

'You guys won the Super Bowl in football. Is that it?'

'We lost the grand final at the Sydney Cricket Ground. That's
like the Vatican. The first time we ever got through that far.'

'You lost? What did they give the guys that won?'

'The blokes who won,' said Delaney, 'are more used to
winning. Winning to them didn't mean as much even as getting
there did to us. We're working-class boys, see.'

'And what's the name of this game you guys play?'

Delaney shook his head. It had amazed him from childhood
that there must be foreigners – 220 million Americans, 280
million Russians, a billion Chinese – who had never seen this
most delicious game. 'It's called Rugby League,' he said.

'How many players to a team?'

'Thirteen.'

'On the offence or the defence?' the girl asked him fixedly,
staring not at his eyes but at his lips.

'The same thirteen play all the way through. Unless someone
gets injured.'

'The whole goddam game?'

'That's right. We're bloody supermen down there. We're not
like those poofters of yours who play two minutes at a time and
all covered with padding.'

'Rugby,' said the girl speculatively.

'Rugby League,' said Delaney. 'They reckon Rugby League
is a game for gentlemen played by thugs and Rugby Union a
game for thugs played by gentlemen. Rugby Union's full of
doctors and solicitors.'

'Solicitors. You mean male hookers?'

'No. Lawyers.'

'Oh. Attorneys.'

'Dead right.'

The door opened and smiling Paul Tuomey, the coach, ran in
like a man doing laps. He wore nothing and Delaney noticed
the way his belly, in no way enormous, disproportioned him

nonetheless. He turned left past the girl and sprinted through into Chicka's room. Soon he would reappear at the now permanently open door of Mansfield's room. It turned out he was running for a bet, an old footballer proving he still had mileage left in him.

After a few circuits he was ignored. Delaney got used to the recurrent gasps which meant he was coming around again.

'What position do you play, Delaney?' the girl asked him.

'Five-eighth,' he said. There was a chance that if they didn't keep importing five-eighths from Queensland, England, or the bush he could play five-eighth in first grade. But he decided it would be too difficult to explain to the girl the concepts involved in that.

As he would assure himself later, he would have been content to spend the evening gently educating the girl within the limits of his interests. Instead she made some obvious pun about the word five-eighth – 'Of a goddam inch or what?' – opened his shorts and, without warning, began to fondle him. The readiness with which her hands persuaded him was a surprise. Ten seconds before, he had felt on a less earthly plane than the two wingers and the Chinese-American guest, than naked Paul Tuomey. Playing cards on the far side of the bed, the lock and the fullback saw what had befallen Delaney and began to nudge and laugh.

'Watch it, Terry,' they yelled. 'The dreaded bloody herpes, mate!'

He begged the girl to stop. Most of the third graders were not expensive imports but Penrith boys whose mothers and wives met Gina in the street. He was also appalled by what the teaching brothers who had educated him would call the 'immodesty' of the event. That did not mean he did not want this girl who lacked an origin or any name that meant anything. Nonetheless, he groaned for her to cut it out. 'Not here,' he begged. He dreaded becoming one of the tour's unlikeliest stories.

Cramped over his erection he led the girl to his room. Stanton had once told him that space-shuttle personnel suffered enormous fats, stiffies untrammelled by gravity. Delaney felt crippled by such a space-shuttle special. But he survived the walk across

Mansfield's room and down the corridor, the small static of derision from the card-players and from red-faced Tuomey, whom they met in the corridor and who asked if they wanted him to come too.

Delaney spent two hours with the girl. Occasionally one of the team would come and knock drunkenly on the door. At last Chicka told a chambermaid that it was his room and he'd lost the key, but all he found beyond the door was Delaney and the girl resting and enjoying a sage conversation. When the Parnassian calm of Maui Wow-ie wore off, he would remember Chicka's intrusion with a shame incisive enough to wake him in the middle of the night.

He would remember too, as a rider to his guilt, that he had discovered only one concrete fact about the girl – that she was a waitress.

Stanton had a good wife. He was always saying so. Yet in Denise Stanton's face a heaviness could be seen, a weariness, particularly noticeable – Delaney thought – as she waited in line for communion at St Nicholas's on Sunday mornings. It seemed to Delaney that two elements were aging her – shortage of cash, and Stanton's wildness, his capacity for mad adventures with strange and troublesome women, dangerous ones, the sort whose friends or husbands carried weapons or received stolen goods – liaisons she could not have known about in detail but which she sensed. A dangerous woman and a knife had been involved in Brian Stanton's resignation from the New South Wales police force. Stanton had told Delaney the story, but Denise herself knew only about the knife and the dozen scar marks on Stanton's body.

The Stantons lived in a little timber house – the estate agent said it had been built before Federation – in Emu Plains. Emu Plains was famous in legend and folk song as a penal station during the days of convictism. There was still a prison farm there – the prisoners lived in little yellow brick cubicles which were said to be very hot in summer. These days so many of them were wealthy embezzlers that most of the cubicles were air-conditioned. The sad and poor of the convict world occupied those sweltering cells which were not already taken by the prison gentry. Nothing very violent had ever happened at this prison farm, except once, when two escapees from another gaol had called in there looking for weapons and had killed a warder. That had been twenty years past, but Stanton would still some-times worry about his women – Denise and the two girls – alone at night in the little cottage, a mile across the paddocks from the prison farm. They were letting so many bad bastards get away with murder these days. So many bad bastards were buying soft options for themselves, paying off prison officials.

At dawn Delaney drove behind Stanton westward to the plains. They could see three separate bush fires burning on the long escarpment above the river. It was hoped that the day's wind would turn them back on themselves and that an afternoon storm would douse them.

Stanton's little house looked hot. When Brian and Denise had first bought it, a large cyprus pine, another survival of the nineteenth century, had shaded it. But that had made the place too cold in winter – the rheuminess and vapours of the old tree seeming to spread into the hallway and bedrooms. Leakage of detergents from nearby drains had begun to kill it, and the past August Brian Stanton had been pleased to rent a chainsaw and, with a few ropes and some help from mates, dismember and fell the tree and stack it for firewood. The lawn looked parched without it and the little house, surrounded by hard-lined brick bungalows, looked naked and bereaved. The tree and the old house had been planted together. Delaney was aware of that, and he wondered why Stanton wasn't and had cut up the pine so willingly.

The house had settled in the earth, so that the path to the front door seemed higher than the interior of the place. In the middle of the path stood a tricycle left there the dusk before by the younger of the Stanton children. From the front door you entered straight into the living room where Stanton's two daugh-ters were watching a Japanese animated cartoon. The younger one, the tricyclist, Sharon, bounced on the springs of the old lounge suite while fixedly watching a dragon push a skyscraper over. Denise Stanton had taken this one to doctors so that they

could find out why she bounced all the time – in bed, on the
lounge suite, apparently on the seat of her school desk as well.
The doctors called her hyperkinetic. They said the condition
often went with mental brightness.

This child, seeing Delaney, launched herself directly at him
from the sofa and landed in his arms, holding on with knees, and
with hands around his neck. It was so instantaneous a vault that
Stanton and Delaney laughed. The elder daughter, Donna, was
not distracted from the apocalyptic cartoon. She watched a tidal
wave swirl people and animals away and down some vast gurgler.

In the kitchen Stanton grabbed Denise from behind. 'This is
my bookkeeper,' he told Delaney. 'They reckon I sleep with
her.'

They halved a can of beer between them, and it was only as
Stanton walked out to the car with Delaney that he began to
talk about the questions raised by their encounter with Rudi
Kabbel.

'Bloody marvellous. Here's a bloke who comes from a place
no one's heard of. "Below Russia". I watch the bloody *Eye
Witness News* like a hawk, but I never heard of "Below Russia".
And here he is giving us lectures about bloody buffaloes, and
employing blokes who all wear this bloody Wog uniform of his.
My people've been in this country four generations and never
worked for themselves. Beats me how the bastards are able to
do it. Straight from Below Russia into a business of their own.'

'They're better at business, that's all,' said Delaney.

But Stanton went on talking as if there were a secret he hadn't
been let into, as if he'd been denied a vote.

Across the paddocks, from the direction of the prison farm,
came the sound of a tractor. Stanton glanced away briefly at it,
and when he looked back at Delaney the grievance in his eyes
had grown.

'Makes me aware I'm a bloody fool,' said Stanton.

But when Delaney was on his own, driving home to Penrith,
he understood that Kabbel had enlarged the night rather than
narrowed it down.

THREE

It became a regular matter – perhaps four nights of the week but certainly three – for Delaney and Stanton to emerge from the laneway behind Franklin's supermarket and find Kabbel seated in his baggy uniform at the picnic table by the bandstand. A thermos and an array of rolls, slightly more than even a large man could eat at that hour of the morning, that security man's lunch hour, waited loosely wrapped on the table before him, as if for sale, as if Kabbel would – as Stanton said – really prefer to be one of those Wog delicatessen owners. Eventually even Stanton let himself drink a full cup of Kabbel's coffee. It was full-bodied and very sweet, a strange robust sweetness. Delaney found himself considering the stuff distinctively Belorussian, a sort of proof-by-beverage of the validity of Belorussian claims to an identity.

'Security,' Rudi Kabbel used to say during these meetings, 'is the wave of the future.'

Delaney noticed that Kabbel often talked in terms of waves, cleansing fires, earthquakes which would leave the earth vacant and pure. But before that great wiping of the slate, the future of security was enormous. Kabbel had been to a security seminar in Los Angeles, and reported from that megalopolis that there security was an industry employing hundreds of thousands. A Beverly Hills mansion, for example, could provide three or four security men with employment. The same was about to happen here, for Sydney was no longer the innocent and distant city to which his father had immigrated. 'The wave that breaks on the West Coast this afternoon breaks on Bondi Beach tomorrow morning,' Kabbel would say.

Delaney's father often echoed Kabbel, though he would never meet the White Russian. Old Greg Delaney remembered Penrith before there were traffic lights on the Great Western Highway. Property lay all night unprotected under the wide rustic moon – for in those days Penrith was considered to be beyond the western limits of the city. What had been in the childhood of Delaney senior the earth's most modest and least thrustful car yards, pharmacies, furniture stores now however required guardians.

Stanton continued hostile to Kabbel's Eastern European palaver, but Delaney enjoyed the meetings. Granted, it was not hard to interest a security man, who apart from a regular soldier had the most boring job on earth.

'A good life, gentlemen,' Kabbel said one night in his perfect though vaguely accented English. 'Society has achieved the point of decay where it needs our gentle services, but not to the extent that we cannot sit here by the bandstand in the true dead of night and eat our red cabbage and sausage. We carry weapons we never use unless, as happens with some security men, we take casual work holding up Westpac branches. But imagine this: the ice-cap in Antarctica melts and raises the level of the sea by seventy metres, destroying the banks, which you notice are always coastal institutions. Foothills become beaches, currency has no meaning – it has no meaning now, for that matter, is kept aloft by a faith which makes belief in the Virgin Birth, say, a small matter. When this happens, no man can pose as Mr Security.'

He bit into a roll. Then he asked, 'Do Castle Security let you take your guns home with you each day, gentlemen?'

'That's the company's business,' said Stanton.

'Ah yes. It is certainly that. The company's business.' At that he laughed a little, as if he had agents who kept him posted on Castle's laxities.

'So you take all your men's guns back off them at the end of each shift?' Delaney asked him.

'I have to. I cannot afford to cultivate friends in the police force who will turn a blind eye. I cannot afford to have my company's weaponry used in domestic disputes and other private enterprises. Two men like yourselves don't worry me. If left to my own devices I would say to you take home your firearms.

This industry, however, is full of disappointed policemen and deluded cowboys.'

In the subsequent silence, Delaney knew Stanton would speak. 'I used to be a copper,' Stanton murmured at last. 'And I'm not bloody well disappointed. Retired on a disability allowance.' Stanton often said that, inferred a pension or insurance. Delaney knew by an accidental reference by Denise Stanton that there was no such leeway in the Stantons' life, that Brian and Denise Stanton and their two daughters, the dreamer and the bouncer, lived without any special benefit from the state of New South Wales. It was a harmless conceit of Stanton's though, and Delaney would not betray it to Kabbel.

'Disability,' Kabbel said. It sounded like fraternal concern.

'Nothing serious,' said Stanton.

'So,' said Rudi Kabbel, 'you've had this valuable professional experience?'

'Too right I have. What about you?'

'Not me,' Kabbel confessed. 'I could say the closest I got to any police force was when my father was Chief of Police in the city of Staroviche in Belorussia. I don't think the statutes there bear much resemblance to those of New South Wales.'

He proffered his thermos of coffee in Delaney's direction. 'You, Terry?'

'No thanks.'

'I meant, have you had police experience?'

'No, Rudi. I'm too young.'

Kabbel laughed at that.

Stanton said, 'He's only filling in time between football matches.'

They all laughed, Delaney especially, since he knew how true that was. When people say that to someone like Delaney a sport is a religion they are uttering something more than a metaphor. A sport could be to people like Delaney not merely a sect but a cosmology, a perfected model of an imperfect world. Rugby League was a game whose laws had been codified by workers in the forlorn north of England; miners and mill-workers of Bradford and Wigan, Hull and Warrington, were invaded by that peculiar genius which concerns itself with the serious business of human games, and produced what was to Delaney the supreme code, a cellular structure composed of thirteen players which mimicked life and art and war so exactly that it *became* them. Delaney had all the mental attributes necessary to the professional athlete. The mystery of why his talent was not greater was one he accepted together with the other mysteries. These other mysteries included the passion and dignity of Gina, the grace of the lemon-scented gum, the literalness of the Incarnation and Resurrection of Christ (since Delaney was of Irish stock), and the question of why the Holy Spirit should descend upon slew-vowelled Yorkshiremen meeting in a second-rate commercial hotel in Bradford in 1888 to decide on rules by which working men could play and be paid for time they took off work to glorify the game.

Delaney's talent, though not of national note, was adequate to double what he earned from Castle Security. The poker machines in Penrith Leagues Club, smelling acrid with the spilled beer and exhaled tobacco of gamblers, and fed eight hours a day with twenty-cent coins – the duck-billed platypus aswim on one side, the monarch whose ancestors had oppressed Delaney's ancestors on the other – these mechanisms were largely what paid for Delaney's occasional brilliance at five-eighth.

Delaney never mentioned his earnings as a professional League player to Stanton because he knew Stanton had to manage out of his wage, had no margin. The scar tissue which showed fish-white on Stanton's chest and abdomen went entirely uncompensated by the state, and the superannuation he had brought with him from the police force had gone into the Stanton cottage.

Stanton himself was to Delaney an example of how a life could be destroyed by an unlucky passion. Delaney intended to suffer no such unlucky passions in his own life.

Stanton had been a constable in Petersham, a suburb of solid old terraces which had begun life as an enclave for British artisans but which, when Stanton worked there, housed men and women of sixty-seven nationalities, many of them volatile both in private affairs and in political memory. Like Kabbel, but sometimes less rationally, they remembered the intricate wrongs of their racial histories. The Greeks remembered what the Turks had done, as did the Armenians. The Christian Lebanese spat at the shadows of Muslim Lebanese. Egyptian milk bar owners mourned Sadat and cherished a memory of the hubris of the Pyramids. Croatians told their daughters not to talk to Serbians, and in coffee shops Serbians muttered complicated curses at Croatians. The domestic argument was run in the same full-throated manner as were ethnic politics. Policemen representing Anglo-Saxon law were faced daily with mad-eyed Mediterranean husbands who believed in a tribal code which said that a wronged husband had the right to impale an unfaithful wife.

On the day they looked into a complaint from a number of neighbours in a row of Edwardian cottages Stanton was the young offsider to a middle-aged senior constable called Gorman. Between spells of work, a Serbian shift-worker had been loudly beating his wife over the past two days.

Gorman, said Stanton later, relating the incident to Delaney, was out to lunch, tuned-off, bored and too fat, with a tendency to beat his own wife but less flamboyantly than Serbs do. Constables Gorman and Stanton approached the house believing they knew what to expect – a peasant baggage of a woman, face bruised with tears and blows, and a dark Slavic banshee of a husband uttering curses even a police translator might find beyond him. Gorman would sit the wife down and try to get a statement from her, while Stanton would – as matter-of-factly as he could – remove the kitchen knife from the husband's hand, wave a truncheon at him, and tell him that in countries where cricket was played they had family law courts for dealing with the matters which in more primitive non-cricket and non-Rugby nations were dealt with by marital disembowelment. And all of it would be a waste of breath, and within a week Gorman and Stanton, or two like them, would be called back to the terraces for a second loud conjugal bout.

It was early evening when Gorman and Stanton knocked on the door. At last it was opened by a Serbian girl with a distended lower lip and bloody mouth. The two policemen at the door saw these injuries for an instant only. The girl raised a bloodsoaked teatowel to her lower face, lifted her head and looked over her threshold as if defying their pity. The house was silent. The husband had already left for his shift at a tyre factory in Balmain. They would be able to ask the Balmain police to call in there and heavy him. Stanton thought that if the husband's exit from home that evening had any of the style the girl-bride showed at the door, it must have been quite a scene.

Neither Gorman nor Stanton was in a hurry to leave the house once she let them in. They sat in the kitchen with her, and she spoke clearly through her damaged lips, which at last she let them inspect but not treat. Her English was first-class; she had done courses at the University of Belgrade. Her husband was of country stock but an engineer. It was very hard for him to get qualified in a new country. That was what made trouble between them – jealousy was his only way, she said, to ease the boredom.

'She sits there at a kitchen table,' Stanton later confided in Delaney, 'with a mouth like raspberry bloody jam. Not touching the tea because it hurts her too much but not letting us know that. I mean Gorman, she wouldn't want to share the sleeves out of a vest with a bloody yobbo like Gorman, and she certainly doesn't want to let him into the secret that she's in pain. We suggest taking her to the outpatients for some stitches but she says offhandedly that a million bloody Serbs were killed in the war and that she doesn't think a cut mouth will kill her. Then she has to excuse herself to go and spit blood down the loo – she moves off as though she's going to a bloody Government House investiture. And this bloody awful dickhead Gorman says to me while we're waiting in the kitchen, "We could both get our end in here." I couldn't believe what I'd heard. "Yes," he said, "her old man's gingered her up and she's ready to go." I told him if he suggested it I'd declare him. I mean he spent an hour a day at the pushing shop down near the railway, rooting himself stupid or *stupider* more like it – our station took 35 per cent of that place, and the young blokes used to have this joke about Gorman eating the proceeds. And now he wants to get his putrid bloody end into this absolutely grade-A Serbian girl. I couldn't stand it – I stamped round the bloody kitchen telling him I'd rupture him. He got very cranky and we left quickly, without giving Danka much good advice. Who were we anyhow? She had the best advice she could possibly get just from her bloody genes.'

The next evening Stanton went back to Danka's house to give her some homegrown legal counselling on her position under the common law of assault. We have the code Napoleon in Yugoslavia, she explained, looking at him limpidly over her healing lips. 'The way she said it,' he would later tell Delaney, 'it sounded like a bloody liqueur or something. It made you want to travel.

'I was gone a million,' said Stanton. 'I thought of leaving poor bloody Denise. Danka thought of leaving her old man. His name was Sima, but at the factory they called him Steve. Danka and I used to daydream we'd shoot through to Northern Queensland and farm or run a little country shop, but she kept saying, I have to see Sima qualified as an engineer first.'

The affair lasted four months. One morning Stanton got a call from her – she wanted him to come to her place. She sounded demented, and he knew that that was uncharacteristic, that a cool fury was her nature. He had known from his visit there the evening before that Sima and some other Serbs had chartered a boat for fishing that day, and would probably be at the time of Danka's call a reckless number of miles out in the variable currents off Sydney Head.

It was summer by now, and the door of the terrace stood open. Stanton went into the deep shade of that hallway. These houses were built not with regard for Australian light and sun but on the British model, as if they were meant to keep out the mists and intensify the dimness of a Midlands winter's day. Stanton, coming in out of the full brassiness of the day, had not been able to see much as he loped up the hallway, confident of his power to soothe the girl. He called out her name as he went, and found her in the kitchen, sitting at the table. There was a strange lack of any answering sound or gesture from her. Stanton laid the keys of the patrol car down on the kitchen table and put both his hands on her shoulders.

He saw six or seven men jogging up the hallway. As they

emerged into the kitchen they stood still. He was aware that at least four of them carried kitchen knives, or perhaps the knives with which they had intended to gut the day's catch. Stanton would never discover what old loyalty or threat they had exploited to force her to set him up. He tried to get his .38 out of its stiff leather holster, but by then Sima had stepped up and put a knife in his chest. Sima muttered away as he plunged the knife in a dozen times. 'I was in this cold tingly shock,' Stanton would relate. 'It was the grating on the ribs I really found bloody disgusting.'

It seemed to Stanton, halfway through this torment, that Sima had in mind an exact blood tax and did not intend to kill him unless it was, more or less, by accident. Towards the twelfth thrust, said Stanton later, confiding in his friend Delaney, Sima's Yugoslav fishing mates began to crowd in, to restrain him from dealing Stanton some coup de grâce. The bastard was throughout, said Stanton, cool as a bloody cucumber, and Stanton could remember Danka saying something like that, that he just mumbled away, and that it was always *her* cries which made the neighbours dial for the police.

Sima stepped away at last. Stanton inspected his tattered and bloody uniform and began weeping and yelling threats. 'I thought, malicious damage to a police bloody shirt. I didn't even think of using my piece. I still didn't believe I'd been stuck a dozen times. An exact dozen, you know, three for every month of bloody rapture. But at the time I didn't feel like he'd done me much damage. I was really hurt that Danka could give me up like that, but you know . . . marriages are very strong, stronger than the buggers that are in them will ever let on. If you're coming in from outside there are rules they don't tell you. You might get into the wife's bed but she doesn't let you see the rulebook.

'I wandered off down the hallway yelling how I'd be back with the whole fucking Central Western Metropolitan Division, but I knew I wouldn't be coming back, no way. The walls began to move but I hung on. I didn't want old Superintendent Monty Walsh to find me stuck like this and laid out on Danka's hall carpet – he'd know what I'd been up to.

'I came out of the door and the sun nearly flattened me. I got

to the wrought-iron gate, creaked it open, creaked it shut, bled
my way across the pavement to the patrol car and found I'd left
the bloody keys on her kitchen table.'

His fear of seeing Danka again was worse than any concern
he had about being further knifed or falling on the carpet in a
coma. He crept up the corridor, no more wanting to re-enter
the familiar musk of that kitchen than the hosts wanted to have
him. He called twice, 'Excuse me, I've left my keys.' When
Sima appeared and thrust the keys into his hand, he suffered a
flush of gratitude so sharp that it nearly took his consciousness.

'Thank you, thank you,' said Stanton.

'I hope the Devil eats your liver,' murmured Sima. And as
Delaney knew, the Devil had.

Stanton drove back to the station and lost his consciousness
there. Much later he entertained Delaney with tales of his time
in hospital and his full-blooded attempt to blame the knifing on
a gang of teenagers visiting from another suburb and looking for
prestige. Knifing a walloper, Stanton told his superintendent,
was as much prestige as most of those yobbos would ever get.
But the story did not stand enquiry. In the end the superintendent knew everything, and Stanton begged him not to prosecute
the Serb. It would destroy my marriage, Stanton said. Old
Monty Walsh told Stanton he would save the marriage – they'd
get the Serb another way. But there were things you could get
away with in the New South Wales police force, and things you
couldn't. To be stabbed on your lover's premises was one of the
ones you couldn't get away with. There had to be an internal
enquiry – the commissioner demanded that. It could be *in
camera*; Denise would learn nothing. But even if he survived
the medical examination he couldn't expect any sort of career.
Not shooting the Serb was the only sensible thing he had done,
but it also demonstrated a lack of presence of mind.

The superintendent therefore let Brian Stanton know that at
the end of his recuperation his letter of resignation would be
accepted.

FOUR

'You should speak about this to Gina,' Father Doig told Delaney.

'Couldn't do that, Andrew,' Delaney murmured. 'No way.'

A bloody parson, not a priest – so Delaney's father spoke of Doig. Father Doig's black hair was styled at the same unisex salon favoured by the Penrith first grade back line the week before televised games. There seemed to be something contrary to faith and morals in that, a priest attending what Delaney senior called poofter-and-dunce barbers. He found it easier still to specify how Doig's behaviour, as distinct from his hairdo, violated doctrine.

Doig had given up hearing confessions in the old-style confessional boxes. Only genial old Father Rushton still sat in his dim little cubicle on Saturday afternoons and wondered about the football score and race results and listened to the eternal temporising of trespassers. On the most breathless summer's evening he wore his cassock, as judges in Israel should. He did not offer counsel, as Delaney's father was proud to say, like some social worker on talkback radio. He delivered judgment and brought down absolution in the old style.

Doig, however, sat at a table by the side altar. He told those who came to him that he was their brother in weakness and commission of sin and that they should call him Andrew if first-name terms would help them speak more freely. He assured them that he had had training in counselling. That's it, said Delaney senior. It doesn't matter a bugger that he's a priest. He's had training in *counselling*! I'd like to know where that leaves poor bloody old Rushton?

'You know, your mother won't go to him,' Delaney senior told his son during a Sunday visit. 'Doesn't feel like she's been to confession at all.' And Delaney wondered, as sons often have, what his mother would have to confess. Mrs Delaney sported a smile which typified what Delaney thought of as meekness – not a failure to address the world, but a sort of quietly gleeful acceptance of it. She wore her hair close-cropped like a helmet, and you would walk into a room and discover her smiling to herself, as if sharing her own joke. He had never had to ask himself was his mother happy. She was not, however, happy with Father Andrew Doig.

'Have you noticed,' she asked one Sunday, 'all the statues disappearing from the church? The one of the Infant of Prague, St Thérèse of Lisieux, St Antony . . . ?'

'You know what he says?' Greg Delaney enquired. 'He says the Infant of Prague is Czechoslovak or something, and that St Thérèse was only patron saint of Aussie while the place was a missionary country, and that's not on any more. And St Antony of Padua . . . that's the best of all . . . he says poor old Antony is used by the superstitious . . .'

'There wasn't any time something was lost in our house,' said Mrs Delaney, 'that it wasn't found by St Antony.'

'I used to use him for betting on the football,' said Delaney's father, without joking. 'Two dollars in the poor box for him every time St George loses a game or Penrith wins one.'

'Why didn't you use him on the stock exchange,' Delaney asked, winking at Gina across the tea table and the opened and exhausted bottles of Resch's Pilsener, 'and make a bloody fortune?'

'Come off it,' said Delaney senior who seemed to have no doubt that a modest pay-off was the right one for him.

Mrs Delaney tossed her helmet hair and said, 'I'm sure Gina's parents would be shocked to hear you talk like that.'

'My father went and buried a statue of St Francis under his first tomato crop,' said Gina, smiling, and charming Delaney by covering her wide mouth with a hand as if her parents were there to chastise her.

'Wog saints are best for tomatoes,' said Delaney, and Gina and his mother laughed and punched his upper arms, as if forestalling the vengeance of heaven. Delaney's father would certainly have laughed except that it might somehow weaken his accusations of heresy against Father Doig.

'Did you see he asked the Wades up on the altar the other day for their fortieth wedding anniversary? He's not a priest, he's a bloody Master of Ceremonies.'

'I've asked him to book a jazz band for your twenty-fifth,' Delaney told his father.

'Not on your bloody life,' said Mr Delaney. 'A marriage is bloody private and so is a confession.'

Yet here was Father Doig not only hearing Delaney's confession at a table in plain sight, but saying don't tell me, tell your wife, I'm not the wronged party. An approach which made sense but was at variance with the Delaney family's traditional system of acquitting their sins.

'It should be the new direction,' Doig whispered. 'Ask the person you've wronged. In some cases absolution's the easy way out.'

'There's no way I could tell Gina,' said Delaney, though he feared others would.

'Tell me if this is none of my business,' said Doig.

Indeed he was nothing like the old-style priests who thundered, 'How many times, was she married or single?' Whose right to know was absolute. Some people thought they got their cheaps that way, but in fact the poor old buggers must have been bored stupid, a lifetime listening to people's sexual small change fall on the confessional floor. Knowing, since they weren't fools, that none of the big operators ever came near a confessional. But never saying to any transgressor, 'Tell me if this is none of my business.'

Doig continued, 'I imagine this was a casual encounter. I mean, almost accidental?'

'It was the team holiday. Hawaii.'

Doig smiled. 'I see. I've been there. Even the priests up there smoke pot. You know, according to some writers it's our serious love we get damned for. Occasional follies are too mean to count for much. But you know that, you're an intelligent fellow. I wonder why you felt you had to mention it. I could still have given you the traditional absolution.' That was another thing

Delaney's parents disliked – Doig used terms like 'traditional absolution' as if there were no real absolution, even though in the past people had thought there was.

'So that's not the issue. What's really worrying you about all this, Delaney?'

Delaney managed to say it; in fact a childhood in which his mother had forced him to the confessional had prepared him to say it.

'It was practically public, and I can't stand that. I really can't stand it. It was what I was smoking. I mean, doing it in front of other people . . .'

'You'd hate Gina to know that.'

'God, I couldn't take it. I let the others see me letting her down. You know.'

'Beasts of the farm yard,' murmured Father Doig.

'Yes,' said Delaney. 'That's about right, Andrew.'

'It's common now, Terry. The video revolution. Group rutting.' It was as well the saints weren't still in their niches to hear such things. 'Look, Terry, this was a risk you took, wasn't it? And one Gina took. Your going away to a fleshpot like Hawaii with the boys of Penrith's third grade. And you were a casualty of that risk. But you learned something, eh? That you aren't quite as cat private as you thought you were. So that in future you'll go forth armed. There's the security problem, I understand that. If ever anyone is vicious enough to tell Gina, please feel you can both come to me for counselling.'

Delaney nodded. He did not quite feel the lightness that followed old-style confession, but Doig wasn't a bad fellow and was compassionate, even if a little of a smart alec. He understood the real world at least, the world in which with very little warning alien women undid your flies.

'Would you like,' Father Doig asked, 'the traditional absolution?'

FIVE

The moonlit picnic table was at Easter piled with hubcaps stacked like pie dishes, and a young man, tall and blond, sat at the table with Kabbel.

'Look, my friends,' Kabbel called as Stanton and Delaney emerged from the lane. 'This is the security business for you!' His boys had found the personnel of a new operation from Parramatta stealing hubcaps from the Audi-Subaru agency down the road. There were rumours they were doing it all up and down the highway. 'This crowd go in to the manager in the morning with the hubcaps and say, we were passing and saw hoodlums, larrikins, hoons levering off your hubcaps. It wouldn't have happened if *we'd* been on the job. Hungry for business, you see, even at this late stage of civilisation, eh? And the fundamental question which arises for us is whether to put the hubcaps back ourselves, which one is not recommended to do with quality vehicles, or to take them to the management in the morning and hope they believe our account of the incident, that we are not pulling the same trick as the Parramatta crowd. What would you say?'

'Take them to him in the morning,' Stanton told Kabbel and the blond youth, 'and if he won't believe you, tell him to get stuffed.'

'Or,' said Delaney, 'take them to him in the morning with a copy of a letter you've written to the Association, complaining about the Parramatta mob.'

'Who don't belong to the Association,' said the fair-haired young man sitting opposite Kabbel.

'Yes. But it gives your story an extra seriousness, eh? An extra punch.'

Kabbel scratched his poll of blond-grey hair. 'Australia's full of private armies,' he said, 'masquerading as security companies. Their purpose is not politics, as would be the case in many other countries, but robust greed. This, gentlemen, is my son, Warwick.'

Everyone shook hands. Stanton clearly approved of Warwick, his size, his accent. 'You're living proof, mate, that Wogs have Aussie offspring.'

But Delaney thought there was still a foreign distance in Warwick. It was as if the boy didn't understand Stanton's fraternal insult, was neither amused or affronted. 'My father's a genius,' Warwick said, with a faint smile. 'That's good enough for me.'

'Oh yeah!' said a relentless Stanton. 'If your old man's such a bloody wonder, why's the company called Uncle?'

'Uncle is my true adviser,' Kabbel said. 'In dangers you would not believe or conceive of, he has been my true voice, my only security. I still commune with him any time I like in a coffee shop in Parramatta. He lives upstairs, an ancient now, a man of indeterminate age.' He smiled. 'He is the genius behind the genius. If my children don't believe in my superior vision, they don't get a job from me.' And he burst into a broad laughter which seemed to Delaney to be itself accented.

'Well, I'm not going to start believing you're anything to write home about,' Stanton persisted. 'So where in the hell does that leave me?'

'No, no, relax,' said Kabbel. 'Of outsiders I require only that they consider me an honest man.'

'Even that's a bloody tall order,' said Stanton, reaching for the remaining segment of a Kabbel sandwich.

Kabbel's son Warwick began to gather up the imported hubcaps. 'I've got to get back to Scott. Nice to meet you, gentlemen.'

Kabbel watched him go, his eyes creased with parental fondness. 'There are grand things ahead of that boy,' he murmured to Delaney.

Delaney was sure neither of his parents had ever said that of him. They had not seen his modest pass in the Higher School Certificate as the basis of a career. His football was to be his career. It would lead him to jobs in Public Relations or writing for the tabloids. His career in security had been a temporary sinecure to allow him time for daylight training. Sydney, however, teemed with brilliant five-eighths, and if they didn't have enough they bought them from Queensland or New Zealand or even from England. (It was axiomatic that any harshly reared Yorkshire boy would sacrifice his gritty origins for the chance to play and live in Sydney.) Delaney's career had not yet flourished as Brother Aubin, his childhood coach, and Greg Delaney, who loved the Rugby League code as if it were an extension of the True Faith, had foretold it would. What had been employment of convenience had had to become a career equal to playing five-eighth. Without one or the other, the payments on the house could not be maintained, the Spanish lounge and dining suite would not adorn the place, there would be no dishwasher. (And Delaney knew by instinct that possession of a dishwasher was the visible sign which separated the spacious from the embattled.)

Neither Delaney nor Stanton thought that Castle much treasured their special talents. Old Kearney the supervisor had once mentioned to Delaney the idea that he might move up to an administrative job. But the company had stood still. That incarnation of the cheese-paring Scots farmer, Malcolm Fraser, had had his thick-knuckled hand on the throat of the economy and was abetted from afar by Maggie Thatcher, Cowboy Reagan, New Zealand's Piggy Muldoon and sundry other exponents of the doctrine of economic constipation. When the era of mild recovery arrived, the company seemed to have developed problems of its own, as if there was a secret which management was trying to keep from the men in the field.

It was an ill-guarded secret, however, and was uttered by Rudi Kabbel in that same week in which Delaney and Stanton saw the hubcaps and met Warwick.

'Have you boys heard there is trouble with Castle? Please, I do not wish to alarm you. But Castle have been forced to consider a bid from Vanguard, and if Vanguard come they will bring their own people.' Kabbel lowered his voice in the vacant park. 'Speak to me if anything goes wrong for you. I have a new and rather fascinating contract. Working for me you would join a family.'

'Would we have to wear your bloody daggy uniform?' Stanton asked. But it was a sort of automatic or reflex irony. Delaney knew his friend was hollowed out by Kabbel's whisper, that it challenged the chancy equity he held in life.

'You could have your wife take in the waist,' said Kabbel, laughing, 'if you want to resemble a hot Steve McQueen.'

'Winter is on its way,' said Stanton.

Delaney's car was at the panel-beaters. Driving him home, squinting into a diffused but vast rising sun, Stanton at last began to speak. (When he and Delaney had met up again at dawn, he had been mostly silent.) 'You know how much you're worth by what you hear and who you hear it from. If you hear from the bloody chairman you're being retrenched, it's a different matter from hearing it from a bloody Bisonrussian in the middle of the fucking night.'

It was Stanton's whimsy to call Kabbel a Bisonrussian.

Delaney said the obvious thing: that it might not be true.

'I don't want to be in that bugger's family. I'd rather be a cog at Castle than a member of *his* family.'

Stanton braked in front of Delaney's white house. The recently planted lemon-scented gums stood still and, he liked to think, vigilant in the first mild yellow light. He was guilty at the elation he felt. The end of Castle forced him to take new chances, the chances he knew he should take while he still could. He kept his lips firmly clamped down on this excitement. He knew Gina was asleep inside. She slept seriously, thoroughly. It was his daily task sweetly to rouse her.

For Brian Stanton, wearing the scars of an earlier cruelled career, Castle was all the breath and bread he and his womenfolk could expect.

Delaney got out but leaned in through the window. Stanton let off the brake and put the car into gear. The activity seemed to cause him pain. 'Sometimes you feel like you're just a whisker away from being nothing, sweet bugger-all. Kiss your ethnic sheila for me.'

When he drove away Stanton emitted not so much exhaust

as a dangerous musk of disappointment. It seemed to Delaney that it was a stench which might attract a predatory destiny.

On the next pay-day the pink retrenchment slip turned up in Delaney's pay-packet. There was a slip in Stanton's too. Even to Delaney it came like the announcement of an expected death and was just as stupefying. 'Two weeks' severance, a month's accumulated leave,' said Stanton. 'I'm not going on the dole. I'm not going to trot down to the Advisory Financial Service in the bloody park and work out how to organise my bloody poverty. That's a particular bullshit sonata I'm not going to play. I'll rob bloody banks first.'

There was in Stanton a dark capability for hold-ups. The management of the company's firearms had been cavalier, and Stanton hoped he would be able to take his .38 with him when he left. He would then have it in his drawer at home: an option. Delaney was relieved when the new supervisor proved finicky and wanted all weapons and rounds accounted for.

Delaney began to apply for the jobs he'd always desired. 'Somewhere in the bullshit industry,' Stanton described Delaney's projected ideal employment. 'You need to be Mel Gibson with an arts-law degree,' Delaney confided to Gina, on the verge of tears in her arms after a week of talking to personnel managers.

Stanton shopped himself around less high-flown establishments than the sports institutes and PR units where Delaney had been trying for a foothold. Men without jobs, said Stanton, were savages. He was a bloody savage. He would have killed for such tear-arse piecework as unloading crates off trucks at the rear of supermarkets, or offsiding on a per-delivery basis for a furniture removalist. 'They should have saved the building of the bloody Pyramids till the 1980s,' Stanton said. 'I would have signed on.'

Early in the third week they set their alarms for 2 a.m. and went down to the park to see Kabbel.

SIX

Rudi Kabbel's business was run from a control room in the front of his old house in Parramatta. The room was brightly painted and had an air of welcome. To come in there after a few weeks of being jobless was a bit like coming home, even Brian felt that. It looked like a professional place too, a good place to bring potential clients in the daytime and say, 'This is where we operate.' There were some easy-chairs, a Spanish-style table with copies of *Guardian* on it – the Association magazine. At one end of the room, on a proper computer table, was a computerised alarm receiver already switched on. The code-numbers of various clients showed up iridescently in yellow on a black screen. A wire led from the computer to a discreet white siren set high up on the wall. In the corner stood a radio transmitter. On the wall opposite the ornately barred window a sturdy arms cabinet was fixed.

Driving down to Kabbel's earlier, Stanton had said, 'I hope to Christ this doesn't turn out to be a Dad and Dave operation, with a two-way radio stuck in the corner of a bloody garage or a laundry.' Delaney had feared it too. Businesses like that came and went. Winged ants in September were less transient. Kabbel's house though, double-brick, Federation-style, looked like a permanent seat of business.

Kabbel welcomed them eloquently and showed them round the room. The two Kabbel boys came in in their turquoise uniforms, the one called Warwick, whom Delaney and Stanton had met recently over a pile of BMW hubcaps, and his younger more compact brother. They signed the gun-register and took their weapons for the night. The young one took the normal .38 service revolver, but Warwick loaded and put in his holster the weapon which was an infallible sign of gun-happiness – a Magnum .357.

'Danielle,' said Kabbel, 'is still packing the washing machine.'

Kabbel began to explain the scope of his business. Two hundred and twenty clients, but most of them in the $20 to $25 a week range. Now he had taken on a chain of chicken outlets – Golden Style. They were concerned about systematic damage to their premises, were certain it was engineered by an opposition fast-chicken company.

'Damage?' asked Stanton. He didn't like the word.

'Minor gestures – tipped garbage-bins. The carpark of the branch at Rooty Hill strewn with refuse. A stone through a window. It's guerrilla warfare at that lower end of the chicken market. Golden Style feel that their former security company failed to patrol energetically enough and that's all they ask of us – surveillance and energetic patrolling. It is not required, Mr Stanton, in a world where so many genuine causes exist, that you endanger your life for Golden Style.'

It was with the flavour of those words in his mind, the redolence of Golden Style, one of those perfect names which are so much richer than the product they attach to, that Delaney first saw Danielle Kabbel. She came in carrying a hardcover book and a notepad, as if she habitually studied while manning – womanning, personning, whatever the feminists wanted it called – while manning the radio. Like the younger of the brothers she bordered on being small. Like him she was perfectly made. And blonde – the family of the Kabbels had that blond gene in a big way. There was a delicate and beautiful furze on her lower arms. Golden Style.

Kabbel performed the introductions. 'Reading?' Delaney asked her, awkwardly but in a way that indicated – he hoped – a sympathy for books.

'I'm doing a novel course at the WEA,' she told him perfunctorily, and then showed how their system worked. If an alarm were activated on any of the client premises the computer screen displayed the code for that particular client, and in case she was asleep (Delaney had an image of her, cheek down on her book, seated sleeping at the computer desk) or in case she was out of the room, the siren on the wall went off. She then called one of the patrolmen on the radio and he inspected the particular site. If a peripheral inspection indicated an intruder, she said, then she called the police and the owner. And that's it, she told Delaney and Stanton. The glamorous side of the business.

'And when do you sleep?' Delaney wanted to know.

'Generally between three o'clock and dawn,' she told him, placing a hand over her smile to keep her privacy. 'I'm like my father,' she said. 'Belorussians never sleep. It's metabolic.'

'We're like that bison I mentioned, gentlemen,' said Kabbel. 'We sleep on our feet.'

'Oh,' murmured the girl, looking up from the radio, 'he's already pushed Belorussian wildlife down your throats.'

On the way home, Stanton looked out at the sulphurous lights burning above the expressway. They always reminded Delaney of migraine. 'A nice little piece, that Danielle, eh?'

PART TWO

SEVEN

137 Ave de Suffren
75724 PARIS
Cedex 15

August 3, 1982

Dearest Radislaw, Radek, Rudi, or whatever they call you there,

I hope this letter is not too unwelcome. I was moved to write it after I met Frau Zusters – remember her? – in Berlin this summer. Albert has an interest in a string of supermarkets in West Germany – Tante Marthe they're called – if a housewife spends more than 65 marks she is given a blow-up plastic model of a cosy-looking woman called Tante Marthe. Albert got the idea from a chain in California in which he has an investment.

Here we are, brother and sister, and haven't written to each other in years, since father died, God help him, and I talk about inflatable damned dolls, as if it were the purpose of the letter. The doll came up though because of its resemblance to my memory of Frau Zusters. I am now older than widow Zusters was when we sheltered in her house and I still consider myself a desirable woman – you'd say that's always been my problem. I make the point only as a reflection on the fact widow Zusters then probably still saw herself as a woman in her prime, even though my memory of her bears a close resemblance to a silly Tante Marthe doll. So during our Berlin visit this summer it played on me: who was in that house these days? Was it still there? Perhaps the Russians did for it in those last few

days? It's age, I think, working on me, and it's made worse
by the fact we had lived through too much fatal history
before we were fifteen. I could imagine myself now going
back to see the DP camps at Michelstadt or Regensburg
the way people go back to an old school.

Fortunately those two *alma maters* – or *almae matres* –
see how well Herr Hirschmann and Miss Tokina taught
me before, in their different ways, they both 'went east'?
– fortunately Regensburg and Michelstadt, with all their
camp spivs and operators, no longer exist. All the Displaced
Persons have been Placed, Europe is finished with that
particular piece of its gardening. I can still, however, make
a fool of myself and go looking for Frau Zusters. The old
house is what passes these days for an easy limousine drive
from our hotel near the Europa Centre. And you know,
I found her without any trouble. The house is divided now,
not into two apartments as in our day when half Berlin
was bombed out, but into four. Frau Zusters occupies one
and rents the other three out to young lawyers and
businessmen and their growing families. She has been
widowed a second time, so perhaps the dear old thing was a
faster mover than she seemed to us to be. Her mind is
clear as crystal. She reminded me of the day when we
all went and queued for her three hundred grams of meat
and that squad of kids turned up and dragged the dentist
out of his surgery and beat him up for being defeatist. She
told me that I sat on the park fence that day yelling, 'I'm
going to go and live in Paris.' 'And you *do*,' she said. 'You
do.'

She took me to the cellar because she said she had
something to give me. She had kept in a trunk all father's
journals. She apologised that the cover of two of them had
grown a little mildewed. I didn't tell her I was ignorant
of the fact that father had been a diarist, but I realised
straightaway he was exactly the sort of fellow who *would*
write up a journal. He was vain enough – no, I'm not being
a bitch, I use the term forgivingly – and really believed
that he lived on what he would have called the cutting edge

of history. And he thought we'd be all coming back through Berlin pretty soon, when the Allies turned on the Soviets. He'd pick them up on his way through back to Minsk.

I took the dozen or so leather-covered notebooks she gave me. I had to. To refuse would have been an insult to her fidelity. I feel no curiosity about them. I suppose I remembered enough. On the other hand, I didn't want to burn them. He thought I was a bad daughter, but if he went to so much trouble to make special provision for them it wasn't my business to turn them to ash. You were the one he considered his heir. I became for ever the adolescent whore who went off with the French sergeant in the DP camp. You were his little Belorussian survivor, and it is up to you now what is done with the journals.

As well as this there is the problem, given that the Allies did not turn on the Russians and recapture Minsk and Staroviche, that Europe may not be a safe place for such memoirs. The names of Ostrowsky your godfather and Abramtchik and other Belorussian leaders appear often in histories of that period. There is a book published recently and written by an American intelligence officer of the era which complains that these men were given undue protection by American Central Intelligence and by the British and French, that Ostrowsky and Abramtchik and Stankievich and all the others are war criminals and should be tried as such. In books of this nature Papa always merits at least a footnote because of a certain massacre carried out by Belorussian police and the SS on the Staroviche–Gomel road in 1941.

Again, we knew very young that events are subtle and that 'war criminal' is a relative and shifting term. It was a term used with a straight face by Stalin, whose crimes against the Belorussians and Ukrainians make the SS seem almost indulgent. Nonetheless I consider it my last daughterly duty to send these journals to a far continent where they are not likely to cause comment or serve as evidence. I place them, therefore, in the care of a loyal son.

My advice to you is nonetheless to burn them. There will
be too much in them about Onkel Willi, and that awful
man Bienecke, and all the rest. I remember you in that six
months we spent in Berlin at the end. You were in a
daze, which was a merciful arrangement given the level of
bombing. But it was not a happy daze. It terrified mother.
Remembering that child, my advice to you is at least to
store them unread and at best to burn them. You and I
know how there are vipers nesting in those pages.

I hope you and your children are well. As for me, though
childless, I have a loving husband. Father thought him a
crook and a child molester, but he has been an honourable
man all these years.

The journals are on their way under separate cover.

Your – believe me – affectionate sister,

GENIA

EIGHT

I am moved at this late hour to produce a history of my family. My purpose is to mark the inroads the struggle for Belorussian freedom made upon the lives of my parents, and so to create the background for my own attempt to prepare a true Belorussia of the spirit here, on this earth which will so soon become a wilderness. I wish as well to place my father's journals in a suitable context.

Let me say first that in Belorussia itself, in certain parts of Berlin, Paris, New Jersey where Belorussian exiles live, it would be a matter of surprise that my father ended in Australia. For he was, while still young in political terms, a minister of the Belorussian government and a familiar of the great Belorussian patriot, Ostrowsky. Most of his government colleagues would spend their later years in South River, New Jersey, as intimates of various intelligence and counter-intelligence bodies – the Office of Policy Coordination for one. Others lived in Paris, trusted employees of the French Secret Service. My father, far from running a research group at a nice address in Rue de Granillers or speaking at anti-Soviet seminars in London or Edinburgh, would finish his life as a guard (retired) on the Government Railways of New South Wales.

When my father came to Australia with me in the late 1940s, it was the theory that he would be a fund-raiser amongst Belorussian refugees in Sydney and Melbourne. The money he raised in this distant latitude was to stand against the day when the Belorussians would return east to their homeland. Money would also be needed by the Belorussian government in exile, still largely scattered around various Displaced Persons camps in Germany. There was always the risk that under Soviet pressure they would be arrested by the Allies and forced to stand trial for various incidents which had taken place in our homeland between 1941 and 1944.

My father was also meant to make friends in Australia of the fledgling Australian security and intelligence groups. There was some contact in this regard. The Australians, like most Western countries, were very frightened of being infiltrated by Communists masquerading as refugees. If the Australian files were looked at, it would probably be seen that for some twenty years my father was an adviser to the Australians on the political probity of this or that Belorussian immigrant.

But the true reason for my father's flight to the antipodes was that by his mid-forties he was already exhausted by politics. It is scarcely too dramatic to say that history had looted him. As well as that, through the incidents I am now going to consider in this history, he had by the time he immigrated to Australia lost all his political influence amongst those arch and crafty Belorussian politicians and patriots. Even as a teenager I knew and understood this. My father was being retired by his colleagues, sent like the early British convicts to a distance from which he was unlikely to return.

Before I look at the European causes of my family's decline, let me say that my father achieved Australian visibility only once, in 1955. In that year Australian Belorussian communities were visited by an old political enemy of my father, Mikolai Redich. Redich had been dispatched on a fund-raising mission. His task was – as they say in this country – to ginger up the Belorussians here. One winter's evening that year, after Redich had delivered a lecture in the suburb of Ashfield and was returning home with my father towards Parramatta, a Sydney suburb where he was being accommodated by old friends from the Displaced Persons camps, Redich fell from a train at Lidcombe station, suffered extensive injuries, and died almost at once.

It was remarkable that at the inquest numerous Australian officials appeared to testify to my father's good character. But amongst the Belorussian community here there was much gossip about the cause of Redich's death, and this event marked both the beginning of my father's decline in health and of our increasing estrangement from other Belorussian refugees in the city of Sydney.

Trains have figured crucially in the Kabbel family history. For all of us they have been vehicles of exile. At the centre of my own history I place our escape from Minsk, together with the families of other Belorussian officials, in a train especially provided by the SS. This train rolled out of Minsk some five days before the Russians captured the city in June 1944. I was then eleven years of age.

Aides of General von Gottberg, German Kommissar of Belorussia, waved us all off from Minsk Central. My mother was not impressed by this show of SS formality. She would not forgive von Gottberg's crowd for failing to attend the funeral of Oberführer Willi Ganz, her favourite guest amongst the Germans, her confidant and – with my father's approval – closest friend. Oberführer Ganz had been Onkel Willi to me. His body lay in the Catholic cemetery in Staroviche – it was von Gottberg's fault that it had never been shipped home. It would now fall to the Russians. His mute grave would go unmarked, or even be desecrated.

It had to be admitted, as my father, until recently police chief of Staroviche, pointed out to my mother, that Oberführer Ganz had been buried in a spring of heavy rains and fierce partisan activity, both factors making a muddy, hundred-mile journey by von Gottberg unreasonably dangerous. She had not been persuaded, however.

The young and highly polished SS men seeing us off from Minsk seemed to imply by the joviality with which they shook hands with our President, Radislaw Ostrowsky (my godfather as it happens), that we were off to some Baltic beach for the summer, perhaps that same one at Puck where we had spent the war's first autumn waiting for Warsaw to fall. My parents, of course, knew better than that. For them it was not the first flight from that ancient and revered city of the Belorussians. For me, however, it *was* the first departure. I took it for granted that I would be back after a month or two, that my parents would then continue the debate about whether to keep that elegant house in Staroviche or, now that my father was a Belorussian cabinet minister, to find a large apartment in Minsk.

The train left Minsk Central a half an hour after first light, an hour when those old cities can look ideal and eternal, especially on a translucent June morning. The spires of the Mariinski shone. Until the train began to roll out my mother had been tense, since this journey was parallel to a physically damaging departure she herself had made with her parents from Minsk to Grodno a quarter of a century before. To add to her anxiety, fighting between Russian partisans and German units had begun the day before all over the city, and as a sort of bass to the partisan activity, Marshal Rokossovsky's artillery had been heard all night hammering away twenty miles distant. Despite all this Soviet bombast Minsk looked itself to me, I mean it looked immutable. There had been some damage to it in the fighting of 1941, some damage by bombing since, but the dawn light seemed to put a gloss over those small defects. *I* knew that Minsk had of its essence to stand for ever.

Other cities look like accidents. Here, in the west of Sydney for example, there is a feeling as of a great red-brick holding camp. The recurring shopping centres could have been dropped from helicopters like military equipment. Here there is no necessity in operation between the earth and what sits on it. Mount Druitt, Rooty Hill, St Mary's, Kingswood – so transient they seem to beg a tidal wave and shall unhappily receive one.

Minsk, on the other hand, on the morning I left it in 1944, was the only possible city which could have lain strung like beads along those bends of the River Svisloch. And so, Minsk defied the storm.

It was known, even as we creaked away from Minsk Central that morning, that the Germans were leaving wounded men behind to make way for us thousand citizens of Bela Rus. For the seat I took, for the second one taken by my adolescent sister Genia, for the third taken by my father Stanislaw Assistant Minister of Justice of the Belorussian Republic, for the fourth taken by my mother Danielle, even for the space in the baggage van taken by our tutor Miss Tokina, five German boys had had to be left to an absolutely guaranteed death. Five simple lads no doubt too young for politics or for world-views, the pitiable cannon of their manhoods only so recently trundled forth, were to be abandoned to the Bolsheviks. On their unwitting, washed-out, lolling features would fall the entire vengeance.

As the railway line skirted the airport road you could see the long scars which I knew by then to be the burial places of Jews and Bolsheviks.

'I wonder what the Russians will make of all that,' my father murmured to my mother. He had spent years in the classic Belorussian dilemma – the choice of working for breathing space with one barbarous nation or another.

To flee by train is a far less satisfactory experience than getting out by plane. In the rear of battlefields there is always too much train traffic. Coaches are sidetracked to let priority freight through. A strange feeling always overcomes the passenger when for a reason no one explains a train creaks and, after many metallic moans, stops; when the engine stops too, and from the summer woods either side of the line, the noise of insects invades the compartment. When this happens and you know that behind you the Soviets are not resting, are devouring townships, then the placid murmur of honey-bees can pierce you like a knife. It pierced my mother and became the abiding terror and frustration of her dreams.

It was after the train had stopped for twenty minutes, that terrible determined inertia, and then started rolling with a will towards the Polish border, a border which in childhood had signified to my mother a certain, relative safety, that she leaned over to my sister and me. 'Not many will be saved from Minsk,' she told us. 'When you pray you should consider what it means that you have been saved.'

My sister Genia, fully adolescent by then, cast her eyes up at the luggage rack.

Genia would be the one who resigned from the role of refugee earliest. My father and mother could not, for reasons I shall soon explain, ever cease to be Belorussians in exile. Because of certain guarantees I received the day Onkel Willi died, I travelled very calmly. My mother had no such comfort. She needed guarantees of safety and would never receive any. My father, as you will see, was in his manner a warrior.

My mother was a native of 'the big smoke' – to use an Australian term. Her family came from Minsk itself. My father was born a little further east, in the provincial city of Rogachev. Both families were clans of lawyers, always political. They lived in a Belorussia which had for centuries suffered partitioning. In modern times we have known only six weeks of independence. During the centuries of servile longing we were 'a divine melon' (my father's phrase) divided always between Poland and Russia. Citizens of Minsk used to joke that their city had changed hands one hundred and fifty times in recorded history. The Poles and the Russians may have considered themselves very different, but were like brothers in their intolerance of Belorussian language and culture.

When my father was sixteen years old and was being taught by Polish Jesuits in Minsk, the delightful news of the fall of the Tsar, ever the enemy of Belorussian independence, reached the city. The German Army, who were then occupying Minsk, allowed my grandfather and various other Belorussian patriots to assemble and found a Belorussian Republic. In its government my grandfather was Minister for Forests. Perhaps he thought he would for a long and tranquil decade govern Belorussia's primeval thickets of spruce and hornbeam, oak and birch and alder and elm. Perhaps he thought that for many seasons he would have the regulation of the deer and the wolves, the lynx, the Belorussian bear and the herds of *zubr*. Belorussians always thought like that, always believed that in the end the world would allow them to breathe.

The Australians are more realistic I notice. They believe that Asia – the Chinese, the Indonesians, the Japanese – will swamp them. Some welcome the idea, most fear it, but all expect it. The Australians are a young race who think like an old one. Whereas the Belorussians, whose country has rarely been more than a concept, a happy phantasm, have always thought with the dewiness of youth.

My grandfather had no time to assert a forest policy before the Bolshevik Army came down the road from Smolensk. And the Germans, who had played a small game of holding off the Soviets by allowing my grandfather and his friends to form a government, now decided to play a bigger game, German staff officers arranging with the Red generals that as the German Army withdrew from the east, the Soviet armies should flood in and fill the gaps. They hoped that if they let the Reds in, the Reds would keep the Poles busy in the east – such was the ploy. It suited the Bolsheviks' fantasy, which had to do with marching all the way to Germany to link up with rebellious German workers and soldiers. It suited the Germans, who knew the Soviets wouldn't make it to Berlin, that the Red armies were too primitive to do more than waste themselves trying to beat a path across Poland.

The Germans and the Russians having made peace, only some White Tsarist cavalry units were, by minor skirmish, holding up the advance of the Reds. And as the Reds brushed these White troops aside, my grandparents on both sides fled west by train with their children. There could be no rest until, on lines clogged with the retreating Polish Army, they reached Warsaw. Even there Polish newspapers carried the terrifying dictum of the Soviet general, Tukhachevski. 'The way to Germany lies over Poland's corpse.'

But Warsaw was as far as he got. The Poles at last burst out along the Vistula south and west of Warsaw and then advanced until they were within a short ride of Minsk itself, the city that lies at the heart of Belorussian dreams. Then the Allies stepped in. In those days it was the British who used to play at being Henry Kissinger. Lord Curzon, the British Foreign Secretary, negotiated a line that ran fair down the middle of Belorussia and gave the territory to the west to the Poles and what lay to the east to Russia. The fashion of the day was self-determination, but as had ever been the case, no one was interested in self-determination for the Belorussians.

My mother and her parents lived in no great style in that Warsaw suburb named Praga, across the Vistula by the Warsaw zoo. My father's family, however, the family of a Minister for

Forests in exile, occupied a somewhat better apartment in the heart of the city, close to the Warsaw Central railway station. Both my grandfathers devoted their exile to Belorussian affairs, in particular to the besetting problem of Belorussian real estate.

Polish landlords had flooded back into Western Belorussia now, claiming ancestral property, being granted it (without the need to pay compensation) just because their grandparents or great-grandparents had once held and exploited that land. (My maternal grandparents, for example, had held large timber and dairying holdings around the *oblast* of Minsk, and had lost part of them to the Soviets and part of them to a noble Polish family with a long memory. Hence the poor apartment by the zoo, with only the dream of a Belorussian homecoming to add opulence to life.)

The Poles liked the Belorussians as much as they liked the Jews, and accepted only a minute quota of them into the universities. My father's education from the Polish Jesuits had been adequate to earn him a rare place in the law faculty at Warsaw. 'To be a Hottentot at Oxford,' he would tell me, 'was like being a Belorussian at Warsaw, with the chance of imprisonment and physical damage thrown in.'

After his graduation he provided what would now be called legal aid for Belorussians, travelling as far as Baranoviche and Staroviche to represent his people in property cases, in municipal wrangles over the building of a new church or development approval for a shed in which to run Belorussian classes. He wrote widely in the barely tolerated Belorussian newspaper published in Warsaw. It ran under a succession of names, for no sooner had one name been approved than the Polish police would prohibit it. So it was called variously *Nation, Independence, People, Freedom, Voice, Belarus, Unity, Survival*. At last the Polish police let them publish for some years under the harmless figurative name *Dawn*. But there was always censorship, and sometimes stories would be blanked out, so that Belorussian readers called it, from its censored patchwork appearance, *The Quilt*.

These Belorussian exiles in Warsaw had to suffer the surveillance not only of Pilsudski's security police but of Soviet agents as well, operatives of Lenin's Cheka and then of OGPU, both of them the forerunners of the renowned KGB. Cheka agents would follow my mother and grandmother to and from the markets in Freta Street. The Cheka would have been delighted to see them steal something, some special fruit of the kind they had been used to affording in Minsk, or a necklace or a scarf. There would have been an immediate denunciation to the Polish police, who would have brought their ample prejudices to the case. It was worse when in 1925 my father began courting my mother. OGPU agents tracked them as relentlessly as chaperones. Any violation of the bylaws governing the behaviour of lovers in Lazienki Park would have brought the Polish gendarmes running.

On behalf of Western Belorussia, my father was elected to the Polish Lower House, the Sejm, at the age of twenty-five years. Only thirteen representatives were permitted from the various national minorities, so that my father's election made him famous in that half of Belorussia which lived under Polish rule.

In the winter of 1927, my father and grandfather were arrested by the Polish police one morning at breakfast-time and charged with belonging to a subversive Belorussian society called GRAMADA. They were taken over the railway line to the Pawiak prison. Here they were treated to the same methods the SS would later use on the Poles themselves – the 'tramcars', cells in which prisoners sat or kneeled like monks in total silence at little benches which resembled *prie-dieux*, while one at a time they were taken out and questioned and beaten and returned to sit or kneel in silence still. My father's jaw was broken here, and the crookedness with which it mended became more pronounced as he grew older.

My father, his jaw attended to by doctors so that he would show no marks in court, stood trial with eighteen other Belorussian deputies and senators, and the outcry from liberals within Poland was such that they were acquitted. The three thousand other Belorussians who had been arrested that January morning were tried en masse – my two grandfathers amongst them – and sentenced to gaol terms. But again the liberal outcry was such that the sentences were suspended. My grandfathers returned from a timber camp in Silesia within a few days. There is that to be said for liberals – they may be in no way equipped for governing the world, but they are admirable in specific cases of injustice.

My grandfather the Minister for Forests would die within a year of his release. My maternal grandfather, also an arrested and then released member of GRAMADA, never again settled to writing articles and attending meetings, the two activities which up to then had sustained him in his exile.

The experience of Pawiak and the trial convinced my father that he should marry and affirm his Belorussian nationality in a way that even the Poles could not proscribe or the OGPU betray – namely by founding his own Belorussian family. The wedding in the old Jesuit church behind the city square was attended by agents both of OGPU and of the Polish security police. For the sake of my grandfathers, who had been so marked by their imprisonment, the families tried to make a joke of those uninvited guests.

NINE

And trains yet again. In the last days of August 1939 – I can dimly remember the excitement of holiday packing – our family left our apartment in Warsaw and went off for what my father said would be a holiday near Puck, a sheltered Polish resort on the Baltic, not far from the great international port of Gdansk. We were to stay in a beach hotel. I was told that as an added excitement we were to find my godfather Ostrowsky already booked in there and waiting, like the presiding genius of our holiday. He had in fact summoned us to the Baltic, and when we got on the train for Gdansk we found we were not the only Belorussians making for Puck, that he had invited half a dozen other families too. The parents all seemed calm and almost maliciously unexcited to be going to the beach so late in the summer, so close to the date when offices, factories, schools returned to full-blast production. The children, however, were feverish with the ecstasy of it, except such older ones as my sister Genia, who seemed stuck halfway between the sober adults and the crazily happy children. She did not tear up and down the corridors of the train with the rest of us. Sometimes she mentioned – with a cool adult sort of yearning – her art teacher, a German-Pole called Mr Beckmann, and surmised that he would be very surprised not to see her in his class the following Tuesday.

It was still very warm on the Baltic beaches, but the wind was turning to the north-east and kicking up sand. The women sat together behind barriers of windproof canvas and talked quietly yet intently, not at all like adults relaxing in the sun. The men sat on their own colony of beachchairs, grouped around the

lean and pallid figure of Ostrowsky, a few hundred metres north
of the women. The water was freezing, so only children and
those interested in self-discipline splashed in and disturbed the
pastel-blue surface and the concentration of the Belorussian
patriots who sat around my godfather.

One afternoon we came back to our rooms on the third floor
of the hotel to find Polish security, plainclothes agents, and
blue-uniformed policemen searching them. Further up the corridor bathrobed Ostrowsky was arguing with a Polish officer who
stood by supervising the plunder. Perhaps plunder is too strong
a word, because although the Poles were raking through drawers
and suitcases, they were not taking anything. They wanted to
know, my father later said, why so many notorious Belorussians
were all together in a Baltic hotel at the end of the season. They
hoped they might find some instructive documentation amongst
our luggage while we were on the beach.

My mother said to one of the agents, 'I suppose you have no
objection if my children and I wait on the patio until you have
had the courtesy to vacate our rooms.' She was a long-boned
and elegant woman. My father used to say she was his image
of a Hapsburg princess. She withered those heavy Poles. I loved
her for being so impressive, for soothing my fear with an imperial
manner.

Two days later the invasion of Poland commenced and all
travel was suspended. Battle resounded very dimly along that
quiet coast. In the pine trees behind the beaches the small
refreshment stalls selling punnets of strawberries, blueberries,
raspberries, stayed open, and we children sprinted back and
forth between the soft fine sand and the wooded paths, buying
and fetching punnets for our parents, turning up at their
beachchairs with our lips stained from the ratio of fruit we'd
eaten as commission. The adults were happier now. They had
at last found the holiday spirit.

We stayed here in Puck, in a hotel now empty except for
ourselves, all through the invasion. One morning at breakfast
the waiters appeared in greenish military uniforms – they were
to go within the hour to their Polish regiments. Some of the
waitresses dropped plates unexpectedly and stepped behind the

drapes to weep. Four or five days later, while an autumn squall was sweeping in over the Bay of Puck, some Gdynia Nazis turned up on motorcycles and in trucks, German nationalists who had lived twenty years under Polish rule, and ran up the sodden flag of National Socialism in front of the Polish post office where up till then all dramatic events had centred on the sending off of postcards of scenes of Puck and Hel and the fishing village at Jastarnia.

As rain squalls became more frequent and the siege of Warsaw continued, we remained guests of the hotel. The possible expense frightened my mother. Through the open door between our room and theirs I could hear them talking about it. Even though I did not understand every word that was said, since I had always been a devout eavesdropper, and since to overhear my parents in their bed, whispering about business, constituted prime entertainment, I can remember the conversation with some accuracy. 'No,' my father said, 'don't concern yourself about it. Ostrowsky assures me the bill will be paid by the Reich Security Central Office.'

My mother's silence indicated a certain disquiet. My father said that both parties hoped to make use of each other, the Belorussians and the Nazis. What other world force to cooperate with? The Soviets? 'We have to come out of this war with a national integrity,' he murmured. And this I remember in particular, though the nomenclature he used meant so little to me then. 'Thank God,' he murmured, 'that through Ostrowsky's advice my contacts have always been with the Gestapo and the SD instead of with those sodomites in the Stormtroopers.'

As the Baltic mists now took over Puck in earnest and filled the corridors of the hotel with damp, as fog rolled in opened doors and windows like steam from a Turkish bath, we yearned to be liberated from the hotel. And in time Warsaw fell and we were able at last to go home, to our apartment which had survived the bombing. Mr Beckmann the art teacher had joined the Waffen SS – Genia saw him in his uniform in the Freta. My father wrote for a new Belorussian newspaper – there was some censorship because the Germans did not want their allies the Russians offended. My father also attended administrative courses run by the Reich Security Central Office in an old Polish government building near the Gdanski bridge. Once he complained that he was sure there were Soviet plants in the course, but the German officers who came to our apartment for coffee and cognac used to reassure him – of course the OGPU had its agents there, but they were fairly supine and inefficient and the SD had an eye on them.

As Central Poland had fallen to the Germans, the Soviets had pushed forward into Polish Belorussia. Belorussia was now once more under the total control of the Soviets – for that had been the arrangement between Hitler and Stalin. My father used to joke at table that this set-up was preferable, since only one intruder now had to be dealt with. The German officers would pretend to be scandalised and advise him against being too openly anti-Soviet for the moment.

My father, of course, knew what would happen. In June 1941 the Germans launched their withering attack on the Soviets, taking all the holy earth of Belorussia within a matter of days. Within a few hours of the capture of Staroviche, my father arrived in that city and took up the post to which the Reich Security Central Office had appointed him, police chief of an entire Belorussian province. A week later, after one of the few happy train journeys in the Kabbelski family history, the rest of his family travelled from Warsaw and joined him in the elegant residence in Drozdy Street.

TEN

'Gunter Grass's *The Tin Drum*,' said a paper on the radio bench at the headquarters of Uncle Security, 'is an essay on the limits of nationalism. Discuss this.'

Danielle Kabbel was not there, in the office, when Delaney and Stanton signed on. Waiting for her to turn up with the key of the weapons cabinet, Stanton lolled in a chair. His younger more restless daughter had been home from school all day with an infection. She had woken him, he claimed, seven times by his count. Once by launching herself from a sideboard on to him. He had woken screaming beneath the sudden weight of the child. He had been dreaming flinchingly of Queensland canetoads and had at first thought she was one, the supreme one, 'Moby bloody Toad.' He was in no state to show interest in the fragments of an education which Danielle Kabbel had left around in the control room. Yet Delaney was hungry for such details.

Grass clearly intends that the midget Oskar should, through his glass-shattering voice, signify and symbolise certain aspects of modern European history. What are these aspects? Whose voice does Oskar's voice stand for? (In your discussions, do not forget the significance of *Kristallnacht* or Glass Night, when in 1938 the Nazis destroyed Jewish property, notably windows and glassware, in synagogues and business locations.)

'Reading her mail, eh?' Stanton asked.

Delaney smiled but did not answer. He was consumed by a desire to read this book about a midget with a voice that shattered glass, as if dealing with the novel was the way to solve and acquit that image of the girl which was always springing up at the front of his brain. He went on reading the WEA notes.

Discuss why it is essential to the novel that Oskar be a midget. First you should consider why it is essential in terms of the dynamics of Oskar's family. Then you should consider whether his dwarfism is a symbol of the deliberately retarded German consciousness which permitted the rise of Hitler.

Delaney experienced, as if watching a worthy documentary on Channel 2 (known to be good for sport, ratshit for everything else), a sharply focused picture of a crowd of women in a living room all talking about the book, understanding everything and nothing amongst the coffee cups, and in the middle of the room, in a floral dress and quiet as nuns used to be, Danielle Kabbel listening with a half-smile.

'Must read this book,' he found himself saying, though he hadn't intended to.

Stanton began to laugh, uncertainly and perhaps with envy. He read Wilbur Smith. He could tell that this was a different kind of book. 'Advanced age bloody student,' said Stanton.

The novel itself lay on the computer table. Delaney lifted it and began to read. The words meant nothing, he felt them as an august flux. Her face was behind them like *Hamlet*'s Ophelia caught – as Delaney remembered vividly from the Higher School Certificate – in a shallow and serene drowning. He understood that he was in some sort of danger, touching her WEA notes like someone with a fetish and looking forward to his shift, so that receiving and signing for his .38 he could pass within the fringes of her dry, sharp, pungent electric field.

FROM THE MATCH DIARY OF TERRY DELANEY

Penrith v Easts, Sports Ground, April 25, 1983 Anzac Day game. Forwards got the Chicka Hays disease, going one out all day, making a bit of ground but always getting caught with ball still in their arms. Also Easts spent entire game inside the five metres and referee didn't seem to care. Lucky thing – what they gained by infringements they lost through lack of good old toe, speed, quickness off the mark. Got a lovely pass away to Eric Samuels ten minutes into second half. I could see Eric going places, so wriggled out of their lock's tackle and followed the old Eric up. He left the centres standing but their winger caught him, fast young kid, an Abo. Eric got lovely underarm pass to me. I thought I was in but their fullback hit me from behind. Going down in slow motion and on way down found Steve Mansfield steaming up on inside. Just put it right into his arms and he scored under the posts. Converted own try. Beautiful. Penrith 13, Easts 4.

*   *   *

Watched first grade. Kevin Hastings played all over Deecock, our Pommy first grade five-eighth. Deecock had it; they can't wait for him to retire and go to North Queensland to captain/coach some Banana-bender team up there. Looks like he'll be the weak link again this season like last. First grade coach Alan Beamish said to me after game, 'Needed you out there, Terry.' I grinned at him, 'Give the local boys a chance,' I said. As if I didn't really mind they'd brought Deecock all the way from Yorkshire just to do local boys out of a job. So first grade a bit of a disaster: Easts 27, Penrith 12.

*   *   *

Gina there. Both felt light in the head after game I'd played. But atmosphere back at Leagues Club tonight like a bloody morgue. Apart from Deecock, they bought that Pommy forward Tancred for $60,000. Tancred's the sort of thickhead who wouldn't work in an iron lung. That's the trouble with Pommy forwards – always knew it was, average bloke watching the game knows it is – they look sort of fast on muddy Yorkshire grounds, but when they get out here on a hard and fast Australian ground they're just as slow as they were back in the quagmire. Yet club officials keep buying them! Good at getting the ball away, but leaden-footed. Tancred never played at this pace before, except in one test match Australia v England, which Australia won 34–7! Yet our heroic club secretary sees him, the Aussie forwards outpacing him all over the ground, and thinks, Ah, just what we need to take Penrith to a premiership.

Lot of mumbling into beer about it in Leagues Club tonight.

When Steve Mansfield made his proposal in the Leagues Club carpark, Delaney had been watching a full and ripe moon hanging over Sydney to the east. It was such a vast fact in the sky that Delaney in his half-tipsy way felt it had to be concentrated on and absorbed. Its presence distracted him from the job he was attempting, the opening of the passenger side door of his Holden. Steve Mansfield, further gone than Delaney, sat on the flank of Stew Reilly's RX-7 and rocked his body merrily as Delaney tried the harsh task of lancing his key exactly into the yielding mechanism of the lock. Gay Mansfield and Gina were still inside the red brick palace, talking in a sisterly way in front of the spotlit mirrors in the women's toilets. Enjoying the status of players' wives, for what that was worth. Even in the carpark, though, you could hear the poker machines whirring and ringing inside. That was where all the bounty and surplus luxury of the lives of the Delaneys and Mansfields came from, from the frenzy of late-night gamblers who could be separated from the machine that chewed their money only by the closing of the club.

Delaney gave up trying to find the keyhole and tottered backwards, slinging his arm around Mansfield and joining him in stuttering hilarity.

'Listen, mate,' said Mansfield when they'd stopped hissing with laughter, 'come back to our place, eh? Gay'd really like that, if you came back.'

Delaney said it wasn't on. He'd already drunk all he could.

'Fair go,' said Mansfield. 'No more booze, that's agreed. No, listen.' He grabbed Delaney by the bicep through the cloth of his best metallic blue suit. 'No, listen. Have you two ever, you know, got stuck into it with another couple?' Mansfield raised his hand, palm open outwards in case the idea provoked Delaney. 'I know you're Micks, but even Micks root around a bit these days. And I mean to say, *Hawaii*, eh, mate? Not exactly a bloody saint in Hawaii, eh?'

He grabbed Delaney round the shoulders and Delaney wondered for a second, did this third grade captain's amazing offer extend to *that* sort of sharing as well. He was grateful when Mansfield let him go.

'Listen, Gay fancies you. She's pretty straight out with these things. I've got to say a great little root, watches those videos and goes off like a bloody firecracker – got to say that, though I'm her old man. I mean it's bloody fantastic, this four-way stuff. Reckon Gina'd be in it?'

Delaney shook his head and could not speak. The immense pagan fact of the moon seemed in alliance with Steve, it bulked up over the urgent line of Steve's shoulder. All that repeated itself in Delaney's head was, If he can talk like this, he can tell Gina Hawaiian stories. And then, How do you talk to each other the next morning?

When Delaney could speak, he said, 'All in the same room?'

'Well,' said Mansfield, 'yeah.' He laughed. 'You don't want your missus getting off by herself with a strange bloke.'

'How in the bloody hell do you talk to each other the next morning?'

'Fantastic. You know. Clears the bloody air. Lets some light in. We trust each other, Gay and me.' Laughter again, laughter that sounded unstrained. 'I don't resent it if she fancies a skinny bastard like you. It's *better* if she's able to say it. Not keep it a secret. I mean, one thing I've discovered – I used to think blokes were rearing to go, but a good woman's a fucking cauldron, let me tell you.'

Ti mon seul desir, Delaney nearly uttered. One day, when he was sixteen, Brother Aubin had brought into doctrine class a print of some ancient French tapestry. A slim girl in a red robe, wearing a medieval headdress, was drawing jewellery out of a chest held by a small maid. Beside the girl, on a bench, sat a silky Pekingese – a rare commodity in medieval Europe, said Brother Aubin, a gift which was a mark of love. Behind the girl stood a rich tent of blue and gold fabric, its flaps held aside by a lion on one side – symbol of honest passion – and a unicorn on the other, symbolising faithfulness, chastity. And embroidered across the door of the tent the message: *Ti mon seul desir,* old French for 'You my only desired one'. Given the stresses on modern marriage, said Aubin, given even the statistics of old de la Salle Brothers boys who had experienced separation and divorce, you boys must be able to say when you come to the altar *Ti mon seul desir* and to mean it totally and to go on meaning it.

It was the only French Delaney brought with him from school, except of course for the fragments anyone had from watching films and listening to music. Delaney could remember that as Aubin talked about the print, the school prop forward Marchetti represented with his hands a great phallic marrow and began jerking it. Delaney, who was secretly melting with the phrase, abominated Marchetti in that second. *Ti mon seul desir* was the banner he wanted his manhood to sail under. That was his nature. Get it where you can was Marchetti's nature.

As Mansfield had already pointed out, *Ti mon seul desir* had taken a beating in Hawaii. But Delaney felt a genuine curiosity about how it could survive a night like the one Steve Mansfield proposed.

'Is it a matter of Gay fancying me, or you wanting Gina?' he asked. He all at once hated Mansfield as much as he had once hated Marchetti and his watermelon dick. 'Italian girls don't go in for that sort of thing,' he said before Mansfield salved his curiosity. It was another way of explaining that after such a night he and Gina would be without a map, without a banner: there were no words they had exchanged up to this stage, no pattern of words, for dealing with the morning after that kind of night.

He was angry too because in spite of himself he had begun to swell.

'Listen,' said Steve, 'we're not bloody perverts or anything. Take Chicka Hays – Gay can't stand a bar of the bastard. He belongs to a rooting club, blokes and birds, who get going by watching snuff movies, Chinese girls getting murdered right on camera, make a decent person bloody spew. Then everyone goes home and makes the kiddies breakfast!'

'Bloody Chicka plays football like that,' yelled Delaney, know-

ing he was being too loud. 'No fucking finesse. All elbows and
making three yards up the middle with half a dozen blokes
hanging on to him. And it's bloody Christmas before he gets the
ball away, can't set up a man coming fast on to the ball. If you
and I had ten kilos less we'd still be fucking footballers. *He*
wouldn't get a social game!'

Delaney saw that the two women had appeared in the avenue
of cars. He could tell Gina by her leonine Italian head. Gay was
not as raw, not as challenging in her looks. She was smaller and
pretty and Mansfield's confessions about her appetites didn't
surprise him – she *looked* more sexual than Gina. She was
laughing at him.

'He's getting stuck into Chicka Hays's reputation,' Mansfield
explained to the women. He sounded tremulous.

'What reputation?' said Gay.

'Coming home with us?' asked Mansfield, having to cough to
clear the question from his throat.

'Yes, come home,' said Gay, reaching her arm up around
Gina's shoulder. Delaney could barely stand to watch the gesture. His skin crept with old-fashioned embarrassment.

'No,' said Delaney. He felt the question would still stand if he
said anything politer. And knew his brusqueness could be
excused because of what he'd drunk.

'I've got to start work early,' said Gina more sanely. 'Stock-
taking.'

Safely in the Holden, Delaney pulled her to him, pushed his
tongue lasciviously into her mouth. She made noises of amused
protest, the kind that promised much once she had attended to
the business of driving home. His hand moved on her thigh and
felt her dewiness beneath the fabric. *Ti mon seul desir*, he
murmured, but as he spoke the aphorism evoked not Gina's
features, at the moment indistinct above the steering wheel,
but the neat-boned face of Danielle Kabbel.

ELEVEN

FROM THE JOURNALS OF STANISLAW KABBELSKI, CHIEF OF POLICE,

STAROVICHE

September 4, 1941

An afternoon meeting at SD headquarters, Natural History Museum, Bryanska Street. Otto Ohlendorf, a really impressive doctor of jurisprudence and economic expert, presently commander of SS Special Action Group D, in the chair. Rank: Brigadeführer. Very young – thirty-three years or so. Story is he fell out with Reich Security Central Office and has been sent to Belorussia to be taught a lesson. Others present were Mayor Kuzich, local SS and SD officers, my division chiefs and the Chief of Police of Gomel, from whom we are borrowing personnel for the next two days. Also there – he says as an observer – Dr Kappeler of the Political Section in Kaunas.

We Belorussians under test. Kappeler is the examiner, there's no doubt about that. All Lithuania and Belorussia presently labelled Ostland. If we hope to have our nation labelled by its correct and desired name, we have to get on right side of men like Kappeler.

The charming Oberführer Ganz, our Kommissar here in Staroviche, so visible at dinner tables, did not attend meeting. Sent an aide instead. It is clear Ganz will be happier when Special Action Group D packs up and rolls on to another city, and when Kappeler returns to the Ostministry in Kaunas.

Ganz's absence noted with a few significant remarks by Ohlendorf. Ohlendorf concerned about other actions carried out using Belorussian police and marked by drunkenness and sexual assaults. (I wonder why he thinks I didn't bother inviting my alcoholic deputy, Beluvich.)

In tomorrow's action, a quarter-litre of vodka is to be the maximum ration per man. I put forward proposal for two shifts of men – 3.30 a.m. to noon, noon to 8.30 p.m., and for a liquor ration to be issued at beginning and end of each shift. No one quarrelled with the idea that the men involved in the action required *some* fortifying.

Mayor Kuzich and Dr Ohlendorf, the latter having already had some experience in these matters, have chosen an area three miles west of the city on the Gomel road. Kuzich made tedious speech about the potential influence of mass graves on municipal water supply – how his experience as an engineer had helped him obviate it.

Made my speech then. Used the term 'Jewish Bolsheviks' a great deal, since it is one much favoured by the Reich Security Central Office. Said that Belorussian patriots had never seen a place for such people in the yearned-for Belorussian Republic, but that our cooperation with Special Action Group D was to be seen not only as a gesture of fraternity, based on common beliefs, but that it should also be seen as yet another element qualifying us for self-government. Speech well received by both Ohlendorf and Dr Kappeler. As, of course, by all Belorussians present.

Got home to find Oberführer Ganz has organised a picnic for tomorrow, in Brudezh forest north of the city. Intended to send Danielle and children on picnic with Kuzich family tomorrow anyhow, but Ganz has horned in. Cannot help feel the charming Ganz very vain – wants the Belorussians to remember him as a beloved and wise occupier. In fact, once the Germans permit us our Republic he won't get too many mentions.

Would have thought his place tomorrow would be, if not out on the Gomel road, at least at his desk in town. There are historical imperatives in operation which no man can evade, even if he can send the children on a picnic. But to go on a picnic himself indicates he does not understand this swine of a century at all. The fact you can't get anything done any more unless you get mud on your boots.

There is also the matter of the Kommissar's Jewish driver. Am broad-minded about personal morality. Hope Ganz's superiors at the Reichkommissariat headquarters in Minsk and way up in Riga are equally well-disposed to him.

Also waiting for me at home, with only half-hour before guests arrive, Jasper, the young Wehrmacht sergeant attached to my office. Seemed distraught, and agreed with uncustomary quickness that he needed a drink. That afternoon he'd visited the ghetto down by the river – he was not supposed to, but some of the Wehrmacht did because there were so many Jewish artisans. Jasper had gone there to collect his shoes from a cobbler who had been resoling them. (Black-market leather, of course, as I pointed out to Jasper, but with a smile, hoping to quieten him down.) The cobbler had been in a state. Said there was a rumour that SS had asked city authorities, Mayor Kuzich, myself, to assist in round-up and execution of Jewish population of Staroviche, and that city authorities had agreed. Jewish deputation had been to see Kuzich that morning (Kuzich had told me of this meeting). Though Kuzich had reassured them and told them he would emphasise to the Germans the good work Jewish Council had done in levying taxes amongst Jewish population, a lot of concern amongst the Jews. Some of the Gentile townspeople Jasper spoke to before coming to see me had also heard the rumours. A greengrocer told Jasper, 'Everyone ought to wait till the Russians are finished off, because those Jews have powerful political friends!'

Jasper looked at me steadily across the desk. 'Herr Kabbelski,' he said, 'tell me if it's true.'

Told him calmly that it was. Observers here from all over Ostland. It would be a model action. Could see him swallowing, trying to deal with his outrage, the same outrage which he had the grace to recognise I felt on many levels as well. Told him there would be exemptions for a small number still considered essential workers. Lest he think of the cobbler, I said, 'Ober-führer Ganz's driver, for example.'

'But, sir,' he said. 'It isn't possible in the technical sense to finish so many people in a day.'

Told him that after some study and on the advice of his
own people, specially Brigadeführer Ohlendorf of Special Action
Group D, I now knew it to be possible, that it had already been
done in Bialystok, Vilna, Pinsk and Brest-Litovskiy – places
where the technique had been developed. It had not always
worked as well, one could say as *properly*, as it would tomorrow.
Some operations further north where Belorussian policemen,
stoked with too much liquor, behaved like barbarians, molesting
women, sodomising children. Even not all of Jasper's people
behaved well, though they'd been in training for this sort of
operation for a long time.

'*They* are not my people,' he said, choking with grief.

I felt for him both pity and anger. 'Then who are your people,
Sergeant Jasper? I know who are mine!' And I gave him a short
history lesson, nothing he wouldn't already have known as a
European scholar, but something to soothe him. If Germans
thought they had a Jewish problem, what about we Belorussians?
The Tsars cramming Jews into these western provinces, forbidding them to live or move outside them, forbidding them to live
even in the countryside! The result? Minsk 41 per cent Jewish,
Rovno 56 per cent, Pinsk 64 per cent, Brest-Litovskiy 44 per
cent, Gomel 44 per cent, Bobruisk 40 per cent, Staroviche 31
per cent. And were they good Belorussian nationalists? They
couldn't give a damn. Stayed put and did business no matter
who came to town. Anti-German by sentiment, anti-Belorussian
because they considered our hoped-for nation a pale of barbarous
peasants. No question that there were partisan cells amongst
them and that if slightest thing went wrong with the German
offensive against Moscow those cells would become dangerously
active. An alien mass in the midst of the endeavour of our two
races, German and Belorussian. Taken as read by us nationalists
that there could be no Belorussian Republic while this mass
remained. Reminded him further that we followers of Ostrowsky
had always made ourselves clear on that point to the Reich
Security Central Office – we were in this whole affair for the
sake of Belorussian independence. So I knew who my people
were. Was sorry if he was having temporary trouble identifying
his.

Mentioned too that I could understand his natural instinct to rush down to the ghetto and spread the word through his cobbler. Two possible results: the cobbler still unable to believe it, and – strangely for such an artful race – the Jews have always found it hard to believe the worst of the Gentile world; second, the cobbler spreads the word and causes a riot. Truckloads of Belorussian police, German Field Police, Special Action people and a few Wehrmacht units waiting by in the alleys off Bryanska Street to guard against exactly such a disturbance. So whole thing would be done whichever way – either brutally and frontally as a result of an indiscretion by Sergeant Jasper, or mercifully and professionally tomorrow.

Finally told him not to be self-indulgent. How did he think I felt? At ease? With the supreme test of my soul, my manhood, due to begin at 3.00 a.m. the following morning? Ganz and my wife and children, together with Kuzich's family, to leave very early, at first light, for a picnic in another direction. If he thought he would have a problem tomorrow, he ought to join them.

Very angry with him when he did not appear at the dinner table, but later turned up in the hallway after all the senior officers had gone off to their beds. Apologised and said he had stayed on in my office, as I'd suggested (though I didn't mean for the whole damned dinner) and fortified himself with liquor.

Promised he would be at his desk at police headquarters the next morning.

Now 11.30. Will go into tomorrow on two and a half hours' sleep. Suppose that's true of all history, that it's achieved on inadequate rest.

TWELVE

Staroviche was a city and *oblast*, or province, sitting south-east of Minsk in a bend of the Pripet river. However hackneyed the sentiment, I can say that there I spent the three happiest years of my childhood. We lived in a solid and ornate villa.

It stood in its own garden and, whatever was happening beyond its brick walls, was its own adequate planet. Only in the summer of 1942 did my mother and sister and I leave it to holiday near Riga on the Baltic. Even though increasing anarchy in the streets of Staroviche would reduce its usefulness to us, we enjoyed too the expensive Hoetsch automobile which went with my father's status as police chief of the city and region, and a chauffeur named Yuri who wore the blue uniform of the Belorussian police. Since children do not watch the calendar, the summers of the garden in Drozdy Street seemed longer than whole decades now, and the winters with their early darkness hardly shorter.

Our best friend in the three years our family lived in Staroviche was Oberführer Willi Ganz. Ganz was Kommissar of the *oblast* or (as the Germans said) the *bezirk* of Staroviche, the same region of which my father was Belorussian police chief. My mother and I became very attached to him, more than to any of the other official guests who came to our place. He was the most sincere of all those German officers and functionaries who liked her landscapes. My sister and I began to call him Onkel Willi, without being asked to, without any embarrassment, practically from the first visit he made to our house.

I remember once when my mother was praising Oberführer Ganz for the sincere interest he showed in us children that my father said, 'Perhaps he laughs too easily.' But he himself laughed when he said it. When I think of poor Ganz after all this time I remember not a set of features but his laughter, which wasn't maniacal on the one hand or careful and mannered on the other. It was like the laughter of a man who doesn't have an enemy in the world. And this from an SS Oberführer, member of a legion of which the world has ever since made a bogey.

He was of medium height, athletically built and beginning to lose his black hair from a rounded, expansive skull. He was the sort of adult who liked to produce little presents from his pocket at times when bedtime is close and a child thinks the main delights of the evening are over.

My sister and I became infatuated with Ganz, as far as I can remember, late in the summer of my parents' return to Belorussia. (To us children it seemed like a return too, though we had never been there before.) The Soviet Union was about to fall – everyone knew that and was excited by the idea, and the atmosphere of cosmic carnival the news created was universal. The Soviet Army had been decimated – we had visible proof of that – two great mounds beside the Staroviche-Baranoviche road under which – as even my sister and I knew, though our parents were not the type to bring such brutal facts to our attention – lay the two Russian brigades who had tried to fight the Germans for Staroviche. Everyone was quoting the saying that the Russian defeat was so absolute that all the Germans had had to do was kick in the door and the whole rotten structure had tumbled in. News that Stalin had been killed by his own people in besieged Moscow was expected daily.

It was safe at that stage for a German official to accompany the wives of the newly installed mayor and police chief of Staroviche, together with the children of both women, on a picnic to the Brudezh forest north of the city. The mayor by the way was Franz Kuzich, one of those whose families had holidayed with us at Puck. Kuzich came from a Germanophile family and his three children also carried German names – Ruta, Bernhardt, Kirsten. They were all knowing adolescents – Bernhardt did not share even the same jokes as I did, would not have been seen

dead laughing at them. Kirsten was a year older than my sister
Genia and used that margin as an excuse for cutting her
dead.

Ganz's picnic was a triumph for us because the Oberführer
wouldn't allow any of the Kuzichs' children's air of higher wisdom
and knowledge to prevail. If they wanted to play with Ganz,
Ganz only wanted to play like a child. Therefore *they* had to
consent to become children again. I remember still how I loved
the man for delivering us like that, for making us fashionable
with the Kuzich children, who might be unfashionably overweight
like their mother but whose opinions meant everything to Genia
and me. Ganz wanted hiding games and chasing games, and as
I ran the woods blurred, a delightful deep green haze, and when
I hid I caressed the bark of the larch trees and the birch, and as
Ganz's pursuing laughter bounced from branch to branch I
thought, *This* is Belorussia, *this* is why we had to come back,
to make childhood possible.

Once I ran, looking the other way, shoulder-first into Ganz,
who grabbed me by the shoulders and clamped me to his chest.
He wasn't wearing his coat and his shirt was white and fragrant.
I could smell his perfume, a mild, male-smelling perfume, and
behind it a further musk. This must be the way warriors smell,
I naively thought. He released me only to clamp me by both
ears again and drag me nose-first against his chest. 'Little
Radislaw Kabbelski,' he said emphatically. 'You are a blessed
child. Let Onkel Willi wish that in all the world's blood and lies,
you will hear only kindly voices.' Then he kissed my forehead
and let me go. I could not have been happier if he had elected
me president.

Later that same delightful day I skidded around the edge of a
knot of berry bushes to find one of Ganz's soldiers urinating
there, a man nearly as old as Ganz, one of Ganz's headquarters
people detailed to guard our picnic against the remote chance
that a few of the world's last Communists should decide to attack
it. 'Forgive me, meinherr,' he said, buttoning as fast as he could.
That also was why we came back. To be meinherr in our own
country. I decided to show the soldier that I was indeed a person
of influence. 'Is Sergeant Jasper here today?' I asked in German

– I had, like many Eastern Europeans of the era, four languages.
'Not today, meinherr,' said the soldier.

Sergeant Jasper was the only German I had seen weeping that
triumphant summer. I felt so endowed with authority at Ganz's
picnic that if Jasper had been in the forest I would have gone to
him and asked him what had been upsetting him, more or less
enquire why he was marring this golden time.

Jasper, an NCO from German Army Intelligence, had been
attached to my father's staff. If any left-behind Russians were
found in the woods by my father's navy-blue-clad policemen,
Jasper was to interrogate them. Any captured Bolshevik partisans and bandits were also to be milked by Jasper. Earlier in
the summer I had heard my father praising him to my mother.
A bright boy, said my father. It was a pity he wasn't com-
missioned, my father declared, because it diminished his standing with the SS officers.

There had been a party at our house the night before the
picnic. It had been a really big affair to honour certain SS and
SD officials from Minsk.

Amongst the guests of whom even I was aware was an SS
man all the way from Riga, another from the Kaunas office of
that same Reich Security Central Office which had paid all our
hotel bills on the Baltic, and Dr Kappeler, an important section
head in the Ministry of the East or Ostministry.

Local dignitaries included the aging heavy-drinking garrison
commander of our town (who my father thought was a fool, but
knew that everyone in the German Army who was not a fool
was presently in front of Moscow), our Kommissar the beloved
Willi Ganz, my father's deputy Beluvich, an old faithful of the
Belorussian dream (my father said) for whom the great chance
had come too late, Mr Kuzich our mayor, and the head of the
Staroviche Gestapo.

Everyone seemed to have brought a wife or a ladyfriend
except Oberführer Ganz, and to an eight-year-old boy Ganz's
failure in this regard was a generous sign that the people he had
really come to see were my mother and Genia and me.

One of the minor guests was Sergeant Jasper, who came

earlier than anyone else and asked the servant who opened the door if he could see my father. My father came downstairs at last and gave Jasper an interview in the study, from which they emerged just in time for my father to greet the other guests. Genia and I were allowed to take round trays of hors d'oeuvres, a trick which brought inordinate applause from all the visitors. Even as we toted the trays around we kept our eyes on two men, Beluvich my father's deputy, and Ganz, for they were the prodigious drinkers in the company. Beluvich and Mrs Beluvich drank vodka in a quiet, industrious way until their faces bleared and they could not finish sentences. Then they would try to light cigarettes – that was the comedy sequence Genia and I did not want to miss.

Ganz drank cognac, and instead of blunting him it seemed to refine him, till his eyes were glittering and all the women gathered round him to listen to his jokes. All the other German officers were more restrained, even the younger ones, as if they were under orders not to drink too much or yield to Ganz's liveliness. I took their resistance as only another instance of the astounding tedium of adults.

In the crush I did not notice Jasper at all.

Genia and I did not have a place at the table, but we watched from the hallway, from the bottom of the stairs, while the Catholic bishop of Staroviche blessed the food. The Orthodox bishop had, to everyone's surprise, after some years of persecution by the NKVD and a jail sentence, left with the retreating Soviets, and a new bishop had not yet been elected. The bishop's departure was taken as a sign of a characteristically Russian perversity, of the same type shown by those two slaughtered Russian brigades who lay along the Baranoviche road.

After the grace everyone sat. My father drank his bortsch very quickly, made excuses to the Ostministry man from Kaunas on his right and the SS man from Riga on his left and rose to call his chief servant, an ancient and loyal Belorussian whom he had found in Staroviche when he first arrived with the officers of Vorkommando Moscow, just behind the first wave of Panzers. We saw my father whisper at the old man and point out an empty space at the bottom of the table. We realised it was Sergeant

Jasper's place and that father was sending the servant to find
him. This qualified with me as delicious drama, as it did also
with Genia, though she tried not to admit it.

We followed the servant as he went searching down the
corridor, in my father's study, in the solarium. He opened the
kitchen door and Genia and I recognised there, amongst a
number of other drivers, military and civilian, Kommissar Ganz's
chauffeur Ya'acov drinking coffee. Most of the Jews of Staroviche
lived in a barricaded section of town – I found out later that
there were more than eight thousand of them crammed in there,
between Braslawski Street and the river. Ya'acov was one of
the few who had outside jobs and lived outside the barricade.
He sat quietly amongst the SS chauffeurs, not volunteering his
name.

But Jasper wasn't in the kitchen. The old servant, with the
Kabbelski children in pursuit, found him on the top landing near
my bedroom, sitting on the floor, his collar unbuttoned, a flask
of spirits between his knees and weeping awesomely, steadily,
stuttering and stammering his grief, on and on.

The servant began to speak to him and Jasper answered
quietly. We heard him say, 'The children, the children,' a number
of times, and we began to fear he meant us. We must have
given off a flurry of alarm because the old servant turned to us
– he was discovering for the first time that we were behind him
– and hissed, 'Clear out. He's not talking to you.'

In the context of that glorious evening, with the prospect of
tomorrow's picnic, it astounded me that anyone under our roof
could be unhappy.

I remember Jasper now more as a representative of that
generation of Europeans who were all forced at great pace to
learn a fierce amount about themselves and their fellows during
those years in the furnace.

THIRTEEN

'Listen,' Stanton said outside the Kabbels' place. The first frostiness of the season was in the air, and Delaney liked that, the arrival of daylight brought with it more the elation of survival. 'Listen, you reckon that girl and her brother might be on together?'

Delaney, gouging for car keys in his pocket, stiffened. He wanted both to hide his face and hit Stanton. Instead he heard himself ask why.

'I went for a leak,' said Stanton, 'and the outside loo's buggered so I used the one in the house. In the corridor there's this painting of the two of them. Signed by Warwick. She's wearing the security company's bloody daggy shirt and they're staring at the bloody camera – or at the brush I suppose you'd say. And there's a wave behind them. He's bloody good at waves, gets the marbling exact.'

By now Stanton was speaking more hesitantly. He could tell his theory had somehow outraged Delaney; he was abashed at having violated some sensitivity in his friend. Then he got peevish. 'Christ, you might as well know these things.'

'In case of what?' There was an ashy dryness, disappointment and the rasp of jealousy, at the back of his throat. Later he would remember this as the first second he would think of himself as her deliverer.

'In case you . . . No, I'm not going to bloody buy in, Terry. I'll show you my scars, if you want. This is the same sort of set-up as the one that rooted my life. It's like playing Rugby League in France – you think you know the rules but you don't.'

He would have liked to ask Stanton whether his love was so clear, like a mark on the forehead which Gina, her parents, his parents could read. But the question itself would be a giveaway.

In the opening chapter of *The Tin Drum* a man is running

from the Prussian police in a potato field somewhere around the borders of Poland and Germany. Delaney intended at some stage to look up the location more exactly, but felt no urge to, preferred in fact for the young fugitive's politics to be vague and for the location to be no-man's-land, a land still to be invented. To escape the police, the escapee slides in under the skirts of the narrator's grandmother, who at that stage of history is still young and is picking potatoes in the field. While the Prussian police run back and forth amongst the furrows, the hidden escapee exploits his privileged position by entering the girl/grandmother. She flushes as the police rage up and down the furrows. She has met her man.

This event recurred in Delaney's sleep. He was running from the persecutors who inhabit dreams, the persecutors who require no names and no motivation. In he rushed, beneath the succouring skirts. Under them lay Danielle Kabbel's bird-boned yet ample flesh. To reach it was to reach home, a stranger home than he had ever known to exist.

These days he drove to work agitated, trying to get there before Stanton, usually succeeding. 'The punctual Mr Delaney,' she told him one night when she was already in the control room and he did not have to go through the boyhood thing, waiting for a particular fragrance, in this case the fragrance of Danielle Kabbel, for that particular gait, a step less robust but all at once more familiar than Gina's.

'The punctual Mr Delaney. If my father had his way you'd be managing director inside a month.'

She had begun reading and writing notes in a new book, a slimmer one, Graham Greene's *Our Man in Havana*. He knew the film – Maureen O'Hara aging elegantly and giving off a high-bred sexual radiance. He remembered the fun and trickery of the plot, and wondered what in her strangeness she thought of it. Later, out shaking doorknobs and shining a torch at mute panes of glass, he fell back on what he knew of the book as a sort of irrational proof of innocence. The atmosphere of the story was homely, humane: there were heroes and villains. Whereas in *The Tin Drum* there were escapees sheltering in weird and joyous places; a mother and an uncle loved each other;

midgets could break glass with their voices; horses' heads squirmed with eels; and a woman ate herself to death with fish oil. In the dark atmosphere of *that* book, adding its power to the dark wave in Warwick's paintings – as reviewed for Delaney by Stanton – you could nearly believe in Stanton's accusation. But not by the calmer light of *Our Man in Havana*.

One night when he arrived, the whole known Kabbel family were gathered in the control room around one of those little machines called scanners. Warwick the artist was tuning the controls with calm delicate movements involving only his index finger and his thumb. Stammers of distorted conversation emitted from the scanner and faded back into static and noises that resembled a saxophone played by an inexpert child. The family was so riveted around the thing that Delaney hesitated at the door and considered going away for five minutes. Then Danielle turned her head. She was frowning as if she wanted to help the circuits inside the machine with her concentration. Her eyes focused, her eyebrows arched, and she smiled, making Delaney welcome to whatever the secret was. A second later Kabbel looked over his shoulder. His eyes glittered. He grinned and waved at Delaney to come closer. When Delaney had crossed the room, Kabbel slung his arm around his shoulder.

'Warwick's been engaged in counter-espionage,' Kabbel whispered, not wanting to be so loud as to cloud anything definite Warwick could get from the scanner. 'Like his grandfather the Chief of Police.' Dressed as a Telecom technician, Warwick had managed to get into the office of Rooster Time, the company at war with Golden Style. He'd even been permitted into the garage where, left alone for a few minutes, he broke into the managing director's BMW and took the number of his car telephone. Kabbel had reason to suspect that the managing director made contact with those who were breaking Golden Style's windows and spray-painting its brickwork and parking areas with offputting slogans like CHICKEN POISON and SHIT FOOD while driving to and from the office.

'How do you know he isn't already home?' Delaney asked. 'Watching *Country Practice* with his kids?'

Kabbel winked, yet again a broad Slavic wink, heavily supported by the rest of his features. 'Scott put a bug in his office a month ago. Ten minutes ago our gentleman called his wife and told her he'd be home in half an hour.'

Delaney frowned. Electronic subterfuge disturbed him. The family looked sinister with their intent, genetically echoing postures around the scanner.

Kabbel increased the pressure on Delaney's shoulder. 'Don't start fretting, I'll never use you for any of these rascal activities.' And then, as if he could spot the growing question in Delaney's eyes, 'Nor do I ever use Danielle. You and she are both too good at what you already do, and that's fair enough with Rudi Kabbel. Warwick, Scott and I are the partisans, the guerrillas, the outlaws.'

Warwick said aloud, 'Twenty-five minutes to his place from the office. He's been on the road for a quarter of an hour so far, and not a word.'

Young Scott, blond as his sister, murmured, 'Might have to bug his house.'

Danielle caught Delaney's eye and smiled opaquely at him. It wasn't as if she condoned the talk of bugs. It was as if all her brothers' hard muscular utterance was beside the point.

All at once the scanner conveyed the sound of dialling, of a telephone pealing distantly, and broke into clear speech. 'Hello,' said a female voice. 'Sweet William,' said the male. (The managing director's name, Delaney would later discover, was William Tracey.) The woman called him darling and in an aspiring voice he asked her about her honeypot, her nectar, and began to use the sort of cheap images you found in letters at the front of *Penthouse*.

'His girlfriend,' said Warwick. 'I don't think we need listen to this.' But what he meant was that he didn't want Danielle to listen, perhaps didn't want Delaney to listen in Danielle's presence. He picked up earphones, put them on. The sound of William Tracey's part-time desire was lost to all but Warwick. Everyone waited in silence for *that* call to finish, and as it did and Warwick removed the phones, Stanton entered and found them all intent and listening to nothing.

The Kabbels got nothing further out of William Tracey that evening. Later, on his own, driving, shining his torch, hoping that no open window or faultily wired alarm would distract him from his torment, he wondered would one of the Kabbels penetrate Tracey's home. He hoped beyond reason that, even given the squalor of Tracey's spirit, they would not try it.

FROM THE MATCH DIARY OF TERRY DELANEY

Penrith v Manly, home game. Good crowd because Manly so full of internationals and fancy imports. Everyone likes to see them get beaten too – they have this reputation for being wealthy aristocrats of League, and they live on the beaches and so on. Old Roy Masters when he was coach of Wests dubbed them 'The Silvertails', and the name's stuck. We were scrappy first half – lots of dropped ball. 'I won't tolerate this bloody dropsy,' Paul Tuomey said at half-time, passing round the Stick-it. I still use resin – that's what Brother Aubin always made us use, and beside him Paul Tuomey isn't a coach's bootlace. Second half our forwards tore into them and I started to combine really well with Skeeter Moore and Eric Samuels in the centre. Faulkner scored a ninety yarder down the sideline with ten minutes to go. Penrith 32, Manly 7.

*   *   *

Slaughtered us in reserves and firsts though. Came on last ten minutes of reserves, but they kept me bottled up. Sent up a few good bombs, but the bounce doesn't suit you when you're being walloped. First grade: no defence from the forwards, no nip from the halves, no penetration from the fullback and centres, and the wings didn't see the ball. Another sad post-mortem at the Leagues Club. Old Dick Webster the copper put his arm round me and yelled, 'Why don't you give this young bloke a run in firsts. At least he bloody tackles.'

FOURTEEN

That winter it would have been impossible to go on the Ganz-style picnics we had enjoyed all the autumn. The weather was not entirely the reason. Genia and I were aware that Moscow and the tyrant had not fallen. I believe we even knew the name of Marshal Zhukov, who had somehow created the crisis which we felt right back here in Staroviche, the crisis being that the survival of Moscow encouraged partisan groups. Genia and I went by car with the Kuzichs to school, two motorcycle police-men preceding the limousine, an armed driver at the wheel, an armed policeman riding with us in the back. This policeman made a fuss of us – he was only a young man, a farmer from the Staroviche area. One day he let us all briefly handle his submachine-gun, take its blue-grey, oily weight into our own hands. The exercise made me uneasy, because I wondered what would happen if the partisans attacked our car then, while the weapon was in my grasp or Genia's.

It was known though that the partisans were forest people. Like goblins they came to town only on the most extraordinary occasions. There was that consolation – the thought of them only caused unease in a darkened room at night. They had blown up some railway lines – we heard that the way children hear most hard news, by eavesdropping hungrily on adults. They had severed for a day or two the Minsk-Smolensk line and even the Staroviche-Orsha rail, closer to home. It was of small importance, everyone said, since the Germans sent most of their supplies by road. So that was established: the partisans were woods creatures who dared not show their faces on a street.

Until on a late January day of black ice – the sort of day on which you would expect goblins to invade hearths, black and white cows to stand suspended in the air, and the crackle of strange laughter to be heard in bare treetops – an eighteen-year-old partisan walked into the Hungry Shepherd cafe in the old town square and shot Mrs Kuzich dead – three shots, I heard my aghast mother whisper. An eighteen-year-old. The wickedness! We knew he was eighteen because my father caught him, a capture which put the world right again.

The Catholic bishop of Staroviche buried the victim and promised us a Mrs Kuzich perfected in death by Christ's Passion. I imagined, as children will, a lighter and less voracious Mrs Kuzich. I couldn't believe that it had happened in the Hungry Shepherd, amongst the coffee cups and the plum dumplings and sour-milk pancakes.

We all sang the Belorussian anthem, a good song for winter forests, a song about yearning for the summer of independence. I was very impressed that the bishop had called Mrs Kuzich a Belorussian martyr. I had always imagined Belorussia's past heroes as incarnate shafts of flame. Mrs Kuzich showed me that they were normal and even overweight people.

It was announced at the graveside that the partisan who had done it had died without remorse the same morning and gone to hell. Therefore an atmosphere of grim satisfaction seemed to prevail at Mrs Kuzich's funeral.

Genia and I could no longer attend the school. Occasionally we made highly escorted visits to SS and Wehrmacht cinemas. And like the Kuzich children, we acquired a tutor.

His name was Herman Hirschmann, a hopeful little man with a moustache. He had been a schoolteacher in a *gymnasium* in far-off Saxony. He taught us German grammar, French, algebra, geography and geometry. No history. History, he told Genia and me, is all up in the air, and no one will know any more what history is until the leaves settle. Every day he walked two kilometres from the ghetto to our house, and was escorted both ways by one of my father's blue-clad policemen bearing a rifle. The Belorussian Jews who had occupied the ghetto had been 'sent east' – our mother used the term without any irony. I think she believed they had been relocated, and that the SS had not in fact shot them. But if the SS had shot them, we children were forgiving about it. The Soviets had done worse things. The Soviets had killed Mrs Kuzich.

The ghetto stood empty for some months. There were rumours that it was infested with rats and typhus. Then new Jews from further west turned up and were allocated a place there: among them Herr Hirschmann and his wife.

One day when Genia was out of the parlour where we took our lessons from Herr Hirschmann, he told me he had a secret, and I could be let into it if I swore to keep it from everyone, even my sister. After I had given the guarantees he wanted Mr Hirschmann opened up the seam of his coat and took out something I had seen only on the uniform of Onkel Willi Ganz – an Iron Cross.

'Are you a hero, Herr Hirschmann?' I asked him.

'So they told me for a while,' he confessed.

'Why did they give it to you?'

'For killing Americans in St Mihiel before you were born. I am a true German, you see. I bear the same first name as our beloved Reichsmarshal Goering.' He made an ironic squeaking noise with his lips, and I looked at his neatly shaven face, his exact moustache, his skin grey from hunger. He and Mrs Kuzich had altered my estimation of heroes for ever.

I was disappointed two weeks later when Genia told me that Herr Hirschmann had shown her the medal. It meant that he was showing everybody, that there was no secret. I suddenly had no doubt that he had shown it to the servants and even to my mother, who sent him back to the ghetto with cake and bread in his pockets.

One night she said, 'We cannot expect God to protect us from the partisans if we are not kind to unfortunates.'

As kind as my mother was, as much as we liked Herr Hirschmann, my father thought he was sly, and one morning called him into his study to tell him so. We could hear father's voice raised. 'Influence the children in this underhand manner,' was a phrase I could hear entirely through the heavy door. Herr Hirschmann gave out only a low murmur of apology.

After that Herr Hirschmann was less given to asides and little anecdotes, no matter how hard we tried to distract him from Euclid. Our lessons became more and more wooden. To compensate, my mother would arrange to ship in children under guard to play with us, but their arrival made Genia and I realise we were very nearly imprisoned in our own house.

There were two escapes. First, the films we saw at the elegant Paris cinema, where amongst the crowd we would spot the motherless Kuzich children. Onkel Willi Ganz often came with us, collecting us from the house in his Mercedes driven by Ya'acov. We made a foursome – mother, Onkel Willi, Genia, myself. Though Kommissar for the province of Staroviche, he seemed to have more time on his hands than my father. Perhaps he lacked Stanislaw Kabbelski's ferocious industry. In the warm darkness of the Paris, between my fragrant mother and equally fragrant friend Oberführer Ganz, cocooned – it seemed to me – in their combined glamorous musk, I gave my pre-pubescent heart to Paula Wessely, the German schoolteacher of *Homecoming*. In *Request Concert* my eyes itched with tears as the young German soldier was reunited with his girlfriend by courtesy of a request programme on radio. It was a film which made the world very safe: *Request Concert* and the partisans who killed Mrs Kuzich did not belong to the same planet. *Ohm Kruger* and *Bismark* were classics which, because Germany lost the war, were condemned in the end as mere propaganda films (as if *Mrs Miniver* was not a propaganda film). After the screenings we would have coffee in the manager's office, and Onkel Willi would tell the three of us stories about the making of the films and details of the lives of some of the stars. I found to my grief that Paula Wessely, that essential virgin of the screen, was married. I remember too that Oberführer Ganz told us Emil Jannings, the star of *Ohm Kruger*, had had an argument with Dr Goebbels, the German propaganda minister. He nicknamed the doctor 'Hinkefuss' – Lame Duck – and had tried to get a laugh by imitating his limp in *The Broken Jug*, a film which Onkel Willi had seen, though Dr Goebbels had tried to get it suppressed. In revenge Dr Goebbels had forced Emil Jannings to act in *Ohm Kruger*, a film largely written by the propaganda minister himself.

One of those lines was spoken by Kruger/Jannings to his nurse. 'If one repeats a lie often enough it is believed.'

Onkel Willi's film anecdotes astounded my innocent mother as much as they riveted Genia and me. It made the stars seem close, as if at any stage they might be seen wandering in the streets of Staroviche. (If they turned up, of course, Genia and I would have seen them only through the thick glass of Oberführer Ganz's Mercedes.)

The other escape during that late winter house-arrest, which would continue into spring and summer and autumn and another winter, were the art classes in the garden. Even on still days in winter it was possible for us to rug up and go out with our three easels. Mother was a landscapist, which meant that Genia and I became landscapists too. Like the cinema, the garden seemed superbly safe when we were in it together with our watercolours. But the great art days were those when Oberführer Ganz turned up. His apparently magical knowledge of the film world was matched only by his knowledge of art. He would sit at Genia's easel and dip the brush and say, 'This is the trick of the *pointillistes*.' Then in lightning speed he would produce a picture of the snow-clad garden. 'Pure Seurat!' he would tell us. 'Now let me show you how to do, even in Belorussia, a very convincing south of France Cézanne.'

Next he would replace the sheet and slash about with his loaded brush, producing a violent and hypnotic abstract. 'This is Kandinsky. Don't be put off by the Soviet-style name. This one lived in Munich.'

I knew that I would never meet another human as clever as my friend Oberführer Ganz.

FIFTEEN

January 31, 1942

Old police problem: don't know whether the boy who shot
Mrs Kuzich is very brave or very stupid. Certainly stupid, a
woodcutter from over Gomel way. Question of his bravery
hangs in balance, though he'll certainly die well. Apolitical. The
Germans unleashed the Latvian militia on his village last autumn
– Ganz speaks with some sense when he says that sort of thing
creates Bolsheviks. Sturdy boy with wiry hair. Opaque eyes, all
the transparency of childhood long vanished.

Two of my men caught him in the lane behind Sorokin's
department-store. Sergeant Jasper had the right to interrogate
him for military purposes. Just begun when Obersturmführer
Harner turned up from SD headquarters next door demanding
the boy. What that undergraduate will find out, said Harner to
me, wouldn't fit under a thumbnail. Said Harner, 'I want to get
at the partisan before Ganz invites him round for dinner and a
little buggery.' Fashionable for the Gestapo to talk like that
about our friend and provincial governor Oberführer Ganz.

As for Jasper, he finds out enough in his quiet, cultivated way.
(His Russian much better than the boy's.) Found out the boy
did not know Mrs Kuzich. Had been given a pistol and her name.
The idea is, he says his commander told him, all collaborators
will be gunned down. There exists a list with all our names on
it. I would not dare tell my wife this. Her fancies are already
adequately tormented.

The news, uttered so frankly across the table by a Belorussian peasant who could have, with equal ease and a slight shift of history, been one of my own men instead of Mrs Kuzich's assassin, goes through one like a knife. One feels like shouting, 'You bastard! I loved my country well enough to supervise the Gomel road liquidations. I saw children squirming in the pit and pregnant girls singing the '*Shema Y'israel*'. I skirted insanity and dishonour for the sake of my nation! And now you want to add to the nightmares which spill out of my own bed and infest my children?'

Asked him, 'Did you know you were killing the mother of three children?'

Intonation flat as he answered, 'My sister was mother of two pups and it didn't seem to cramp the Latvians' style much.'

The other information Jasper got from the boy was that a party official from Gomel, in hiding since the Russian military withdrew, had moved into the area of the five villages the Latvians had been let loose in and had formed a partisan band out of the males and few surviving young women. The group was armed with one hundred rifles left behind by the retreating Reds. The boy spoke with some pride of their small victories: severed railway lines, an attack on a small party of German engineers near Rogachev, the execution of five Belorussian police on a road west of Bobruisk. He told us matter-of-factly that only twenty-four out of the nearly seventy who had joined the partisan group were still alive. Patently useless threatening him with death.

Was almost politely doubtful he should give us his leader's name. Said the leader complained a lot about lack of instructions from either the Red Army or the NKVD. This killing of Mrs Kuzich the first time they'd been ordered from above to do anything specific. 'Was your leader Trutkov?' asked Jasper, and I had to admit to myself the sergeant had a gift for interrogation – a telegram had just arrived from Rogachev announcing the capture of a wounded partisan, previously a party official under the Reds and named Georgi Trutkov.

The boy looked at Jasper as if he were omniscient.

'Trutkov has been captured and killed by the SD in Rogachev,' said Jasper, improvising a little.

After that the boy opened up. Towards lunchtime handed him to Obersturmführer Harner so that SD could get their slice. Boy bowed to Jasper and me as they led him next door. 'Poor little bastard,' Jasper told me. As if all the children were still children and harmless. Jasper, as always, the Bavarian sentimentalist. At least the SS – people like Brigadeführer Ohlendorf – understand what life is like here in the East, that the rules of history and even social exchange have always been different here. Said to Harner it essential for morale of my co-nationals that Mrs Kuzich's killer be executed by *my* police. H replied absentmindedly that that seemed appropriate.

Afternoon, had to open a Wehrdorf, a fortified village at Krotinitsa. Idea pioneered by Ostrowsky himself – put in a tough section of our Belorussian police, create a local watch or village militia, install a patriotic mayor. Surround the place with redoubts and barbed wire. Impossible for partisans to penetrate at night and apply muscle to the villagers.

Drove out there and shared the platform with Ganz. Very enthusiastic about the Wehrdorfer programme. Told me, 'I favour pacification in the literal sense, my dear Kabbelski. Not in the sense the Roman legions and the SS use the term: to make a desert and to call it peace. Its only limitation is that it fails to appeal to the hate glands.'

We travelled in convoy with an armoured car – Ganz has been assigned one.

When I got back at dusk found that Gestapo – i.e. our friends Bienecke and Harner – had hanged the boy partisan from one of the pipes in their cellar. Barely an apology from them.

SIXTEEN

Delaney got a game going with Danielle. He was allowed, according to the game rules, to lean over her shoulder and read a few paragraphs of whichever novel she was studying. So he encountered by a game of stealth Muriel Spark and her school ma'am Brodie, Salinger and his acned malcontent Holden Caulfield, and one from his schooldays, Graham Greene's whisky priest, a priest light years away from Doig, and in whom Brother Aubin had claimed to find manifested the grace of God.

'Why two Graham Greene's?' he asked Danielle. He could smell her hair, which struck him as more vegetable than Gina's – Gina's hair had an honest carnivore smell to it. Sometimes she complained of the unsuitability of various shampoos. It was the olive oil of her Sicilian ancestors seeping from her pores, Delaney would tell her.

'Why two?' Delaney asked Danielle Kabbel again.

'It's the style,' she told him. 'Ron says that he's got the best style in the English-speaking world and is also the best narrator.'

'So there,' said Delaney.

'So there,' said Danielle.

Delaney was not as anxious any more about Warwick. The incestuous, he reasoned, encountering a randy conversation on the scanner, would not protect their sister from hearing unless that sister was a sister in the traditional sense. Warwick's painting, which Delaney – since told of it – had gone out of his way to avoid viewing, was therefore a painting of an intense brotherly feeling, but there was no horror in that. Delaney's concern had therefore switched itself to the opinionated Ron of the WEA, a young writer who had done occasional episodes of *Sons and Daughters* and was trying to write a novel up at

Hazelbrook in the mountains. Sometimes Delaney saw him as a pole to himself – a sort of third grade five-eighth of literature. Once a week Ron drove down to Parramatta to conduct Danielle's WEA course. Delaney hoped he was a faggot, but since his own contacts with Danielle were all beneath the shadow of world-famous prose-style, and although some of them featured crudities in their first paragraph – Holden Caulfield took five lines to get to 'crap' – there was something in the unspoken regulations governing the delicious contacts Delaney had with Danielle that made it impossible to ask questions about (as they said on the current affairs programmes) Ron's 'sexual preference'. What he feared, of course, was that Ron's sexual preference was Danielle.

Delaney had courted Gina through his junior football games, the competitions which bore such names as Jersey Flegg and President's Cup. (If you belonged to a Jersey Flegg team you had honour in your neighbourhood and your future was limitless.) Gina – maybe because her body and blood had been laid down in an island which had seen so much hectic action – could be excited by warrior skills and physical courage. On the Sunday nights of their courtship, when he was bruised and his thigh muscles ached, she admitted him and herself closest to the peak, and a few times over the crest and into the valley of calmer touch and conversation beyond. In that way too, therefore, the workers' game, Rugby League, had been kind to him.

But the Kabbel family seemed to exist outside the hemisphere of sport. It was, Delaney thought, the strange Belorussian seriousness of the father. Delaney's meagre renown as a five-eighth seemed to be one of those things the Kabbels didn't choose to look into, any more than into the rhythm of his breath or the fluctuations of his pulse.

Some nights when Delaney arrived, Warwick, Scott and Rudi would have already finished listening in on the scanner to the chicken king Bill Tracey's homeward progress. On other nights Stanton and Delaney stood with them while they studiously listened to Tracey's hot talk, and the low laughter and breathiness of Tracey's girlfriend. 'I get a fat just listening,' Stanton confessed. 'She might be a stupid bitch but you can tell she bangs like a windmill.'

If Danielle was in the room, Warwick would put on the earphones and sit with the fingertips of his left hand to his brow, while Danielle inspected the arms register and booted the computer for that night's vigilance.

Delaney was there when at last Tracey's voice was heard in tones that meant pure business.

'That you, Stevo?' Tracey was heard asking.

'That's Jack Stevens,' said Warwick, whispering as if Stacey, cocooned in his BMW, might overhear and be warned. 'Former copper sacked over a towtruck rort.'

'Now he vandalises for profit,' murmured Rudi with a wide smile.

'Stevo?' Tracey asked again.

'Here,' a second voice stated.

'Wanted to talk to you about Blacktown. Doing a lot of business in Blacktown. I mean . . . reckon you could get inside and bugger up some of the stoves and rotisseries and so on?'

'Not inside, mate. Don't want to buggerise round in there with alarms going all round. Paint job and glass. That's the limit.'

'Windows as well though?'

Stevo said he meant the usual – windows, and broken glass all over the parking lot.

'And graffiti?' asked Tracey, wanting his money's worth.

'No worries.'

'Walls and parking area?'

'If time allows. Don't always have as much time as van bloody Gogh.'

'And I haven't spoken to you, right?'

'Listen, just take it easy. I drink with the local superintendent. He knows I have to make a bloody living.'

Tracey said he wanted the sort of damage they couldn't afford to go on repairing, wished Stevo goodnight and could be heard putting the phone down between the bucket seats of the BMW.

'True police work!' sang ecstatic Rudi to his children. (Delaney saw Danielle smile and shake her head.) 'Tonight we make democracy safe for fried chicken!'

SEVENTEEN

No later than half an hour past midnight the total manpower of Uncle Security had encircled the Blacktown branch of Golden Style. The way this had been achieved made Delaney uneasy. After all his speeches about not involving them in this sort of direct operation, Kabbel had offered Stanton and Delaney double-time and asked them after all to take part, to make up the numbers. 'In the end,' he said lightly, 'it's no more dangerous than the standard business of being a member of the species homo sapiens.'

Now in the shadow of the railway bridge sat Rudi Kabbel's Toyota, Scott in the back hunched between the seat and floor, armed with Polaroid and flash. Warwick Kabbel, whom Delaney and Stanton had now privately and innocently nicknamed the Censor, sat appropriately alone in the middle-aged Datsun in the corner of the Franklin carpark, where the fronds of one of those stocky Queensland palms that resembled pineapples caused any vehicle parked there at that hour to look like the car of lovers or of someone staying late at a nearby party.

The back of Golden Style was separated by a narrow ditch from the Blacktown Workers Club, a red-brick palace of Babylon. In the carpark, a short step from the ditch, Delaney and Stanton waited in Delaney's Holden. Arrived at his station, Delaney now began to enjoy himself. The Workers was redolent for him of grand political excitements. When he was eleven his father had brought him here for the launch of the political campaign of the Labour demagogue Gough Whitlam. They had stood in a packed gallery for two hours and had seen Gough's speech only on a television screen, but the crowd, in a strangely unAustralian ecstasy, a frenzy more appropriate to some other and less stable nation, kept the younger Delaney agog. Later the hulking leader appeared below the gallery on his way to the bar – political assassinations were unknown in Australia and politicians could safely drink with any of their fellow Australians.

Whitlam had fallen bloodlessly three years later, half the people rejoicing and half choking with nationalist shame. But the excitement of his rise would always be associated with this unlikely building, and its memory tonight was augmented for Delaney by the likelihood of Stevo's nearing discomfort. These were lesser elations though: they were nothing beside his wider Danielle obsession.

Stanton slept. His daughter, this time the one who was always calmed and hypnotised by television, had been home all day with a violent stomach virus. He had argued with Denise. He was very pleased with this chance to lie still. 'What do you reckon the Kabbels talk to each other about when they're on their own?' he had asked earlier. 'Bloody Rudi and the Commonwealth Censor? Do you think they talk about bloody Russian buffaloes?'

But he had not wanted to pursue the matter. 'Police work!' he murmured, already half-asleep but quoting Rudi. 'This isn't bloody police work's backside.'

What did Rudi say to Danielle? Delaney asked himself as Stanton tossed and slumbered unhandily in the back seat. Their conversation couldn't be imagined. As he attempted to imagine it the earth cooled around him until he was shivering, the smells of the day's exhausts and fried food congealed in the shopping centre's sulphurous night and he felt berserkly happy.

Some time after two a station wagon crawled across the Workers carpark and halted a few hundred yards from Delaney and Stanton. Delaney woke Stanton. Like cops in television dramas they sat low in their seats. From the station wagon appeared a large and, by the sharp light from the street, jowly man of middle-age and two ratty-haired blond young men. Stevo, according to Kabbel, had a pool of employees who all drank at the Station Hotel in Parramatta. By the blare and fluctuating light of such rock bands as Split Enz, Flaming Hands, Australian Crawl, Stevo did his interview and set the terms of employment.

Stevo opened the back of the wagon and took out the raw materials of his trade – some heavy hessian bags of broken glass. The big blonds lugged them across the ditch into the parking spaces of Golden Style and emptied them on the bitumen, spreading the fragments with sweeping movements of their feet. To Delaney their work seemed leisurely. Leisurely, Stevo shook the can of spray-paint in his right hand and wrote SHIT TO EAT on Golden Style's side wall.

Two honks from the direction of the railway bridge told Delaney and Stanton it was time to move in. As they left the car and jumped the ditch, one of the blond boys had taken up a rubber-coated mallet for eventual use on the windows. Stevo strode to the front of the building to write a further slogan, this time on the paved and tabled area set aside for al fresco devouring of chickens. Delaney felt wonderful and deliciously waited before crying out his prepared sentence, 'Fixing the site, gentlemen?' He had in his line of vision both the oblivious blonds and Stevo the professional vandal.

Before he could speak he saw Rudi and Scott Kabbel appear behind the man. There was a sharp burst of light from the camera in Scott's hands. Then the whole event, as Stanton would later pungently detail it, burst open like a garbage-bag dropped from a height. One of the blond boys began to run back towards Stevo's station wagon, and Delaney brought him down with a classic head-behind-the-hamstring tackle, as if it were turf and not gravel and tar which were waiting to receive them as they fell. Delaney slid painlessly across the glass-strewn surface of the parking area. He heard cries of pain, however, from the boy he had felled and saw him lift to the street lights the cut pad of his right hand. The damage was not enough to stop him from retrieving the mallet and bringing it down on Delaney's shoulder, emitting as he did it a grunt worthy of the martial arts. As Delaney rolled on his side and vomited on to Stevo's pavement graffiti, he could hear the evil breathless screams of someone savagely hurt rising behind him. It happened that Stevo had sent a blast of acidic paint fair into Scott Kabbel's eyes.

EIGHTEEN

November 21, 1942

Children and Danielle went under escort to a party thrown by Willi Ganz at his apartment. Occasion: young Radislaw's ninth birthday. Delightful event. I looked in and spent over half an hour. My leisure not as great as our dear Kommissar's. Pathetic to see the joy of young Radek – a joy threatened on all sides by the partisans. Last night, for example, in fortified village of Krotinitsa, the jewel of our pilot scheme, partisans raided police outpost and took my men to a barn and shot them. Left them obscenely arrayed, flies open and hands placed as if engaged in self-abuse. Cold night, and villagers did not dare move the dead; hence found them frozen this morning in these horrendous postures. Spent the morning lying to their relatives in town here.

Partisans further hanged the Krotinitsa mayor from a telegraph pole. Have moved in a stronger detachment of my men, and Kuzich appointed young Daskovich from the city office here to look after Krotinitsa's civil side since none of local people willing to take risk. All this barbarity continues, both Germans and Russians behave like savages; we bear it for the sake of Bela Rus. And in the midst, like the well-known jewel amongst the dungheap, my son smiles. Genia more sullen, no longer a child, suffering the double assaults of womanhood and the awful life we are forced to lead here.

Ganz fantastic – parties are his especial gift. Got out his violin and played the famous theme from 'Midsummer Night's Dream', even though Mendelssohn, grandson of a Jewish philosopher of

assimilation, is scarcely on the approved repertoire for SS
Oberführers.

Anyhow, really waltzed the theme along and the boy's eyes
glittered in a way that would have brought pure joy to any parent
if it were not – as I say – for the omens which surround us. The
Russians counter-attacking in the Don bend – Comrades Vatutin,
Rokossovsky and Eremenko. German Sixth Army now isolated
in Stalingrad, and if *that* place falls, far as it is from Staroviche,
increase in partisan activity will stretch us till we squeak. SD
documents say sixty-five thousand partisan operatives are loose
in the Ukraine and Belorussia. A German debacle in the Don
bend could double that figure. Ganz still pushing the Wehrdorfer
and the plausible concept that when the SS and SD try to get
even with a village which has harboured partisans by sending in
the Correctional Battalions composed of German, Austrian and
Hungarian psychopaths, partisan numbers are actually swelled
(*vide* the assassin of Mrs Kuzich).

And in the midst of all these monstrous balances, my son listens
to jazzed-up Mendelssohn with such certainty of a bright future.
Have such certainty myself, though by now a little tainted.

Was just about to leave and return to office when Wehrmacht
sentry came pounding in. Something in the Herr Kommissar's
garage across the courtyard had exploded. The place was in
flames. Asked was it partisans but was told consensus amongst
my police (including my driver Yuri), who were fighting fire with
Ya'acov, was that a can of shellac had exploded.

All the children clamouring to attend fire, but self and Danielle
forbade it. Self, Ganz, ran downstairs. Saw string of German
soldiers and Belorussian police handing buckets across the courtyard until they reached Yuri's hands, who threw them into the
face of fire surging through open doors of garage. Ganz's driver
Ya'acov stood by screaming orders at Yuri – I could not catch
what he was saying. In the end, though, Yuri tipped three
buckets of water over his head, cursing the Jew as he did it.
Ya'acov then stopped pestering Yuri and, taking a breath like a
man about to dive, raced into the banks of chemical-looking
smoke. 'Shit my aunt!' screamed Ganz uncharacteristically.
'Leave it, leave it!' He ran across the courtyard. The bucket

line had heard his roar and thought he'd been talking to them. On orders from the Kommissar they were quite willing to let a garage burn down. Level with Yuri and staring at the revived flames, Ganz yelled, 'Pour it on, you fool!'

Saw that the children had now arrived despite orders, and Danielle grabbed Radek and tried to cover his eyes in case Ya'acov ran out of garage burning.

Ganz's limousine all at once emerged from fire and smoke at perhaps thirty-five k.p.h., nearly skittling poor sweating Yuri. It rolled two-thirds of way across courtyard and braked. Ya'acov toppled from it, wheezing horrendously, hacking and retching. Ganz stood by him clapping his back and occasionally lifting his right arm upwards as if Ya'acov had just won a race or a prize-fight. When Ya'acov breathing well enough to stand upright, Ganz pulled him to him by the shoulder and kissed him on the side of the face. There was nothing sexual in the kiss. Nonetheless Ganz ill-advised to break his country's race laws in front of so many men.

If anything fire added to Radek's excitement in the day.

Got home that evening to find wife upset. Seems Hirschmann the tutor has been showing children his Iron Cross as a means of acquiring leverage over them. Radislaw started on Danielle in Ganz's car, the one rescued by Ya'acov, on way home. All the more embarrassing for the revived and scrubbed Ya'acov being the driver. Hirschmann and his wife exist through my intervention – most of the rest of their shipment has 'gone east'. Seems Radek reminded of Hirschmann by sight on way home of fifteen Jewish escapees being marched down Bryanska Street, a sight in which Ya'acov may well read his own potential fate. Radek on seeing them began to weep and cry out, 'If I ask Daddy as a special birthday present, will he let Mr Hirschmann stay? Mr Hirschmann is a hero and killed twenty Americans . . .'

Shall speak to Hirschmann – that part easy. What to say to Radek, how to explain the limits of my influence? What does Radek know of SS activities? Possible, of course, for children in a sense to know more than they actually *know* they know.

If Hirschmann has told the children anything distressing it's the end of him.

NINETEEN

November 28, 1942

Meeting called by Ganz at provincial hall. Present: Dr Kappeler of Political Section of Gestapo from Kaunas; Bienecke of the Gestapo and SD Staroviche; Harner ditto; the present garrison commander Lustbader, an elderly colonel who tells me his men had a frightful time in the Voronezh sector six weeks back. General Golikov destroyed 70 per cent of this paternal old gentleman's battalion, now being brought back to strength by conscripts who arrive daily in Staroviche, not bad-looking men though a few older than me – Germany not yet at bottom of its remarkable barrel though. Lustbader not likely to survive another such shock, however, as the one he suffered on the Don, so can't help hoping he'll never be posted to front again.

Also present at Ganz's meeting: Mayor Kuzich the widower; Daskovich whose administration of the armed village of Krotinitsa has provided him with some interesting insights on what should be done in the Belorussian countryside; my aging deputy Beluvich. Subject of meeting: forthcoming clearance of ghetto and relocation of inhabitants in labour camps.

Ganz said he was as devoted to solution of Jewish and partisan question as anyone – 'hard and ready' was the way he put it. But there were standards which civilisation had the right to exact. There should be no extraction of gold fillings from prisoners' mouths – we should all be above such animality. Though there were channels through which the property of prisoners could be dedicated to the war effort, personal looting was not to be countenanced. Many instances of such behaviour last year when Staroviche Jews expelled from ghetto and sent to site in the forests near the Gomel road. Bedding and items of jewellery taken for personal use – the delinquents included some of my men, some of Bienecke's SS squads, and some army personnel involved in the action.

Resented this reference to my men because my control of their behaviour very firm on that occasion. Fully aware that Ganz mentioned my men first just to salve Bienecke's vanity, because his men and some of the Wehrmacht *did* loot. Ganz simply massaging the unfounded German sense of superior morality, confirming the image of us as temporary barbarian auxiliaries. Let it pass for moment.

Ganz further complained of reports of sexual licence at certain execution sites – assaults on partisan women captured in the raid on the barn at Bonachev, for example. (Raid carried out by the Staroviche SS assisted by a platoon of my police under one of my deputies.) He was aware of frightful excesses committed against forty Latvian Jewish women who had turned up in Staroviche as part of a transport the previous spring.

'These acts carried out by our Latvian or Belorussian allies?' asked Bienecke with apparent innocence.

Ganz: 'By members of our own corps, Hauptsturmführer Bienecke. Acts unworthy of German manhood. Acts of literal sadism.'

I was beside young Harner, and saw him write on his pad, 'Acts unworthy of the culture which produced Offenbach and Mendelssohn.' Knew then Ganz would be better to keep silent.

Bienecke said in way that seemed conciliatory: 'With respect, Herr Kommissar, I don't think administrators understand the stress that operates within a squad of men assigned to these sorts of duties. We are faced with inhuman tasks and required still to retain our humanity. Many of our men are heads of families, older than is desirable for combat purposes. Others are boys but of the type who lack the fibre or initiative for conventional battlefields. What can I say – it is not always possible to wage war as a philosopher would. Schopenhauer and Kant are not members of the security forces, even though many of the leaders and senior officers of the Special Action Squad are doctors of philosophy and divinity. Now the men of the Special Action Squads have a particular cross to bear. They do their duty and are reproached by a variety of administrators with such terms as "sadism". It is their fault, it seems, if the world's estimation of Germany is ruined. So not only are they faced with the necessity of performing particularly nasty jobs [here Bienecke suddenly became more heated] but they have to be the target for mud-slinging. I protest most emphatically against the Herr Kommissar's last accusation.'

Ganz stayed calm throughout. 'Leaving that aside for a moment, though I should warn Hauptsturmführer Bienecke that I have testamentary evidence to support the accusation he finds objectionable, there are instances not only of barbarity, but of what is worse from a military and political point of view: folly. The fifteen wounded Latvian Jews who recently crawled their way out of a mass execution site and, on being recaptured, were led covered with mud and blood through the centre of the city to the Mogilevska Street prison! I don't believe that *this* didn't happen since guests of mine – including two children – saw the procession while being driven home from my apartment, and were naturally very distressed by it. The effect on the civilian population of such wanton and careless displays can be guessed at. We are virtually confessing that we cannot do these things humanely. *That* first of all. We are also encouraging partisan recruitment. My point is, gentlemen, that to the benefit of all of us I would like the *bezirk* or *oblast* of Staroviche to act as a lighthouse of wise and humane policy. I am grateful to Dr Kappeler that he found the time to be here for what I consider a crucial discussion on this very concept.'

Ganz put his argument. Recent report of anti-terrorist sweep in Sluzk region shows 9,500 supposed partisan sympathisers slaughtered and 492 rifles discovered. These were characteristic figures for such sweeps. In what could be called by other names but what he himself chose for the moment to call excessive zeal, said SS and Belorussian raid in the Sluzk area might have justifiably unearthed some 750 partisans and partisan informers to match the 492 rifles. But the security forces had liquidated thirteen times the credible number of people it should have. The Belorussian countryside abounds, says Ganz, with such instances of extreme reaction. In the Mogilev area certain leaders of the security forces boasted of the destruction of 150 villages. It is the witnesses of this sort of behaviour, and the tithe of survivors, who turn to the partisans as to their only recourse.

Dr Kappeler spoke next. Said there was good reason in the Herr Kommissar's argument. But what about the partisans themselves? They thought so little of their fellow countrymen that they had planned to poison the water supply of Vilnius. If they wished to recruit a village that had thus far proved loyal, they killed Wehrmacht or SS men in the area just to invite retribution on the place.

All the more reason, said Ganz, not to play into their hands with excessive retaliations.

Kappeler said in emphatic scholarly way he didn't entirely agree. These tricks were amply described in the press and on the radio and the populace was warned not to be taken in by them.

But have you seen some of these villages? Ganz protested. Only the priests are literate and possess a radio!

'I take it then,' said Kappeler, 'that in the *bezirk* of Staroviche you have pursued an active policy of engaging the assistance of the clergy at village level, as outlined in the December 1941 directive of the Political Section of the Ostministry.'

Ganz now sighed too dramatically and called both on myself and on young Daskovich to comment on the role of the priests in maintaining social order in the villages. Daskovich was very happy with his relationship with the Orthodox priest in Kroti-nitsa, a pastor actively committed to the survival of his flock. The man was capable, said Daskovich, of drawing on an Ostministry directive for a sermon text. He was a strong Belorussian nationalist, and regularly took the line with his flock that the hope of nationhood could only be fulfilled through cooperation with Christian Germany in an unremitting attack on Jewish Bolshevism.

My very point, said Ganz, is that hundreds of such right-thinking people had been slaughtered in retributive actions carried out by the German penal battalions, by the Latvian militia, by our corps of twenty thousand anti-Bolshevik Cossacks, by the Kaminsky Brigade which, while annihilating villages, wears the St George Cross, red on white, the symbol of Belorussian nationalism. It is not the people who die who are a problem to state security. It is the proportion of survivors who see the White Russian nationalists and the Germans as suddenly less desirable than the Bolsheviks, who abandon the Cross of St George for the Red Star. And for each one who makes that shift, units which could be more profitably engaged at the front have to be detailed for anti-terrorist action.

Ganz then called on us all therefore to show restraint and wisdom. Wants this policy of moderate severity and judicious but civilised force to operate within the limit of Ostministry and Reich Security Central Office directives. He is grateful to Dr Kappeler for coming over to Staroviche to attend our meeting and hopes that the Political Section will watch with interest the successes achieved by the security forces operating in the *bezirk* of Staroviche under the twin policies of strength and moderation.

Cannot help but feel Ganz ill-starred. Behind him lies a divorce – his wife was Viennese – and a slightly tainted career – from 1937 till February 1940 he was *kreisleiter* of Bohemia. He may have displayed there the same fulsomeness of speech so odious to servants of the state such as Dr Kappeler. In any case Staroviche is something of a demotion.

His argument has some force, and might have an outside chance of being implemented if it were not for this evening's events. Young Daskovich ambushed and killed on the forest road back to Krotinitsa. Have just been out to the site, for all the good that does. A mean, low stretch of road with slushy snow on it, that whorish snow which will turn to ice tonight and to mud tomorrow. The forest never looked more dangerous, not even in a child's nursery story where forests are always full of imps and deep threat. It's a squalid stretch of road to lose someone like Daskovich on, a man so young and educated and coherently nationalistic. Hauptsturmführer Bienecke likes to say the 42 per cent of Belorussia controlled by partisans is all solid forest and so doesn't count. But when you're out there in a foul dusk beside D's corpse, that 42 per cent becomes a very weighty figure.

Amazed at the vehemence of my wife's reaction to tonight's news. She barely knew Daskovich except as a peripheral guest, the young man from Kuzich's office who was brighter than Kuzich. Clearly D's death just another piece of bad news to go with all the other bad news, but this the item which drove her over the limit. Wept pitiably and needed sedation, but would not go to sleep until I'd prayed for her – insistent on that, one decade of Sorrowful Mysteries for the repose of D's soul, an Act of Contrition for ourselves, the enunciation in her case slurred by the dose of brandy and laudanum.

She rarely paints in the garden now, rarely goes out there with the children and the easels unless Ganz drags them all out. That is why I am glad Hirschmann, for all his faults, is still in the ghetto. Can't be denied he provides companionship for my besieged children.

TWENTY

Danielle's stand-by for the control room was Bernadette, a plain girl in her late twenties who went to the WEA with Danielle, worked in some state government department, and was saving to buy a spinster's unit in North Parramatta. Delaney knew these details from Stanton, who flirted with, disarmed, and teased Bernadette in a way which Delaney thought proclaimed too clearly, You're no threat. No one will raise a knife for you. Bernadette was willing to be called in an emergency at any hour, and the blinding of Scott Kabbel with paint was an adequate emergency.

Danielle Kabbel arrived at Westmead Emergency almost as soon as the column of defenders from Golden Style. Delaney saw her appear in the lobby as Scott Kabbel was forced down yelping with fright and the pain of his seared eyes on to a trolley. Delaney himself sat crookedly in a seat in the waiting room, favouring his shoulder and wondering if he could play on Sunday. Past rows of empty chairs, Danielle ran to the trolley's side as it disappeared behind a curtain, lunged and made transitory contact with Scott's hand and was satisfied, as if her touch and her scent were enough for her injured brother.

Likewise she said nothing to Kabbel, but came and stared into his eyes. 'They don't know yet,' the Kabbel patriarch said simply. 'He took photographs of the vandal which any superintendent of police will find hard to ignore.'

Stanton's doubting voice seemed sacrilegious cutting in. 'They'll challenge them as evidence,' he said.

'Evidence?' said Kabbel – the voice sounded fierce but came out tremolo. 'It's not for evidence he took these photographs. I have no hope in court in these mad days. I give the photographs to Golden Style who send copies to the police. Who say to the barbarian, "Enough, Stevo!" I am not interested in transforming the dungheap into gold, dear Mr Stanton. Only in moving it from one corner of the farm yard to another. I shall arrange an X-ray for Terry.'

He announced it like a hospital functionary, but he did not yet move, instead planting a muscular kiss on the middle of Danielle's forehead. Delaney flinched. Easy! he nearly said, fearing that the shield of bone beneath the girl's forehead was thin as a membrane. As often as he'd envisaged putting his mouth to her brow he had never imagined such a pile-driver kiss. 'You understand,' Kabbel continued to his daughter, 'they won't know anything until they have put dye in his eyes to tell the extent of the burns. They can't use anything strong, anything chemical, since it would react with the acids and alkalis in the paint.' Again, Delaney thought, he sounded a little like a supervisor, a consulting physician, something like that.

The curtain around Scott's cubicle opened, and a doctor who seemed no older than Delaney came out and spoke to the huddled Kabbels.

'World ahead of him,' murmured Stanton. Delaney had thought the same thing – I could have been that young quack if I hadn't once been mistakenly sure I'd play five-eighth for Australia and enter the pantheon.

'By the end of the century,' he said, echoing his father, 'doctors won't earn any more than a fitter and turner. Society won't be able to maintain them at their present level of luxury.'

'So,' said Stanton, 'the little bastard has sixteen years to make a killing. Wish I could say that.'

The young doctor said, with that authority doctors still had though priests had lost it, that as far as he could tell the burns would cause no permanent impairment. Scott Kabbel lay behind him, visible through the parted curtain, pads over both eyes. 'You're fortunate it didn't happen at home. When these things happen at home people run for boracic washes, which increase the area and depth of the burn. People are brought in here screaming. It wasn't a Turk who sprayed your son's eyes?'

Kabbel said, in a voice deliberately accented, as if declaring war on the Anglo-Saxon dominance, 'It was an *old* Australian who did the spraying. Someone who learned to be a barbarian *here.'*

'It's a favourite weapon of the Turks and the Armenians out this way.' He looked tired all at once and not as assertive. 'My parents were Italian.'

Scott had to remain under observation, said the young doctor (now exposed as a voyager like everyone else in the casualty ward). The eye specialist would have the final word in the morning. Even then the burns could take some weeks to heal entirely.

Reassured, Kabbel now began to think of his clientele, whose property had gone unsupervised for the past two hours. He sent Warwick and Stanton back out on the job. At first Stanton resisted the idea. He tried not to say so, but Delaney and the Kabbels could see that he thought Kabbel might be sending him back out on the road so that there'd be no one but Kabbels present when the question of Delaney's medical expenses arose.

'My God,' Kabbel said, casting his head back and looking at the roof, 'I am no bushweek organisation, Brian. Do you think I keep a company health insurance going because I am in love with actuaries? Everything he needs will be met by my insurance.'

'Well then,' asked Stanton, looking away but sticking fraternally to the business of Delaney's interests, 'what about his match fee if he can't play on Sunday?'

'Please, please. Does anyone carry such insurance as that, Mr Stanton? *Games* insurance? Please go and see that the new anarchy has not ruined my business. I shall look after Terry like a son or a cobber.'

Though Delaney's shoulder still roared he kept his eyes on Warwick, who had hardly spoken since the Golden Style fracas. It was another case of the Kabbel family's stillness, its lack of gestures. Excepting Kabbel's own plentiful gestures.

So Warwick and the appeased Stanton left together, murmuring to each other beyond the glass doors about the order of business for the rest of the night. Delaney saw the loveable and doomed earnestness of Stanton, nodding, nodding, a good employee. A brisk nurse appeared with a wheelchair and told

Delaney to sit in it. Kabbel and Danielle fussed him into it. Within seconds it was hissing down empty corridors towards Radiology, Danielle pushing him. Kabbel had remained by his blinded son, the nurse had stayed in Casualty. It seemed reasonable at this hour, in this set of events, in a short-staffed hospital, that Danielle Kabbel should be hurtling him past closed doors marked ENDOSCOPY and VENISECTION towards one of the race of radiographers Delaney had met so often after football injuries. He considered beginning a conversation with Danielle about how radiographers were the most consistently bored people he had ever met, bored with their techniques and their machinery, with telling the human race to hold its breath, bored (when it came down to it) with pain. In their company you could practise conversation with Danielle Kabbel and they would not know what you were doing, they would not be diverted. They were lined with lead – like most of their equipment.

'How great is the pain?' he heard Danielle ask him. It sounded a strange sentence, as if she'd been influenced as a little girl by her father's oddity of speech.

'It's all right till I move.' He did move, trying to crane around to see her, and his injury sang.

'Silly fellow,' she told him, and taking her right hand away from the chair handle pushed his head downwards and to the front, to the exact angle at which the pain turned off. As if his movement and flinching was a form of doubt she said, 'My father *will* pay for everything, you know. It's a matter of honour. People from Eastern Europe are like that. They have these rules, different rules from us.'

'I trust your father,' said Delaney. 'You can't blame Stanton for sticking up for me.'

'Who could blame Stanton?' she said, and she laughed fondly.

Delaney said Stanton was a good bloke who'd had too many disappointments.

'So he's your old mate?' she asked with a gentle edge.

'That's right.' But you, Danielle Kabbel, you are more than mateship, blood and bride, you strike sharper than snake or coronary inside the chest cage. *Ti mon seul desir.*

The radiographer carried in his eyes the misty lack of engagement Delaney had expected to find there. He asked Delaney to enter a cubicle and take his shirt off. Danielle Kabbel protested. 'He doesn't have the use of his left arm.' As Delaney stood in the doorway of the cubicle she told him to raise his right arm while she took his blue sweater off it. 'Now over your head,' she instructed him. He was dazed and happy to fit in with her orders. She eased the sweater off his left arm and then, while he watched her small hands, undid the company shirt and took it off his back.

The radiographer positioned him against an X-ray plate and told him to hold his breath. He could see with a corner of his vision Danielle standing behind the radiographer smiling as if to encourage the tissue of his damaged shoulder. He thought, You will be with me when I'm my father's age, and everything is going – waterworks, old footballer's joints. When they fill the aging Delaney with barium meals you'll be smiling behind the new generation of X-ray technicians.

She dressed him again and wheeled him out. An hour later the young doctor of Italian parentage told him it had turned out to be no more than savage bruising.

TWENTY-ONE

FROM THE JOURNALS OF STANISLAW KABBELSKI, CHIEF OF POLICE,

STAROVICHE

September 16, 1943

Asked to lunch. Kappeler visiting again from Kaunas. It's him, Bienecke, Harner, at SD/Gestapo headquarters, Natural History Museum. They have Moselle wine – it is astonishing the things that come east at a time when the front is imperilled, especially in the Don/Donetz area. I have not finished the first glass when they ask me about Ganz. What do I think of his theory of anti-terrorist behaviour?

I am fortunate to be able to say what I now *know*. 'This is a test of savageries, gentlemen. I believe that to hope that a policy of mildness will somehow inhibit the recruitment of partisans is a seductive but impractical recourse. Above all, I am sure that young Daskovich – if he were here – would argue against it. He ran Krotinitsa in a rational and exemplary way. This made him *more* not *less* of a target. It would be nice to administer this *oblast* in an Aristotelian manner. Unhappily the partisans will not join the dialogue.'

Might have been mixing my Plato with my Aristotle, but Kappeler did not seem to mind – seemed delighted with my response. He rang a small bell which sat beside the cruets of oil and vinegar. His secretary appeared, carrying a file. Kappeler told the young man to hand the file to me. Its cover was marked by a system of abbreviations and numbers. There were a few intelligible words – *Juden, Ganz*, the initials RMORKO which all Ostministry documents carried, and *Bstar*, the symbol for Staroviche. Inside, many letters sealed up with tape, so that file

opened straight to a copy of a letter written last March by Dr
Kappeler to Oberführer Ganz, going something like:

> I request a report on the Jewish situation in the *Generalbezirk*
> of Staroviche, especially about the extent to which Jews
> are still employed by German and Belorussian agencies as
> interpreters, chauffeurs, tutors, mechanics, etc. I would
> appreciate a prompt reply because it is the intention of our
> office to order a swift solution to the Jewish question in your
> area . . .

The answer from Ganz came two months later, in early June,
Ganz doing his trick of implying the discussion was theoretic,
like an exchange of chess moves by letter, and had nothing to
do with daily policy. In cooperation with the security forces in
the *Generalbezirk* of Staroviche, he was subjecting the question
of further repression of Jewry (he used the word *Zurückdrängung*, a word both too gentle and too direct by Ministry
standards) to constant exploration.

Could have told Kappeler but didn't that last summer, when
Danielle revived and began to take the children to the garden to
paint in the afternoons, Ganz was there every afternoon, rallying
her spirits – for which I am grateful – but hardly exploring the
idea of subjecting Staroviche Jewry to further *Zurückdrängung*.
In any case, wrote Ganz, concluding his letter, the reduction of
the Staroviche ghetto with its remnants of skilled Jewish labour
was a slow, grinding process.

A further letter from Kappeler asked for regular reports on
the speeding up of this slow, grinding process. No report or
reply was, however, visible in the file. In September Kappeler
wrote asking for news of progress. Ganz's reply was that the
skilled Jewish workers remaining in the ghetto had been now
reduced to a level beyond which the war effort and the welfare
of various agencies would begin to be affected.

In the end Kappeler wrote straightaway to Bienecke to ask
him whether Special Treatment had been carried out on the
Jewish population of Staroviche. Bienecke replied quickly saying
that apart from some new arrivals from Latvia in June, who

had been immediately subjected to resettlement (*Aussiedlung*, Bienecke's euphemism), the population of the ghetto, added to the small number of Jews who lived outside the ghetto to perform special services, had remained steady as a matter of the Kommissar's, that is Oberführer Ganz's, policy.

The last item in the file was a recent confidential memo addressed to Kappeler from Dr Lohse, Kappeler's chief. Lohse had been to Minsk and been in conference about Ganz with Generalkommissar Kurt von Gottberg, Ganz's superior and with SD Chief of Belorussia, Obersturmbannführer Eduard Strauch. Lohse explained in the confidential memo that Ganz's equivocations in the matter of the remaining Staroviche Jews were demonstrated to these two distinguished leaders through the letters Ganz had written. Obstf Strauch, notoriously brutal and a bad enemy to have, is reported in this confidential memo to have said that Ganz reminded him of the late Generalkommissar Kube, who had been similarly slack in this matter. Strauch had complained so bitterly to the minister about Kube that minister had sent one of his secretaries of state to give Kube a serious warning, and Himmler himself had been pressing for Kube's dismissal and disgrace when the partisans had done everyone a favour – one of his chambermaids had planted a bomb under his bed and it went off at three in the morning. The point is, said Strauch, you could not really depend on the partisans to deliver the Reich of a second great embarrassment – Ganz. Generalkommissar von Gottberg had concluded the conference by saying, 'Lohse, I recommend that your office initiate an executive measure aimed at Oberführer Willi Ganz.'

When finished reading, Dr Kappeler asked me what I thought. We all knew what an 'executive measure' is, *Exekutivmassnahme*, a classic 'soft word' whose intent can be convincingly denied long after the corpses are counted. The truth was that the two most powerful men in Belorussia seem to want poor, soft, amusing Ganz assassinated, though no one could say it in those terms. Given that he is a familiar at my house and that since last July twelve months my men have been engaged in his protection, with only a token SS guard participation, the thing can't be done without my cooperation.

First reaction to the proposal is to think of Danielle and to realise with a clarity I have not enjoyed until now that Ganz has in fact taken from my shoulders the task of attending to the mental well-being of both my wife and children. The whole bleak, besieged experience seems all at once intolerable without this gentle fool, who obviously has the talent but not the stomach for government, government as it is practised in this brutal world, in this penultimate age of the history of man.

Found myself growing irritable. 'You expect us to go on giving and giving,' found myself saying to Kappeler. 'You take advantage of the fact that the Belorussian view of man and his destiny coincides so closely to your own. What are you really offering us for all our cooperation, all our engineering of society?'

Kappeler said, 'You people are *prodigious* patriots.' He was smiling when he said it. Then he told me that the final meetings between von Gottberg and Ostrowsky were in progress to set up a Belorussian National Parliament in Minsk. Told me, 'You can easily check since Ostrowsky's your boy's godfather, I believe. All I can say of this happy circumstance is that your exemplary work, Herr Kabbelski, has been one of the determining factors in the evolution of Belorussian independence.'

Naturally ecstatic myself. Bienecke seemed to take a load off me by saying, 'All we want is for Mrs Kabbelski to ask Oberführer Ganz to your house to drink tea.'

Realised gratefully that what they wanted in first place was not Ganz himself, but merely his Jewish chauffeur. I temporised, saying that to alienate the Kommissar might place my police force in an awkward position. Knew, however, even as I left Bienecke's office, that for political reasons of my own I would make the arrangements Kappeler and Bienecke required.

September 17, 1943

SD headquarters in one wing of old Natural History Museum. You approach Bienecke's office through a door in main façade protected by sandbagged emplacements, then through galleries of dusty cases containing wolves stuffed and mounted at the end of the last century, and heaps of stone axe-blades as used by our swamp-dwelling neolithic ancestors. Always the impression that you're entering a medieval bestiary when you come in here – ambience must have a strong effect on the feelings of prisoners brought here for interrogation.

Bienecke and Harner both in office and Bienecke's secretary Lena, the tidy dark-haired girl who always seems so proper. Beluvich says she responds to drink tempestuously – B saw her sitting on Bienecke's lap with her blouse undone during the interrogation last month of the mechanic found with explosives in his garage. Bienecke's office during interrogations a venue which, in spite of the stereotypes the public applies to those who have the task of grilling the enemy, would not normally be considered romantic even by a policeman's woman. Lena's posture can't have contributed much to the seriousness of the boy's examination. However, demeanour of all parties very correct today.

Was able to assure Bienecke Ganz would be out of his office from 10.45 tomorrow morning, would be at my place drinking coffee with Danielle. Harner repeated his earlier tired witticism about how wonderful it is for a man as busy as I to have found a continual and proper companion for his wife. Looked them both in eye and said that I treasured Herr Kommissar's friendship and that I was sure that in his way he loved Danielle. They did not dare smile, and Lena nodded as if touched by noble sentiment.

'Further,' I told them, 'it is essential for my relationship to the Oberführer, who is after all the provincial governor, that it be clear that the order for tomorrow's action originates here with the SD, or if you wish with Dr Kappeler's Political Section. I do not wish my Belorussian police blamed for the initiative, or put in bad odour with Herr Kommissar Ganz.'

Bienecke gave assurances. We planned allocation of squads for tomorrow – two platoons of my men to operate with SS in ghetto, groups of roughly section-strength to collect interpreters, mechanics and so on scattered round the city. Party of Russian POWs preparing site this afternoon on Mogilev road. Bienecke and Harner show their contempt for Ganz by code-naming the operation *Kaffee-aktion*.

Got home early to find Hirschmann there, tutoring away, treating Radek and Genia to French irregular verbs. Called him into my study – clearly Hirschmann expected reprimand over one or other aspect of his educational approach. Gave him half-packet of cigarettes and filled him a glass of brandy. Thanked him for taking my earlier remarks concerning the content of his teaching to heart. Thanked him for the influence he was having on Radek.

After three astonished mouthfuls of his brandy, he said, 'Sir, I regret I have not been altogether as successful as I would have wished in your daughter's case. Her interest has been diffused both by the terrible state of the world and if I dare say so the first flush of womanhood.' Says it's a phenomenon he has become professionally accustomed to. Said it with such military forth-rightness and correctness – even after all this time in ghetto – that I remarked, 'I have had the exact same thoughts about her. I can see, Herr Hirschmann, that with your intuitive grasp of others you must indeed have made a good soldier.'

So encouraged, he began chatting. 'In battle,' he said, 'in battle all your values are different, they are all related to death. Death seems as reasonable – or worse still as insignificant – as sneezing. Coming out of the lines and seeing women again and having leisure – that was painful to me, like being reborn.' He smiled. 'I was more troublesome at such times.' I really didn't mind him talking with such familiarity. He was a man who understood how things went. He was saying, your children have restored me to the values of life, but I know that is temporary, that in the end I have to go into the line.

As much as any educated man, Hirschmann is aware of the direction of history. I let him take the rest of the bottle back to the ghetto to console himself. I sent a covering note in view of fact he would inevitably be searched.

TWENTY-TWO

One morning Herr Hirschmann, winner of the Iron Cross, failed to arrive for the start of our classes. Mother had sent us into the parlour to get ready for the day's work, which I did and Genia – deeply set now in the sullen rebelliousness which had begun in the war's first autumn – didn't. When it was a quarter past nine I began to quiz her about what could have happened to our tutor. Now she took the usual delight in not answering. I began to feel the sort of choking panic the young feel when they are lost from their parents in strange territory, and then – since I was less than ten years of age – I began to cry.

'Huh!' said Genia and laughed a little to herself while sharpening a pencil. I heard the telephone pealing in the living room.

My mother came in a few seconds later. She was thinner now – her hair was wispier, and I believe I could see for the first time what she would look like when she was old. There was also a forced liveliness in her voice, the sort that was associated in my mind with the phrase 'making an effort for the sake of the children'. Papa had called and said Mr Hirschmann would not be there today. He had meant to let us know earlier but had forgotten. She put an arm around me. 'What's the matter, Radjiu?' she asked me. Genia said, 'He wants to get his day's supply of algebra from that old Jew.'

Mother screamed at her. 'Don't talk in that brutal way!'

She soothed me then with the news that Willi Ganz was coming for morning coffee, and we could join the party. Genia uttered a word I had never heard before, and before I could ask for a repeat and a definition, mother had again screamed, and I knew it would not be the same as coffees and painting sessions of the golden past, even of the sweet besieged period after Mrs Kuzich's murder, as distinct from the bitter besieged period we were now enduring.

The Kommissar arrived early, to my mother's obvious pleasure and mine. Yet I felt throughout the coffee and the cakes, delivered that morning from the same Hungry Shepherd cafe where Mrs Kuzich had been gunned down, that Onkel Willi was constrained, would have preferred I wasn't there. I suppose every child has that experience: waking up to the fact the adult who has always been his special familiar finds him a bit of a nuisance. Onkel Willi would spend time talking to me fairly loudly and jovially, then turn away as if I had been for the moment adequately served and distracted, and speak quietly and urgently to my mother. I heard partisans mentioned, the Crimean Front situation, a despairing letter he'd had from an old Party friend working in Odessa.

He enumerated things that were happening which wouldn't have been permitted by his old friend Kube whom the partisans had blown to pieces, a dear man, a man of taste and of all the people the partisans could have chosen to assassinate it was Kube! He'd been given a good funeral, but really they hadn't found enough of him to fill a bucket. Then there was the small-minded malice of men like Bienecke. Bienecke was the kind who had brought shame to the race. Bienecke used the 'electric methods' pioneered by the SD in France – not the sort of scientific advance to crow about.

Naturally I did not then understand what Onkel Willi meant by 'electric methods' and imagined Bienecke, a crude man I felt a certain distaste for also, experimenting in a laboratory and wearing a white coat.

He talked also about the affair between Hauptsturmführer Bienecke and his Belorussian secretary Lena, a widely known scandal which disturbed my dreams in ways I could not then put a name to. Onkel Willi raised these matters in a kind of code, and if he had been anyone else, if tears of disappointment hadn't been at the back of my throat, I would have run inside, hidden behind the curtains, and spied on him without restraint. What I would have learned, however, would have been no consolation for the loss of that Willi Ganz who could impersonate the Impressionists and the Fauvists and who had hidden and sought in the Brudezh forest.

When it was time for him to go, Genia was coaxed into kissing him goodbye, but I followed him and my mother, without understanding why I should, without being able to break away, out through the porch to the front steps. The sergeant of police who had charge of the security of our house was waiting idly there.

'Your car, Herr Oberführer?' he asked. For Ganz's car was not in sight.

Ganz asked with some peevishness where it was. The sergeant told Ganz that an SS officer had turned up and ordered Ya'acov to park beyond the gates and out in the street.

'For what cause?' Onkel Willi demanded.

The sergeant could not say, but he sent one of his men to open the gates and fetch the car back in. When it rolled up the driveway there was an SS driver at the wheel.

Onkel Willi knew at once who to blame for this transmutation. 'This is Bienecke's doing,' he told my mother. He asked the driver where Ya'acov was.

'Wanted down at the SD, sir,' said the SS private.

'No,' said Onkel Willi. 'Wanted *here!*'

And he jumped in and ordered the man to drive him to the Natural History Museum.

Out of the back window, he waved at us once, absent-mindedly.

He came back early in the afternoon, flying into the house as if he did not wish to be stopped by children as he crossed the lobby. My mother and he locked themselves in the living room. I knocked at the door, but my mother told me not to enter. I heard Onkel Willi grow louder and, at last, dissatisfied with the consolations he was receiving from my mother, burst out into the hallway.

His broad face was awesomely red and blurred and bloated with tears. He moved like a drunk, surging towards the door, but he baulked when he saw me. Kneeling, he grabbed me by the shoulders and seemed to try to crush me laterally. 'You poor

little soldier,' he said. 'They have done something terrible,
Radek. You should block your ears, darling. You should refuse
to listen ever again to any of us.'

His voice was hot and astringent from the cognac my mother
had fed him. Beginning to shed tears again, dreadful tears to
see, tears which super-saturated his face and altered it beyond
decency, he let go of my shoulders, put his arms entirely around
me, and kissed me hard on the mouth. His lips seemed enormous
and worked away at and overpowered my mouth. I thought he
was trying to spit some unwelcome truth deep into my throat.
So it was at first with a sense of rescue and delight that I saw
with the edge of my vision the blue sleeve of my father's coat
and, more centrally to my confused sight, his kid-gloved hand
descending firmly on Oberführer Ganz's shoulder. 'Please,
please, Herr Kommissar,' I heard my father say, that tautness
of his voice sounding welcome yet alien. Today, I thought,
everyone around me has turned into a stranger. 'I warn you,'
father continued. 'Today above all days is one when you should
show a calm face. Believe me, Herr Kommissar!' He hauled
Ganz to his feet. I could not raise my eyes, for I had been party
to what I thought of as Ganz's shameful act of the mouth.
Because I did not know how it had happened, I carried the guilt
for it.

Ganz asked, shuddering with tears, his voice in fragments,
'You or Bienecke?'

My father did not answer and Ganz raised his voice. 'You?
Bienecke? That bastard Harner? Some NCO?'

'Control yourself, Willi.'

'I trust it was you, Stanek. Since you are the only one with
any humanity.'

'No,' said my father. His voice had narrowed further. He
seemed to have lost respect for the Herr Kommissar. 'Of course
it wasn't me. It was done in an impersonal manner.'

'Impersonal?'

'A method tried in Minsk last month,' said my father in that
adult shorthand or 'shortspeak' I had been hearing all morning.
'Pioneered by that famous barbarian Nebe of the Reich Security
Central Office.'

'What?' yelled Ganz. 'What method?'

'Dynamite,' said my father.

I still avoided watching my father, but my eyes were on Willi Ganz, who opened his mouth, grabbed a pedestal on which a bust of Chopin stood, and vomited on the carpet.

I felt my father's hand on my head. 'Go and play, Radek,' he told me, while Onkel Willi hawked and gagged.

I went solemnly, not wishing to flee like the culpable, not breaking into a run, in fact, until I got to the stairs. As I ran, I performed the mental equivalent of feeling myself all over to discover what was left of the child I had been the hour before.

At suppertime, I came downstairs again, wary as a hunter. My father was standing at the living room window, a tumbler of vodka in his hand. He watched the Belorussian rain numbing and darkening the garden. These were the rains which had washed the Grande Armée and, two autumns past, given the Wehrmacht its first halt.

I knew my father was waiting for the half past six news on the *Deutschlandsender*. Later on in the night he would attempt to pick up the more distant BBC news transmitted in Polish.

He saw me. 'Ah!' he said as if meeting me after a long separation. He smiled and extended his hand towards me, and obediently I went and stood by his side. 'We'll pull the curtains soon,' he said, 'and put the lights on and have a happy evening. Cards? Shall we play cards? I've never taught you whist.'

I said nothing, leaned against his hip, heard him finish the glass and give that sigh which comes with the first radiance of liquor in the blood. With his hand on my shoulder, I felt delivered from shame and sin. 'Herr Hirschmann won't be teaching you any more. I'm going to have to find you a good tutor from somewhere in the city. As yet I don't know who it will be.'

'Where has Herr Hirschmann gone?' I was able to ask.

'The Germans sent him east,' my father answered.

I understood he was lying for my sake, and for the first time I felt a shadow of that onus he had taken on himself for the sake of Belorussian independence.

TWENTY-THREE

She had driven him home in his own car a little after eight. Her father had given her her taxi fare back to North Parramatta, which meant she had to come inside the house to call a cab. Delaney knew that Gina had already left for work – he had been working so much overtime for Kabbel that his non-appearance would not have alarmed her. As he led Danielle past the gum trees in his front yard he had the feeling that if he admitted her to his house and its minor secrets – the front door key, as an instance, waited under a yellow bucket in the laundry at the back of the house – it would be as definite, as final an act as sleeping with her. Yet there was no avoiding it. 'Could you get the key?' he asked her. 'Under a yellow bucket in the laundry around the back.'

She let them in. Even her use of the telephone, putting her mouth in the place of Gina's, seemed to cement the business. He felt a shortage of breath in the shut house as she told the cab where to come. 'Quarter of an hour wait,' she told Delaney with a philosophic grin. She offered to make tea, but Delaney said he'd had enough at the hospital. If she were let loose in the kitchen among Gina's things – so his suspicion went – life would no longer be controllable.

She filled in the time until the cab looking at his family photographs – the wedding photograph outside St Nicholas's, himself and best man Eric Samuels in sky-blue formal wear, Gina and her girlfriends beautiful in a brittle way in layers of taffeta, muscular pretty girls who would never dress like this again, unless it was for their own weddings. 'Your wife is very pretty,' said Danielle. It sounded like more than politeness, like genuine and gracious envy of Gina's well-organised substance. 'She looks like a woman of character.'

'That's right,' said Delaney. 'She's an honest woman.'

But he wasn't there to praise Gina. Gina was praiseworthy without his opening his mouth, and the fact made no difference.

Danielle inspected the photographs of all the teams for which Delaney since babyhood had made openings, found touch, backed-up, got the ball to the centres. 'It must be strange to have a *game*,' she said. 'I can't imagine what it must be like to have a game. Something that's there year after year.'

'You've got your game,' said Delaney. 'Warwick and his scanners. Your father. You can't tell me it isn't a game. Trapping Stevo. It was like what your father told me about his old man. Hunting Russian guerrillas.' Delaney laughed. 'You crowd have a game. You've just got to see you all together in the control room to know that much.'

She dropped her head towards one shoulder, making a brief and genuine try at seeing the business of Uncle Security as sport. 'No,' she told him. 'It's too serious, I'm afraid.'

'So is Rugby League when you're in it for a living. And if I could make first grade next year my life would be transformed.'

'More glamour?' she asked. In her mouth it sounded a pretty strange word.

'More business opportunities. If you take them. You can always get a job as cellarman at the Leagues Club but that's dead-end unless you'd got the talent to rise. Besides I hate the atmosphere of clubs. Disinfectant and spilled beer and the pale stains on the carpet when some idiot cried ruth. I couldn't spend my life there. No, there's real estate or there's even journalism or Public Relations.'

'And we'd lose you at Uncle?'

'Don't hold your breath. Anyhow I'm carving out a career there teaching the boss's daughter to read novels.'

'Oh yes? Pretty dense, is she?'

'Bright as a button.'

He watched her as she stood by the hall door reading the Papal Blessing which hung there, coloured scrollwork on a parchment-like material, a coloured disc with the Pope's head on it above wording which invoked the Divinity to enrich the lives of Terrence and Gina Delaney. His mother had sent away for it through old Father Rushton and it had arrived – in spite of go-slows at the Redfern Mail Exchange – eight days before the wedding.

It occurred to Delaney for the first time that the bear-like Polish Pope resembled an older Kabbel, had the same sandy Slavic face, basic issue to Eastern Europeans. Danielle Kabbel, one blonde Slav, contemplated another, Christ's Vicar who had lent weight and strength to the Delaney marriage.

'Stanton reckons,' Delaney told her, 'John Paul should have gone to Poland when they declared martial law and dared them to arrest him. That would have been real Solidarity.' Though Delaney knew that the reason Stanton idolised Lech Walesa was that he showed what a working man could do, could shake a dark empire and get on the front page of *Time*. Solidarity, to Stanton, was the political equivalent of *Star Wars*, and the old warrior who possessed the force had let the hero down.

Mrs Delaney, however, loved the Polish Pope. He had delivered her of a tyranny she had lived under since childhood – the necessity of explaining to unbelievers why the Pope was always Italian. She forgave him, if ever she thought of it, for squibbing on high noon in Warsaw or Gdansk.

Danielle shrugged. 'He isn't a free man,' she said. 'Infallibility isn't sufficient.' She had her father's gift for uttering arresting sentences. You could wait a lifetime and not hear such a sentence from a slag like Gay Mansfield.

Outside, Danielle Kabbel's taxi honked. Delaney got up from his chair even though she told him not to. At the door he dragged her into his arms and kissed her unhandily on the forehead. She held him at the stretch of her arms and inspected him with that gravity he saw in her all the time. She gave out a small yelp and two parallel tears ran exactly down her face; no messiness, no lack of symmetry and barely a sound. He asked her why.

'I wish you were a member of the family,' she said. She left the house. He hoped briefly that the cab driver wasn't someone who knew him from the club. A girl his mother would describe as 'dainty' running from Delaney's place, tears in her eyes at such an odd hour!

He was still awake, sore in the shoulder and afraid, at noon.

Training was to begin at five. He would go early and get Wallie the club masseur to treat the damage with all his old fashioned linaments with their ancient labels featuring goannas and emus and hinting at Aboriginal and magical healing substances. Wallie would be good for the spirit. He treated the bodies of footballers as if they were the temples of the Lord.

Danielle's last sentence, when turned end to end, meant nothing and meant too much. You could imagine a girl like that, bearhugged by a footballer within arm's length of wedding shots and of John Paul's blessing, naming Gina as an impediment. But her regret wasn't for Gina. It was because he was no Kabbel.

He fell asleep at last wondering if she was saying – in the indirect, arse-up Kabbel manner – that she wished they were married, that he was incorporated in the Kabbel tribe in that way. He left unexamined, sitting in the dimmest corner of his surmises, the idea that she might be telling him she wished he was her brother.

TWENTY-FOUR

FROM THE JOURNALS OF STANISLAW KABBELSKI, CHIEF OF POLICE,

STAROVICHE

November 30, 1943

Further meeting on Ganz problem today at Natural History Museum next door my office. Was amazed to find Kuzich present. Since his wife's death our mayor has got by quite happily with occasional solace from Mrs Dorovina, the department-store owner's wife, but today he *looked* bereaved, red-eyed and badly shaven and angry with fate.

'We've got him!' said Bienecke quietly to me, not wanting to seem to crow in front of the widower Kuzich, but his face alive with that excitement peculiar to police work, when events and people seem to cooperate to deliver up to you a long-cherished target. Have not relayed to Bienecke my disgust at excessive aspects of Ganz's personality nor my horror at the foul pederastic kiss he imposed on Radek. Even if I were anxious for the Kommissar's destruction I would not share such intimate concerns with Bienecke.

It seems Bienecke has enough to go on from other sources though. Two months back, within an hour of what Bienecke still calls the *Kaffee-aktion*, Ganz turned up at Bienecke's office to accuse him of murder and chicanery. Ganz had already met young Harner in the lobby and, seeing some blood on his trousers, called him a swine. Both officers – Bienecke and Harner – then in a condition of shock since Bienecke's fore-doomed experiment had not gone well, and some of my men and a platoon of Lustbader's had to be sent round to end the misery of sundry victims. To have a tear-stained hysteric turning up and yelling accusations at such a time very hard to take for proud and narrow men like these two.

Later, more calmly, Ganz tried to get even with Bienecke on procedural grounds. Wrote to von Gottberg, to Lohse and to Kappeler saying that Jews from his office had been executed but that those working for Oberst Lustbader and the Wehrmacht have been left quite alone, and that this distinction constituted a personal insult to him as Kommissar.

No doubt Bienecke will win paper war. Already has powerful Dr Kappeler on side. Also sent off to von Gottberg photographs of Ganz and his driver Ya'acov in over-friendly stances, including one of Ganz congratulating Ya'acov, holding him by the arm, the day of Radek's birthday, when Ya'acov rescued Ganz's Mercedes from burning garage. Seems this constitutes a race crime adequate to excite someone like von Gottberg. Other photographs and testimonies Bienecke has collected concerning Ganz-Ya'acov connection must be enough to blow von Gottberg's hat off.

Bienecke, after giving me a summary of the further complaints everyone now had with Ganz, let the remarkably pensive Mayor Kuzich begin to speak. There's a secretary in the town hall named Drusova. One of the clerks had informed Kuzich that Drusova was stealing stationery, secreting it in the lining of her jacket and even beneath her blouse and underwear. Kuzich had his chief secretary, a middle-aged woman, detain Drusova at the end of the day – that was yesterday. Kuzich and chief secretary thought they were dealing with ordinary pilferage, but also found on the girl's person carbons used in typing up a number of documents – the names and personal details, for example, of appointees to administer the various Wehrdorfer in the *oblast* of Staroviche, lists of invitees to the mayor's Christmas party, memos from Kuzich to me on law and order matters, memos from Kuzich to Bienecke on partisan matters, memos from Kuzich to Ganz on ghetto matters.

Obvious the girl was passing this species of intelligence to the partisans.

Drusova has been prisoner since last night. Can't suppress a surge of pity for her, though Bienecke says that 'for obvious reasons' she hasn't been touched. Asked, of course, what the obvious reasons were. He said, she could be used to draw the partisans to Ganz. Asked how he intended to turn her, how to ensure that when she speaks to her partisan contacts she will not include a code-sentence which will tell them she's been caught. Had he any relatives of hers for surety?

Bienecke said, Of course, her fourteen-year-old brother. He is hostage. Drusova's been told he'll be released if she does her task properly.

My pity's now transferred itself from Drusova to the boy.

Kuzich said, 'She's the one who sold my wife to the bastards. My wife's social and official itinerary was typed up in the office. Tell her any lies you wish but don't keep any promises you make to the bitch.'

It's clearer than ever how strongly Kuzich also is set against Ganz and his policy of moderation. The man doesn't have an ally in Staroviche, Kaunas, Riga or Minsk.

Bienecke's method is this: he releases the girl. She tells the partisans she has been chastised for stealing paper and expects to be civilly tried and fined for it. She says that her boss the mayor pleaded for leniency to apply to her case. In a short time, within a few days at the most, before the partisans are aware that the boy is a prisoner of the SD and not away in Gomel with his grandparents, she will give her partisan contact a rundown on the feud growing between Ganz and everyone else, and advise them that through Kuzich's correspondence with us she knows the Gestapo and I both intend to withdraw our protection, leaving him merely with two or three of Lustbader's middle-aged asthmatics.

This fatal thinning of his protection would happen either outside his office or more likely outside his apartment. Question Bienecke asks is whether I will cooperate and withdraw my men?

Even then not certain. Ganz profoundly flawed. Don't want him near Danielle or the children. But still a man of brilliant promise. In the end I asked for a few hours. It is not good for my Belorussian purpose to be too supine to the desires of the Gestapo and SD.

Telegraphed Kappeler, asking for further assurances that a Belorussian National Congress *would* be called and seeking an urgent reply. Three o'clock this p.m. telegraphic assurances from Kappeler arrived on my desk. Have decided to assist Bienecke in what is probably essential for the ultimate security of this *oblast.*

TWENTY-FIVE

FROM THE MATCH DIARY OF TERRY DELANEY

Penrith v Balmain. Least said the better. 37–8. Missed a crucial tackle which set up their first try after twenty minutes. Tuomey, of course, his usual charming self. 'If that shoulder's not up to it, tell us and we'll bloody take you off.' Kabbel tells me from his intelligence sources the blond hoon who did it copped thirteen stitches in the hand, so that's some comfort.

Sluggish in attack today – couldn't get anything going in the back line and Steve Mansfield and forwards slow and let the others penetrate up the middle. Reserves and firsts won. Deecock for a change brilliant at five-eighth. Most of our tries from bombs though. Not from real penetrative football.

Shoulder so fierce by tonight Gina and I didn't go to club. Bugger that blond with the hammer!

He pretended greater shoulder pain than he felt and avoided touching Gina that night. The late-night television news he sat up watching was full of lumpy footage from the American networks which the local stations boasted of as 'the full resources of our worldwide satellite hook-up'. There were garish ruins in an unimaginable town in Mississippi in whose main street a chemical tanker had exploded. A scrawny dog owned by an obese couple in Orlando, Florida, could use a home computer to do basic calculations and draw diagrams. That was the quality of the stuff for whose sake Delaney avoided Gina's bed. A yellow flicker bounced across the room from the face of the dog-owner as Gina stood watching Delaney from the door. 'If the damage is permanent, you'll just have to sue Kabbel,' she said.

When he came to bed at last he lay straight and still. He was pleased his status as a professional athlete, that his body was not any body, that people paid at the turnstiles to see its tricks, gave him the extra authority to lie like a board at Gina's side. Sometimes he would glance at her to ensure she was sullenly asleep, her back to him, her shoulders assuming a hunch which belonged to an older woman, some widow of the future. The sight filled him with bewilderment and misery. He felt an urge to ring his mother, to get her praying, repetitive prayer on which Mrs Delaney could spend a whole day, a tide of repeated formulas, of sympathetic utterances.

'There is nothing wrong with magic,' Father Doig had told his shocked congregation once. 'Magic is *meant* to be potent in all societies, in our society as in Aboriginal society. Magic – the Rosary or some other tribal incantation – can kill a cancer, save a marriage, revive the doomed.'

'Now we're bloody Myall blacks!' old Gerry Delaney had complained, and had spoken – as he often did – of writing to the cardinal about Doig's heresies.

But that was all Delaney wanted – what Doig had talked about. Someone to take the curse off.

He did not wake until she was getting ready for work. The brisk sound of her dress going over her shoulders and down her body brought him around. It was already after eight and Gina was hurrying. He gave her like charity the small news that his shoulder had improved. He tried to set up the lying impression that *that* was their reward for not touching all night. The mortgage payment was safe – he would get a match fee on Sunday. She said that was good. He watched her frown at him, her doubt that that was all the distance between them, a few bruised sinews. He grinned candidly, and panic crashed his heart against his ribs. I can't keep up the lies, I haven't got the guts for it.

Then it came to him that it would be better if he'd *had* Danielle Kabbel, acquired something definite to lie about. Something you could say in a sentence.

That night Delaney returned to the control room from Blacktown in the middle of his shift. Danielle Kabbel was dozing on the

couch, an old-fashioned quilt covering her lower body, a sky-blue
cardigan crookedly over her shoulders. On her thigh sat an open
spine-up copy of *Catch 22*, a novel which Delaney had once read
and been shocked by – the lunacy of its love and war and death.
It amazed him to think of her reading it, figuring it out. Yet she
was deeply into it, the meat of the book spread evenly across
her leg. She gaped and then smiled when he woke her.

He said, 'I believe there's a painting Warwick did of the two
of you.'

'Yes,' she said. 'Why?' She stretched, yawning on the word.
Her breasts lifted within the cardigan.

'I wanted to see it. That's all.'

She swung her legs off the couch and found her shoes. She led
him into the hallway and towards the Kabbel kitchen he had never
seen. The inner part of the house was immaculate and cold. On
either wall were dim and ancient black and white photographs –
the Kabbel ancestry, Delaney supposed – and shiny coloured
prints of the Kabbel children. Danielle turned on the light and
Delaney saw the painting. 'Good, isn't he?' Danielle asked him.
She smiled again. Delaney was delighted with the smile. He saw
in it the simple arrogance of kinship, nothing more.

Stanton's description of the thing had been pretty exact.
Danielle and Warwick were blank-eyed. But that was because
Warwick's craft didn't stretch to living eyes. The wave breaking
over the Harbour bridge and the ugly Centrepoint tower, sil-
houetted like a vast folded clothes-hoist, was beautifully marbled
with sea-spume and had a depth to it. It was the sort of schoolboy
painting that was hung on construction hoardings in the city
during Education Week. If you saw it there, you'd guess that
the blue costumes with the four brass circles on the collars were
the uniform of some minority group high school.

'Hey, you never wear the uniform!' said Delaney.

He heard a faint sigh of fabric as she shrugged. 'Warwick must
have thought he'd put me in it for some symbolic reason.' She
laughed quietly. 'It isn't as if I don't slave for the business.'

'Why the four rings?'

'That's symbolic. My father's design. It stands for the four of us.
Interlocked. My father goes in for that sort of thing. It's the . . .'

He knew what she was going to say. 'The Belorussian in him, I suppose.'

She laughed again. 'Exactly, Terry. You're catching on.'

'I love you too, Danielle,' he said, hoping it would loosen somehow the Kabbels' interlocking rings.

Danielle said, 'Oh,' made a little squeak with her lips and put her hand to his jaw.

'Can I be your lover?' It was a strange thing for him to say. He had never used that term with Gina. With Gina he had always been his honest, Delaney, five-eighth self. Such a word as 'lover' may have alarmed Gina or seemed to crowd out the boundaries of life so that there would be no space left for practical matters, including practical marital affection.

Danielle Kabbel's hand closed on the flesh of his cheek. 'You can be my lover,' she said. 'Certainly you can be my lover.'

He had that feeling he'd had the morning before, the feeling he often had with the Kabbels, that the rest of his life didn't count with them, that they viewed it with what he thought of as a giant innocence, with the sort of flattened-out eyes Warwick had painted, and that these did not take in his marriage. With disappointment and joy he knew he would never have to explain Gina away to Danielle Kabbel, would never have to plead that in spite of his crimes against Gina he was an honest man.

'Where?' he asked. 'Where, Danielle?'

'My room,' she murmured. She reached up and drew her lips across his cheek. 'My room, please.'

It was a reasonable plea from a sensitive girl. Please, nothing alien, no motel, no vinyl car seat, no park embankment.

Her room was that of a schoolgirl – she still kept all her school textbooks, and a gold on blue pennant hanging on her wall, midway above her bed, announced Danielle Kabbel had won the Under-15 800 metres at Our Lady of the Sacred Heart in Parramatta in 1978.

Ecstasy is such a ridiculous state (so he would tell himself later) that he forgot to wonder if her good Catholic 800 metres, so proudly and singularly stated on her wall, prevented her from taking the sort of precautions even he and Gina took these days.

TWENTY-SIX

FROM THE JOURNALS OF STANISLAW KABBELSKI, CHIEF OF POLICE,

STAROVICHE

December 1, 1943

Arranged. Drusova has assured her contacts that after the Kommissar arrives at his apartment for lunch tomorrow, *c*12.30, Bienecke and I will be withdrawing the normal guards. Kommissar will be left only with a few Wehrmacht sentries who have not seen combat or really encountered the Satanic determination with which Oberführer Ganz's apartment is likely to be assaulted. Even partisans must know Willi values lunch highly, so that Bienecke's choice of the apartment for the appropriate location very deft.

No one in SD or in Dr Kappeler's office seems to care the partisans will milk Ganz's liquidation for all it is worth in propaganda terms. Bienecke intends to cancel any partisan sense of triumph by surrounding those involved in the attack as soon as they have fulfilled the intentions of the Reich Security Central Office towards Oberführer Ganz. I imagine friend Bienecke will keep no promises to Drusova or her brother either, unless he wants to use Drusova for future security work. Surmise he may send Drusova and brother east out of pure vanity, however useful Drusova might be in future, just to show partisans they've been used by Bienecke. Bienecke, like most men of limited intelligence, out to prove even to Bolsheviks that he's smart, that we're all smart on this side of the fence, that we possess dangerous cunning.

Both Radek and Danielle still confused and depressed about Ganz's outburst. As gentle a soul as Danielle is, believe she has been distanced from him now.

BBC news came through clear in Polish and even if halfway unreliable is alarming. At least even BBC say German Fourth Army holding in front of Orsha. More optimistic officers you meet speak of defeats in southern Russia as if they are positive blessings, creating a shorter, more rational, more defensible line. The threat to Smolensk has weighed on Danielle – you can see the fright and a sort of yellow insomnia come up in her eyes whenever I turn the radio on. Smolensk is something intimate to Danielle. Before the first war her family had interests in a brickworks there and she visited the place as a child. It is the first city of the East, she always said, the place where the last traces of those Catholic allegiances which connect us to the West end, and that other world emphatically begins. It is also – as am always saying to reassure her – a good three hundred and fifty kilometres from Staroviche, and on this front that seems a great distance, even though in the south last summer the Russians would make advances of seventy kilometres in a day.

Am taking heavy dosage of laudanum tonight. Don't want to face tomorrow with the usual ashen fatigue.

3.00 a.m. woken from heavy sleep by telephone call from Ostrowsky in Minsk. Wanted me to know that final plans for a Belorussian Republican Congress *have* been thrashed out with von Gottberg's office and with Political Section in a meeting which went on in Minsk until an hour ago. Wanted me to know. 'If there's anyone likely to resent the hours he spent in sleep while this glorious news hung around his bed unspoken, I knew it was you, my dear Stanek.'

Poor Danielle waiting in corridor, a wraith in her nightdress, sure the call was bad news. We celebrated with brandy and then slept happily in each other's arms till dawn.

TWENTY-SEVEN

Delaney could tell there was a window ajar at Dyson Engineering. Beyond a yard littered with trailer bodies and the frames of caravans – Dyson's business – stood a two-storeyed brick blockhouse, and the window that was open declared itself, on the top floor by the stairs, in a faint stutter of metal venetian blinds. Delaney stood in the deep shadow of a compressor and considered the window. There was something like a shimmer of light up there, but whether it came from inside or was reflected from a distant source across the rooftops he could not decide. This degree of inspection was called in the industry 'a perimeter survey', and unless someone emerged from the window carrying Dyson Engineering's petty-cash box, patent drawings or photocopier, he would be justified in holding this position until the police came.

After ninety seconds of further observation, he walked back to his car in the laneway and switched into base. There was the huskiness of sleep in Danielle's voice when she answered. He pictured her, blanket dropped around her bare ankles, leaning towards the mike. In the cold car, he intoned, 'My bride!'

'That place is alarmed,' she told him. 'Something should have shown up here on the computer.'

'The wiring could be out,' he said. Love talk, he thought.

'Or the intruder disconnected it. Terry, stay clear. I'll call St Mary's police.'

'I love you better than anyone living,' he said. Because she never mentioned Gina he was liberated to speak fantastically, the way he had always wanted to. *Ti mon seul desir*. I love you better than anyone living. But he never heard back from her any wild utterances, nothing like that. And she never used his name. She used his name in sentences like, 'Or the intruder disconnected it.' He knew that she was the most strange woman, that when he married her people would say that behind his back.

He let himself inside the gate again and stood in the shadow of the compressor. He knew that from the outside, from the point of view of a perimeter survey, his intention to marry Danielle Kabbel made him a deadshit, a despicable bastard. Even Stanton would use such terms. Double bloody deadshit to string Gina along, to play at being married when a stench of indifference filled the house in Forth Street, threatened to warp the timbers and poison the lemon-scented gums by the roots. He thought that if he waited there might turn up a kinder way to let Gina know than he could think of today. But he couldn't think anyhow. All his mind went into Danielle Kabbel, his mind was absorbed and jangled. As the monster's brain sitting in a glass retort in Dr Frankenstein's laboratory, his sat and waited in Danielle Kabbel's schoolgirl bedroom. He spent his time at home joking, singing, sometimes slapping Gina on the hip or shaping up to her like a boxer. Rowdiness – he wanted to fill the house with it to cover for his lost head. On his nights off he sheltered in the bathroom until Gina had fallen sourly asleep. Soon it would be the Sunday after Corpus Christi, the date of the elder Terracettis' marriage in Palermo. Their son and daughter, with spouses and children, were required to visit the tomato farm in Bringelly and drink grappa and eat sweet cakes. How would he occupy a day like that? With a confused and suspicious Gina in the shadow of the Terracettis' monumental marriage.

Still no one appeared at the upstairs window. Delaney saw a police Commodore rolling towards him down the laneway with only its parking lights on. He slipped out the gate to meet it. It held two young constables wearing the sort of moustaches favoured by American police on television. He trailed the two of them up the outside stairs and watched them wriggle up through the open window in their tight-arsed navy-blue trousers. He followed himself, feeling the residual damage in his shoulder during the second his wrists took his entire weight on the window-sill.

Delaney and the constables now stood in an outer office. There were three desks and the usual dowdy office furnishings.

A small indefinite light shone through from the boss's office. The cops did not bother to tread softly. They strode over, and one of them threw the door open.

Looking past the cops and through the door, Delaney could see that the light came from a two-barred electric radiator sitting on the floor. Within its small nimbus was a two-thirds full flagon of red wine, and two polystyrene cups. Beyond them, in the direction of an old three-seater lounge, violent movement could be seen, and Stanton, wearing only the Uncle Security shirt Denise had tapered down for him, stepped into the light cursing, his hands joined over his genitals. One of the cops now found a switch and turned a full and merciless light on the office. A woman sitting on the lounge reached, her arms cramped across her breasts, for pieces of clothing. 'Turn the fucking lights off!' roared Stanton. The young policeman considered him. 'Turn the bloody lights off till the lady gets dressed.'

Delaney recognised the woman, a tired-looking but pretty widow who worked at Franklin's. There were cruel dimplings across her abdomen from the children she had borne for her late husband.

Delaney said, 'Turn off the lights, constable. It's one of our blokes.'

'Jesus Christ,' said the one near the lights, whistled and, in his mercy, switched the lights off. The cut-price seduction venue returned to an appropriate and kinder dimness. Stanton could no longer be seen as he had a second before, the humiliatingly swarthy legs and blue prick. 'Jesus, Delaney, did you call the bloody law?'

One of the police asked without any malice, 'Do you blokes bring sheilas to your client's premises all the bloody time?'

'Do you expect me to hire a fucking suite at the Regent?' asked Stanton.

Delaney found himself weeping, the phenomenon terrified him. He made no sound and covered his mouth. Tears for his friend's humiliation, or perhaps for his own desperate and joyous situation. Swallowing away furiously in the doorway he managed to stop the flow. 'There's no need to take any action on this,' he heard himself saying. 'I'll keep special watch on the place

and we'll rewire the alarm in the morning.' It didn't sound
authoritative, so he said, 'Brian here is an old walloper himself.
He's got kids . . .'

'Frig you, Delaney!' shouted Stanton, savaging his trousers,
throttling them, the belt buckle tolling against his knees and a
shiver in his voice, desire and claret and a two-bar radiator
no longer adequate for the biting night. '*He* fucks the boss's
daughter,' he told the constables. 'But they let him do it at the
office.'

Delaney felt the blood burning in his face and heard the widow
from Franklin's crying softly behind Stanton.

The constables surprised Delaney by remaining lenient, as if
they accepted Stanton's proposition, that we're all sexual comics
sooner or later and that it was uncomradely to put too much
stress on the discovery of an old cop with his pants down. Both
young men accepted a glass of the claret. The woman was
excluded from this general atmosphere of absolution. Her shame
went unrelieved. She dressed quickly in the toilet in the outer
office and vanished. It was to a closing outer door that Stanton
called futilely, 'Let me see you to the car, sweetie!'

'She never takes anyone to her place,' he explained to the
cops in her wake. 'Doesn't want her kids to know.'

He cleaned up quickly and left the premises, as they were
called in industry and police terminology, locking up as he went.
Delaney, the silly bugger who'd called the police, was a fringe
member of the fraternity which flourished briefly in the dark
yard of Dyson Engineering as Stanton, no longer foolish, the
flagon held frankly in his hand, thanked them for everything.
They had even helped him pick up the trail of tissues the widow
had left. They would make a report, and it was agreed Delaney
would too. Some kids had broken in and done no damage.
Delaney would tell it that way to expiate for calling the police
before checking up on whether it would make his friend feel
stupid.

'Listen, mate,' one of them called to Stanton from the doorway
of the patrol car, 'next time better make it the back seat of your
Holden.'

The Commodore crept away. Stanton might never have to

face those two young coppers again – they might be transferred to Botany or Brewarrina. Delaney, however, was a friend. Every night he could bring to work, wilfully, an image of bare-arsed Stanton and his blue phallus exposed by fluorescent light.

'Well, thank you, cobber,' said Stanton. 'Thank you, gentleman rooter!'

'How do you know?' Delaney asked. 'Danielle and me. How do you know?'

'Read it in the bloody *Sydney Morning Herald.*'

From his years of football, Delaney had learned the game's butt-end range of skills. He liked to depend on penetration and speed, but there were as well eye-gouging and ball-crushing, winding and knees in the back, the clenched arm across the shoulder-blade and the uppercut on the referee's blind side. From this underworld of Rugby League Delaney produced an elbowing action which left Stanton gagging and devoid of breath. 'What do you mean, they let me do it at the office?'

Stanton laid the bottle down, gasped for a while and said like a man with laryngitis, 'Do you think that old Rudi doesn't know? You think you creep back at midnight and root his daughter and he doesn't know? He knows who the chicken king's fucking but he doesn't know about Delaney? You stupid prick! He wants you *in*. He wants another son. Good God help you, you poor bastard.' His breath had revived now. He stood upright and spoke calmly, as if all the spite he felt as an interrupted lover had evaporated in an instant. 'I know what I'm doing. A poor lonely checkout bitch and a flask of red ned. You don't know what in the bloody hell you're doing.' This was worse, pity from a recent shirt-tail crackler, a trouserless goon. Delaney hissed at him – stuff about Stanton having enough disasters of his own without worrying about Delaney's. This is the end of all friendship, Delaney thought.

In the morning, signing off his .38, he asked Danielle to follow him to the car. 'Does your father know?' he asked. She stood blinking in the sunlight. He had never seen her before with the sun in her eyes. It was one of those sharp, sunny winter's mornings. 'The world's best winter!' said promoters of Sydney, not always exactly, since it could rain like a hose.

'Does your father know?' he repeated. And Warwick? Who had listened calmly to the erotic chat of the chicken king.

'He knows I make my own decisions,' she said. She bravely raised her jawline to the sun. He would long remember both the claim and the gesture. She said, smiling beneath her lowered eyes, 'You never think other people are catching on. But they do.'

'We ought to get out of the house. Out of your room. We ought to go somewhere else.'

'Where would that be?' she asked.

'I'll look around.' It was impossible to see himself and above all Danielle booking into some motel. The Travelodge? The Pasadena? The Rio Bravo? (Here in the west of Sydney motels seemed to be named after movies, Clint Eastwood kind of movies.) It was impossible to see *this* pair of lovers disconnecting the alarms at Dyson Engineering and climbing through a window to the mean comfort of an old lounge and a two-bar radiator.

'What I turn up with will be all right with you?' he asked.

'Yes,' she said. She considered her hands and smiled again. 'Yes. Within limits.'

TWENTY-EIGHT

It was after midnight, in the meat of Delaney's shift. Warwick found him in front of the Datsun dealership in Blacktown. 'Quick, Terry,' he said. 'Leave your car, I'll drive you back.'

Delaney asked him why. But he could not complain that his routine was being broken. It had been broken often enough since he became Danielle's lover and sole desire.

'Something you'll be interested in,' said Warwick. 'Promise you that.'

Is this the family intervention? Delaney wondered. I'm driven to a paddock behind Rooty Hill and shot in the head with cold Warwick's Magnum. All done with that same smoothness you saw when he switched over to earphones on the scanner.

Getting into the car beside Warwick, he placed his hand, for the first time in his security career, on his .38, stretching against the handle of the thing as if it were a walking stick.

'I thought you should see this,' said Warwick, driving off. 'Since Scott's still got his eye problem.' Scott had gone to a little shack the family owned out beyond Lithgow to let the burns heal. Scott, Kabbel had said, loved the bush. In the meantime, Warwick seemed to be arguing, Delaney was the substitute Scott.

Warwick turned the car back down Main Street towards Seven Hills. Delaney had to be careful what questions he asked. He did not want to provoke any reference to Danielle. He didn't want to hear what Warwick thought of the affair, whether it amused or outraged him.

'Come on,' said Delaney in the end – an ordinary formula but painfully chosen – 'tell a man where in the hell we're going, eh?'

Warwick reached between them and switched on a shortwave under the instrument panel. The bell-clear voice of a taxi dispatcher filled the car. 'Lalor Park to Ryde,' it said. 'Marsden Hospital to Girraween. Blacktown Tenpin to Merrylands.' Warwick switched the volume down and smiled modestly at Delaney. A prince of technology. 'Our mate Mr Stevens has just called a cab from Wentworthville Leagues Club.'

'Oh yeah?' said Delaney, liking less than ever all this lifting of soundwaves Warwick was so keen on, this electronic thievery. 'We're five minutes from Stevo the vandal's place in Pretoria Road,' Warwick told him. 'We'll be there long before him.'

'No,' Delaney yelled. 'No way. I'm not here for any of that.'

Warwick kept on in a level clinical way. 'You were injured, after all. Getting pictures which some clown of a boozing mate of Stevo's loses down the back of a filing cabinet. I mean, Delaney, we can go round pretending we're saving society by shaking hands with doorknobs and shining torches at windows. We don't make a dent on the core of things, you know, the protected species.'

Delaney writhed in his seat. 'Jesus, we've got protected judges and casino owners, and bookmakers and politicians shovelling smack straight into the veins of sixteen-year-olds in King's Cross, and you want to bring the axe down on poor bloody Stevo. I don't care enough about him. I won't touch him. I won't let you touch him. I mean it, Warwick. Bloody hell!'

Warwick clucked at Delaney's extravagance. 'Neither of us'll touch him. How's that for a promise?'

Delaney hauled himself across the vinyl seat closer to Warwick, inspecting his face. A handsome, studious face. It broke into laughter. 'Honest, Terry,' said Warwick.

The houses of Pretoria Road sat low amongst the telegraph poles. I am the happiest man in Australia, berserkly in love as I have always wanted to be since old Aubin brought the print into class. I have found the woman in the pavilion surrounded by lions and unicorns, kangaroos and emus. The woman at the middle of things.

Yet the world had never looked meaner or more a cause for shooting yourself than it did in Pretoria Road after midnight. At the heart of each bungalow a love which had soured and flaked together with the first hopeful nuptial coat of paint, which had spawned large hoonish sons whose mag-wheeled and reducoed wrecks were parked everywhere on pavement and lawns. A street of no manners, no grace, no hope. The street you'd expect to find Stevo living. All his connections and barbarisms and old mates hadn't brought him further than this. You just had to look at the place to know that Stevo had brought his own vengeance on himself.

Warwick parked close into the pavement by a corner house and beside some kid's scarlet Torana. 'See the place down there?' he asked Delaney. 'Open carport, low brick fence. That's Stevo's castle. His wife's a diabetic and on holiday in Queensland. Stevo celebrates by visiting all the licensed clubs. He'd like to find a woman to bring back with him in the cab, but they still haven't made them that low.'

Delaney said, 'If you try to run the poor loveless old bugger down I'll get in your way.' He grasped the parking brake between the bucket seat and jerked it on two extra notches.

'Anyone would think,' said Warwick, 'Stevo was a relative of the Delaneys.'

And in a way he was. Stevo was a man Delaney had till recently thought he could never become. But now that Delaney was the happiest man in Australia any disaster could overtake him.

'Just so that you're clear on that,' said Delaney.

'How much in match fees did he cost you?'

'Not a cent. The coach cursed me last Sunday, but even a champion's entitled to one bad game.'

'It might all come against you later,' murmured Warwick.

They saw a taxi then, edging along Pretoria Road from the other direction, the driver looking for letter-box numbers with probably damn-all help from a drowsy Stevo. The cab found the place and braked. Stevo took an age to emerge. Watching Warwick keenly for any mad movement, Delaney pictured Stevo grunting and farting and trying to find his money. By the light of a street lamp Delaney saw him open the door – the front seat door, Stevo willing to be the cab driver's mate all the way home from Wentworthville Leagues. Stevo stood by the driver's window for a time, chatting, settling on or arguing about a tip.

Through all this Delaney went on taking readings on Warwick's face. It remained composed, empty of any berserk intention.

Stevo went to his gate, leaned on it, swung it. It exploded with a small neat phosphorus flash about the size of a bowling ball and a noise adequate to turn sleeping neighbours over but, in a street of bombs and hotrods, not to wake them. Stevo stood under the street lamp holding his right hand up by the wrist. It streamed blood. Even at that distance Delaney surmised that segments of Stevo's fingers were gone. Stevo flopped on to his hip but continued to hold and examine his hand. The cab driver ran to him.

'There you are,' said Warwick. More or less in the shadow of the scarlet Torana, he backed his car slowly around the corner, did a casual turn and drove away, not, however, putting on his headlights until he had rounded a further corner by a high school.

'God Almighty!' said Delaney, finding his voice.

'Well,' said Warwick, beginning to breathe more loudly, 'he blinded Scott. In older societies he would have been blinded himself. I mean, Delaney, there's not enough obvious retribution these days. That's what drives people mad and makes everyone sick. I'm not going to be made sick.'

Delaney yelled at him. His fury though was partly aimed at himself, for losing his way in a foreign tribe who booby-trapped front gates. 'You stupid prick! Your brother's burns will heal. You going round to give Stevo back his fingers then?'

'Come on, Delaney! You're upset because a no-hoper like Stevo lost his aerosol finger?'

He laughed. He knew exactly that it was a lack of bearings that worried Delaney.

'How did you learn to do that sort of thing?'

'Survivalist manuals from the States.'

'Survivalist?' Delaney asked, feeling nausea, his stomach, heart, lungs, all those parts they called in the Bible 'the reins', blazing and churning, and the delicious and terrible hook of Danielle in his gills. 'Surviving what?'

'The wave. The *tsunami*. Everyone knows. There'll be one in the end. Nothing surer.'

'A wave? How do you know there'll be a wave? Are you a scientist?'

'I use the term as a figure of speech,' murmured Warwick, pausing at the lights on the Great Western Highway and watching the semi-trailers roar by, laden with beer and sheet metal for Bourke or Broken Hill, drivers intent on death or a bonus. 'There'll certainly be an end to all this madness.'

TWENTY-NINE

My father found it hard to find an appropriate substitute for Herr Hirschmann, since the whole population seemed to be swept up into war efforts of one kind or another. He located at last a seventy-year-old woman, living in retirement in a house in Pushkina Street, who had graduated in law and letters in Cracow in the days of the Austrian Emperor Franz Josef whose empire then controlled that city. She must have been a prodigy in her day, even to the progressive Austrians, and she had taught most of her life in Warsaw and Vienna. Staroviche was the town of her ancestors to which she had retired. My father would sometimes say to her after a drink, 'Never retire anywhere near the Warsaw-Minsk-Smolensk highway. There are always Goths and Vandals marching up or down it.' But the advice came too late. Her name anyway was Miss Tokina; she had a serene face and an instinct for controlling Genia as if the age difference between them were only a few years instead of over half a century. She got Genia reading the German classics – turning my sister's inchoate adolescent energies on to Heine and Goethe.

Miss Tokina, however, did not come until just before the final scene in Onkel Willi's life. Because of the events of Kommissar Ganz's fall, I would for most of the period of Miss Tokina's tuition in the house be in a privileged position, like that of a recuperating survivor of a shipwreck or of an African hunter who has emerged wraith-like from the tyranny of a swamp fever caught on safari. My Belorussian education would by that stage be virtually at an end. I could pretend nausea or a headache and my mother would exempt me from Miss Tokina's sessions. I believe that my frequent absence from her classes bound

Tokina and Genia closer and that her ultimate death of malnutrition and pneumonia in the Michelstadt Displaced Persons camp in 1946 would help drive Genia away from the family and into the arms of Sergeant Pointeaux. But to mention Miss Tokina's death and Sergeant Pointeaux's venality is to take the family history ahead by years and not by days. I return, therefore, to the early winter of 1943, when the great news had just been telephoned to my father in the middle of the night by my godfather Ostrowsky himself that a Belorussian Republican Congress would hold preliminary meetings before Christmas in the Minsk Opera House.

This information transfigured the household. I would hear my mother sing in the mornings, and there were a few days when she began to sketch with charcoals even though it was that point of time when the year seemed darkest, between the last of the rain and the first of the snow. My father's vision of the world improved, and I remember a suppertime when he uttered the peculiarly rosy view favoured by most of the visitors to our house – the Germans and their allies would hold indefinitely their shortened line from the Leningrad front through Vitebsk and along the lower swamplands of the Pripet. Give or take a mile or two, the Russians had stalled along the borders of godly Bela Rus, and this seemed to my mother like an answer to prayer. The Russians spoke grandly of their first, second and third Belorussian fronts, but Bela Rus remained intact. It was said at our table by many a Belorussian official and even by the colonel of our garrison, Oberst Lustbader, who understood military affairs, that 'the antiquated bludgeon of the Red Army had now outrun its logistical possibilities.' It was a formula that seemed to bring great satisfaction to everyone at the Christmas party my father held early that year, since he had to leave for Minsk to confer with the great Ostrowsky and with General von Gottberg.

So there would be a stalemate in the East, a negotiated peace in the West, one of the codicils of that peace being America's, Great Britain's, everyone's recognition of the independence of a Belorussian Republic under the Presidency of my Lincoln-like godfather Ostrowsky. Finally there would be a devotion of all the world's resources to the destruction of Russia, and then a thousand years of peace and sanity.

This hope seemed to flame around me, particularly in the days immediately following the terrible events in Onkel Willi's apartment, and the freezing air was full of a brightness which hurt my eyes and which seemed like a reflection of the voice I would encounter, the promises I would receive.

After his period of mourning had passed, Oberführer Ganz turned up again at our place and my mother took him into the living room. It was the late morning. There was a point on the stairwell which was one of my spying places – once a ventilator had been located there giving straight into the living room. It had been taken out when the staircase was replaced and the workmen had simply covered it with a thin plate of painted deal. When I sat on the appropriate stair this plate was at knee-level, and conversations other than the most cautious would rise from it to my ear.

Onkel Willi had come to beg my mother's pardon for his earlier demented behaviour. My mother denied there was any cause for him to apologise. 'I was beyond control, my dearest Danielle,' Oberführer Ganz insisted. In this terrible phase of history, he said . . . it was, as I have indicated, common for people to invoke history in our household: there was more credibility in their doing so in Staroviche in 1943 than there is here in Penrith now . . . in this terrible phase of history he had only two polestars of sanity. She understood perfectly, he said, that one of these polestars had been extinguished through the chicanery of Bienecke, who had achieved his goal in the cruellest manner anyone could devise. (Here Willi Ganz made a short reference to dynamite and a groan escaped my mother.) She had never judged him, he said, for his friendship with Ya'acov, her mind rose above the comic-opera narrowness of those who had devised race laws. What he would not be able to live through now was her rejection, if because of his demented behaviour he lost the pure affection which had till now prevailed between himself and the Kabbelski family, especially the unsullied understanding which existed between my mother and himself.

I remember what he said then, not because it was different

from all the oblique adult references I had been hearing lately, but because for the first time the words seemed to me to carry an adult freight of meaning. It was as if I had cracked the code at last.

'Believe me, Danielle,' said Herr Kommissar Ganz, 'your husband has nothing to be ashamed of. He has acted from motives of the highest nationalism. He has done what he can to moderate the savagery of the Kappelers and the Bieneckes. As time passes his view of things, like mine, might come to prevail. I look forward to a time when we can work together not simply to administer a region and maintain the anti-terrorist struggle, but to restore the honour some of our colleagues have forfeited in the past two years.'

My mother assured the Oberführer that there was no way in which her friendship for him had been diminished. 'We are all unworthy,' she said – I could not quite understand how. 'And we all have secrets.' I could hear tears in her voice as if she were the one seeking pardon. 'I think we ought to pledge that we will always be friends, no matter what, in war and after war and whatever we reveal of ourselves.'

'I pledge that now,' said Ganz, his voice breaking.

A week before I would have taken an august conversation like that very seriously, whether I could have understood it or not. With the memory of Ganz's furious mouth on mine, the words were transformed, the way the seaside around Puck had been transformed one day in 1939 after I placed my finger in the maw of a hungry sea anemone and felt its alien ravenous grasp and understood that the sea was not just passive but was a hungry element.

And my knowledge of Ganz's strange hunger made the conversation between him and my mother sound like something a little overdone, like a conversation in one of the romantic radio serials about a typical yet noble German family whose sons, sad and wise, were always coming home on leave from the Eastern Front and talking about honour and history, endless forgiveness and a phoenix future rising from the ashes.

'Let me take Radek to lunch,' said Onkel Willi without warning. 'I am well escorted – SS and your good Belorussian outriders and Wehrmacht guards. I am afraid I rather disgraced myself in front of Radek that day and I would like to gain lost ground. Also, Danielle, you must find being trapped in the house with such an active boy quite exhausting.'

I tried the novelty of thinking of myself for the first time as an active boy. I had not accustomed myself to the idea before I heard my mother calling for me. I disappeared upstairs as fast as I could and reappeared more loudly a little later, thumping on the steps as if I had come sprinting from my room. My mother was waiting by the parlour door at the bottom of the steps, smiling at me. 'Herr Kommissar Ganz has invited you to lunch,' she told me. You could not have said her smile was radiant, but it had no ambiguity, she was not smiling at me in that preventive way she had when some visitor offered me over-rich confectionery too close to bedtime: the smile that said, 'Refuse politely.' I was both appalled and delighted that she had heard nothing from my father about Oberführer Ganz's weird grieving kiss.

Onkel Willi's broad face appeared behind her shoulder. 'Will you join me, Radek? A gentleman's lunch. Cigars and cognac afterwards.'

My mother's laughter committed me. I got an overcoat and we creaked down the drive in the back of the Oberführer's car, preceded by four SS men in a limousine, flanked by two sidecar motorcycles manned by my father's men, and followed by a blitzwagon carrying an army corporal and a private. Even in this dangerous winter, it occurred to me, we have so many men to stand guard over Onkel Willi's visits to the Kabbelskis'.

I sat still on the seat, very taut. There was the unthinkable risk that Onkel Willi might beg my pardon too, that the kiss might become an open subject between us.

Herr Kommissar Ganz employed a cook housekeeper, a heavy Czech spinster named Fräulein Hradek. As Onkel Willi and I sat at the dining room table, Fräulein Hradek recommended the menu to us, listing dishes like a waitress in a restaurant. 'Gentlemen, a full-bodied bean soup, followed by carp in a sweet and sour jelly and then hare in sour cream.' As she recited all this Onkel Willi groaned and rolled his eyes comically at me.

It was a richer lunch than anything the Kabbelskis were

eating that lean December, but then Oberführer Ganz *was* the Kommissar of Staroviche. In any case the plenty of his table partly reassured me. Since it was the sort of fare appropriate to an official guest, it elevated me to that status. And a provincial Kommissar could not weep in front of an official guest or kiss him full on the lips.

A pale young SS private wearing white gloves appeared and served us our soup and then vanished. Woodenly I spooned the food in. It tasted of my embarrassment and Onkel Willi could tell. He reached for my free hand and enclosed it in his. An immense hand, it could have been a stevedore's or a boxer's if Onkel Willi had come from the appropriate background.

'This is lunch between friends, Radek,' he told me. 'Your Onkel Willi lost a good friend in the most cruel manner. Therefore I behaved like a wounded beast. But I must assure you that no one in the Kabbelski family will ever be knowingly misused by me. And I've changed my tack now to a determination that those who were responsible for the cruelty will suffer. You agree the cruel should suffer? Now, eat your soup, unless you don't like it.' He withdrew his hand and clapped, struck by an extravagant idea, the way the *old* Willi Ganz so often was. 'Why don't we make a compact to dislike it together, exercise our freedom of taste? Take on the soup dragon together. A Hanseatic knight and the White Russian champion. In league.'

'No,' I said with something like a natural smile. 'I like the soup and I don't think we need to go to war with anyone.'

I thought there was gratitude in his barking laughter, as if we were really going back to hide and seek in lightly guarded woods. The dining room possessed, in fact, the same solitude which had existed in Brudezh forest. The SS waiter was not to be seen, Fräulein Hradek – without Hanseatic knights to battle – sat silent in the kitchen. The apartment block was largely empty – the ground floor a sandbagged storeroom, and two civilian officials from Oberführer Ganz's Kommissariat office occupying the next level. On the top floor both apartments belonged to the Kommissar himself, so that what had once been the hallway between two separate dwellings was Onkel Willi's lobby.

In a busy world, surrounded by busy causes, we sat at the

core of genteel silence. That was my impression anyhow.

He began to ask me 'when you grow up' sorts of questions. These were similar to 'when the war is over' questions. Would I ever consider emigrating to America? Marrying an American? I raised the problem that I was their enemy and so they were mine.

'Won't always be like that,' said Onkel Willi, bread in his mouth. 'What if we made peace with the Americans? What if within a year there were British and Americans here, in the streets of Staroviche?'

Because of American films I had seen, because of the glamour of the name, I felt an obscure excitement at the idea. I imagined smiling, loose-limbed boys in Bryanska Street, lolling on tanks adorned with America's white and Christian star.

'I predict it,' he said. 'By next midsummer. And . . . it will make some people at the Natural History Museum behave better than they have up to the moment.'

I concluded he must have meant Hauptsturmführer Bienecke, a man I agreed with Onkel Willi in disliking.

'We might all end in California,' murmured Onkel Willi with a misty and conspiratorial grin. 'Learn a little English and make our living as horsemen in cowboy films.'

I tried to envisage Oberführer Ganz without his uniform and realised that he would have made a very good sad heroic Indian chief.

THIRTY

FROM THE JOURNALS OF STANISLAW KABBELSKI, CHIEF OF POLICE,

STAROVICHE

December 2, 1943

Removed police guard from outside Kommissar's apartment 12.30 p.m. – sent them to search suspected partisan safe house near Gomelska bridge. Since three arrests made there, my action in removing guards will cause less comment, even if it has been guaranteed there will be no comment in any case.

Units of SS and my men ready to move on Ganz apartment *post factum.*

Called Danielle at house and discovered to my unutterable horror she permitted Radek to go to lunch with that sodomite. Lost control perhaps twenty seconds, raged at Danielle – she will never understand why. Fortunately my screamings conveyed little hard intelligence. 'I don't want my son with him!' I ranted.

Despaired for Radislaw. Called on Yuri to get the car and drive me full-speed to Ganz's apartment, Marka Street. Armed squad following behind. Self and Yuri armed Gewehr automatics. These plausibly adequate to save son if Wehrmacht guards also alerted. To hell with von Gottberg, Kappeler, Bienecke *et al.* Let them get the Kommissar another way!

THIRTY-ONE

The luncheon conversation with Onkel Willi had – through my host's efforts to settle his young guest down – reached safe ground. I could talk films with great ease, and Onkel Willi had the grace to pretend he had not seen *Stagecoach*, which I had been taken to at the Paris cinema in Warsaw the month before the war began. As a result I was able to begin a ramified account of the storyline, subplots included, even snatches of dialogue from part actors.

My narration was interrupted by the sound of some outer door in the apartment slamming twice. I heard Fräulein Hradek exclaiming with unexpected passion and then a torrent of sound from the stairway and front hall. I saw Onkel Willi's face turn bloodless and the corners of his mouth hang anciently as he stood. The door between the dining room and the kitchen opened, and through it fell the pale young private with the white gloves. Nothing could be heard except the furious sound of what I knew, yet could not believe, were guns, though indistinct yells and screams lay behind the noise. I saw Onkel Willi's lips frame the words, 'Jesus Christ!' When the row stopped for a second, I heard boots entering from the kitchen and the living room.

Onkel Willi pushed me under the table. Kneeling aghast in the under-table dimness I saw two triangles of reality – furniture legs, the base of a sideboard, drapes, the bottoms of Oberführer Ganz's knife-sharp trousers – segmented from each other by the cornered hang of the tablecloth. I felt as if buried alive, and chewed for comfort on the back of my hand. The boots ceased to move – a pair of them entered the left-most of those three lightning-sharp triangles of mine. Onkel Willi spoke in Russian as if he were talking to a plumber or a housepainter.

'Well then,' he said.

A young voice said, 'Fascist sowfucker!' Then the tower of intolerable sound fell on me once more.

Then for the first time in my existence I was delivered from the awful geometry of that kind of event, from the limits of earthly peril in which I found myself. It was as if there had been a gravity in my blood, pulling me down to boot-level, dragging me against the cutting edges of the triangles. And then the gravity was released. In all the racket, the universe produced a voice which made the earth habitable. I say a voice, and I would always claim it was a Belorussian voice. But it was more as well, it was a firm hand in the small of the back. It enunciated this to me: Keep still. This isn't the only place you're going to see in a long life.

To speak of an unspeakable experience is impossible to do without debasing it. Nonetheless I can say that no other voice has ever made me so welcome to the wide world. For some reason I responded to it by uttering one word. 'Uncle.' I was aware of laughter. And, like a hand in the small of the back, the sentence, 'After the wave breaks, you'll still be in place'. I knew at once what the wave was. It was what would cancel the benighted politics which were killing Onkel Willi.

An instant later, I suffered the experience of being lifted on a fountain of light high into the corner of the dining room. I could see the ruined meal, the tubercular private, and Onkel Willi staggering. The grief I felt for him was that he probably did not possess any elevated view of the act, such as I enjoyed from this vantage point. He likely felt in his last seconds as I had when I first perceived the triangles beneath the table, and my grief for him was not for his death so much as for his terror.

The stupefying sound ceased. Now that it lifted like a curtain between Onkel Willi and his assassins, I saw them for who they were. One looked like a peasant, another like an intellectual. These two were perhaps in their early twenties. They wore caps and overcoats, both sets torn, but the provenance of one of the overcoats was better than that of the other. The intellectual had extremely child-like puckered lips, as unsuitable for terrorism as Mrs Kuzich's hips had been for martyrdom. Their leader was a man my father's age. There were no embarrassing immaturities in his face and I had the impression that he was an army officer in mufti, since he looked as strange in his street clothes as Bienecke did in a suit. There was a second of awe as they considered what they had done – even the leader had to give in to it. Onkel Willi's broad brow faced the ceiling and – tidiest of men – his good white shirt had been torn loose from his trousers and hung bloodied over them as if he'd been caught before he had tucked the tail in. From the throat to the waist he was not recognisably a human being. The tubercular private's body had suffered more lightly. Through a corner of the kitchen door I could see Fräulein Hradek's horizontal and homely ankle and thought what a terrible world it was when the making of hare in sour cream carried with it the fatal penalty.

I saw the senior assassin, the one who was already in my mental vocabulary The Soldier, lift the corner of the tablecloth and peer under the table at the child beneath, that child who lay galvanised beneath the tyranny of the triangular view. This child felt he should explain that Onkel Willi was not a target, was not Bienecke, was not even Chief of Police Kabbelski, was only of relevance to children and to women widowed by their husband's career. Was an extra in a Western, as it turned out: with his broad, nearly Mongolian face a certainty for the role of a firm young adviser to the elderly Sioux chief who has seen the buffalo hunting-grounds shrink. The Officer looked in under the table at the child panting animal-like on its four limbs and the child could not manage a word.

The Officer said, like an echo of the 'unclesome' voice, 'Keep still!' Then he turned to the baby peasant, the baby intellectual. 'It's the Kabbelski kid.' The word he used was in fact halfway between the English 'kid' and 'brat'. There was no animus in the way he used it. The wonder was that in all the carnage he had time to know my tag, whose 'kid' I was at all.

'Stay still there,' I saw him tell the child beneath the table. They left by the kitchen, all three of them, making for the courtyard where Ya'acov had once saved Onkel Willi's

Mercedes. I maintained my high point of view in the corner by the kitchen door. I heard it all with great dispassion – The Officer, The Peasant and The Intellectual perishing in a surge of noise on the back stairs as Chief of Police Kabbelski arrived from the direction of the front lobby, roared when he saw Onkel Willi, but then with open mouth and prodigious frown such as I had never seen him wear, stepped over the Rubicon of gore from the Kommissar's body, lifted the tablecloth and saw the child. The grunt of delight he uttered was quite as animal as every sound he had made since entering the apartment. He grasped up the child, forced its head into the crook of his shoulder as if he would willingly prevent it from seeing anything more of the butt-end of politics, and galloped out through the living room, the lobby, hurdling the bodies of two middle-aged Wehrmacht privates on the stairs and reaching the pavement. He sat the child on the ground, stood back from it, gasping with delight, bending with his hands on his knees. 'Thank Christ,' he intoned. 'Thank Christ!'

Still stuck in my high corner of the room, I yelled, 'Me! Me!' Though he thought he had found me, he hadn't. Disappointment – that's what I believed then anyhow – caused me to faint and fall. It was a brief business. When I found my head again I was on the pavement. A dozen or so Belorussian police stood around, a dozen or so SS men. I could see Obersturmführer Harner frowning at my father's celebration of his son's survival. Past him, at the corner of Marka and Bryanska Streets, I saw an elderly peasant, looking at all of us with fierce concentration. When he saw my eyes were on his he spread his hands and grinned. 'Uncle!' I murmured, but he turned his back and walked away down Bryanska.

THIRTY-TWO

From the night Warwick blew Stevo's hand off, Delaney achieved the unimaginable and began to take Danielle to a hotel in North Parramatta which, he knew from the casual fornicators and adulterers he played football with, catered for 'short-term residency'. The middle-aged brunette on the desk had introduced Delaney to the term. Danielle waited in the car outside – it was late afternoon on a non-training day – and the brunette asked the question with a fake propriety, as if she were running the reception desk at the Regent. 'An overnight stay, sir? Or a short-term residency?' Short-term residencies were two-thirds the price but still too much for Stanton and the widow to afford.

Delaney hated the place as Danielle did. But Danielle seemed to consider it her fault they'd been forced to it. She would apologise to him as they trembled under the blankets waiting for the radiator to take effect. Behind them hung a print of two white horses running through breakers while the sun set unnoticed on a jagged horizon, a horizon which looked like a peril to shipping. Delaney knew it was an awful picture, standard in every room. He had avoided hanging that sort of thing at his place, and now it mocked his confusion, his desire, his delight. It did, however, remind him without mercy of Warwick's *tsunami*.

Here for the first time he raised the question of precautions. Strangely the maiming of Stevo made it easier for him to ask self-interested questions like that, as if the Kabbel family now owed him a moral debt.

As they did. He had lied firmly to the Parramatta CID at the beginning of shift two nights after Warwick's small ball of fire had maimed Stevo. Two detectives arrived, inspected the Kabbel operation, and took Stanton and Delaney aside separately, asking them if they knew whether Kabbel kept explosives anywhere. 'If they've got it hidden anywhere damp it'll explode spontaneously,' a detective sergeant told Delaney, 'and you'll be playing five-eighth in a bloody wheelchair.'

'Did they talk much about getting even for the damage to their brother?' one of the detectives asked, enabling Delaney to give a cunning answer. No, he'd never heard them talking about it or having fantasies. (Warwick didn't dream. Warwick *did.*)

The composure of the Kabbels under this sort of pressure, their certainty that Delaney would be loyal under a CID grilling (Stanton knowing nothing to start with), irked Delaney.

'They didn't worry you, Terry?' asked Kabbel afterwards with that overdone Belorussian twinkle.

'Yes, Rudi, they bloody did. But not as much as Warwick does.'

So the Kabbels owed him perhaps the knowledge of whether Danielle was taking precautions or not.

'Now, yes,' she said, 'but not at first. The pharmaceuticals don't agree with me. I had to go to a doctor and get a device.' The old Kabbel correctness of speech: 'pharmaceuticals', 'device'. 'Does it worry you?' she asked him, echoing what her father had asked him about the CID. For a second he thought: That's the Kabbels. They know there are certain things that upset normal people – attention from the police, unexpected pregnancies – but they don't understand why.

'If you get pregnant,' he said, 'I'll marry you and we'll run away to one of those Barrier Reef towns up north. I could be the local football star.' It was a daydream charged with aquamarine and pawpaws. 'Some people would say it's not all up to you. I could wear something.'

'No.' She put a hand on his wrist. 'No.'

But he may even have been owed something further. 'You read about Stevo?' he asked.

A brief write-up in the *Sun* said Stevo had lost two fingers and the top joints of two others.

'Of course,' she said. 'Warwick did it.'

Delaney absorbed that for a time. 'Where does he keep the

stuff? Fuses and all that. Plastic or dynamite? Where does he keep it?'

'He's got a few oddments of that sort out at our little hut near Newnes. Uses it for cracking rocks. Exactly what he does I don't know. Explosives are *his* department. He's very safe and he has the right manuals.'

'He wasn't so safe for Stevo,' Delaney said. 'Do you approve of what he did?'

She looked at him. She was calm and intense and did not try to equivocate. He felt a strange temptation to give in to her code, or her brother's, in which the explosive disfingering of Stevo seemed a reasonable act of war. 'Most certainly I approve,' she told him. 'The reasons are obvious.'

He laughed, trying to seem tolerant. His secret scheme though was to snatch her out of her family, to slice off at one motion all the rugged Kabbel loyalties. 'Do you say that sort of thing to Ron when he asks you questions about all those books? "Ron, the reasons are obvious."'

But in spite of her certainty about the rightness of Stevo's punishment, in that room, below the neap-tide horses, she took to weeping regularly. The tears were not noisy but seemed to Delaney like full-scale grief, not mere shame or girlish nostalgia. The tears grew out of the secrets of that Kabbel culture in which he was a stranger and barely held a visa. Stanton had warned him the whole bloody thing would confuse him, and he was confused.

'It's just a general sadness – it comes over me,' she told him the first time he kept at her for a reason. 'Because I already have a baby,' she said the second time.

Hearing this, Delaney lay still under the rampaging Clydesdales. The fact that there was a baby somewhere was not a small matter, especially not for someone from the Delaney family, Irish and Australian and RC. Where was this child? Did the fact he had never seen it mean that she was an innocent and entrapped girl or a callous mother? It was too dangerous for him to speak.

She said, 'When I left school I rebelled against my father. I thought he belonged to another world. He kept talking about partisans and Belorussian buffaloes and independence, but it didn't mean anything in North Parramatta. If it did he wouldn't have married my mother – she was a very straightforward Australian girl he met at a dance when he was working in the railways. He would have looked wonderful then – he was twenty-four years old, and yes, he was a Wog and torn between the old world and the newest of new worlds, Australia. So he married her, and she didn't leave home until I was eleven years old – it wasn't his fault, it wasn't hers. They were brought together to produce us, part of us called Scott and Warwick and the other part called Danielle, and once that was done there wasn't much left over to do. I think he scared her a bit, there were too many layers to him, you know.

'I took up with this man when I was seventeen. I know you don't believe it but I was troublesome at school, except in English, history and economics. In mathematics and physics I was an urban guerrilla. I worked in Coles afterwards, and the man I met was assistant manager. He was a decent man, Terry. He was a man worth spending the rest of a lifetime with. He was possessive though. My father asked us to go to a weekend in Melbourne, and my friend or my husband – however you want to define him – was very opposed. I went to Melbourne – Rudi was working there at that stage – and when I got back here found that I was locked out of the flat. The father of my child took great legal pains to prove me an unfit mother, and the longer I was away from the flat the easier it was for him to prove that I was negligently absent instead of just locked out. There were a number of family court hearings in Parramatta, and in the end I had to be reconciled to not seeing my own baby.'

'Not at all?' asked Delaney.

'Once a week was permitted, but in his presence. It was beyond tolerating, and the sorrow made me sick. I found myself in Northmead psychiatric. There was no other way of doing things but becoming reconciled.'

'But why would anyone resent you going to Melbourne to see your old man?' Even as he asked it, Delaney could see there might be reasons.

'He'd quarrelled with Rudi.'

'But what were you all doing on this family weekend?' Perhaps an explosives refresher course, Delaney couldn't help surmising.

Danielle began to examine the rim of the bedcover and inhaled, acquiring oxygen for choosing her words. Even athletes did not breathe deeper than that. You would think the brain, even the neat brain of Danielle Kabbel, was a bellows. 'Rudi had a dreadful childhood. The Poles, the Germans, the Russians.' What worlds of oppression shone in those three names, though lately, especially with people like Stanton, the Poles had become heroic. 'We grew up in a different sort of place, a place where there was no politics.'

'No politics. What have Gough Whitlam and Bob Hawke been doing all this time?'

'I mean the sort of politics that kills people in the street.'

'They reckon us rich countries export deaths by not exporting our wheat,' he murmured, as if he wanted to slow the argument down.

'Once Rudi was in a room where the partisans killed three people. And another time he was more or less buried alive in a pit and left there for ages. And his problem was to make all that seem *real* to us. Now you probably don't believe in any of this, but in Melbourne there was this Belorussian woman, seventy-two years old, and she was a medium. You know, she holds something like seances. Or she *held*, I should say, she died last year.'

Delaney's legs seemed to him to contract, he felt an electric touch at the back of the neck. He was far from home now, with this foreign woman from a weird clan. 'He got you to go to Melbourne for a seance?'

'Not a seance. Not talking to spirits. Though in some ways, yes. We all sat together, linked hand to hand, and the old lady made it real to us, the things that separated us from Rudi.'

'Did you hear voices?' asked Delaney in dread, breathing harshly himself now.

'It was more that we all felt the most terrible terror and then the greatest relief and safety. So it wasn't like a voice. It was like Rudi had predicted: a powerful hand against the small of the back.' She smiled as an apology. 'That's the trouble with the

Kabbels. None of us ever felt as secure, really secure, as we did that night.'

'If you felt secure as all that,' Delaney asked, the logic crackling at the back of his throat, 'why did you end in Northmead?'

'I hadn't worked out what to do,' she explained. 'Which way to jump. I *was* a good mother, Terry. Being called a bad one was the price for the other thing.'

'The other thing? The hand in the small of the back?'

She smiled up at him. 'You're a very bright fellow, Delaney. I love you very much.'

Delaney felt the awful bleakness of that Melbourne seance, he could sense the foetid cold of some old Coburg terrace, smell the strangeness of the clothing, picture the old medium's creased lips.

'Why did he need a seance?' asked Delaney, remembering something he had heard from Kabbel on the night of the hubcaps. 'I thought he could talk to this old uncle of his in Parramatta any time he chose to?'

'This old man – the one in Parramatta – Rudi only found him a few years back.'

'And do the lot of you sit on the floor and listen to this old fellow and do whatever he says?'

'Of course not. We can't speak Belorussian for a start.'

'Is he the one who suggested to Rudi blowing Stevo's hand off?'

'Don't be ridiculous,' she told him, choosing to laugh. 'We don't intrude between Rudi and the old man.'

'Does the old man talk about the bloody wave, Danielle?'

'Everyone does, Terry. Even the afternoon papers.'

He considered where he could take Danielle, what Rugby League and pearl-diving port in far Queensland where she would be safe from calls to seances. Where she could live on a beach beyond the radius of Rudi's terrible Belorussian infancy.

THIRTY-THREE

FROM THE JOURNALS OF STANISLAW KABBELSKI, CHIEF OF POLICE,

STAROVICHE

December 2, 1943

Would not let them question the boy. To hell with Bienecke!
What can he stand to learn from the miraculous survival of my
son? Since he had urinated and was shivering, I wrapped Radek
in a blanket and drove home with him. Behind us, Bienecke and
Harner had the bodies of the assassins placarded and hung from
lampposts.

Radek pop-eyed and wore an excited half-smile. You'd think
he'd been given a present. 'Shock,' Yuri told me with heavy
wisdom. He reached his hand over into the back seat as if he
would gladly offer it when needed.

Halfway home boy began to babble like a sleepwalker, using
bits of words, putting syllables and ideas together with their
wrong partners. Shook him gently and at last he stopped. Then
held him against me – he lay half across my lap. What he told
me then astonished me somewhat. 'The oldest one,' he said –
you'd think he was telling me an exciting detail of an excursion
– 'looked under the table and said, "It's the Kabbelski brat."'

I blinked and gave thanks the absolutely reliable Yuri was at
the wheel and not some Bienecke-planted spy.

Leader of the assassination team is believed to be Semyanov,
major in the NKVD. Credible he might know the members of
my family on sight, though to believe so makes me feel naked.
Harder to understand his acquitting of Radek from the same
sentence he had just imposed on Willi Ganz. Both sides in these
brutal exchanges have not stopped before for children. Both

sides have raised the stakes to include the very young, the very old, all women including and, by report, especially those bearing children. Semyanov therefore had every ideological reason to do to Radek what the SS have done to the children of villagers. That he didn't could be a temperamental thing, a pulse of compassion and therefore, in partisan and NKVD terms, a lapse.

Already concerned that whatever happened in Ganz's apartment, Bienecke might conclude Radek had had some form of exemption, and would ferret away at that idea. We have already done enough for the man without feeding him fancies as well. So hastily put together a compact with Radek in the back of the car that we would not tell anyone about Semyanov's words, that it was to be a secret like Hirschmann's medal but better kept.

Willi Ganz buried quickly. Disgraceful funeral – all the Belorussian officials but no one from Minsk or Kaunas, no one from General von Gottberg's office and only a minor secretary from Dr Kappeler's Political Section. Messages of condolence from von Gottberg to the people of Staroviche on the loss of their beloved Kommissar were read by priest during sermon of Requiem Mass, likewise messages from the Ostministry. But everyone supposedly too busy with current emergencies – hardly more intense than the emergencies of the past six months – to come to Staroviche and say a Pater Noster for poor sybaritic Ganz or to throw a clod of Belorussian earth into his grave. Fool of a cleric preached on Jeremiah: 'Ye have scattered my flock, and driven them away, and have not visited them: behold, I will visit upon you the evil of your doings.' He predicted the Soviets would be smitten specifically for this death, which is a little unworldly of him if he really believes so. I'm sure Willi Ganz, at least in his better days, would have preferred something a little less vengeful and grim. Maybe something about many mansions and seraphim and cherubim, a heaven of sweet Italianate limbs and good food.

Miss Tokina, children's tutor, insisted on attending with Danielle, and but for them would have been no tears at Ganz's grave. Danielle has begun to speak as if Ganz had offered his life for Radek's and it would be too cruel to disabuse her.

Bienecke stayed away, not out of sensitivity but from contempt, and sent his deputy Harner. Major Gnauck, a young one-armed officer – we get lots of physically or mentally maimed garrison commanders here – newly appointed to command the Staroviche garrison, told me Willi Ganz's ancient father and former wife petitioned von Gottberg for the return of their son/spouse's corpse to Germany but that request was denied on 'war effort' grounds.

Only when, having briefly celebrated my son's deliverance, was travelling to Minsk in a convoy which included old Oberst Lustbader's battalion – they going into transit camp for eventual posting to the front, Staroviche receiving Gnauck's even more geriatric garrison in their place – only then had time to consider particular implications of Semyanov's (it *was* Semyanov) words: It's the Kabbelski tiddler, brat, kid. One implication that my family has some kind of immunity, that I am somehow understood by partisans, that they see me as a moderate influence. They did not, however, see the even more moderate Ganz in such a light.

Other possibility that occurs is that they want to save me for show trial if Staroviche falls to Soviets. They are saving all their cruelty, including that which would usually be directed against Radek, till then. They might intend the same for Ostrowsky and other of his lieutenants. They should know we are professional exiles – will go into exile again, and when the Soviets fall to the West return again, carrying – it can confidently be expected – guarantees of Belorussian sovereignty. So reprieve of Radek, and what Semyanov said, goes largely unexplained.

Bienecke though would love to know all this, would play with the suspicion I am somehow in communication with *partizanskie kraya*, the partisan machine. Wouldn't seriously believe the idea but would use it as a lever. In even more desperate days than these, could use it as pretext for my assassination.

THIRTY-FOUR

It was nearly noon and not all the mists had risen out of the groins of earth in which Aldo Terracetti grew his tomatoes. Spiked with wooden stakes, the Terracetti land ran at a small cant down towards a creek called Lowes Creek, and under all this vapour looked something like Delaney's mental image of rustic Italy. Delaney himself stood on a cemented embankment outside Aldo's pool room and unofficial winery and sipped a Resch's Pilsener, eschewing the Terracetti grappa. Aldo, his brother Eduardo and his son Joe, drank beyond the glass doors behind Delaney. His hands were numb, except for the middle finger of his right hand, which he had corked against the spine of a St George centre the day before. It sang like a stone bruise in the cold air. As well a shoulder ached and the muscles of his lower abdomen, subject to the various strains of his true profession, his new fear of the Kabbels, his true and foredoomed marriage with Danielle, his unterminated and cruel marriage to Gina, tolled with pain.

Yesterday's game had been played on St George's hard ground in front of a fanatic crowd. He seemed to himself to spend all the time tackling, preoccupied with the deceptive thighs and upper legs of their young lock, the seventeen-year-old the club heavies said would play for Australia before he was twenty. The kid had all the confidence of someone who doesn't know yet that the game was a furnace, that it was fuelled on unrefined talent, and few gave a damn if unrefined talent was consumed in the flames.

According to the administration of the game, Saturdays were reserved for the second most important game of the round. It was a rule of thumb hard to believe in when Penrith first grade had lost the last five on the trot. That statistic detracted from the glory of Delaney's team, which had won the last seven, and through gruelling defence and a small margin of very ordinary brilliance made it eight in a row against the Saints. Delaney had not even bothered to write the game up in his diary. He supposed he never would. Love of Danielle had made the game petty and brutish to the happiest man in Australia.

Gina was inside like the rest of the family. Upstairs where women were loading the tables with ham and salads, she stole glances at her eternally wed aunts, the skeletal one Uncle Eduardo had married, for example, and wondered how they had managed it, why their marriages were like institutions – the stock exchange, the Vatican – and why the gates of hell had not prevailed against them. It was cruel to watch her with a smile on her face, rushing about with plates and forks, pretending to be one of them, hoping to pick up the tricks they had not yet confessed to. To Delaney Gina possessed the horrifying look of a woman already widowed.

'Hey,' he heard someone call from a point directly above where he was standing. He looked up to the sundeck upstairs. Gina's sister-in-law Susie was standing there, blowing smoke into the cold air. 'The Italians won't let me smoke inside,' she told him. 'Mama Terracetti says it buggers the *prosciutto*. Come up and say g'day to your old sister-in-law.'

He couldn't say no.

Susie was what Delaney's mother called 'well-groomed'. She was proud of her husband's career (state sales manager, greeting cards), proud of the two sullen and intelligent children she had borne. She lived in North Rocks in a good street. In company she made indirect references, with lots of eyebrow-raising, shaking of the head and small innocent moans, to the fact that Joe Terracetti was endowed like a draughthorse and drove her to the craziest roaring peaks. She represented therefore all the news, all the certainty Delaney least wished to hear this Sunday of the Terracettis' wedding anniversary.

'How's the football?' she asked.

'Like the Vietnam War. We're losing even though we're winning.'

'First grade next year?'

'If they don't bring in a Banana-bender or a Pom. They probably will, you know. They only pay lip service to the local blokes.'

'Most important question of all, what's wrong with Gina? And with you, if it comes to that?'

He couldn't say anything. He couldn't manage even a lie like 'teething troubles'.

'Listen, Terry,' said Susie, 'you know I'm a woman of healthy desires. By the same token I don't go around talking in a pornographic way, I've got no interest in that. But what I'm going to say I said to the husband of a friend of mine when their marriage looked absolutely *finito*. It's this. The clitoris is a rudimentary penis. All right? That should tell you what a woman needs. All right? Forgive me if I offend you by being direct. But it's probably something the Marist Brothers didn't tell you.'

Delaney began to laugh, not because she was funny; her seriousness was worth respecting. He laughed with a sort of longing for the innocence Susie had, the idea that a willing hand properly placed could heal. Clutching the wrought-iron railing he rocked and wept, and then with horror saw Gina staring at him from beyond the glass of the living room, an awesome grievance in her face. It was clear when she slid the glass door open and stepped out on to the verandah that she took his laughter as an insult large enough to justify what she had not intended to do at her parents' anniversary – parade her injury in front of frowning relatives, weep openly, yell reproaches. Her shoulders were straight and her hands gathered into fists. 'You put me to shame in front of my parents,' she said.

'Oh bugger!' said Susie. 'Do you want me to leave you to it?'

Gina closed her eyes. Her long lips were set in a line of exquisite sorrow. It was terrible to face her dignity. He was awed to discover that the happiness of a thoroughbred like her could depend on a third grade five-eighth and security man.

'Don't stand around laughing,' she told him. 'Don't do that. Denise Stanton tells me Kabbel's got a daughter, a nice little blonde. Is that the problem?'

Delaney said, 'Yes.'

Gina had made it easy. She stumbled against one of the

outdoor benches and sat sideways on it. Her face contorted and she began to wail. His mother had never made a sound like that. It was a foreign sound – Delaney thought of it as subterranean somehow – it had run underground great distances and for eternities before emerging from Gina's mouth in Bringelly and startling the party.

'Oh God,' she cried, slowly pounding the bench. 'What can I do?'

Susie put her hands on Gina's shoulders. She looked paltry beside Gina, her flesh speckled with the wrong expensive make-up.

Delaney stood muttering. Everything he uttered sounded like a provocation. Her tears became less controlled. There was no limit to how terrifying they could become, and Delaney had an urge to run downstairs and out to the car parked beyond the farmhouse gate. Three women brought their Sicilian faces to the living room door – Gina's mother, the skeletal aunt, a Terracetti cousin from Gymea. They seemed like a chorus in an opera and their faces looked beautiful in ways which had not been obvious to him early this dismal morning and which increased his impulse to flee. Downstairs even old Aldo appeared on the concrete apron outside his pool room, looking at his grieving daughter for some seconds, and disappeared again. 'Gina darling,' her mother called, 'why don't you forget it for today? Put your arm around her, Terry, and bring her in here.'

Gina threw up her hands. 'I don't want the arm of that whoremonger around me. He . . . he has had foreign whores in Hawaii. Everyone knows that, everyone in Penrith!'

Delaney was aware of his stupid blood blazing in his face.

Gina was fearsome and went on screaming. 'Everyone knows it! Adulterer! Whoremonger!'

His gorge heaving with shame, Delaney forced himself to the door and told Mrs Terracetti he was going home. 'I don't want to be impolite . . .' he said.

'Impolite don't matter when my daughter is bleeding.'

He made for the steps.

Mrs Terracetti's accent thickened, as if falling back on some terrible Sicilian sense of honour. 'Would you want your worst-a enemy to cry like that?'

Downstairs he made more quick apologies to the men, backing as he went. He hoped they had not heard much of the Hawaiian news. Joe Terracetti urged him fraternally to come and stew himself on grappa. By lunchtime Delaney would love every bastard on earth, said Joe. By four o'clock he would be sick and by seven too tired to fight with his wife. Delaney continued to back. From upstairs Mrs Terracetti called, 'You need children. None of this waiting until you got all those things – dishwasher, video? Whatsa your video doing for you today?'

At last he was out on the Northern road in his freezing Holden, making for the Blue Mountains, where the mists would be heavier and he would be protected from such gazes he had just suffered at the Terracettis'. He switched on the radio and filled the car to the limits of its steel and glass with the manic warmth of the Match of the Day commentators at Belmore Oval. He worried away at the propositions that he was the happiest man in Australia and that he would not treat an enemy as he was treating Gina.

Somewhere beyond Lawson, where the mist and the narrow highway made self-aware driving a matter of necessity, he decided to resign from Uncle Security. He was not sure what this would do for himself or Gina or Danielle. But because it was a direction in which he could move without causing harm, the idea filled him with serenity.

THIRTY-FIVE

'Let me tell you in confidence, Terry,' said Kabbel, serenely chewing. 'I am pleased you have chosen to go back to your wife.' Beyond the windscreen it was drizzling coldly. Even Kabbel couldn't sit by the bandstand in this weather, playing windproof and waterproof Belorussians, exposing his Belorussian certainty to the weather.

Delaney, sitting in the passenger seat, a cup of the usual Kabbel peculiarly fragrant coffee in his hand, said nothing. He still had no idea what in the hell leaving Uncle Security meant – the first move in separating Danielle from the family or a move back to Gina. He didn't want to strengthen Kabbel by arguing with himself about that point aloud.

Anyhow it had made Gina something like happy, it had produced in Delaney's white and Papally blessed house in Forth Street an atmosphere of dull misery in which Delaney was able to sleep beside his wife, to regret occasionally sending his hand down the line of her back as if he were settling a Labrador. He knew it was all criminal but believed it gave him time to think.

Thinking wasn't possible. Everywhere – it seemed to Delaney – the air discouraged it.

'You would have had to go back in the end,' Kabbel went on, crowing. 'Danielle sees herself as so inseparable from the lads and myself . . . She did tell you, my friend, she was more or less married before, didn't she?'

'She told me about some seance in Melbourne.'

Kabbel started to laugh. 'Jesus Christ!' It was a rare expletive with Kabbel and Delaney knew why he came out with it, to get Delaney on his side in laughing at the way women exaggerated. 'I wish she wouldn't use that term.'

'What should she have called it?' Delaney asked, refusing to join in any 'Oh, women!' stunt.

'That's the trouble,' said Kabbel. 'It was the sort of burning family experience you could never understand, Terry, even if I tried to explain it. I don't mean you aren't intelligent and I don't mean you aren't a good bloke. I mean it would be like a foreign language to you.'

Delaney felt his face redden before Kabbel's glistening confidence. 'Why don't you give up this mystifying bullshit, Rudi?' he yelled. 'Why don't you let Warwick and Scott find Australian girls with big tits and sunny bloody temperaments? Why did you have to force Danielle to go to Melbourne to see bloody ghosts? They're zombies, those poor little buggers, you're like a bloody pillow over their faces. Get rid of the bloody explosives manuals, Rudi, and let in some bloody fresh air!'

Kabbel leaned over in his seat and looked frowning into Delaney's face. 'Is this a declaration of hostilities, Terry?'

'I don't know what in the bloody hell it is. Listen, Danielle has not once mentioned my wife.'

He understood straightaway that it was a mistake to mention that, even a betrayal. What he meant it to be was an accusation against Kabbel, because he kept them so locked up that they didn't see anyone out there beyond the edge of the Kabbel clan campfire.

'So you wish Danielle *would* nag you about Mrs Delaney?' asked Kabbel, with that shrewdness again which made Delaney want to hit him. 'Adultery occurs everywhere and in every age and in spite of women's sisterly concern for each other. You are actually complaining, Terry, that Danielle does not weep hypocritically for your wife?'

'I'm complaining that you stunted the poor little bitch!'

Rudi Kabbel sighed, laying his head back against the rest, the extension of the seat which was designed to prevent whiplash injuries. Returning from setting booby-traps, the Kabbels would be safe from spinal damage.

'Sometimes, Mr Delaney, history *does* make its claim on people. In places like Los Angeles and Sydney people try to live in an eternal and very base *now*, without any memory of the

dead. The barbecue and the sun are *all*. Games are *all* – a game
is *all* to you. But you have to face it: sometimes – I restate it
so that you will know – sometimes even here history can't be
avoided, history comes up and grabs people. Outside coffee bars
in Auburn where Armenians wait with knives for the Turks to
come out – there it can kill people. What I say is, don't try to
marry Danielle. It will never work. She belongs to forces you
can't negotiate with, Terry. I tell you that as a friend. I too wish
it were otherwise. But there can't be any Aussie cosiness in life
for her.'

Mouth open, Delaney was considering making the challenge,
yelling 'we'll bloody see' and all the other worn terms of a
struggle between a lover and a father, when Kabbel changed
direction.

'I was going to tell you, anyhow. I'm selling out, Terry. The
business and the house. I want to buy property – forests,
escarpments, meadows. The line can no longer be held, Terry.
The line against barbarity.'

'And poor damn Brian Stanton?' asked Delaney.

'He'll work for the new owners. I have to get out, Terry.
There is a valley beyond Newnes – two and a half hours away
from here if you drive sedately like me.'

'Farming? Or a bloody munitions factory?'

'The bottom land can be farmed and carry livestock. There
are great sandstone gorges, made by glaciers when God was
young.'

The mention of glaciers signalled Delaney. 'This is all for the
sake of that wave you crowd talk about!'

'Everyone knows it's on its way, Delaney. Every cretin
restocking the shelves in supermarkets from Tasmania to Fin-
land. Everyone knows it's on its way.'

'So you don't live *now*, like sane people. You live for *afterwards*, you stupid prick, Rudi.'

'Said like a good Catholic, who doesn't enjoy fucking now, if
you will excuse the term, so that he can fuck without worry in
heaven.'

'So you cork up the gorges to stop the rest of us getting in,'
Delaney observed. 'You put up a gate and anyone who touches

it gets the Stevo treatment. The gates of bloody heaven, eh?
And the unworthy get their mits blown off. You know what shits
me about you, Rudi? You look at me, a professional player, but
that means sweet damn-all, a poor stupid bugger who's worked
well and taken deep bruising at the bloody chicken house for
you, and you think pity about poor Delaney, he's done for, might
as well write him off. I've been inside your daughter, you old
sod, and it doesn't mean a thing, I'm just another one of the
damned. And what will you do out there with Danielle, in bloody
Newnes, in Kabbelburg? A woman, Rudi, a really lovely and
healthy woman? Will you give her to Warwick so they can bang
out a few cross-eyed kids while you're waiting for the bloody
surf to break over the Blue Mountains?'

He noticed Kabbel was regarding him in a strange deliberate
way and understood with delight that the man had lost his
temper. But it was not the hot loss Delaney had hoped for.
There was no chance of punches or screaming. The Kabbels
never gave you that.

'Give me your gun, Delaney, and I'll sign it off. Call for your
pay and bring your uniform in tomorrow night. Though you do
not think so, I give Danielle her freedom so it is her matter
whether you meet in the future. I don't think we should meet
again.'

There was nothing Delaney could say without losing ground.
He put his beeper and his .38 on the seat beside Kabbel. Still
struggling for a fit last word he opened the door. As he stood
up outside the car astringent rain struck the back of his neck.
It brought him something like a satisfactory answer.

'You're a bloody fool, Rudi,' he called, 'and you'll die unhappy.'

Kabbel shrugged, nodded, and drove away.

THIRTY-SIX

FROM THE JOURNALS OF STANISLAW KABBELSKI, CHIEF OF POLICE,

STAROVICHE

December 21, 1943

Fourteen of us gathered in the boardroom of Minsk Opera House. We constitute the Belorussian Central Council – Ostrowsky to take our names to General von Gottberg for ratification by Christmas. Easy to be fanciful at such a time. Not impossible though that on this day in the future Belorussian children will honour our snow-clad graves.

Minor humiliations. We have to confer in German for the sake of the two German observers, Dr Kappeler and Oberführer Riese, von Gottberg's deputy. Ostrowsky is occasionally summoned to go and talk to von Gottberg. It is like being called away to the headmaster's study.

We strike our blows for independence though. Earthy old Stanek Stankievich came back from morning coffee to make a speech. 'German military disasters are one thing, the Belorussian Council is an entirely separate entity. Its continued existence depends on German victory but its destiny is its own. It ought to be understood Germany could be destroyed, but the Belorussian cause would still exist.'

Ostrowsky rushed in to assure Kappeler and Riese Stanek's German creaky, that he really meant to emphasise our only immediate hope was the policy of alliance with Germany.

Both sides knew nonetheless that a message had been passed.

Ostrowsky came back from one of his sessions in von Gottberg's office across the square at dusk. Planes of his face impressively lit by chandelier as he detailed final terms of our independence. There is to be universal conscription of Belorussian males over the age of eighteen into a Belorussian Defence Force. This force to wear both the double-barred cross and the SS insignia. Basis of this force will be the twenty thousand members of our police forces, to be run from Minsk by our old friend Franz Kushel. Ostrowsky says he told von Gottberg he did not want to have to negotiate with the civilians who had worked for Kube, the Generalkommissar of Belorussia preceding von Gottberg. (Kube a friend of Willi Ganz apparently, and like Ganz in philosophy; was blown up in his bed by the partisans.) I've been used to working with the Greens, said Ostrowsky – by which he meant Wehrmacht authorities for whom he had administered Smolensk. Von Gottberg pointed to his own green SD uniform and said, You're working for the Greens again, Radislaw!

We're going to fight to extend the Wehrdorfer system, garrisoning the countryside with our expanded armed forces. In return, villages who take part in the Wehrdorfer system will be exempt from requisitions of grain and livestock by the army. Could not help but think, Why didn't Germans let us do this years ago, instead of waiting for this late stage when their authority – as ours – is diminished?

Same thought raised by Mikolai Redich that evening. Took me aside during a party arranged by Kappeler at Hotel Europa. Redich has been administrator of Rogachev for past two and a half years. His reputation is strong. A large man who stoops down to talk to people, even to tall people like myself. Has a very engaging and forgiving irony in his eye. Kappeler's party was first-rate and at time Redich approached me, would have guessed he'd already taken too much herring and vodka for anything he said to have more than sentimental value. In fact, though his breath was fiery and wavered around my ear, his intent very political.

'We young ones, Kabbelski,' he said, flinging his arm around my shoulder, 'have to consider the realities of our present situation. It's like old Stankievich says – not only might we fall with the Germans, we might also find ourselves labelled with their crimes. Old Stankievich himself, he organised events in

Borissow which the British and Americans, when they become our allies next year or the year following, may find they can't countenance.'

He was referring to the Borissow action in late 1941 when Stankievich's Belorussian police were given too much work to do and too much liquor at same time. All this leading to the sort of barbarism against which Ganz always inveighed and which, I can testify in front of any tribunal, I have always attempted to avoid in the *oblast* of Staroviche.

'Even Ostrowsky,' said Redich then. He even winked. 'Ostrowsky may have too many so called "crimes" on his slate to be acceptable to the Western nations.'

Asked him was he trying to lobby me to support an alternative to Ostrowsky. 'Don't misunderstand me,' he said. 'I know Ostrowsky is your son's godfather. I am simply raising the possibility that the Allies might not see Ostrowsky and Belorussia as exactly the same entity, even though we are in the habit of so doing. Ostrowsky has become so thoroughly identified with the German cause.'

'So – even though they can't say so yet – are the Allies,' I suggested to Redich.

'We'll have to see about that. America, we should remember, is in some ways more Jewish than the Pale of Settlement itself. For one thing, they run the film industry, and like Dr Goebbels do not for a minute underestimate the power of that medium. We may like to think of ourselves as brethren of the Americans. When we think of them we think of Bostonian gentlemen and Minnesota Swedes. But what are Lieutenant Biberstein and Captain Goldberg going to think of us, in particular of our respected leader whose activities in Smolensk are so well documented, so widely witnessed, so resented by the Soviets who *are – de facto* and either for the moment or for ever – the Allies' comrades-in-arms?'

Got very angry at this defeatism, this hypocrisy. 'Let's not have this brand of cowshit! We all with equal alacrity threw our cause in with the Germans. Two short Christmases ago the Soviets were reeling and the Waffen SS were in the suburbs of Moscow.'

He said dismissively, 'Do you think I forget the chimeras and delusions of that winter? But I don't want a man of your quality, Kabbelski, to continue to delude himself.'

'But if Ostrowsky will offend the Allies because of his anti-Soviet activities in Smolensk, I will offend them because of mine in Staroviche, and you likewise because of the cooperation you gave – of your free will, I emphasise – in Rogachev.'

He spread his hands and dared to wink at me. 'I was simply a civil administrator. I was a Belorussian governing a populace who saw a chance of honourable independence in the events of 1941.'

'Forty-two per cent of that populace were Jewish. Perhaps Hollywood will ask in its powerful way where they are now. And if Hollywood asks, so also does Roosevelt.'

'Damnit, Kabbelski,' said Redich. 'You're no political novice. You and I are not responsible in law for the activities of the Special Action Squads, and responsibility in law is all that matters politically. A case could be made against Ostrowsky which could not be made against us, and I am not speaking of a case in moral terms but of one in legal terms. You, for example, were a friend of Herr Kommissar Ganz who championed moderation and protected Jews in his home and his office. You yourself protected certain Jews. There was a sergeant in German Military Intelligence name of Jasper shot down in the Staroviche railroad yards by partisans last month – surprisingly Ganz was shot by partisans too for all his moderation! – and in Jasper's belongings was a detailed account of certain Staroviche events in late summer 1941, including a conversation he had with you. That document you wisely destroyed.'

Astounded that he possessed this sort of knowledge, but said nothing for moment.

'To protect Ostrowsky and make him acceptable to the Allies,' Redich went on, 'you would have to destroy enough documents to fill a library. Messing about with the jottings of a mere sergeant in the intelligence wouldn't suffice. These are the facts.'

Asked him, 'Whom do you represent?' Knew the answer I might get, but surprised nonetheless the faction involved had spies in the Staroviche police – *vide* knowledge of Sergeant Jasper's belongings, and implication that Jasper's assassination might have been connived at by someone, Bienecke or – I suppose he intends to convey this – me. Accusation scarcely worth dignifying – idea that I am fearful of a distressed young man's jottings, that they could sap my authority, is contemptible. So limited myself to asking Redich only the political question, since he makes such fuss about being purely a politician rather than a moral being. 'For whom are you lobbying me, Mikolai?' A good lobbier, I think, a true bullying political gangster.

'It's the Vatican Group, of course,' said Redich. 'You don't need to be told that.'

Vatican Group so called because apparently supported by Vatican funds. Led by Abramtchik, a good Catholic but a former Communist – his brother still works for Soviets. Abramtchik has powerful French intelligence and Vatican connections, or so his supporters like to claim. Ever since his conversion back to moderation, he's made fuss about those of us who are Catholic sticking together. The Orthodox, including Ostrowsky himself, are apparently culturally the inferiors of the Jesuit-educated. Have never tolerated this view myself. 'So you are prepared to use the religions of our oppressors as a tool to divide us?' I asked him.

'We have friends in the West,' said Redich. 'If the Reich cannot hold on to Belorussia, do you think we should continue to be unilaterally loyal to a defeated power which until now hasn't shown much loyalty to us? Ostrowsky talks like a habitual servant of the Reich, come what may. Perhaps he has no choice. We, however, possess magnificent contacts back there, in the heart of civilisation, and are helped in that regard specifically by our Catholic background. You don't think we need friends in the West? Our friends in the East we can hear right now?'

Tossed his head, referring to the continuous wail of police cars in the street, referring also to the way explosions and shouting and either far off or close gunfire could be heard, adequate to wake even a good sleeper four or five times a night.

Our conversation interrupted at this stage by Dr Kappeler, who made a speech of welcome. But like a true political messenger, Redich came to me again before the end of the evening, shook my hand and said, 'Keep an open mind, eh? And a nimble set of feet.'

It sounded like his political philosophy.

Ostrowsky came to my room hour ago, 2 a.m. Resembles a man who has just got over a fever – or more like someone whose body has gone to sleep but whose brain blazes on. So at the one time enormous energy and almost unspeakable exhaustion in way he talks. His face ageless and hollow. Says he wants me to direct his favourite programme – the extension of the fortified village set-up, the reclaiming of the countryside. Has absolute guarantees from von Gottberg that SS and other German security arms will not be admitted to fortified villages except at Belorussian request in emergencies. Such Belorussian forces to be placed in fortified villages as to enable them to come down with vengeance on disaffected elements in surrounding countryside. This policy tried up till now on an ad hoc province-by-province basis, sometimes by mayors, sometimes by police chiefs. Now to be centralised effort under control of a cabinet minister. Since whole business will require a certain amount of shifting around of rural populations the title will be Minister for Relocation. This process essential in all aspects – economically, to ensure a harvest; in terms of security to make partisans' hold on the countryside so difficult that at least they will again be restricted to the deepest forest areas.

My reflection is that this at first sight a Ganz-like policy, but will enable everyone found outside the fortified village system to be pursued and harried with a most un-Ganz-like vengeance. Partisans will on a national level be separated from their recruiting base and so wither on forest floor.

I'll be working with Franz Kushel, who'll have command of the Belorussian Defence Force. Remark to Ostrowsky all this could have been done two years back if Reich had then let us form a Belorussian national army, as they were so belatedly permitting now. Ostrowsky said, 'Radek, you must not call it a Belorussian national army except when you are amongst friends.' He smiled. 'The term terrifies von Gottberg.'

Cannot sleep for happiness. Feel I will have in my hands once Republic is proclaimed, and even earlier – once conscription begins – the most complete means to defend the nation, which has till now been increasingly defined for me in terms of Danielle, Genia, Radek. So be it. Truth is that through this portfolio, I can liberate the children of Belorussia back on to the streets!

THIRTY-SEVEN

When Denise let him in, the hallway of Stanton's place felt cold, so the sacrifice of the old tree the year before had been for nothing. Denise looked creased and pretty, so much a sister to the widow at Dyson Engineering that Delaney suppressed the memory and turned on the jovial uncle act. He carried under his arm a carton of Resch's Pilsener and a bag of small, gob-sized Violet Crumble Bars for the Stanton girls. A man so burdened (he meant to convey to Stanton) did not come to your house to dob you in, betray your secrets. He was cementing loyalties. By all the rules of mateship, *that* was visible. 'Where's your old man?' asked Delaney, putting his lips to Denise's cheek and finding it very cold.

'Shaving,' she said.

'I didn't think he worked tonight.'

'He says he might have to go out.' She believed it with all the glands of her belief, the terrifying trust of women burned for a second in her.

'Well,' he said, 'they'd be a bit short-staffed now.'

She led him into the living room where all the heat of the house was localised. The warm Stanton girls were in their dressing gowns, ready for the night which pressed against the window beyond the television set. Remarkably they were playing a game – a board and plastic markers and dice lay on the floor. Into the midst of it all Delaney irresponsibly dropped the bag of goodies. 'Have to ask your mother,' he said, too late.

'I've got to watch the little one,' said Denise. 'Confectionery sets her off.'

It was the older one, the one whose attention could be taken only by serious wonders like television and Violet Crumble Bars, who tore the bag open with a dark ferocity that reminded Delaney of her father.

'Glad you came around,' whispered Denise. 'He's not happy with that Kabbel crowd.'

Stanton appeared in the doorway. He looked pink-faced from the razor. 'Well,' said Stanton. 'It's the Governor bloody General. And I see he brought his own bloody beer.'

'Which I can't drink much of. Playing in reserves tomorrow.'

'Jesus.' Stanton was distracted from fear of what Delaney knew to an honest envy for Delaney's match fees. Denise rushed in with best wishes. It was a little like the poor praying for the economic health of BHP or Conzinc Riotinto.

Denise stayed with the children and let the men go out to have serious professional talks in the kitchen. Stanton drank his beer gratefully, for the glow, even though the weather was too cold for it. It stuck like porridge in Delaney's gullet. Gagging, forcing the words up past the gaseous liquor, Delaney expressed his regret over the Dyson Engineering fiasco.

'What a thing for mates to fall out over,' said Stanton, and made a speech Delaney had heard from him in the past. 'Look, Delaney, I could live happily with just enough cock to knock out a few kids and keep your missus happy. They say that's what it's all for, but then they give you twenty times more than you need. It's like driving a fucking sports car in a twenty-five k. zone. Got me beat!'

Delaney suggested he might find Doig understanding to talk to, but Stanton laughed that off. It struck Delaney that Stanton didn't like his sins understood or lessened. If you fornicated you had to break and enter an engineering plant to find the right place for it, the right level of daring. Maybe that's what saw to the success of the fornication motel in North Parramatta. To face the brunette in the front office and tell her you wanted a temporary occupancy was a kind of adventure.

'I suppose you want to know how Danielle is?' asked Stanton.

'No. I wanted to tell you Kabbel's selling out.'

Delaney could see by Stanton's bewilderment that Kabbel had not yet told him. Despite himself, he was pleased to kick off the friendship again with such a painful favour. 'He says your job's safe – that's one of the conditions of sale. But maybe you should start looking around anyhow.'

'Oh yes. Maybe they need a new heart surgeon at St Vincent's.'

'Rudi's a man of his word, in his own way.'

'But he's out of it, you know, off the air, and I wondered why. Out of the office all the time except when he turns up with heavies from other companies. Bloke from TNT there the other night.' Stanton ground his forehead into the pad of his hand. 'And bloody stupid Stanton still doesn't twig, just happy to be working twenty hours overtime a week!'

'Rudi's buying land. He's selling Uncle so that he can afford a pastoral bloody kingdom.'

Stanton shivered – the beer and the cold were adequate but not likely explanations. 'I don't think I'm on his mind much,' he said. 'I'm not much on any of their bloody minds. Warwick runs the rosters now, but he's no company. You know, I said the other night they'd have to find two new men – Scott hasn't come back from the bush – and the bugger looked right through me. Danielle's OK, over that flu she caught, but she's not too lively at the moment. They really choked that off, didn't they? You and Danielle. Strangled that one at birth. Never bloody mind.' He dropped his voice. 'You know I got so desperate the other night that I fell back on poor old Bernadette – Danielle was still in bed sick. Took Bernadette out to the old shed that used to be control room when bloody Rudi started the business. Poor bitch kept saying, "Brian, what if there's an alarm while we're in here?" Promised her I wouldn't be that long, and she said, "But I might be." The old Bernadette! Must have it off amongst the filing cabinets at work.'

Delaney was somehow shocked by the idea of Stanton making what hay he could in the shadow of Danielle's illness. All sexual pride suddenly drained, however, from Stanton's face. 'Lot of good all that's going to do me.'

'Danielle better now?'

'She's all right. Compared to the others. Jesus, Rudi had a fit just after you left.'

Delaney laughed. 'Upset, was he?'

'No, a fit. A fair dinkum . . . you know . . . fit. What do you call it? Paroxysm.'

Stanton explained how, at the start of a shift, Rudi Kabbel had appeared from the hallway whimpering and biting his lips, and a stream of urine falling crookedly down the legs of his deep blue pants. His hands were raised in front of his face and were trembling very fast, which made Stanton think of epilepsy. He whimpered like a child. Danielle ran from the arms cabinet and dragged him roughly from the room by the hand. Later she came back and told an amazed Stanton that it was Rudi's childhood. He'd suffered awfully, she said.

This news aroused in Delaney a vague and painful urge to rescue Danielle from her father. But before he could ask too many questions about this incident, about Rudi's trembling and his unleashed bladder, Stanton reverted to the sale of Uncle. 'You can't tell me that if one of those big companies want to buy without any encumbrances that Rudi will stick out for poor bloody Stanton.'

Delaney couldn't tell him that.

'This time I'm going to apply for my own gun licence. I'll rob banks.'

Delaney smiled and patted Stanton's arm. His friend had said that before, but apart from his innocent intrusion into Dyson, society remained safe from him.

THIRTY-EIGHT

The last Staroviche winter was sweet and by no means seemed to me to be the last. The house was full of Miss Tokina's instructive voice and of Belorussian police billeted in servants quarters upstairs and at the back of the house. They were very happy to be here instead of thrust forward into some frozen village amongst partisan-ridden forests. My mother treated them with an absent-minded generosity. They flirted with Genia. They spoiled me – it delighted me to see they knew I was the kid the partisans had nearly finished, it enabled me to adopt a certain style. Even at night I was not afraid of bullets, yet I needed to sleep with my mother, given that I dreamed so often of that awful sense of a large mistake, of myself transfixed in the high corner of Onkel Willi's dining room and my father rescuing from beneath the table the wrong child, the shell of Radislaw, the stranger.

As I said earlier, I was safe from tutors. It seemed to me that because of the shock both of Onkel Willi's kiss and of Onkel Willi's murder no one would ever have the right to try to make me learn algebra again.

My father was back and forth to Minsk almost continuously that January. He attended meetings of the Belorussian Central Council and talked to the various regional chiefs of the Defence Force. He was the foreshadowed Minister of Relocation. The *Minsker Zeitung* and the local Belorussian papers both said so.

I have to confess I was pleased he was away so often. I felt that I could no longer pose as his little boy. Events had made me a brat, as Miss Tokina had converted Genia into an occasionally charming, less hormonally stormy adolescent. The feeling that my father knew too much about me, had seen me in too many extremities, had not abated. That he was locked up in the Hotel Europa in Minsk and was planning the Belorussian Republic and all its works and all its pomps seemed entirely suitable to me. I was at ease. I did not foresee the spring, as my intelligent mother did.

There had been winter Russian offences in the south, but the Smolensk front on which we depended remained steady. The combination of oil and railways down south made assaults inevitable. Up here in the north we were innocent of oil and the Germans still held all the railway junctions. So it looked like a situation that could last for ever: the Germans encompassing Leningrad and holding far Novgorod and Staraya Russa, a Belorussian garrison in the house, my father away on most important Belorussian business, Genia neutralised by Miss Tokina, my mother anxious in the tradition of mothers but never with a blade to her throat, and no threat of a blade developing.

We went to Minsk for Easter, travelling by troop train. It was slow – a small locomotive travelled ahead at an eking pace, looking for tampered-with rails and hauling a tender carrying a German railway repair unit. Once we were parked for two hours while track was replaced. Towards dusk, as we edged along, shots were heard from the front of the train and an officer came through to our compartment and asked us to lie on the floor. Genia and my mother obeyed him so thoroughly that I was able, in the spirit of the guarantees I had received under Onkel Willi's dining room table, to look out through the shuttered window. I saw, edging through long grass and cornflowers, a strong detachment of German infantrymen from our train. I saw them all pause and pour fire into the woods. These fellow travellers of ours were on their way ultimately to take up a line along the Beresina south of Minsk, should that be necessary. It was yet another of those lines which the more knowledgeable of our house garrison said could last an age.

We reached Minsk towards midnight, and my father was there to meet us. We heard klaxons on the way to the Hotel Europa. My father smiled at my mother. 'It's never quiet at night,' he said. That Easter morning we heard Mass in Latin at the church of the Bernardine monastery. It was a sharp, clear Resurrection Day. For two such nationalists my parents had an unselfconscious preference for the Latin Mass over the Belorussian-Byzantine style, for a French Christ resurgent over a Russian or Greek one. For my parents were amongst that 20 per cent who used Belorussian only to communicate with their fellow nationals but who believed that a knowledge of the Latin responses made one an heir to Western culture and was as good as a visit to Paris.

In the car on the way to breakfast at the Europa, my father told my mother, 'You should stay in Minsk. General Busch intends to make Minsk into an irreducible stronghold. Besides, I'm only nominally police chief of Staroviche now.'

We drove past a strongpoint on a corner guarded by young Belorussian conscripts in new but shabby uniforms which echoed those of the SS.

'I don't want to give up the house in Staroviche,' I was delighted to hear my mother tell him. 'And Genia must have Miss Tokina or she'll go mad.'

'Don't misunderstand me,' said my father, smiling and indulgent. 'We won't relinquish the lease on the Staroviche house.'

We haven't relinquished it to this day.

THIRTY-NINE

Old Greg Delaney had been able to come in off the road at the age of forty-five when he achieved the post of dispatch clerk at Pioneer Frozen Foods in Parramatta. Here his days began hectically – if he dropped dead on the job, he always said, it would be between seven and nine in the morning – but the rest of the shift was calmer. He had time to read two newspapers and be opinionated as drivers and supervisors from the factory drifted through his office. What gave him piquant joy was that he knew management were relaxed about him, that he kept the bookwork and the drivers straight. That freed them from suspicion and him from supervision. The managing director had come down to his booth by the loading docks the week before Christmas 1982 to hand him his bonus cheque, to sip a scotch with him and to assure him that an independent consultant had discovered that Greg had saved the company $98,000 in pilferage during the previous tax year.

That visit from the management intrigued Delaney – the fact the man had uttered a specific sum and that it was large enough simply to be equated with riches in Greg's mind, but that Greg considered his $1,500 bonus abundant reward. And that the managing director knew that, knew that the figure he reeled off would not appear to Greg an achievable or possessable sum, meant to Greg no more nor less than say the number of light years between Earth and Alpha Centauri. And this was not because Greg Delaney was stupid. It was because he was a happy man and therefore incorruptible.

His son made him professionally uneasy by asking him for a job.

'It isn't what your mother had in mind for you. Driving a truckload of frozen peas round Sydney.'

'Tell her it's only temporary,' said Delaney.

It was possible old Greg didn't want his son crowding him in at Pioneer, invading his glass booth, making special claims on him.

'Mrs Terracetti called your mother with a pretty garbled story about some brawl between Gina and yourself. That's what this is all about, isn't it?'

Delaney admitted it.

'You know she's a bloody wonderful girl, Gina.'

Delaney nodded. 'Do you think I'm going to say the opposite?'

'Don't come into Pioneer. Start something of your own. I should have made you go to university.'

'My aggregate wasn't high enough.'

'Then to one of those advanced education places.'

Delaney said that he needed a breathing space. 'After that I'll go and found my own multinational.'

Whatever his reasons, Greg Delaney continued to fight the idea.

'Look, Pioneer's minting money. There'll be a generation of kids who believe vegetables grow in little plastic packets with a bloody pioneer wagon on it. But I ought to give any job that comes up to a married man.'

'Shit, *I'm* a married man.'

'A married man with kids. Listen, a word of advice. Not the word you're expecting. Don't take your problems to that idiot Doig.'

'Well,' asked Delaney, 'is there a job?'

'Will be in two weeks. A Greek driver's going back to Salonika. Reckons the standard of living's better there. What have they done to our beautiful country!' (This was a constant exclamation of Mrs Delaney's.) 'I'll get you an application form.'

'Will you put a word in for me?'

Old Delaney – a man who had saved his company $98,000 and was willing to save them from his son as well – snorted and said nothing.

He had seen it in films.

Films had in fact provided the bulk of his education, outside marriage and his affair with Danielle, on these matters, and he wondered if people now made love, mimicking the erotic gestures of Julie Christie or Burt Reynolds, in a different way than their grandparents.

Or even than their parents. For the Delaneys senior tolerated pictures only from the '50s in which June Allyson and Cary Grant shared twin beds and displayed towards each other lots of amiability and not an amp of passion. Questions of potency and orgasm did not arise. But in a Goldie Hawn movie a husband dies of a heart attack at climax. And in others there was a modern standard scene where an unsure hero gets a spectacular woman to bed, there is a cut to her wistful and him ashamed, and she sighs, 'It could happen to anyone . . .' It was always a comic scene and the audience laughed, delighted to find confirmed that which their homely wisdom and honest women had already taught them: that too much desirability can freeze a man's engine.

In the fornication palace at North Parramatta, on a Tuesday evening after training, Delaney found that this scene from comedy, this take from that other effete and sated world parallel to the real world and never touching it, had interposed itself between himself and Danielle, and that Danielle was saying, with less flagrant disappointment than the movie vamps, 'But it's nothing to be worried about . . .'

That afternoon she had bravely appeared in time to meet him, asserting herself, her own woman, but it seemed to Delaney that the withdrawal of Rudi's approval reduced everything, made the whole business meaner. Despite himself he began to hear noises from other rooms, a jovial voice, a murmurous discussion of erotic preferences, a sound of furniture bumping harshly, a post-coital shower turning on. It had been necessary to Danielle Kabbel and Delaney both, one of the basic terms of their infatuation, to believe that everyone else in the place was a lover of a different and lower order than themselves. *They* were fated, but the people next door were just in it for the fun. The illusion lifted now, the whole arrogance of the affair vanished. The walls grew thin. Delaney could see a sort of stain of weariness on Danielle's forehead, and his own dumb seed failed to move.

That first.

The following morning Gina did not let him sleep late. She woke him by placing on his bare shoulder one of those frozen plastic containers of coolant people put in their Eskies and picnic baskets to keep the beer and the meat fresh. They were going picnicking, she told him grimly, even if it cost her her job.

She dragged him into the kitchen and showed him what she'd gathered – ham, tomatoes, mozzarella, sundry dips, a barbecued chicken in a foil bag, two beers, a bottle of Frascati. 'Well,' he said, 'you Dagoes know how to put a picnic together.' But he was blind with misery. How could they find their way to a cliff-face and force this stuff down their throats? He tried to restrict the time she might demand of him. 'Why don't we go up to Springwood at lunchtime?' he suggested.

'Bugger that!' roared Gina, pointing at him. You'd almost believe a curse was in it for him if he didn't go along. 'We're going to the beach.'

He groaned. The cement promenades of Bondi rose in his mind.

'Palm Beach,' she said. 'You know, there's a lighthouse there. We're going up the lighthouse. Come on, no resistance. You're supposed to be fit, Mr Delaney.'

It was better than he thought, a clear winter's morning with a sort of frank bland light which didn't suit that species of crucial conversations Steve Mansfield called 'deep and meaningfuls'. In the spirit of the enforced expedition to the beach, Gina drove and made careful and polite talk.

When Greg Delaney had driven his adolescent son to Palm Beach on summer Saturdays it had always taken two hot hours or more. Delaney and Gina got there this winter's day in one and saw the whole long strand of ocean beach all but empty under the sun. At the northern end a shred of sand-dunes ran towards a great and separate headland, almost its own island, on which the lighthouse stood. Delaney felt an instant wistful urge to climb to it but wasn't sure how you got up there. It was as if Gina had read the guidebook though. She parked on the edge of the dunes, on the inland side, by the great sweep of water named Pittwater after one of those British ministerial Pitts, Delaney wasn't sure which one. 'Hands out,' she ordered him as she landed the picnic basket in his arms. She led him off along a narrow stillwater beach, the sand soft, the surf from beyond the dunes resonating in his ears. The wave, the bloody wave. It would drown the filament of dunes and lap the sandstone ledges of the headland. To Kabbel, therefore, all this lovely shore was already done for.

'This is beautiful,' said Gina, walking unevenly beyond the tidemark.

There were fishermen's huts ahead, below the cliffs of Barrenjoey headland, on this back side of Palm Beach. Delaney suspected there weren't many fishermen left in the area and that the shacks were probably leased by trendies from the eastern suburbs. Whatever the case, past the first one Gina led him right and up a track fringed with tall boulders, by banksia and vines, acacias and melaleucas, and other arrantly Australian vegetation.

'Ancient,' said Gina. 'Ancient country.'

They climbed the uneven sandstone track. Walls of scrub and great boulders did what they liked with the sound of the sea, blunting and slowing it at one bend, bouncing it at them fast at another. Rosellas skittered across their vision, leaving a stain of scarlet and blue. There was no one else there. It was as if the guidebook had promised Gina there would be no one.

The lighthouse seemed smaller when they reached it, but the mouth of Broken Bay immense, and the illimitable coastline swept away northwards. Gina clung to him for a while in case space devoured her. Off amongst the low salt-tough bushes sat terraces of sandstone. They were exactly the places to spread a picnic blanket.

Delaney and his wife went looking off in the scrub for the right slab for them. They moved stooped over on an overgrown track – the spiny vegetation needled their arms and legs. On their right a fenced grave appeared – Fred Mulhall, born in 1815 in Somerset, made the long interstellar journey to Australia, kept the light on Barrenjoey till the light took him – a bolt of lightning frittering him in the 1880s. His wife was laid with him.

Conjugal lessons seemed to be following Delaney even into the bush.

They defused them by sharing a laugh at poor Fred's epitaph.

> All ye who come my grave to see,
> Prepare in time to follow me.
> Repent at once without delay,
> For I in haste was called away.

They found a platform at last, open to the sun and lightly fringed with wax-tongued banksias.

He read the Rugby League news in both *Herald* and *Telegraph* with at last, after weeks of being adrift, some sense that it was – as Danielle had once said – *his* game. In the *Herald*, a piece on Bernie Swift, the St George five-eighth. Delaney had once played against him, Metropolitan Catholic Colleges versus Combined High Schools, curtain-raiser to Australia versus France at the Sydney Cricket Ground. Swift had had everything then – wonderful understanding with his halfback, could scurry and then open up with a change of pace like a centre. Brilliant on the little kick. So I had the message when I was seventeen that there were blokes better than me. Perhaps I thought the buggers would move to Queensland. No, what he had thought then, when he was seventeen, was *I will learn, I will learn*. The sun, however, spread its consolations across the page. Besides, he had some of his father's tranquillity. When it came to ambition he had not been swallowed whole.

As he found out after eating lunch and urinating grandly like Adam from the edge of the rock, this was Gina's seduction venue as Dyson Engineering had been Stanton's. Delaney was dazed by a full-blooded winter sun, by half a bottle of Frascati and by an unusual sense of the world being right. Gina moved with that same knockabout gruffness she'd employed to force the picnic on him. She had been sunbathing topless (as her mother had never done in the Mediterranean sunlight), a bathrobe around her thighs. She shifted and laid herself across his lap, and later it occurred to him that if he had not shown any interest she would have lost everything, the day, her pride, her friendly calm, and been forced to hurl the bottle at him and curse and gouge him. He touched her breasts and found her honest moisture nearly without thinking, certainly without thought of the Kabbels and Danielle. What he said after these opening movements wasn't what he meant to say. He tried to assert a sort of fidelity to Danielle, but that didn't come from his mouth. What came from his mouth was, 'I'm not out of the Kabbel thing yet.'

She wasn't any fool, he would later tell himself. The 'yet' was a dead giveaway, as good as a promise. It was not quite ecstasy up there on the rock platform. It was not intended by Gina for that purpose. It was the meat, bread and greens of love, meant to build the boy up after too long a time on an alien and over-rich diet. It was a negotiation. It made ordinary life more or less possible again.

On the way down the headland she said, 'I'm sorry for broadcasting the Hawaiian business to my family.'

The remaining shame of that old misdemeanour crackled across his skin like a failure of warmth. Mrs Terracetti would always look at him sideways from now on.

'I don't go around bumping everyone I meet, you know,' he told her, squirming through the powder sand, laden with the basket. 'I smoked pot. That brought it on.'

'I'll buy some straightaway,' said Gina solemnly.

'Gay Mansfield wanted me to try her on, and Steve wanted a crack at you. And I knocked them back.'

'Ah,' said Gina, 'that's why she told me.'

'*She* told you?'

'She took me aside after the last Cronulla game and said she reckoned I ought to know. "You can't forgive what you don't know," she told me.'

Gina winked across Pittwater, as if at the pilot of a floatplane which was just rising from the green water. 'You shouldn't have knocked Steve back without telling me,' she said. 'He isn't a bad-looking fellow.'

Delaney reached the car and rid himself of the burden of the basket. 'You know I'll have to see Danielle one more time.'

That made Gina solemn. 'I suppose so,' she said in the end.

FORTY

FROM THE JOURNALS OF STANISLAW KABBELSKI, CHIEF OF POLICE,

STAROVICHE

June 20, 1944

First session of Belorussian Central Congress, under Czech cut-glass chandeliers of Minsk Opera. As humiliating as I feared. Oberführer Riese on the gavel. They sit on our faces! Parallels the trouble I have had, being permitted by von Gottberg's people and by lean Kappeler to draft plans to take the countryside back, but being allowed to execute nothing. Am able through my standing as Chief of Police, Staroviche *oblast*, to experiment in my own garden, as it were. Against the tide, terrorist incursions in villages and railway yards in Staroviche province have fallen since Easter!

Know Ostrowsky had to submit his speech to von Gottberg's office and that Redich and his Papally-connected crowd go round muttering that he should have refused. Saw Redich at lunchtime. Explained how Ostrowsky can't win on the matter – has to establish Belorussian Republic before Germans leave Minsk (if, of course, they do). If central government isn't established before Russians come there can be no official government in exile, no government to offer the Americans, British, French, no government to return to Belorussia with these potent Allies as they turn against the genuine enemy.

'And,' asks Redich, stating the old problem, 'are the Americans likely to respect a head of state who in the Minsk Opera House pledges eternal dedication to Hitler?'

'They'll know he had to, that *that* was written for him. They're realists.'

A consummate conspirator, Redich stooped in front of me and whispered, 'A pincer movement is coming in on Vitebsk. Likewise Zhlobin. We should hear the gunfire by tomorrow. German intelligence says the Russian forces are highly mechanised now with vehicles supplied by dear old Henry Ford and the cripple Roosevelt. You see, *that* alliance is stronger than some people think.'

Afternoon session, Ostrowsky showed true political style, got Kappeler and Riese on wrong foot to my considerable delight. Rose and made speech of his own, saying that the Central Council had now finished all it could do within the limits of power permitted it by General von Gottberg. Therefore intended to resign and call on the convention, the thousand patriots sitting in Opera stalls, to elect new president.

Riese jumped like a shot rabbit, knew that Ostrowsky's resignation would reduce the convention to factional chaos and von Gottberg would blame him for letting it get out of hand. He ran to Kappeler and began muttering in his ear like a penitent. Uproar of conversation in body of theatre. Ostrowsky went serenely back to his seat beside old Stanek Stankievich in the front row of stalls, only few metres from where I sat in aisle seat second row. I was placed, because of seat on aisle, to rise and walk solemnly round front of stalls and publicly urge Ostrowsky not to abandon us to the factions, but felt that he might not want me to do that. He looked like a man in good control of things. Saw him nod and smile moderately at something old Stanek said. Saw also Redich leaning over to speak in ear of Abramtchik, head of Papal gang. Abramtchik's hands clasped, imperceptibly waving an index finger. No, he was saying, no, we don't have the numbers. To my surprise, he rose, climbed the stairs to the stage, whispered briefly to Kappeler and Riese and while Oberführer Riese punished the table with his gavel, came to the microphone. Had to admire him. He too, like Ostrowsky, acting by political instinct. It was unthinkable, he said, that the father of the Belorussian Central Council should now, as a Belorussian Republic appeared to be a possibility, remove himself from the leadership. He understood what pains and stresses had operated on this great patriot during the past six months, but he urged him to take the burden on his shoulders once more. He called on the delegates to elect Ostrowsky president of the convention by acclamation.

The acclamation was enormous. Delegates climbed on their chairs and wept and shouted, reached towards Ostrowsky as if they wanted him to cure them of blindness. Part of their ecstasy was their knowledge that Ostrowsky had demonstrated to the Germans how absolutely they needed him if they were to hold or, at the worst, ultimately return to Belorussia.

Riese tried to get control back by chiding delegates for forgetting to send loyal greetings on occasion of Herr Hitler's fifty-fifth birthday last April. Amidst gales of laughter and the singing of birthday songs, greetings were moved and carried.

In the afternoon we began to form committees. At one end ballet rehearsal room, chaired, or more exactly briefed and informed, relocation and security committee on draft plans. At four o'clock heard the first thunder from beyond the Beresina, but such was our absorption in our work and such the general noisiness of Minsk that we did not at first recognise it for what it was.

Tonight late summoned to Ostrowsky's suite. Since Danielle and children moved up here he has the courtesy not to call in at an hour which might disturb their sleep. Conditions at the Europa already bad enough. Delegates are three to a room and rowdy. Not content to drink, shout, play cards behind closed doors they leave the doors open, maybe hoping that the racket and the sight of their tumbled bed linen will attract other roisterers in. Worse still, if they want to sing they come into corridors to do it. No riot from Ostrowsky's suite though, and door closed. Knocked, and admitted by one of Ostrowsky's secretaries wearing the new uniform of Defence Force, very like the SS uniform but the red double-barred cross on the collar. That another cause for complaint: that SS will when it suits them try to subsume the Bela Rus Defence Force straight into their ranks.

Two of my fellow cabinet ministers asleep on camp-cots in one corner of large reception room. Wall bracket lights on above them. Their faces have a yellow stain of exhaustion. Across the room Ostrowsky at large desk with doughty Franz Kushel, chief of our forces, a man who's impressed me in past months with his moral strength. A number of maps wide as carpets on the desk, uppermost a map of the city. The aide went to Ostrowsky and told him I was there. Ostrowsky signalled me over without taking eyes off the map. 'Thank you for coming, Kabbelski,' he said when I reached the table. 'Grievous business. Russians threatening the Minsk-Moscow highway. General Tippelskirch's Fourth Army in danger of encirclement. Franz here tells me Wehrmacht wants to blow everything – the cathedrals and the Bernardine monastery, the town hall and the Belorussian library, the Natural History Museum, the Opera House, the lot.'

Kushel smiled. 'They want to deny the Soviets culture as well as installations.'

Ostrowsky covered his eyes with a hand, said to Kushel, 'Want you to make it clear to General Busch's office' (Busch has just taken over Army Group Centre) 'Belorussian Central Council will not let its troops be used for destroying cultural treasures.' He handed Kushel a sheet of paper. 'That's what I'll tolerate – the armoury, the Svichloch bridges, the radio station, the control towers at the airport, the power stations, the fuel storage depots and the railway yards. We will not declare war on our past.'

The forthright Kushel waved the sheet of paper Ostrowsky had signed. 'It's important for me to have this,' he said simply.

Ostrowsky smiled thinly at him. 'Remind them that even if we go we're all coming back,' he advised.

'Some of them don't believe it,' said Kushel. He rose, looked smiling absently at me, then switched the smile off and looked away. If all this meant some sort of embarrassment it is first time I ever saw him show any. 'I'll use the telephone in the bedroom and make an appointment for early morning.' He left without saying anything further.

Aware, since we had worked together in adjoining offices in town hall for past two months, of his unusual constraint tonight. Told myself, however, that with exhaustion, the Soviets, the partisans, the Germans and the carousers in the corridors, there were plentiful reasons to explain it.

Ostrowsky looked at me. A bleak face but it always has been. Lincolnesque. The mask for a soul who has never known a moment's rest. 'Stanek, I have something very grave to ask you to do. You are the most junior of my ministers. This afternoon's election by acclamation was not merely a vote for me, but a vote for Belorussian unity. It means that the Western faction – what I've heard called the Papal gang – have accepted my leadership in a manner which they cannot in the future deny or revoke. But as you can understand Abramtchik and his aides did not support me for no price at all. They want their faction represented at all levels of the cabinet. This has forced on me the sad necessity to adjust the cabinet I would have wanted. I have to ask you, Kabbelski, to resign as Minister for Relocation.'

I opened my mouth to speak, to tell him that this was a portfolio to which I was dedicated not merely as some opportunist politician might be but with my Belorussian fibre and with all my desire to make Belorussia safe for the Genias and the Radeks to walk abroad. But shock had slowed me and he spoke first.

'Stanek, the Soviets are about to retake Belorussia. Busch had these plans for making Minsk a fortress but it was never realistic. The Panzers are finished. It was in the front of the Third Panzer Army, the champions of 1940 and 1941, that the hole was knocked, the salient which puts Tippelskirch at risk. It could be a year or even two before we return in the wake of the twentieth century's final cataclysm. Your portfolio has no meaning until we do return. For that reason I ask you to surrender it to one of Abramtchik's faction and to take the relatively minor post of Minister Assistant to myself and Deputy Minister of Justice.'

I knew there was no one else for this task of mine. Only way I could hold out hope to Danielle of a return to Belorussia, a return in which she could take her easel wherever it suited her, was in my capacity as Minister for Relocation. She would trust a Belorussia in which I held such an authority. She could trust no other Belorussia. From childhood she had dreaded the status of refugee. All I could provide her with was Minister Assistant to the President. And that was not enough for a return. While I hold present post, can guarantee her the villages and the forests. Now Ostrowsky wants to pass them over, for reasons of factional convenience, to someone else. But did not have the gift to express all this to someone as austere – a genuine political monk – as Ostrowsky.

'President Ostrowsky, I have drafted the relocation plans and drawn up a scheme of administration. Am I either to see them brutalised by someone else? Or someone else claiming them as his own?'

Ostrowsky sighed. 'Stanek, vanity at a time like this!'

'Not vanity, Mr President. I belong to this project body and soul.'

'We could call it the Kabbelski plan if that would make the pill sweeter to swallow. It is normal in cabinet government, Stanek, for a new minister to inherit his predecessor's plans and to go on with them or not. Besides that, as I said, we will be very lucky indeed to implement any policy in the near future, we will be very fortunate indeed if Minsk is held and our portfolios become more than mere names.'

I buried my face in my hands. Ostrowsky is very perceptive and could sense what the gesture meant. 'You and your family will be evacuated in good time. I have von Gottberg's word.'

I smiled so that he would know I was not being self-indulgent. 'If it weren't for Danielle I'd just as soon join one of the better Defence Force battalions and make a stand.'

'I'm not going to throw Defence Force battalions away on romantic stands. Kushel's division, made up of all our twenty thousand policemen, will retreat with the SS and the Wehrmacht. And you – do you think we can afford to lose you?'

'Only from a specific portfolio,' I said. 'Is it the case, Mr President Ostrowsky, that Abramtchik approached you before your election today and offered support in return for senior places for his hacks?' Because my impression was Abramtchik taken by total surprise!

'He approached me afterwards.'

Thought about that. 'What could he offer? He'd already been manoeuvred into supporting you. Sir, it seems to me bad business to pay afterwards for a favour which has already been freely done.'

Ostrowsky smiled wanly down on the vast map of Minsk, the various colours of cathedrals and sewers, squares and generating stations. 'He offered me continued support. You don't have to be told. Abramtchik built up a powerful Belorussian support in Paris between the wars but does not have the influence with the SS that we enjoy. As well there is the fact that his brother is a NKVD official and also that he himself was a Communist in his boyhood. Some delegates here would swear to you that he is a Soviet plant. All these questions have the power to tear us apart when we need a show of unity to present to the Allies. What if we reach the West and are negotiating with the Americans, being taken seriously by them, when unresolved factionalism causes the Papal gang to found an alternative Belorussian government. It will be recognised by French intelligence and by the Vatican, and the Americans and British will become confused in their attitude and fail to recognise us. It is prodigiously important, Stanek, that that should not happen. To prevent it, I am willing to make a substantial gesture. The substantial gesture is your position in the cabinet. *They* know you're like a brother – that this is therefore no light accommodation for me to make.'

'They tried to lobby me but I was loyal.'

'For that I thank you. But in cabinet matters, Stanek, loyalty must be its own reward. By appointing you Deputy Minister of Justice under myself, I shall make you unofficially my cabinet aide, a position from which I can credibly promote you in future.'

'Which of his faction is to inherit my plan?'

'We should know by tomorrow. Resign, please, Stanek, so that they can never say you were dismissed.'

Found myself wishing I could yield, but the plan too intimate to me – as I'd warned him. Also felt that I needed to resist, not to go voluntarily – otherwise could not work out pattern of future alliances or bear the diminished lustre Ostrowsky now held for me.

Gasping for air, told him, 'I regret you will have to dismiss me, President Ostrowsky.'

Which he regretfully but immediately did.

Found out before morning session Redich to take over the Relocation Ministry. Feel that in my political landscape all the signposts have been reversed.

FORTY-ONE

Delaney called Uncle after nine at night, an hour when Danielle should have been there alone, reading a novel, the yellow codes of all the clients glowing on the computer screen by her elbow. Warwick answered, however.

'You're not making an offer for the business, Terry?'

'Not unless it comes with a stock of explosives,' said Delaney.

'You're what they call a droll bugger,' Warwick told him. Warwick seemed to be laughing.

Delaney asked to speak to Danielle.

'No,' said Warwick. 'She wouldn't want you to. What can you do, Delaney? Meet in a carpark for a last embrace? She's got too much dignity.'

'Put her on, Warwick. If that's what *she* says, then . . .'

But Warwick refused. In the living room Gina pretended to watch an American comedy about a boutique whose owner, a bright-eyed anorexic girl, was in love with a weightlifting fruiterer. At least it was meant to be a comedy, but when love was threatened everyone grew earnest in that awesome American way, and earnestness prevailed and, because everyone on the screen expected it to, healed all. Gina expected nothing from earnestness, but for the sake of her pride she needed to pretend an interest in the comic-strip love affair. Delaney wondered what women did in these circumstances before the television age. Read the classified ads, pretend a deadly serious interest in Births and Deaths, Furniture for Sale, Houses and Land/ North Shore Line, Machinists Wanted?

'Put her on,' Delaney insisted, knowing that a sort of decency demanded that, yet already pleased at the idea of Warwick and Danielle graciously saving him the pain of hearing the voice of his sole desire.

'No, I won't,' said Warwick. 'Do you know what my father thinks of you?'

'No,' said Delaney, half hoping again that distracting insults would fly.

'He thinks you're an honest man. And you know I'm one too. So you'll know I'm not lying when I say she has a severe respiratory infection and wouldn't be able to come to the phone if she wanted to.'

He began to ask frantic questions about her health. 'Of course she'll get better. We Kabbels weren't made to succumb to flu. Goodnight, Terry.'

He hung up. Delaney felt at the same time deliverance and the sense that he was committing treachery. He rang the number but it would not answer. He rang it again. Gina rose in the living room, came out past the wedding pictures on the dresser, past the Pontiff's benediction, and looked at him once in a way which seemed to convey certain questions. What are you doing? Are you tempting Destiny? Don't you understand the unanswered telephone is a gift? He didn't. He dialled once more and there was nothing. Gina had returned to the living room and he went and sat beside her.

'I wasn't even interested in her,' said the muscle-bound actor to his beloved, whose legs were as thin as those of Central Australian Aboriginal women.

'Well,' said Delaney, as the live audience on the television sighed at the last sentiments of fidelity uttered by the weight-lifter. 'That's settled.' He knew it was true enough to say, yet it was harder to believe than any of those doctrines Doig took apart each Sunday. He suffered that awful sense of seeing himself from the outside, seeing exactly the volume of air he took up – a slight, lithe fool, hollowed out from the chest down, drongo, no-hoper, silly-bugger, deadshit. This self-claustrophobia mercifully lifted after a few seconds. Taking breath, he saw ahead of him the marital landscape like a plain far from featureless, an earth adequate to live off but at this stage both hard to discern and, of course, empty of surprise, every corner of it covered in the deeds. A decent habitation and, as his parents might say, his lot in life.

'I hope you'll forgive all the grief and messing around,' he said.

'You don't have to worry,' said Gina. She didn't want him to go on. A commercial began and she buried her eyes in the non-news of the evening paper. There was, thank Jesus, no great surge of reconciliation and mad joy.

FROM THE MATCH DIARY OF TERRY DELANEY

Penrith v Norths at Kalahari desert, as they call North Sydney Oval. McPhail out with hamstring so played full game in reserves. Really good centre, Paul Borissow (some sort of Slav but not much like Rudi). Beautiful working with him – intelligent player and good at busts up the middle. Like all the good ones doesn't need opening wide as the Harbour bridge and a printed invitation, just needs a chink of light and goodnight, nurse! Other player I combined with was second-rower, bloke from the bush, Gilgandra or somewhere, name of Greg Gorrie. Worked wide a lot and fast as a winger, big powerful thighs. Borissow and Gorrie two tries each in first half. Regathered a grubber myself thirty metres out in second half and scooted over for one of my own. Reserves: Penrith 32, Norths 8. Beaten in firsts again. Bloody club secretary faces the Channel 10 cameras with straight face and tells them how all we have to do to make semi-finals is win six on the trot. Deecock his old leaden self. Everyone muttering round the dressing rooms saying, 'Selectors have to do something.' Some chance of promotion for one Delaney.

Magic day, best for weeks. Gina there. Life's honest pleasures.

FORTY-TWO

For some reason our stay at the widow Frau Zusters' house in a tree-lined residential street running off Kaiserin Augusta Allee in Berlin seems more remote than my remoter early childhood. I do not remember it as I remember the holiday at Puck instigated by my godfather Ostrowsky or the Ganz picnic in the Brudezh forest. Frau Zusters was kind in a dazed remote way that suited my state of soul and made me think of her as ancient, even though I now realise she was no more than forty-five years. Her husband had been an engineering contractor working with the Wehrmacht in the oil-fields of Romania and had sadly been killed in a daylight raid by the Americans. I realise it was her widowhood that gave her her agelessness and put anxious tucks in the flesh of her face.

My father worked assisting Ostrowsky in offices provided by the Germans in Alexanderplatz, somewhere over to the east of the city, a place I would never visit. I heard him complain to my mother, 'I'm a damn housing and supply officer. Mrs Stankievich came to me to complain she couldn't get ham! No one's happy with their apartments, they think they're back in Minsk. I have to say, Look around you! Is this a city with a housing glut? They're behaving so badly. I suppose it's shock.'

They say that Dr Goebbels in the late summer of 1944 sent an album of air-raid damage photographs to Hitler, but that Martin Bormann sent them back to Goebbels with a note reading, 'The Führer has no time to occupy himself with irrelevancies of this nature.' I suppose I suffered from the same sort of detachment. I imagine myself as a small blond boy with a Slavic face sitting composedly in Frau Zusters' cellar while the Allies

pounded away at the Chancellery, the Reichstag, the War Ministry in Bendlerstrasse – in fact at the fabric of everything. This
child reads and even sleeps through the terrible noise, which
seems to occupy a great part of the day and a crucial segment
of the night. He spends most of his waking time looking through
Herr Zusters' stamp collections – the widow lets him take them
with him into the cellar. He wishes he could have known Mr
Zusters, who must have been a character. Between the wars
Zusters worked and collected stamps wherever there were
oil-fields – East and West Africa, the Persian Gulf, Mexico,
Borneo, Texas. In his photographs he wore long thin moustaches
and crooked ladykiller smiles. He had married a house-proud,
housebound girl, perhaps so that he knew there was an ordered
home in Charlottenburg waiting for him when he needed it. Now
he was another dead cowboy, like Onkel Willi.

I had my nightmares during the silences, the pauses in the
bombing, when in the small street it was almost as quiet as a
suburb in a time of peace. My mother associated the dreams
with the air-raids and with my Belorussian experiences. She
was wrong about the air-raids, right about the other. They were
not nightmares, to do with being under Oberführer Ganz's table,
but rather dreams of being riveted high in the corner while my
father bent amongst the shambles to extract *that* child from his
place beneath the cornered tablecloth.

My mother would discuss my bad dreams, the excessively
bad dreams, the ones involving trembling of the limbs and loss
of bladder control, with Frau Zusters. I was aware that they
were a comfort to each other, the two women, as, to quote
Frau Zusters' homely but exact image, the world fell apart like
a boiled onion. But it did not occur to me how scared they were,
how scared Genia and Miss Tokina her tutor might be. The
state of the city shocked the Kabbelski women. The great official
buildings all around Tiergarten were in ruins. In residential
streets grey-faced men and women in what had once been
good summer clothes pushed wheelbarrows loaded with broken
furniture. Everywhere very young or very antique firemen were
digging for the dead, or for those who might be happier dead,
the trapped. My mother had known things were bad in the East,

that the Russians were racing to the San and the Bug, but she had not expected such visible chaos at the heart.

Most of the bombed houses in the district were further to the east, Frau Zusters had noticed. She used the term 'further to the east' as if she were referring to Poland, instead of to collapsed houses only a block or two away, towards Moabit. Frau Zusters proposed that the survival of her house may have been due to its being only half a kilometre from the Charlottenburg palace. 'They are not total barbarians, you know,' she would tell my mother.

This axiom of Frau Zusters seemed to give the women no help once a raid began and they were forced to sit in the cellar, sometimes caressing, sometimes catatonically drawn back from each other. Yet though it may sound foolish, and in spite of the 10,000-kilo bombs the Allies would sometimes drop on the city, trying to crack the crucial cellar, the serpent's egg of a bunker where Hitler sat, there was no bomb capable of shaking the composure of *that* little boy, of the Kabbelski brat.

Except therefore for the nightmares and my envy of Bernhardt Kuzich, whose father had allowed him to be conscripted as an anti-aircraft gunner to a battery in the Grunewald, I was totally free of any destructive emotions, and looked forgivingly at the terror of the four women (my father only rarely there) with whom I was locked up every day.

We had special ration cards provided by the SS and most of our food was obtained by my father at canteens and stores around Alexanderplatz and brought home in the crowded limousine reserved for ministers of the Belorussian government in exile. One day, however, just for morale reasons, we all went out to queue for food with Frau Zusters, who had a normal ration card, as did Miss Tokina. All rations, theirs and ours, were then democratically pooled. My mother, as much as she appreciated the better quality meat and preserves my father brought home, had told Frau Zusters that she missed the therapy of shopping. The shopping queue, she said with an apologetic laugh, was the only way you could discover that you really *were* better off than others.

This day, a sharp morning in the autumn of 1944, Genia and I sat on a park wall opposite a grocer's while the women gratefully immersed themselves in the sisterhood of the food line, exchanging histories, particularly the histories of their menfolk. Genia and I noticed a squad of young men wearing some indefinite security uniform turn up in a Volkswagen at the door of a dental surgery two doors from the grocery. They rang the bell and, when the door was answered by an elderly man, pushed past him and into the building. They returned to the street quickly, dragging a young man in a surgical coat, the dentist, who hobbled unevenly into the centre of the street. One of the young gang addressed the shopping queue in an educated voice, 'This man has been spreading defeatism to his patients. You all know how it is, ladies. First he numbs their mouths and makes them open to full stretch. Then he breathes his poison into them.'

The young men then began to beat him, cracking him over either ear with truncheons, driving the blunt end of their sticks into his midriff. He fell crookedly, and with a metallic noise, to the paving. Genia left her perch beside me and ran into the street screaming at the young men in Belorussian, curses she had never learned at home. I remember that I focused at once on my mother over the road in the queue, saw her excusable instant of hesitation before she ran into the street and grabbed the spitting Genia around the upper body, begging pardon in accented German, saying, 'This poor child has had awful experiences in the East.' She dragged her back to the fence beside me, though I confess I did not want to be associated with the embarrassment. I understood perfectly why my mother had taken this direction, hauling Genia towards the park instead of into the queue. She was trying to emphasise that Genia was a mere child, beneath the age of queuing for essentials. That was embarrassing too, I knew the young squad would see straight through it.

But they paid me little attention. Before they crawled back into their car, they pulled up the dentist's left trouser leg to show an artificial lower leg and a strange metal knee. They unstrapped the brace which attached the apparatus to the dentist's body, lifted it and dropped it clanking across the man's stomach.

Genia was weeping. 'I've had enough. I'm going to live in Paris,' she told my mother and Frau Zusters. All the queue were looking at her, more than they were looking at the defeatist dentist. The sight of him raised the obvious question of who was going to restrap his leg and get him off the street. Whereas you could exercise a responsibility-free interest in that foreign girl over there.

'You're not going home?' my mother asked placidly.

'I'm going to live in Paris,' yelled Genia, 'and read all the time.' Some of the women in the queue laughed.

FORTY-THREE

Deecock, the first grade five-eighth, after coming off with nausea before half-time, was diagnosed as having a mild case of glandular fever. Late the following night the club secretary announced to the press, who were interested because the club had won four of the six they needed to achieve the semi-final berth, and who were throwing around such imagery as 'Cinderella team', that they were going to run young Terry Delaney at five-eighth next Sunday. It was a reward, Delaney could not help believing, not for virtue but for returning to the life cut out for him. His elevation seemed to put the Kabbels at a distance and served as a distraction from the ache for Danielle. It was a victory for his game over the games of such as Warwick.

There were two journalists and three photographers at the loading dock of Pioneer when he got there the next morning. 'Listen,' Greg told him, 'don't say you work here. Tell them you're helping me out. I don't want your mother carrying on because you're called a truckdriver in the newspapers.'

'What does she want me called? A computer expert?'

'I reckon she wouldn't object to that. This could be the start of good things for you. Don't let the world think you're some sort of rouse-about!'

The photographers, however, wanted to get him loading frozen dinners into the back of the truck. It was a standard device to interview newly promoted players at their workplace, toting barrels, carrying bricks, at the controls of an earthmover. Smiling on the tailboard he could see Greg staring wanly from his glass booth, beyond a line of other delivery men whistling and yelling, 'Show a bit of leg, Terry!'

Pioneer gave him Friday off, since Alan Beamish, the first grade coach, wanted the team to spend the day together looking at videos of Manly's last six games. Manly's fullback was poor under pressure and both their second-rowers played too wide, like centres, for most of the games. Their game plan was for the heavy men to take it up the middle and soften the defence, and then spread it wide and play merry hell. Above all their five-eighth, the old-timer Warren Thompson, wasn't to be given room to distribute the ball. Terry was to be given a private video showing of the way Thompson moved, backed up, and got away placement kicks. It had all been edited for him by one of the committee-men. The videos ran silently, no movie-projector clicking or ratchetting to distract the players from the essence of the enemy's game. The tension and glamour of first grade football! What Delaney learned, of course, was no more than he already knew, no more than Alan Beamish said to him late on Friday night. 'On his bad days he gets swamped by the defence. But on his good ones he's slippery as a pig in grease and he reads the play as if it was the bloody stock exchange report.'

It was one of Thompson's good days. Not at first. For the first ten minutes Delaney was relentlessly on him, smothering tackles under which the old international went down without struggling. It was as the videos had shown though – their big fast men probed up the middle to soften the defence and found it fragile. Then they picked up speed and threw high looping passes to the centres. Delaney could not believe the mysterious submissiveness of his own forwards – it reminded him of all the stories of rigged games, of players running dead. In reality, he was sure, it was a sudden loss of soul, and leading the moral decline was the vaunted Yorkshireman Tancred. After Manly's first try Delaney raged around the in goal listening to Tony Ellis, the captain, haranguing his failed pack. He wanted to yell, 'Don't pick today to run lame!' But he knew that wouldn't be tolerated. Their slackness could ruin him just the same. When short of breath and trying to swamp Thompson, he had the light-headed certainty that that incompetent Penrith pack could debase the game for him and raise the option of the Kabbels again. 'Fucking *tackle*!' he screamed at a prop who had once played for New South Wales, while a Manly second-rower broke two more tackles and scored near the posts.

When Delaney himself put up a little kick and regathered amongst the tired Manly forwards and danced over in the corner, the commentators said – so Gina would later tell him – it was a reward for not giving up all day. He should have been delighted, would have been a year ago. All that entered his mind was: small rewards. There wasn't enough nourishment in them.

They played him one more time in firsts, a successful game against Cronulla in which he played adequately but without ridding himself of that malignant doubt placed in him by his own pack, six forwards lacking speed and heart and grandeur. Then Deecock recovered from his mild bout of fever and Delaney was returned to reserves. It was a matter of course, involving no culpability on Delaney's part. Greg Delaney seemed to suspect though that his son had been given two chances to play blinders and had decided instead just to play well. Delaney himself felt he had been taken to the heart of things and had found it hollow. He made up for it in reserve grade with a new unremitting toughness and a high tackle count, which delighted the reserve grade coach. 'Bit of the true Panther, eh, Terry?'

Stanton found him in the club after training one night. 'Buy an old mate a beer?' said Stanton. It was a stratagem to get Delaney to the bar alone. 'I'm out on my arse,' said Stanton. 'None of the big blokes bought Uncle – they've stopped buying into the little stuff, they don't need to. Crime's booming.'

'The Kabbels are keeping it on?' asked Delaney.

'They're walking away from it. They're taking the computer and scanner with them when they go bush. What a bloody crowd! They just let the clientele fall away and the house is on the market, and that's it.' He lowered his voice as if letting go of the final secret. 'The job market's tighter than last time we did this. Yet they talk about bloody recovery, the newspapers are full of recovery talk. Will you ask your old man if there's anything?'

Delaney said he would. He knew there was nothing. Stanton was the married man for whom Greg Delaney had wanted to keep Delaney's job.

'They're just walking away from Parramatta?' Delaney asked, returning to the Kabbel question.

'Just strolling off with apologies. Like I said, haven't seen Rudi for weeks.'

'Danielle's there still?' Delaney couldn't stop himself asking.

Stanton looked away, staring at a wall of team photographs, the slick-haired players of the '50s, the close-cropped foot-ballers of the early '60s and, from Vietnam on, a range of styles, the wild long-hairs and those with unisexed locks. Stanton took stock of all these teams grinning, flashing the combined radiance of their expected triumph.

'What about Danielle?' Delaney insisted.

'Danielle's pregnant,' said Stanton. 'But listen, they're not up in arms about it. I'd sit tight if I were you.'

Delaney drank calmly. It was the word he had been waiting for though. Everything he'd thought solid – marriage, two runs in first grade – had run to water. His fatherhood dominated all. And there was this added in: Danielle would not protect herself from the other Kabbels, but she *would* protect a child.

'It mightn't be yours,' said Stanton.

'Don't tell me that, Brian. Don't give me that incest bullshit. It's not on. I don't want to hear it.'

'Jesus, you don't meet many men who want to claim a bastard.'

Delaney envisaged the child. It would be born fair. When it was two it would show its mother's solemn smile. Joy briefly distracted him, as Stanton could tell.

'Sling her a bit of money if you like. First graders can afford that. But don't turn your life upside down.'

Delaney took a $20 bill from his pocket. It had always been such an unaccustomed denomination that its sandstone orange hue signified bounty to him. He pushed it towards the pocket on Stanton's shirt.

'Listen, let me . . .'

'Not on your sweet life,' said Stanton, knocking his hand away. 'Listen, I have my plans.'

Delaney wanted to make friendly declarations – I won't let your kids go without or want things at Christmas. But he knew Stanton couldn't tolerate that sort of thing. Across the bar one of the heftier poker machines began to bleat like a siren and flash garishly. In imitation of all human forms of relief, hundreds of coins fell from its maw into its metal tray. A middle-aged man wearing a business suit looked across the bar at Stanton and Delaney, as if inviting them to share in his self-congratulation. An Australian hero. A jackpot winner.

FORTY-FOUR

September 18, 1944 – Berlin

Have neglected journal. Busier here than ever in Staroviche or
Minsk. Am treated as de facto housing officer by all wives of all
members of Belorussian council. Mrs Hrynkievich wants me to
complain to SS about her blocked cistern. Ostrowsky seems
amused by my predicament. Told me, 'See how much trouble
you're saving me!'

Another major part of duty is dealing with Dr Franz Hilger,
the Foreign Office's liaison with the SS on matters to do with
émigrés and governments in exile. Hilger from the same mould
as our old associate Kappeler. His doctorate is in humanities,
like Kappeler's, like Stankievich's, for that matter. For some
reason too long an association with the humanities, which are
meant to make man subtle and humane, seems to stultify people.
Hilger has trouble, given his lack of understanding of our history,
in distinguishing us from Russians. In conversation with me,
throws out such lines as, 'All you Russians show the same
stubbornness!' Cannot understand, despite repeated explanations, why we will not affiliate with NTS, the Alliance of
Russian National Solidarists, a council of aging White Russian
officers who have waited here and in Paris for the Great Return,
who thought it was at hand in 1941, and who for different reasons
think it is at hand today. If returned to Moscow, they'd consider
Belorussia their front garden, as they always have.

'I want to bring all the Russian émigré groups under the one
umbrella,' Dr Hilger tells me, as if we're being abstruse and

untidy to oppose it. The fact that history, religion and culture all cry out against such neat bureaucratic mergers means nothing to the man.

Hilger also keeps sending round all the others – the Ukrainians, the Estonians, even a Dutch fascist council – to look at our model operation. A united and factionless government in exile!

Have grown to like and admire Abramtchik, whose office is along the corridor. Met there a German officer Otto Skorzeny, famous for his rescue of Mussolini last year. Skorzeny apparently training young officers of Belorussian Defence Force for infiltration behind Soviet lines. This an indication that Ostrowsky considers all talk of Abramtchik's Soviet connections to be mere talk. Otherwise would not make him minister responsible for such an enterprise.

Drove out to Dahlwitz to look over this training camp with Abramtchik at latter's invitation. Camp very impressive and intense. 'I can create havoc along the Polish-Belorussian border,' says Skorzeny, walking us down the orderly paths amongst the pines. Felt an absolute lust, after the chaos and sourness of the city, to be here instead, in this well-scrubbed camp with its air of a mission, of certainty, of brave confidence; to stay here and learn encoding and how to destroy a railway bridge.

Met squad who are going in first. They call themselves Black Cats. Led by young police officer from Vitebsk, Mikhail Vitushka, a fine type, a practical intellectual. He and his party, parachuted in, will stay there, operating from those same ancient forests which were the strength of the Soviet partisans, until the Allied armies arrive. In Staroviche there will be a Soviet police chief whose problems over the next year will mirror my recent ones!

Abramtchik and Vitushka tell me Redich has been out here a lot to Dahlwitz discussing with the Black Cat squad how to set up secret organisations in the villages and towns. Apparently sees the *relocating* of the Black Cats into the Berezhina forest as within his area of concern. Would be more useful if he applied himself to relocation of Mrs Stankievich into an apartment of her choice. On way back home, Abramtchik began to speak to

me quite freely about what he sees as Ostrowsky problem. 'The
Germans will train saboteurs for Ostrowsky, but will the Allies
continue the training?' he asked.

It had been such a pleasant day I felt emboldened to answer,
'They will if you vouch for him.'

Abramtchik laughed. 'Can you see Pope Pius setting up a
parachute school in the Vatican for an Orthodox Belorussian?'

'I can't see the Pope doing *that* for anybody.'

'You're wrong,' he told me. 'The Pope has undertaken to be
host within the Vatican to a training school for loyal Belorussian
Catholics.' He began laughing. 'I can show you the correspondence or arrange a meeting for you with the Papal Nuncio in
Berlin.' He gestured with a hand, deliberately overdoing it. 'We
shall drop from the skies like angels!'

Astounded at this news but did best to hide it.

'I don't want Ostrowsky to fritter all these chances we have,'
said Abramtchik.

Asked how Ostrowsky would do that. Abramtchik replied O
would do it by committing our twenty thousand soldiers too fully
to set piece battles against the Americans or British.

'I would be very grateful,' Abramtchik told me, 'if as means
of employing the Belorussian battalions are suggested to our
good Orthodox friend by the War Ministry and the SS, you could
inform me of the nature of such suggestions and directives. I
take it you approve of the Vatican and the French, and even the
Americans, ultimately training our men. If it's to happen, I
should know what pressures are being put on Ostrowsky by the
Germans so that I can apply corrective pressure.'

Implication is Ostrowsky is easy meat for the Germans.
Abramtchik does not understand how O fought Himmler for
control of the Belorussian battalions. They now carry the title
Waffen Sturmbrigade Belarus and are under Ostrowsky's control. And all this, I felt like saying, achieved without reference
to the Vatican! It is true though that War Ministry want to throw
them in against Americans. It makes sense that Abramtchik be
kept informed of real developments, not just of the developments
Ostrowsky and Franz Kushel decide to pass on to other ministers
at cabinet meetings.

Strangely, sensible decision to pass on intelligence to Abramtchik tastes like betrayal on the palate. And this despite fact Ostrowsky has betrayed me beforehand.

FORTY-FIVE

The house in Parramatta from which Uncle Security had operated carried a 'For Sale By Auction' sign with a date which had already passed. Diagonally across it a red and white 'Sold' sticker had been pasted, so that all the sign did now was satisfy the pride of the estate agent. Delaney noticed the notation 4 B/rms and suffered an image of the gold and blue pennant of the Sisters of Mercy declaring Danielle's triumph in the Under-15 800 metres. The sweat and tension of that contest, forgotten by now by the nuns themselves, struck him like a fragrance, like something uncorked she had left behind her when packing up.

He drove over the Blue Mountains the next Saturday morning. The lies were on again: he told Gina it was a conditioning run at Katoomba for the whole team, who had a bye that weekend. It was credible. Some of the forwards needed it. He crossed the mountains morbidly. The switchbacks above Lithgow, which he had once greeted as a trying ground, going into them with a Nikki Lauda style, terrified him, looked set to silence him before he'd spoken to the two women who had to be spoken to. When the suicide bends at last brought him down to the plains, he turned north. Either side of the road, which soon turned to dirt, great grey ledges of sandstone rose covered with dull green foliage – 'ancient, ancient', as Gina had said at the lighthouse. Farms looked large and vacant, the sort of farms at whose core, in the farmhouse kitchen, sat a crotchety owner with a shotgun to hand. It had never been a great place for crops and cattle, but that gave it its grandeur and a loneliness which, if you were pushing down this rock-based red-dust road for the fun of it, you could find lovely and intriguing and say to your wife, 'I wish we had a weekender here!'

This was the country you would choose to hide in too if you

were certain the world would unravel. It was easy to believe *this* would remain no matter what else befell the balance of the world. He stopped at the pub at Newnes to ask about the Kabbels, and a tanned cooperative drinker wearing a blue singlet drew a map for him. 'Little shack on two acres,' said the drinker, drawing a roof.

'He's got more than two acres now though.'

'Not yet. Bought up all the country behind, Heather's Gully it's called. But they haven't got round to exchanging contracts.'

The road got so rough that Delaney wondered how the stone marks and the dust on his car could be explained to Gina. The cliffs narrowed in to verge the road, gum tree roots grew thick and sinewy across its surface, and his car ascended and descended platforms of rock. At last he had to leave it for fear his sump would be punctured, his muffler cracked. He began to jog, watching his feet. A professional shouldn't run in uneven country, but the breath of night was in this defile. He wanted to be back at the car by dark.

At a point where a cliff rose on his left and another fell away below him on his right, he came on the gate. It sported an orderly sign, good lettering, none of the consonants running from too much turpentine. 'R. W. D. S. Kabbel – Trespassing Prohibited'. You could vault it, but was there a minefield beyond? The Kabbels had taught him to ask questions of that kind. You could jiggle the lock but would it leave you with your thumb intact? He was a professional footballer and his limbs were his fortune. Even if they weren't, the gate terrified him, and he looked over the edge of the road, into a gully already filling with turquoise shadow, and felt an urgency to get out, hose his car, sit with Gina all evening.

For the child's sake he levered himself upright on the crossbar of the gate and saw down into a widening valley, a natural pen, a perfect pound, gulch, hole-in-the-wall. Down in the bed of the pound, sheltered by she-oaks, an old low-sunk farmhouse waited with vacant windows. No smoke came from its chimney. There were no farm boots lying around drying on its verandah. Behind it on a rise sat a newer structure – cement-based, steel-framed – you could see the steel roof-tree emerging from the eaves.

Secure, well-ventilated, waterproof. 'If they store it anywhere damp,' the CID man had told him, 'you'll be playing five-eighth in a wheelchair.' But the Kabbels had too much professionalism to store it somewhere unsafe. Especially if the kingdom afterwards depended on it.

People would drag their desperate limbs up this road only to have them blown off by Warwick. They talked in those terms, bearded and well-built young men Delaney saw on the satellite news, infecting the world with their cool blue-eyed panic. They had no doubt that once the wave struck or the sun fell they would have to defend their chosen acre against those other members of the race who stumbled up to the fence. They couldn't wait. You needed a wealth of landmines, plastic, shotgun pellets, because the darkness – or so they boasted – would last an age.

Delaney began to call but knew there was no one there. His voice went racing away into that gorge beyond the house, into that unownable country on which the contracts had not yet been exchanged.

FORTY-SIX

He met Doig in the new coffee shop opened in Main Street that winter by two women rumoured to be lesbians and so, in Penrith terms, fantastic creatures. Doig, boyish in his white shirt with the crosses on its collar, seemed to enjoy a rapport with them he lacked with many of his older parishioners. 'Their carrot cake is a ripper,' he confided to Delaney, and Delaney dutifully ordered some.

After a handsome girl in overalls and headscarf had served them, Delaney tried to explain that Doig was the only neutral party he could talk to. He rushed to say he did not seek confession, or what they called these days 'the rite of reconciliation'.

Doig put a firm hand on Delaney's elbow and spoke urgently through the residue of crumbs which had half glued his mouth up. 'Wherever two friends talk to each other,' he said, 'that is a rite of reconciliation.'

It was September, and what Danielle called 'his game' was over. Delaney had played in the semi-finals – again it was only the third graders who carried the honour of Penrith to the Cricket Ground. There were rumours that Alan Beamish, the first grade coach, would be sacrificed in the manner of unproductive generals in armies and football teams, would be replaced by an old international from Queensland, and would take into exile in his hometown, Cobar, the blame for the failure of all strategies. He would also take away with him a regard for Terry Delaney. After Deecock's fumbling season, a new coach would probably make it one of the conditions of his contract that he be let go, and being unfamiliar with reserves such as Delaney, would probably have some Queenslander in mind as a replacement.

This scale of development would have once put Delaney into

a fever. Now it seemed a minor matter. What was significant was that the Kabbels had vanished from the earth. On weekends he tried to trace them at the pub at Newnes, but they were not in residence in their sandstone canyon. Yes, said all the drinkers, contracts had been exchanged now, settlement had taken place. Did any of them know if the Kabbels had used a local solicitor to manage the purchase for them? A lawyer from Lithgow, say? No, none of them knew that.

It seemed to Delaney that the place in the wilderness was reserved only for after the catastrophe. So, where were they dug in now? He called directory assistance for Sydney and Penrith every day in the hope that a telephone had been connected. Now and then he would call a string of county councils – waiting for the wave, the Kabbels would need electricity. He would pretend to be a clerk in a hire purchase company. As he told the story, one R. Kabbel had applied for a hire purchase agreement on a refrigerator and he wanted to know if R. Kabbel paid his electricity account punctually. With some councils it worked, but there were no Kabbels, no Uncles, not under any initials. No Kabbels at all. No Kabbels switching lights on anywhere.

Delaney explained all this to Doig. Coffee grew cold as Delaney stated what had to be done. He had to leave Gina. Even if the Kabbels had disappeared for ever – and he knew they hadn't – the claim of Danielle and the baby made Gina's life awful, absolutely bloody degrading.

'Claim?' asked Doig. 'What sort of claim?'

'To be rescued,' said Delaney. 'You know. From the other Kabbels.' The urgency took him over once more, making acid in his stomach as he spoke. 'Rudi Kabbel believes there'll be something – a wave or a flood or some damn thing – which will finish off the known world. Then the Kabbels will be king. He'll breed – or the brothers will breed – from his own daughter. The idea of that sort of thing is in the bugger's head already. Where does that put my child, Andrew? Eh? Tell me that.'

Doig asked the usual questions. If the Kabbels thought like that, was he sure the child was his?

'It's certainly mine,' he said.

'Why certainly?' asked Doig. 'From what you say . . .'

Delaney felt he could not convey his instincts about Danielle, not to a priest or even to a swinging heretic like Doig.

'Gina can live on if the marriage finishes. It's the other two who don't have a future.'

Doig said, 'Are you telling me you're going to give up a marriage so that you can dedicate yourself to a search for people who might have gone anywhere – Tasmania, New Zealand? They're both good places to await the end of the world in.'

'No. The Kabbels are still here. They've bought land on the other side of the mountains. For when it happens, you know. And it won't happen. So what will Rudi do then?'

Doig groaned. It struck Delaney for the first time that Doig might be a man of compassion and not just a fashionable priest in an unfashionable parish. 'You may have to leave this girl and her child to destiny, Terry. You have a marriage contract, and *that* is binding. Whereas your responsibility to the girl is vague.'

'No,' Delaney said. 'Sorry. It's the other way around. For Christ's sake, it's the kid, don't you see? I can't let it be born into that lunatic family.'

'What if Gina had a child?' Doig seemed for a second pleased with himself for coming up with this new and unsettling idea. 'Yours? What would that do to your plans?'

Delaney shook his head. It was obvious Doig believed a crucial blow had been landed.

'Pardon me if I speak like an old-fashioned priest,' he said.

He didn't want to, was fearful that Delaney would storm out. In fact Delaney was excited that at last Doig might be about to do his professional duty, bring down on him a condemnation he could react to, use as a springboard. 'Look,' said Doig, 'I blame the church for a lot of this.'

So he reneged instantly on his promise of severity.

He said, 'You are taught from babyhood that sex can destroy you. If you believe it, then you'll be destroyed. *I* have been nearly destroyed in my time, believe me.' He paused and inspected the bowl of amber sugar crystals. 'But sex is a matter of rational negotiation, like buying a car or a house. You have to be deliberately calm. If you think you're going off to save this woman, Delaney, don't make it a matter of fated destiny, of rescue on a grand scale. You're going off for your own sake. Because there *are* other possibilities. You can rescue her and not marry her. You can support the child without leaving Gina. You see, a rational balance.' Doig frowned. 'Do you get what I'm saying?'

'I can't do it that way.'

'No. Because the church told you your sexual passions were runaway monsters which would tear your house down. You have to tear your house down now that the monster is out of its cave. Now that there's such a thing as desire, you have to throw Gina away.'

'She won't stand for it. Support of a bastard. Support of a girlfriend or an old girlfriend. She can't take that, and I can't hide it from her.'

'Bring her to me, Delaney. The two of you . . .'

'No. No.' Didn't he understand anything about Italians? 'She couldn't take the shame.'

Doig pushed his chair away from the table. 'You've decided she can't.'

'No. I know she can't.'

Doig grabbed Delaney's wrist. 'I want you to bring her to me. We'll make an arrangement, the three of us.'

His belief that he could make a peace they could live by was so child-like Delaney did not like to trample on it. But he knew there wasn't any compact anyone could draw up. 'I'll see if she'll be in it, Andrew,' Delaney lied.

FORTY-SEVEN

FROM THE JOURNALS OF STANISLAW KABBELSKI, CHIEF OF POLICE,

STAROVICHE

February 2, 1945 – Berlin

The lieutenant we visited today at Dahlwitz in bad way with pulmonary inflammation and thigh wound. He lies in his own room in infirmary at commando school. He would be better off surrounded by other humans in a general ward, but his superiors believe he would spread alarm.

Last time I was at Dahlwitz was just prior to Christmas, when out there with Ostrowsky to review Black Cats and other Belorussian operatives soon to be parachuted home. Atmosphere then very sanguine, confidence high, men looked magnificent. Hard to believe the proud personnel of that day have been reduced to this one gibbering officer.

He looked up from bed at us and said, 'You can't go back, no one can go back! No use threatening agents we left behind, no use saying go on working for us or we'll spill the beans to the Soviets. The Soviets know everything. I tell you, every damned thing!'

This statement of faith, delivered from clogged lungs and a constricted throat contracted during what must have been a pitiless and unhingeing escape through the frozen Belovezh forest, across Poland, across occupied Germany, flashing forged papers, hiding his thigh wound, surviving by wit. Now his wit is at an end.

Ostrowsky sat beside him like an uncle, calming him. In no time the boy was again calling him Mr President. 'Tell us precisely what you believe the problems are back there,' asked Ostrowsky soothingly. 'In the homeland.'

The boy began by weeping, but his account was clear. Clear too that what has happened to Black Cats is largest Belorussian reversal since last December at Biscenson, when Germans unwisely insisted on throwing the Belarus brigades up against General Patton's armour in a blessedly brief encounter. (For which, of course, Abramtchik unjustly blames Ostrowsky.)

His face therefore a mess of tears and unnatural sweat, the lieutenant began to tell us how the Soviets manage security. The lieutenant and his squad parachuted into the Kaminetz area on midwinter's night. They had been given the names of Belorussian loyalists still supposedly to be found in the villages north of the Pripet and the Bug. They found the villages totally deserted and empty of food. It had been intended that they live off the villages. Now, within two days of landing in the woods, they were in a desperate and famished condition. They moved north looking for Vitushka's platoon. On the way they met a very frightened, very elderly charcoal burner, living with his wife in a hovel in the woods, who told them that the Russians had simply cleared the area. Along the Belorussian-Polish border, they had emptied every village and relocated the villagers in encampments to the east. Hence they now knew that anyone found in the woods was a fascist spy. The old man and his wife, who had escaped this extraordinary relocation, were terrified that that would be *their* fate.

Starving and ill from exposure, the lieutenant and his men located Vitushka in the woods near the Pruzhany road. Vitushka confirmed the old man's story. Along a border of two hundred kilometres, and to a depth of seventy kilometres, everything had been cleared. Ostrowsky agents in the villages had been executed. Travel by urban people in Grodno, Kaminetz, Brest, Kobrin and so on was not permitted. The city dwellers were locked up, the villagers were gone.

Could not help feeling an awe and admiration for such a degree of thoroughness. This *is* relocation on a scale which would be beyond my resources and Redich's gifts.

The boy related that a supplies drop on New Year's Eve and a few successfully stalked stags saved them from starvation. It was apparent, however, that they had a choice only between dying in perfect security in the forests or trying to contact Ostrowsky agents in the cities.

Moving south now they encountered a Russian patrol-in-strength at night while trying to cross the Brest Litovskiy-Minsk highway. Only six of them escaped death or capture and, after two more cruel days had passed, stood on the northern outskirts of the city of Kobrin. Vitushka and two others decided to penetrate the city and make contact with the Ostrowsky cell there while the wounded lieutenant and the others waited in the woods. Vitushka, he said, had behaved very well through all their sufferings. When he could, he did his party trick, which was to sing black American jazz songs in a gravelly Negroid voice. The lieutenant described how in his peasant coat, Vitushka emerged from the woods on an edge of a country road. Away in the dimness of late afternoon was that most miserable of low-lying Belorussian towns with its shabby wooden suburbs and its unkempt timber mills. And Vitushka stood there for a moment singing for the benefit of the two going with him, and the others who would wait, 'Please Don't Talk About Me When I'm Gone.'

During the night one of the lieutenant's two companions swallowed his cyanide pill. It was after dark the next night before one of Vitushka's small party turned up again. He too was ready to end his life. Soviets had a ten thousand-man intelligence division in the town – at least one man attached to each household. Nothing in the slightest way remarkable could happen in Kobrin or in any of the border cities. Vitushka and one of his men had approached the Kobrin address given them during their training at Dahlwitz and had been instantly captured. The third man, the one who had now reached the woods again in a state of moral collapse, had been posted in the doorway of a grocery shop and had seen the arrest. He had instantly tried to cover his connection to Vitushka by showing his papers to the grocer and buying one of the few items which were for sale – a can of pickled cucumbers. These he took to a timber yard, where he spent a miserable night in hiding. Somehow he talked his way through a patrol next afternoon. By then loudspeakers were announcing that the fascist Vitushka and one of his lieutenants would be publicly paraded through Kobrin and that the parade would be filmed by a newsreel camera crew.

The lieutenant lost one more of his companions through suicide and another was shot by a Russian sentry near Bialystok.

Ostrowsky continued to comfort the lieutenant during our time with him today, but we need no intelligence officer to explain to us the significance of the boy's experiences. Belorussia must be recaptured frontally. It cannot be recaptured by infiltration. The President's network of agents has been obliterated.

Ostrowsky continued to hide his true feelings from me. Atmosphere dismal in the car returning to Alexanderplatz. On arrival the President asked me not to go home yet but to join him for a drink in his office. Matey drinking after office hours was not at all characteristic of him, and the oddity of the request made me accept.

Poured the vodka himself, rather quickly, in case I changed my mind and went home to Danielle. Both of us drank first shot at the same hectic pace. As they say, if ever men needed it . . .

Ostrowsky said, 'There are agents, Soviet agents, working amongst us. It is amply apparent that they're from the other faction.'

Wondered if it was amply apparent, but Ostrowsky too tired and heartsick to argue with.

'It's essential the Americans don't find this out. We must be able to offer them networks. We can tell them later the networks have gone and have to be rebuilt. But in the first instance, at the first meeting with them, they must not know what happened to Vitushka or what the lieutenant found out.' The proposition that it is as well the lieutenant will not live to meet the Americans hung for a moment in the air.

Remarked that the Soviets themselves might let the United States know. But Ostrowsky is sure that the Americans will believe us and not their Godless and temporary allies.

'Two men,' he said, 'of whom I can be sure neither have Soviet affiliations. Yourself and Hrynkievich.'

Do not consider it a compliment being compared to

Hrynkievich, who runs Belorussian self-help here in Berlin. The good Dr Hrynkievich cunning, venal, not very clever.

'I call upon you again, Stanek, for something of a special contribution. At a given moment, I would like yourself and Hrynkievich to go as my representatives and to make contact with the Americans, preferably with Patton, in Bavaria.'

Proposal is of course attractive. But thought at once of Danielle. Asked a question which in my goodwill towards Ostrowsky I would never once have asked. 'Hrynkievich to lead the mission?'

Ostrowsky nodded. 'He has seniority as my Minister of Welfare.'

Mentioned to Ostrowsky Danielle's unease about the coming flight from Berlin. Her anxiety would treble if she knew I would be gone somewhere to the West and that she had to make it unaccompanied.

He poured another glass of liquor like a supplicant. He would be very grateful, he told me.

As I drank second glass, became increasingly enraged at him. He would shackle me to a barely competent minister like Hrynkievich and send me out on the roads of Bavaria to offer the Americans a non-existent agent network. Later he might be able to say to General Patton, 'After all, I cannot be responsible for what a fool and a junior minister tell you.'

Idea was that I should discuss the thing with Danielle and give Ostrowsky an answer – no doubt a positive answer – in the morning. As I drank, found the true answer came out of my mouth of its own accord. 'I regret, Mr President, that any idea of leaving Danielle behind me in Berlin would amount to a betrayal worse than adultery.'

'But I would see her safely to the West when the appropriate moment came,' he assured me.

Delighted to find myself unrelenting. 'I am afraid that those are guarantees that in the circumstances would bring her no comfort, Mr President.'

Leaving his office, felt more of a free agent than I have in a dozen years. In back of car on way home, found myself saying aloud, 'Let him send Redich.'

FORTY-EIGHT

As the weather turned humid, Delaney found his own flat in St Mary's. Gina resisted the urge to return to Bringelly and adopt the status of wronged child, preferring to live on in Penrith as a wronged woman, too proud, however, to speak openly of the damage which had been done to her. Delaney's flat was one bedroom, no phone. He had to continue his search for the Kabbels from public telephone booths. He drove a $1,500 Holden with rust problems. You had to avoid poking it with your index finger lest you knock a hole in the door panelling.

In it he travelled around Parramatta, looking in ethnic coffee bars for Kabbel's Belorussian 'uncle', the one he'd heard about from Danielle and from Kabbel himself. Swarthy men of indefinable origins watched him, his Celtic fairness, as he approached the bar-owner and asked did he know a man called Kabbel, a Belorussian who perhaps visited and chatted with any elderly relatives the proprietor might have. Searching for a Belorussian coffee-shop owner with an uncle he travelled as far east as Auburn, even though they were mainly Turks and Armenians there.

With half an absent mind on his career he went to his parents' place for dinner twice a week, knowing that the dormant player within him needed Mrs Delaney's comprehensive meals. An air of baffled forgiveness made the evenings painful. Once Mrs Delaney stood over him and asked plaintively was there any chance of he and Gina reconciling, but then fled the kitchen in tears as he prepared a flinching answer. Old Greg poured Delaney a beer and said, 'You've got to remember the sort of place Penrith was when your mother and I were young. You could walk for miles, pass gate after gate, fence after fence, and every adult was married and stayed married.' Old Greg winked.

'Of course, there was plenty of misery and boredom though. Not hard to come across the old misery!'

Delaney played cricket on Saturdays for the sake of his sanity. He had once liked to believe that if he'd had an inch or two more in height he would have been a good pace bowler. He was beyond such vanities now. But his medium-pace deliveries, the occasional wrong'un thrown in, earned him some respect from local batsmen.

On a night of berserk heat in January, Delaney sat on the apron-sized balcony of his bachelor flat drinking beer and watching the migraine-yellow lights along the highway. On such a night he had first met Kabbel, and this happened to be very nearly the anniversary. Somewhere out to sea, beyond the harbour, a merciful south wind was said (just as on that night of the meeting with Kabbel) to be gathering itself. The Penrith squads were already in training in this sub-tropical stew of humid air for a winter which seemed even more remote than the promised cleansing wind. When his door knocked he went to it without enthusiasm. It was Stanton, sweat standing up in globules all over his face. One of his arms was thrust up against the door jamb for support and he was panting. His left hand held a shopping bag.

'I'm sick,' he said. He ran to the tiny bathroom – it sported in fact no bath, just a basin, a loo, a shower, with space between them for someone slim. Delaney heard Stanton run his hip against the rim of the basin. He did that himself every time for the first few weeks. While the shopping bag stood abandoned in the middle of the hallway, Stanton was sick near the base of the water closet and lay for a time gasping, with his head against the cool tiles. Delaney went and got him some iced water. On the way with it he toppled the bag with his foot, and could make out inside it notes in bunched form and the muzzle of something like the .38 with which he and Stanton had armed themselves every night of their career at Kabbel's.

'Bloody hell!' Delaney said. 'You've done it.'

It was Stanton's office in life to talk about these things. You had to have other talents altogether to *do* them.

Stanton seemed to agree. He began to weep. 'I've been hurt

once before. Hurt a dozen times if you count the bloody scars. I'm shit-scared of bodily damage.' His face contorted further. 'I can't do any more of them. I can't do any more of the bastards.'

'How many have you done, for Christ's sake?'

'This is the second. I *had* to do one at Christmas, Terry. The kids don't understand economy. It's those bloody irresponsible television people. They show the kids one goodie after another on the bloody box. There's no mention of these things costing cash – the message is that everyone has these things as a matter of bloody course. I stole a Commodore in Villawood and held up a service station in Liverpool. I didn't mind that one. The bloke was a student or something – he was reading an accounting textbook. It was like doing business. I asked for the money and he gave it to me very politely. Only $380 – they have people running around to those places all night so that the money doesn't accumulate in the till. The boy knew what it was worth, knew what the exchange rate was. I was buying Christmas and he was buying a future in a nice brick house in North Rocks and a nice wife and two ankle-biters. A really sensible, business-like kid! Listen, Delaney, do you have scotch or brandy or something?'

'Come outside,' said Delaney. The bathroom did not smell fresh.

'I'll clean it up after my scotch,' Stanton offered, rising painfully from the tiles. His face was still swollen and muddied with tears. The picture of a man doing his duty as parent, husband, wild colonial boy.

Outside, at the doll's table large enough, as Delaney often told himself, for four anorexic Vietnamese, he poured some whisky for Stanton. He had placed Stanton's bag at *that* end of the table, against his friend's leg. Stanton's match fees, appearance money, premiership bonus. 'And tonight's little raid?' Delaney asked.

'Stole a car in a quiet street in Lalor Park, drove it to Wentworthville – a little too far, I reckon – and another service station. This bloke scared me. He was on speed or something. They reckon those blokes are dangerous to be mugged by, but it's dangerous to hold them up too, they're likely to do anything.

He obeyed everything I said but he kept laughing in a slow, stupid way, as if he had an alarm or a weapon behind the counter. He was slow and bloody theatrical as hell emptying the till – it was more than $600 – and when I was running to the car I was sure he'd do me some harm, shoot me in the back or run after me with a knife. I was in a hell of a fright – otherwise I would have thought to lock him in the men's loo. Had an awful drive back to Lalor Park, to where I'd left my car. I was wearing driving gloves, see. In this weather! Not during the hold-up, but driving.' Because his fingerprints were filed from his days as a cop and his career as a security man. 'I would have stuck out like a dog's balls if a patrol car came alongside.'

Tears appeared in Stanton's eyes again. The man was ready for a merciful hospital, a sanatorium. Delaney told him he could loan him $50 a week, and pride temporarily seized up Stanton's tear ducts. A loan, a loan, Delaney insisted. Till April. One of Pioneer's older hands was retiring in April. (It was at least a fantasy and at best a chance that Stanton would get the vacancy if old Greg could be mobilised to use his influence.)

'Look at it this way. You can't do any more of these Ned Kelly stunts. You've nearly killed yourself tonight fetching home $600, and that's less than $30 a week between now and April. Take a loan from a mate for more, eh? It's less dangerous.'

So now, Delaney realised in bewilderment, I am maintaining three homes, and I won't get a match fee till the end of next month.

The whisky and the release from fear seemed to make Stanton sentimental. 'You're a fucking saint,' said Stanton.

'That's about right.'

Then Stanton hard-headedly asked Delaney to keep the cash for him. In case the police were waiting for him outside the house in Emu Plains. He was sure they weren't. If Delaney did it that way though, he could put it in envelopes and hand it to the Stantons in instalments with his weekly loan. Then Denise wouldn't have to worry where in the hell the sudden money had come from.

'And the gun?' asked Delaney.

'I'll take that. I've got a licence.' If the police were waiting, he said, he'd tell them he'd been out to the Gap, contemplating suicide. 'Not far from the bloody truth,' he said.

That is a moral lever I must use with old Greg. Stanton, in spite of his terror of scarring, talked like someone with suicide in mind. 'If driven to extremes of want,' Delaney later found himself saying aloud, as if rehearsing for conversations with his father. (He was then rinsing the surrounds of the loo with Pine-O-Cleen and had a handkerchief tied over his face for fear the stench would unsettle him.) 'If driven to extremes of want,' he repeated, soothed by the muffled words.

He had not considered how hard it would be to hide the money. At last he packed it inside the screw-on base of a trophy he had won as a schoolboy. He would have an explanation – savings, match fees.

He was still awake and dreaming of Danielle's rescue when the southerly raged in from the sea and through the balcony window, upsetting one of the lightweight chairs.

'They were here,' said Delaney's source at the Newnes pub when Delaney visited it the following Saturday. Delaney had begun to beg off cricket so that he could come searching for the Kabbels in Heather's Glen more often. 'Looked like they'd come to stay – two cars towing two trailers.'

But they'd left two days later, said the man. Same arrangement – two cars, two trailers, the four of them.

Delaney pressed some dollars into the man's hand. 'Call me reversed charges as soon as they come back.'

He fled the bar. He desired the loneliness of the drive back across the mountains. In the space it gave him he believed he could puzzle out this brief Kabbel apparition. But more than an hour later, driving down Main Street, he had still not been able to discern any meaning to it.

FORTY-NINE

FROM RADISLAW KABBEL'S HISTORY OF THE KABBELSKI FAMILY

Yuri was the genius of our escape to the West. He arrived outside Frau Zusters' house in Charlottenburg, Berlin, one evening in late April 1945. The passenger seat in the front was piled high with ordnance maps and my father was alone in the back, sharing the vehicle with no other member of the Belorussian government in exile. I noticed this exclusivity at once. In spite of the noise from the east of the city, it signified something like a return to normality. My father had filled the boot of the car with ham and tea and cognac. I suspect that behind the lightshades, the upholstery, even the hubcaps of the vehicle, he had placed a few further small treasures, bullion or diamonds, though being a genuinely political man he had never owned much of either. Neither he nor Yuri carried any weapons. It was, as Yuri would say during the journey, like farting in the wind, carrying weapons at a time like this. My father's intention was to reach the salient in the south, cut out by General Patton's Third US Army, and to surrender to them, to the sundry John Waynes, to the chewers of grass, gum, and tobacco whom I had last seen just before the war in indelibly remembered films at the Paris cinema in Warsaw.

My father and I fitted in the front with the ordnance maps. My mother, Genia and Miss Tokina took the rear seat. There was room for Frau Zusters, but she was so firmly identified with the house that none of us expected her to join us. Neither did she, though she wept and speculated on destiny.

I mentioned Yuri's genius earlier. He worked us south past the wreckage of houses and automobiles, towards the point where the Kurfurstendamm turns south on the edge of the

Grunewald, the woods where Bernhardt Kuzich would tonight, as he had been doing all day, send flak into the sky. From there Yuri found a way by country lanes towards Wittenberg and Erfurt, avoiding the main roads blocked with convoys and refugees. It was a normal story of flight therefore, except for Yuri and his back roads. All Europe seemed to be on the sunset trail that spring, looking for the Americans, whom they still considered innocent and fair people. Sometimes, in the three days of our search, my father would bribe our way into a military convoy travelling towards a front which had by and large become illusory. I slept enormously throughout this journey, but I remember the deserters hanging from the newly leafing trees, and sometimes SS men and police also hanging where the fleeing proletariat of the Wehrmacht had overpowered them. Even Miss Tokina got sick of exclaiming at such sights. I remember my father holding me, semi-conscious, upright, while I relieved myself at dusk at the edge of a ploughed field near Bamberg.

On the evening of the third day we stopped with a horde of other people, many of them soldiers, in the town square of the Bavarian hill city of Forchheim. A mass instinct had halted people here, as it halted us. Even though the noise from the front was not as extreme as what we had heard coming from the east in Charlottenburg, there was a sense that a resolution was at hand, something more precious than deliverance. No one need walk or drive further. Yuri's ordnance maps were now finished with.

Yuri, with some of the merchandise from the back of the car, bought Tokina, my mother, Genia and myself a space to sleep in a cellar beneath a Renaissance schoolhouse near the town hall. Yuri and my father stood guarding the car all night and, at a given hour towards dawn, strapped a Belorussian standard – the double-barred cross of white on a red background – across the side of the car. By seven o'clock in the morning, when they came to the cellar to collect us, they had been found by the Americans and had even had a conversation with an American political officer called Major Knowles. My father seemed radiant, now that he knew that the future was negotiable.

*   *   *

I do not have my father's journal as a guide to this period. But I was aware of some of the factors influencing our lives in the Regensburg Displaced Persons camp in which we found ourselves. Perhaps from the conversations of my elders, perhaps from continuing even on the edge of puberty my childish habit of eavesdropping, I was aware that there were some Americans – Major Knowles in particular – who respected the Belorussians because they were anti-Soviet, and another darker faction of Americans, represented by the Counter Intelligence Corps, who were more interested in the fact that for the sake of their independence they had worked with the SS. It was taken as granted in the huts of Regensburg (the place had originally been a Polish forced labour camp under the Germans, but the Americans had made it more habitable) that the forces of light represented by Knowles, a beefy avuncular Southerner who attracted droves of displaced children wherever he moved, would triumph over the others. In case they did not, one of Ostrowsky's junior ministers, a friend of my father's from Minsk, set to work to provide us all with forged identification papers. Hence we became the Kowolsky family, and our grandparents – those devout Belorussian patriots – became, for the sake of protective colouring, Poles.

My father and sundry other Belorussians interred in Regensburg became, through Major Knowles's benign influence, officials of the United Nations Relief and Rehabilitation Agency. There was Franz Kushel who, according to camp mythology, had told his men at Eisensteinstadt to fight their way through an SS division and link up with the Americans at Zwissel. There was Redich, who had also acquired Polish grandparents and whose name had become Radic. And then there was my father. They seemed to me to run the camp, and I am sure they did. The easy-going Major Knowles and the officers of the US supervision battalion, who were meant to control Regensburg, managed only the perimeter and were pleased with the arrangement. For they could not believe their luck. Children endowed with cigarettes and gum and stockings, they found themselves triumphant in a corner of Bavaria which had been little marred by war, in which the Gothic parishes and baroque town halls still stood.

Because of all his veterans who filled the camp, Kushel was elected camp chief. Under his supervision were the canned foods; the medicine balls; baseball bats; parallel bars; blackboards; gym shoes; Bibles in all languages; garish-coloured comic books detailing the adventures of Moses, Tom Sawyer, Superman; the pianos and piano accordions; the antibiotics and contraceptives; the bicycles and chocolate bars – all of it the bounty of UNRRA. We lived at the apex of that heap of plenty. There was a special mess for camp leaders and UNRRA appointees and their families.

I had no awareness that anywhere in the pyramid anyone went wanting. Regensburg was to me a happy kingdom, an Aristotelian model of a state. It worked better and more benignly than Staroviche had, nor were children restricted to their own gardens.

This rational kingdom had its army. Not the American Army, not the supervision battalion which had borne its virgin arms across France and into Bavaria, not Major Knowles with his oiled and unused big Mauser on his hip, so different from the firearms of Staroviche, so much an ornament. Kushel had the army. Wisely, he called it the Boy Scouts. All youths from thirteen to twenty years belonged, and marched and wheeled on the three playing fields. Above us hung the limestone cliffs of the Danube valley, and the river itself was merely a short walk away, that river which connected us to the East, to our beginnings, to those unassuaged longings which had burdened all our lives. By that strand of water one day soon, we would – as by a rope up a hillside – pull ourselves home.

The Americans, we knew in the meantime, had cornered the riches of the earth, were an unfathomable trench of abundance. So too, through the Americans' touch, was UNRRA. To provident Slavs like us it was reasonable that some of this excess of cigarettes and razor blades, of clothing and medicines, should be sold to provide us with what political parties call 'a fighting fund'. Major Knowles agreed with this concept.

Every few weeks therefore I would travel with my father, Yuri and Major Knowles, socketed between their respective male musks, on the wide front seat of a two-ton truck as it made for the city of Regensburg. We would make stops at warehouses on the north bank of the Danube. Goods would be unloaded from the truck while Major Knowles and my father and Yuri stood about smoking. Then we would cross the Danube towards the old part of the city. Major Knowles loved this crossing. There would still be warehouses to visit, but the sight of the spire of the Dominican church would set him off.

'You've got no idea, gentlemen,' he would say, 'how distinct all this here is when set beside the city of Goldsboro.' That was the name of his town in North Carolina. By his description it was low country, beset by coastal swamps. He seemed to have no idea that we too came from low-lying earth, from the most ancient fenlands of Europe. Regensburg he knew by all its names. By the Roman name of Castra Regina, by the old name of Ratisbon. He used all the terms – St Emmeram's and the Schottenkirche were Romanesque, though St Emmeram's had been done-over in baroque. He used the term 'done-over' as if at some time in the eighteenth century wallpaperers had come in. The Dominican church and St Peter's cathedral by the old stone bridge were pure Gothic. In Goldsboro, he told us, there wasn't any Gothic – though there was a taste of it in the Presbyterian church and the Oddfellows Orphans' Home. Goldsboro though, he said, and the whole of Wayne County (which I had no doubt was named in honour of the hero of *Stagecoach*) was innocent of baroque and rococo.

On some of our Regensburg excursions he would take us to old sausage restaurants by the bank of the river. These would be full of American officers.

I was delighted to see that they resembled Major Knowles in temperament. They were generous and sentimental men. I believe that my father and other Belorussians thought whenever they saw such collections of smooth, open-faced, splendidly uniformed Americans that they had found the right ally at last, men who were persuadable and whose hearts and minds were in the right place. Knowles was the sort of ally Hauptsturmführer Bienecke had never been.

I knew, again not by what I was told but by what I overheard, that the ancient enemy intended to mar the Regensburg idyll.

There was the rumour that a Russian mission would be permitted into the camp to look for Belorussians who had worked with the Germans. Right-thinking Major Knowles received requests from his superiors, who had received them from a Soviet NKVD general named Sedlov, to look in Regensburg and other places for people called Ostrowsky and Abramtchik, Stankievich and Sobolewsky, even for Redich and Kabbelski. He was pleased to tell them that there was no one of those names in Regensburg; his right-thinking superiors were pleased to pass on to the Soviets the same news.

Polish intelligence officers from General Anders's Polish Army, which had campaigned with the Allies, began to turn up in Regensburg, eat in the mess with the camp leaders. They carried a warning that agents of the Soviets who had influence in the Western press were leaking and printing stories about how lax General Patton and his American officers had been in pursuit of the so-called war criminals of Belorussia and other places. These old enemies, the Poles, were suddenly our brothers too. They too were waiting for the Allies to turn East.

One afternoon in early autumn Knowles turned up in a fast jeep and called a meeting of camp officials in the mess. My mother, Genia, Miss Tokina and myself waited dressed in our best clothes in our suite at one end of a hut the Americans themselves had had built for camp officials. Ordinary internees – even those who had families with them – lived in men's and women's quarters, but someone as eminent as my father enjoyed a space of ten metres by four of which separate rooms could be made through the use of shoulder-high partitions. It was an arrangement which had for me the solidity which the house in Staroviche had never enjoyed.

That night the young, highly polished Americans of the supervision battalion withdrew to their barracks and did no duty on the camp perimeter. Our family and others travelled in a truck with Major Knowles westward towards the French zone. The French, it seemed, were not under the same pressures to betray us as General Patton. The womenfolk and I spent a day uncertainly at a large confusing transit camp. Ostrowsky was there – he had come from the British zone to talk to everyone.

He was full of enthusiastic news, it seemed, some of which seeped down to me. The British were right-thinking also! My father had an hour's conference with him.

I believe it is as a result of that conference that we ended up in Michelstadt DP camp, which I think of now as the European terminus for us all, Michelstadt being a flame which consumed and transmuted our politics, our loyalties, our childhoods. Such decisive events were to overtake the Kabbelskis there that I see Michelstadt not so much as a European location but almost as a stop on the Parramatta–Penrith line.

Michelstadt – not the camp but the valley in which it and two other DP camps stood a little to the east of Stuttgart – was by no means physically squalid. It stood amongst splendid woods. On excursions from the camp you always met young Germans on their way to hike in the hills between the Rems and the Kosher. The camp was run by the French Army, and from my mother there was a small flutter of excitement at being able to exercise her grasp of that language which above all – like so many Slavs – she loved and respected.

There were by now age and harassment lines either side of her mouth, and her upper lip seemed puckered into a question. The question was of course the old one: whether the quick flights would ever end, whether she would find an address. She could no longer risk too great an enthusiasm. Even though my father was immediately appointed Refugees Rations Officer by the French commandant, my mother never ate well. She saw UNRRA's bread for what it was, the bread of exile. We were all therefore ecstatic, even frail old Tokina, when during a morning walk around the compound my mother encountered Galina.

Mother had begun school with Galina at the age of five, before the first exile. Galina's father had been a Russian timber merchant, her mother Belorussian. In that first loneliness at the start of their schooling, under the eyes of a sober young Polish nun, they had held each other upright on a bench in Baronoviche.

The day we met Galina, we were promenading in our normal manner – Genia and Tokina walking ahead, the old woman's ear bent towards Genia, my mother and myself a few metres behind, my mother already wearing (though it was only mid-August) the coat with the fox collar she had brought with her in the limousine from Charlottenburg, and I, proud of my pre-pubescent tallness, an adequate escort for her. Galina was more than twenty paces away, across a circular patch of grass where young Belorussian policemen were playing loud soccer. Mother recognised Galina, so she said, by that open face and the way she carried her head. In that mass of people the recognition was a little like reading a foreign newspaper, my mother said, and finding the one word you understood, the word – amongst the masses of meaningless digits – which was radiant with significance.

The feat of recognition was even greater in view of the fact that Galina, my mother's childhood sweetheart, was not dressed like a camp eminent, but nondescriptly, in the remains of a black suit. It went well with her black hair. I have to confess that I had noticed her too through the mêlée of footballers. She was both one of the most beautiful women I had ever seen, but also, as I admitted with a shock, tougher and so, visibly younger than my mother.

Coincidentally but not remarkably so, ten years after their first meeting the two of them had met up in one of Poland's excellent *gymnasia* – or high schools – in the 1920s. There is a worldwide school joke – the joke about the outrageous student who reduces the pompous teacher to human dimensions by putting soda bicarbonate or any fizzing salt likely to react with water in the teacher's chamberpot. I have heard Australians tell the same story, so that it must be a universal recourse hit upon by the right sort of student. The first time I heard it, however, was during the reminiscences of my mother and Galina. Galina had of course been the one who introduced the salts into the headmaster's chamberpot in the apartment on the top floor of the *gymnasium*. My mother had been her most enthusiastic applauder. And where had Galina been between this chamberpot escapade and her appearance on the far side of a circle of grass occupied by Belorussian cops-at-play? She had been married to a Polish Volksdeutcher who had been killed serving with a Ukrainian regiment near Millerovo, west of Stalingrad. (I thought it appropriate then that anyone who had the beatitude to lie beside Galina should die a warrior's death.) She had received her doctorate for a thesis on the old stone-age inhabitants of the Belorussian swamps. Since then she had been teaching paleolithic history at the University of Breslau. Until those new stone age people, the Soviets, had driven her out of her classroom in Silesia.

This personal history all absorbed hungrily, no one more hungrily than me, while we drank tea in our hut. 'And do you have anyone now?' I was astonished to hear my mother ask.

Galina answered in her superbly husky voice that her fiancé was in another camp, Backnang, fifteen miles along the valley. He was a Pole – he had taught with her at Breslau.

My mother, indiscreet with joy, said, 'We are all Poles!'

Galina sucked on an American cigarette my mother had offered her – they were the ones to which my father had access in his stature as Rations Officer. She laughed not at the front of the mouth but with her throat, a sound which filled me with a delicious languor. 'It's better that we all be Poles,' she said. 'The Allies have an idealised view of the Poles, who are all victims and martyrs. Whereas we Belorussians are considered either Soviet or fascist collaborators.'

The weight of that sadly true caricature hung on my mother for a moment. Galina saw this and rushed to say, 'But it doesn't matter. Aside from that bomb the Americans hurled at the Japanese last week, the future is quite golden, Danielle. Believe me. Golden.'

My mother had an urge in the following weeks to do favours for Galina. I was subtly pleased when Galina refused them, except for the occasional hospitality, glass of brandy, American cigarette. First my mother suggested she was sure her husband could arrange to have Galina's Polish boyfriend moved down the valley from Backnang to Michelstadt. 'But there are so many Poles there,' said Galina, 'that he can teach for UNRRA. He also drives a truck to Stuttgart every week for UNRRA and collects me on the way through. Even if he came here, and we married,' Galina continued, 'I wouldn't be allowed to live with him.'

I shuddered at the frank statement of her desire for cohabitation with some Pole unknown to me.

Similarly my mother offered to find her a job in the camp school, at least a part-time one. 'They'll never take me,' she laughed. 'There are already too many Belorussian doctors of philosophy teaching the seven-year-olds.'

And finally, as the autumn progressed and the dormitory huts began to display their potentialities for draught, my mother decided that Galina must have an apartment of her own. But Galina again gutturally refused. 'But I like the women in my hut,' she said. I knew my mother thought of them as crude, big-boned wives of crass Belorussian officers. But Galina could see the value of loud laughter amongst exiles. So, throughout the winter, she was content in the general dormitory and, by leave of the elderly French officer who commanded Michelstadt, her weekly journey by truck to Stuttgart.

I believe that Ostrowsky's reason for asking my father to come to Michelstadt was to prevent it from becoming a stronghold of the Papal gang, the Western faction, the Abramtchik-Redich push. It appears from his journal that by the summer of 1945 my father might have been disenchanted with both factions. But he was still on balance an Ostrowsky man.

I would hear him talk to my mother, however, about how pleased he was that nowadays he did not do everything Ostrowsky asked him. His decision to stay with us in Berlin until the last (especially with my mother who would have been terrified to flee alone, with just Tokina and two children), his refusal of Ostrowsky's request that he go west with Hrynkievich looking for Patton's army, had been one which placed family above political duty. He may in fact have been a little guilty at not having travelled with Hrynkievich and therefore took uncommon comfort, told with uncommon gusto, the story of how Patton's military police, searching Dr Hrynkievich, discovered in his pocket the ration cards the SS had arranged for Ostrowsky's Belorussians, a ration card bearing the sort of insignia likely to excite American counter-intelligence officers, who were instantly called in.

Much later Belorussian historians would regret the fact my father had not gone with Hrynkievich. My father would have acted as some brake on the man. As it was, the counter-intelligence people used Hrynkievich's ration card as a lever for extracting from him a picture of the cooperation between the Reich and Belorussian patriots. That description was apparently on file, and only such right-thinking allies as Major Knowles protected us from its consequences.

In Michelstadt both sides understood there had to be a balance between Ostrowsky people and the Papal gang, between Redich and my father. Redich was elected camp leader with the help of the votes of various policemen who had served under my father in the *oblast* of Staroviche. In return my father was appointed the camp's senior UNRRA official. Behind this visible balance there must have been other arrangements factional and per-sonal, particularly personal ones, for my father was in the last year of his ambitiousness and Redich would never lose his ambition till the day he fell from the train near Lidcombe station in the west of Sydney in 1955.

Again, briefly, because of this apparently friendly balance and of my mother's revival at the discovery of Galina, Michelstadt appeared to be a reasonable model of society. But as in Regens-burg DP camp, between Eden and the Fall lay only the briefest interval.

FIFTY

At the height of summer the new coach arrived. His name was Barry Golder. In Delaney's childhood he had been a famous ball distributor and maker of busts up the middle. Now he was unbalanced by weight, had an alcoholic's complexion, was earthy, jovial, crafty. They gave him a new house at Lapstone with a kidney-shaped pool, and he moved in with his blonde wife and quiet daughters.

He summoned Delaney to the club one evening. 'Believe a bit of the tiger came out in you at the end of last season, Terry? I like a bit of the bloody old tiger, even though silly buggers who get suspended make me ropeable. Listen, I'm bringing in a five-eighth from Brisbane. You know us Queenslanders, we can't help ourselves doing things like that, just to show you buggers down here we still exist. He's a year older than you and got heaps of talent. I'll probably start with him, but one bad game and he's out on his arse. I might be a Queenslander but I'm not as fucking stupid as that, eh?'

'One bad game, you reckon?'

'Well, maybe one and a half. And the same rule applies to you. When we go north next month to have a trial run at Port Macquarie I'll play you in the second half. You're going to earn good wages this year, either way.'

These rumours of success came too late. They were barely a whisper of wind across the surface of his flesh. To maintain Gina whether she wanted it or not, to do the same for Stanton, to pay his scandalous rent and have cash in hand for the rescue, he would need to earn like an orthopaedic surgeon.

'Believe your marriage broke up last year?' Golder asked him halfway through a second beer.

'Yes, that's right.'

'Won't wreck your concentration, will it?'

'That's when the tiger started.'

'Bugger me!' said Golder. He began to laugh, and raised his glass. 'Here's to plenty of woman trouble for you then.'

On the strength of this chance of riches, Delaney called the Parramatta enquiry agents, Fielder and Drane. He'd employed them for a week the previous December, as Christmas bore down on him like a deadline. Through the estate agents who had auctioned the Kabbel house in Parramatta, one of the agency's employees, an earnest, sweaty man in his early thirties, stuck with the unpromising name Ralph Margin, exactly the sort of flawed being Delaney had feared would be given such a minor job, had found the lawyer who had handled the sale for Rudi. Margin had been unable to get a Kabbel forwarding address from the solicitor. It was the investigator's suspicion that the lawyer would let it slip for a sum. He gauged the sum would be $500. Delaney authorised him to make the offer, but the solicitor was offended, threatened to report Fielder and Drane to their professional organisation, and threw the investigator out of the office.

'I wouldn't worry,' Margin told Delaney. 'It's probably only a box number somewhere, and no one can watch a box number twenty-four hours a day. You'd have to be Kerry Packer to afford it.'

Now Delaney called Ralph Margin and told him to offer someone in the solicitor's office, a secretary or an articled clerk, $1,500. 'So there is no embarrassment, you should deposit that amount with us first,' said Margin. 'We would give you a receipt for it and return it to you if the transaction doesn't take place.' That was the way a reputable business operated.

Flying to Port Macquarie through choppy columns of humid air, Delaney had not yet received any definite answer from Margin. It was not a rowdy flight, like the one to Hawaii eighteen months before. These were first graders, saving their chemistry for the game, not wasting it on noisy mateship or on the floral uniformed hostesses. Delaney sat beside Gorrie, the second-rower who would also be given half a game. Gorrie slept, sunlight jiggling up and down his face as the plane jolted past thunderheads. North of Newcastle, that depressed, depressing city of coal and steel, the coastline lay in primary colours below. The beaches seemed immense and unpeopled. High plumes of white smoke rose out of the mountains – remote, travelling bush fires. Along this coastline lay the escape route he would offer Danielle. It couldn't be more than a few weeks before the child was due. It would have its flight into Egypt, or Rockhampton or some such place.

The team were to eat at a seafood restaurant beside the water that night. It was something Golder had mentioned at every training session that week. Gorrie and Delaney were dressing for the dinner in their motel room, grunting as they eased their blazers on over all their muscular soreness, both of them with a competent second half behind them (67–7 over the local team), the local television news having just highlighted a sixty-five-yard movement in which they had both had a hand. They were ready to leave the room and go to meet Golder in the bar when Delaney saw the Stanton house on the screen. At first it seemed to him somehow a welcome familiar accompaniment to the afternoon the game had given him. He ran to the set and turned the volume up. A young television journalist, his back to the house, his eyes unmarred, was talking faster than Delaney wanted him to, getting the story through. Even on television the little house cried out for its tree.

A man had shot someone. The *householder* had shot someone. It had been that morning. A prisoner from Emu Plains low security prison farm had driven to Flemington markets in the company of a warder to sell a load of tomatoes. The truck had broken down on its return trip, not far from the prison farm gate, in fact in front of Stanton's place. The warder had worked on the motor and sent the prisoner inside to ask the people in the house if he could use their telephone. The wife had explained her husband was asleep on the lounge in the same room as the telephone. The prisoner could use it if he was quiet. He was obviously a silver-tail prisoner and was in fact an embezzler with a year of his sentence to run (the television newsman supplied these details). The prisoner had been calling the garage at the farm when the husband awoke, surmised that the prisoner had invaded the house and was holding the wife hostage, withdrew a .38 pistol from beneath the lounge and shot the prisoner dead. The husband had been taken away by Penrith police and, according to the boy newscaster, would be charged with murder. 'Murder?' Delaney yelled at Gorrie. 'That's not bloody murder!'

The wife had said (again the newsman talking) that her husband had been unemployed, and the risk of dangerous criminals breaking out of the prison farm had preyed increasingly on his mind.

A young female journalist interviewed the dead man's wife at her home in Killara. The embezzler had two daughters aged nine and ten who had been looking forward to their father's appearance at the next parole board hearing.

'Looks like bloody murder to me,' said Gorrie.

FIFTY-ONE

In the interests of finding a pattern to the confusing events of Europe's first winter of peace in Michelstadt, I have consulted my sister Genia. She had then already begun to spin away from the gravitational pull of the Kabbelski family. The spin was in the direction of a French sergeant, Albert Pointeaux, only seven years older than her – though it was a gap which made him seem middle-aged to me. Genia, from the time she fell in love with Pointeaux, saw us therefore with something like an outsider's critical gaze.

I add her letter to this account.

Paris

January 27, 1984

Dearest Radek,

If I had half a brain, I would have understood that of course you would want to translate father's journals. You are a good son and a curious one, and I suppose that to translate a document is the next most intimate connection with it other than actually writing the damn thing.

Needless to say, I remember that winter vividly. It was at a screening of *Beau Geste* in the recreation hall that Sergeant Pointeaux approached my father between reels and asked him would he permit me to sit beside him, with all the other French guards, in the second row. Albert, as you know, was not acting out of propriety but on a dare from the other soldiers. Father told him to clear out.

They knew each other already though – Albert did all
the paperwork on UNRRA – quite self-educated, a man
of natural talent. He had a senile commandant and a lazy
and venal lieutenant called Pucheu, who let him do
whatever he wanted as long as Pucheu himself got a cut.
That's why Albert will still say – though sensitive to my
grief over mother – that for him Michelstadt was as good
as a university education.

I thought Albert was wonderful from the start. You could
all tell that I thought he was wonderful. Despite the
loutish angle of his cap, the greased hair, the minute strand
of black moustache. Despite all his legerdemain with
cigarettes. I know now – I knew then but could not express
it – that he could tell that we were a family marred by
history, that it was compassion as well as honest lust which
drew him to me.

That winter some of the elderly Belorussians, the ones
who were too old for politics but had not wanted to live
under the Soviets either, went to the commandant, Colonel
Nouges, and complained that there were inequities in
the distribution of rations, and that some people were
going hungry. The elderly wife of a professor of philology
from Lwow died in early December of malnutrition,
and ordinary camp inhabitants believed it was due to
racketeering, not by father but by Redich. A post-
mortem which showed that the old woman had a tumour
of the stomach did not defuse the rumour. Colonel
Nouges, the sort of old fool who only wants reassurance,
called Redich and father in to tell him it wasn't true. Of
course father kept solidarity with Redich but was, I
believe, secretly outraged.

Father then approached Albert and discovered that
Redich had been raiding the UNRRA warehouse, taking
truckloads of goods for what father would have called
factional rather than national interests. Albert had
covered up with the bookwork. He says my father raged
at him. 'Why didn't you tell me straightaway! Redich has
no authority! Etc, etc.' But Albert says he did not want to

buy into the conflict he could sense between the two
wedges of Belorussians. He knew enough from his
childhood in Montparnasse to understand that Redich and
some of his heftier sergeants were the type of people who
could arrange for disappearances. His instinct would soon
be borne out by what happened to you. Albert didn't want
to die for Belorussian politics. I think his attitude
supremely sensible!

Father, the idealist, went to Redich and had a screaming
row. In your dream world, halfway between John Wayne
and Galina, you may not have noticed. But it was the talk
of the camp and amongst ordinary people it did father
great credit. He asked what in hell the Abramtchik faction,
the Papal gang, needed extra black-market revenue for
if they had such good friends in the French government, in
General Anders's Polish contingent and in the Vatican?
Some Ostrowsky people had also been beaten up in
inter-factional fights. Our father told Redich this sort of
divisive nonsense was to stop. Otherwise Papal gang people
in camps that were dominated by the Ostrowsky faction
would find life uncongenial.

Meanwhile Albert, circling the camp on his old Czech
400cc motorcycle, continued to court me. What I was
attracted to was that he was not a tragic and dedicated
figure. He did not believe in tragedy, he did not pick his
wounds like the Belorussians. He was an unheeding and
generous lout – exactly what I wanted. He already
foresaw a future – and he was more accurate in
crystal-gazing than any of the Belorussian dreamers in
Michelstadt – in which we lived well and had no politics.
To me, he was the liberation. He did not propose endless
returns and exiles, coalitions, changed names, midnight
flights. He promised a good time, and unlike most other
men in the world, he delivered it.

You must forgive the inevitable tone of censure, or of
mockery of my parents' views, in what I tell you. It is
not intended, I am merely trying to prove to my brother,
who would at the time have absorbed my parents' view

of the romance with Albert, that I wasn't acting out of pure wilfulness.

By the end of the winter I was pregnant, but with Albert's access to black-market goods it was easy for us to find in Stuttgart a highly qualified obstetrician to help us out. Neither of us liked the idea, but Albert knew that if things were not arranged this way it was likely that some of father's huskier Staroviche cops would fall on him one night and at best leave him neutered. Pressure was perhaps increased by the fact that he called me Heloise, and even though he was no Abelard, he remembered what Heloise's uncle, the Dean of Paris, had done to the body of that great philosopher out of jealousy and vengeance.

Our parents as it turned out knew nothing of my pregnancy. Security on the matter was absolute. As you were to find to your grief, you poor little fellow, security on other matters was dubious.

This has got to be a rather long-winded letter. It has been very cold in Paris this February and I am getting to an age where despite central heating the ice at the core begins to be felt. I shall continue this letter in the morning.

FIFTY-TWO

It was as Golder promised. The young Queenslander became briefly famous through dazzling his way past two disoriented defences in the first games of the new season. 'You watch,' Eric Samuels told Delaney. 'The opposition's going to wake up to him. Sure, he's got a few nice tricks. But he's brittle and his side-step's too easy to read. You watch, you watch. The first good lock he plays against is going to kill him.'

To Delaney the success of Golder's Queenslander was only a token annoyance and stood for the deeper derangement of the world. He had therefore played two tough and vengeful games in reserves, and through this accident found himself much praised in the clubhouse, as if his new ferocity were a deliberate tactical choice he had made based only on considerations to do with the game.

In the third encounter of the season, the Queenslander met the good lock Eric Samuels had foreshadowed and was choked off all day and left the field limping. According to Golder's promise, he would now have only half a game left to recover form. Delaney, however, did not quite believe Golder's promise, or anyone's.

In the fourth game, before a rabid crowd at St George, a tendon snapped in the Queenslander's calf. Delaney came on five minutes after half-time and helped halt a tide of St George tries. It was announced on the evening news that the Queenslander would be on crutches for six weeks. The following Tuesday night a *Herald* photographer came to training and took a photograph of Delaney running with the ball. It appeared with the announcement that Golder would be using him at five-eighth for some time, perhaps for ever.

*   *   *

There was always a ferocity in the air at Redfern. They called this team the Rabbitohs, after the Depression days when the unemployed of South Sydney used to hunt rabbits in that low country of sand-dunes and sell them door to door. Half the crowd seemed to have the toughness of Depression survivors, old men with the shadows of a hard life on their faces, old women who knew their football backwards and wore green and red beanies on their heads. And then, lots of dangerous kids, the kind you saw rioting on English football fields in the evening news. It was exactly the sort of fierce crowd Delaney welcomed that Sunday – an away game, and the world against you. And a new ferocity inside.

Once when he was young he had met a great St George forward and asked the man what he did on the morning of a test match against the Poms – what time he woke, what he ate, what he told himself. The forward replied that he got up about nine, ate a steak half an hour later, and when he ran on to the Cricket Ground he repeated the proposition, 'I'm the toughest bastard here.'

The young Delaney had been a little shocked. Five-eighths got by on craft, by niftiness. A five-eighth could not credibly promise himself that he was the toughest bastard there. The young Delaney himself was not in it for the aggression, had been sure he never would be.

These days though he understood the veteran. As he ran on to Redfern Oval, down the wire-caged walk placed to prevent the crones of South Sydney from attacking players or referees, his jaw was retracted, his teeth slightly parted, his mouthguard tight in his fist.

Gorrie, the Gilgandra boy, was playing second row that day, in tandem with Tancred. The selectors still stuck with Tancred. On a heavier winter day like today, he had time to pull his Yorkshire tricks.

And he was certainly good weight in the scrums. Penrith won the first two but were cramped – the Rabbitoh back line standing at least a metre offside, forcing Delaney to run too wide, and the referee too intimidated by the partisans in the grandstand to chastise the local team. Delaney found himself cut down brutally from the flank by the South Sydney centre, the young one called Lynch, another whiz-kid. Lynch had all the tricks, all the savageries. Before getting up, he gouged and scored Delaney's eyeball with his blindside thumb. A home crowd would have seen it and protested. This crowd cheered.

Delaney had not regained clear vision when Lynch took the ball in midfield and ran forty metres with it, leaving the forwards standing. Except for Gorrie who, being young and from the country, did not know when he was up against a champion, and so ran the man down ten metres out from the goal line.

Now came a passage of frantic defence, the ecstasy of the crowd breaking like a surf behind the goal line. Delaney himself was in an ecstasy, tackling expertly low, letting the ones who didn't know how drag the Rabbitohs down brutally by the shoulders. Lynch wore all the time a cat's smile on his face, and if possible, when tackled, always levered himself upright with a hand placed across Delaney's face. When the Rabbitoh try came, it was the result of a movement between Lynch and their young second-rower, their fast Queensland winger. Even Gorrie was left shamed and standing. Tancred blinked, flat-footed and bemused, like a parent whose children were beyond him. By half-time it was 12–0, the crowd were singing a taunting chant – 'Look at the scoreboard!' Delaney knew that the commentators would be saying that the Penrith lads were lucky it wasn't 24–0. Golder's half-time exhortation was full of obscenities, and Delaney found himself, for the first time since his childhood, very nearly denouncing another player to his coach, very nearly accusing Tancred of stupidity, cowardice, malice.

Delaney ran back on head-hunting for Lynch. As Golder had said, the bastard was opening up the defence as if it was a can of bloody dog food.

The Rabbitohs, it seemed to Delaney, were winning all the scrums now. Running on a diagonal, gathering an intimidating speed, Lynch was coming through, yelling to his five-eighth for the ball. Delaney felt a lightness, a certainty. Sometimes, when you're out of oxygen and elated and fierce, you got those certainties, the pattern became apparent. He was sure he could stop Lynch and that no one else could. It was one of those rare times when you did not worry about position, and you ran any distance to achieve the ordained result. He had Lynch's measure. He knew which way he would turn with the ball before the ball was even in his hands. For a time he was certain that he would go in low, but three or at most four paces from Lynch he realised it must be high, in case Lynch had a colleague further out moving at that same pace, and got the ball to him. Exultantly, Delaney straightened, brought his arm up to collect Lynch's shoulder. He felt nothing but raw delight when the arm took Lynch's face and something parted there and Lynch's clever eyes glazed.

Lynch lay flat and unmoving on the paddock. Delaney heard with a strange surprise the ranting of the crowd, saw the referee waving someone off the field. In a few gasps, with a little more oxygen to the brain, he understood it was him. He looked at the referee's hands, fixing on the fingers, which would tell him whether he was gone for five or ten minutes. But the referee did not use his fingers, used merely a back-handed gesture of total banishment. Leaving the field, Delaney would not have survived the hatred of the harsh natives of South Sydney if not for the wire cage.

FIFTY-THREE

The second part of the letter from my sister, reflecting on the events of 1945–46, follows.

Paris

January 28, 1984

Dear Radek,
A fierce wind today and I saw from my window three gypsy children move in on a woman and steal her purse with enormous skill, so deftly that she was left in the middle of the pavement with her hands extended, weeping. But that piece of news does nothing to soothe your confusion about Michelstadt, so I shall take that business up from where I left off yesterday.

At the end of the winter of 1946, two of Redich's men, both of them former police lieutenants from Rogachev, and one of them – Gersich – a delegate from Rogachev to that famous meeting in the Minsk Opera House where Ostrowsky outfoxed Abramtchik, were called to Colonel Nouges's office to find three armed officers of French counter-intelligence and two American officers of Twelfth Army counter-intelligence, similarly armed, waiting to arrest them. My unofficial fiancé of the time, Sergeant Pointeaux, filled me in on the tragedy of that arrest. Gersich and his friend were tumbled straight into the back of a truck, driven to the border of the Russian zone north of Bayreuth and handed over to officers of the NKVD, the

forerunner of the KGB. The camp doctor back in
Michelstadt had to sedate Mrs Gersich that night. She
knew her husband had disappeared into the void.

There was a great deal of anxiety in Michelstadt that
other arrests might take place, and that 'Belorussian patriots'
– as some of those coarse clowns called themselves – might
be seized and sent prematurely east. (Remember that
term from our childhood in Staroviche? Sent east?)

Our father suffered from this fear, of course. But there
was the additional problem that the Papal gang suspected
that he or someone else in the Ostrowsky set-up had
betrayed Gersich and his colleague to the Soviets. As
you know, most of us were masquerading as Poles, or as
humbler refugees from Belorussia than in fact we were.
Subtle mis-spellings of our names, forged papers, the
general goodwill of the French and the Americans, gave
us protection. For Gersich and his friend to have been
arrested, someone – and Redich was certain it was someone
in Michelstadt – must have betrayed Gersich's and the
other man's identities, must have sent information and
photographs to General Sedlov. Someone in Michelstadt
must therefore be a Soviet agent. Redich wanted that
agent uncovered and punished. That is why Redich
kidnapped you and put you in the pit.

Because Sergeant Pointeaux was courting my sister, I was
treated as something of a favourite by the guards. I would sit
with them in the guard-house, read their comic books, both
French and American, and shamelessly extract chocolate from
them. My father might have abominated Sergeant Pointeaux,
but my connection with both men gave me more stature than
probably any other brat in Michelstadt. It did not occur to my
father, to Albert, or to me that I might be used for leverage
between the factions, and so my liberty to wander in the camp
and beyond it was virtually unrestricted.

I was returning from the guard-house to my parents' suite in
Hut 11C one early dusk. It is very likely that I was singing or
talking to myself. In both Regensburg and Michelstadt I had

returned to being what my mother called 'a normal child'. There had been cessation of the mild seizures which had occurred fairly regularly in the last days of Staroviche and in Frau Zusters' house in Charlottenburg. So, a normal child, I sang my way home towards a plentiful supper.

On this particular late February dusk the camp had already begun to recover from Gersich's capture by the Russians. The mess halls, where I would sometimes eat with other children, telling by instinct that they liked me better if I avoided the mess where the camp leaders and their families ate, were full of talk of immigration. The first officials from Canada, the United States, Australia, were just beginning to appear in places like Michelstadt, touting their version of the new world, looking for faces that would fit it. New York, New Jersey, Boston, Montreal were invoked. Of Australia people knew little other than kangaroos and genial Aboriginals. The vacancy of what was known made the place seem highly desirable to many people in the mess, people who never again wanted to be at the storm's eye.

That evening, I was equally at peace both with the idea of a future of prairies, exotic wildernesses, deliciously serrated city skylines, as with the present benefits of Michelstadt.

Four huts from home I was intercepted by a beefy young Belorussian, probably in his late twenties. He told me that he had served with my father in Staroviche. My father didn't want me to go home – instead he had sent this man to tell me to meet him in the recreation hut for some exciting news. 'A surprise, a surprise,' said the young former policeman. 'Though I suppose you're nearly too grown up for surprises now.'

I walked ahead of him but was aware, as if he had bifurcated, that there were now two of him. I looked around to see a second young man, thinner but equally tall. The second young man was smiling too. I smiled back. They were full of a sort of peasant goodwill. They seemed to be following me precisely so that they could witness that first flush of amazement on my face when my father announced the unexpected.

They told me, in the vicinity of the crudely built Catholic church, that my father wasn't really in the recreation hut, that he was in the old part of the camp. To get me to him they intended to put me in a garbage-bin and pass me off as refuse when they came to the French sentry by the soccer field. It was of course essential for this escapade that I remain quiet and still. With all my soul I pledged quietness and stillness.

So they found me a garbage-bin and I sat in its yellow reek of early putrefaction as they toted me past the sentry. I heard them nominate a destination beyond the old huts, the huts which would have been primitive accommodation even in the days of the German forced labour.

Beyond these ancient huts was a covered row of old latrines. That was where they took me. They set me down and dragged the lid of one of the pits away. I was tumbled forth from the bin. There was no father. There was only the dirty snow and the burningly cold earth. The genial-looking policeman who had first approached me said, lifting me by the armpits and lowering me into the dark, 'You're going down, sonny.'

I told him no. Nonetheless I fell into the dark earth, landing at last with a fierce jolt on a deck of planks someone had placed halfway down the pit. I could barely see the monitory faces of the two Belorussians high above me in the lesser dark of a February dusk. 'If you get thirsty,' said the one who had done all the speaking, 'you'll find lumps of ice on the walls.' Saying that, they threw in two blankets, and I wondered straightaway whether these would be adequate.

Then they dragged the lid across the pit. The darkness was absolute. Without being dramatic one could say that I was buried alive.

The earth could not accommodate my terror, but man is such an efficient machine that in the end I felt for moisture on the foul walls. Even in a miasma of terror I pursued the mechanics of being human or, at least, animal. Given time on my platform of deal deep in the pit I would have become a hunter, scrabbling for worms and bugs in Europe's subsoil, delving for the insects which had maintained their wise politics through all Europe's surface changes, the changes which only *we* believed to have penetrated to the centre of the earth. I was astonished that it had happened again in my life so soon: I believed that the guarantees I had been given beneath Oberführer Ganz's dining room table had exempted me from all future anguish of this scale. It was all very well for that Belorussian voice named Uncle to have promised me a wave. In the pit, the wave was no consolation.

I did not begin to feel cold until sleep, normal functional sleep, began to overtake me. I fought it since I believed this sort of unconsciousness would not give me any height from which I could look down on the child in the hole.

I was blessedly wrong. Asleep, I wavered atop a light pole above the ancient latrines. A dead light bulb, one which had probably shone in the days of the Polish slave labourers, sat in the mantle by my right shoulder. I was aware of the radiant anxiety of the child in the latrine, that child affrighted to sleep. I could see the lit camp and hear voices and jazz music. They were not alarmed voices, they were not voices asking where Radek Kabbelski was. They were voices full of the expectation of America and Canada. They were voices more stimulated now, since the Allies had failed to sweep on over the Russians, by the prospect of New South Wales or Winnipeg or Massachusetts than by memories of the forests and the Belorussian buffalo.

There were very few people in the open, for it was a dismal evening. The drizzle which descended from low, soggy clouds would turn later to sleet. I saw my father walking quickly past the playing fields, around the perimeter. Stopping to talk to a French sentry, he was – on account of his stature – permitted out the gate and into this old section of the camp. The ground in this area was, I was aware, littered with the debris of condemned huts, timber and iron roofing stacked for some further use but never taken away. My father advanced halfway across this wasteland. My sister Genia, I saw, appeared behind him on the playing fields, striding straight across the middle of the soccer pitch. As my father looked behind one pile of stacked lumber and then another, Genia began to speak animatedly to the young sentry who had permitted him into the open. My father turned, saw her and strode back to the gate. He began gesturing to Genia, shouting, though I could not catch what he said. I could see though that the sentry was embarrassed. I was astounded, aggrieved enough to curse him, as I saw him gesture

Genia back towards the huts from which the music and the voices rose. He had been distracted from finding me by the easy delights of chastising Genia, of calling her a slut.

I believe that later in the night he returned with two of his police officers, one of them being Yuri, and searched the open land – there were reasons why he could not come back with battalions and torches. I would not be aware of this later search, however, just as I was not aware of what a busy night in general it would become for him.

The last event I saw from my vantage point, as the camp was becoming quieter, was Galina and my mother rushing along the fence, my mother stooping to look under the older huts by the playing fields. They spoke for a while to the sentry, but he seemed to have become bored with the Kabbelskis and their friends by now and answered only briefly, ultimately turning his back to them.

Halfway back across the playing fields, in the shadow of the clinic, Galina and my mother began to argue. I was absolutely diverted by the strangeness of this. Galina became increasingly angry, took my mother by the upper arm, pushed her this way and that. It might have been a re-enactment of a school yard scene, I naively thought. Then mother, pulling away from Galina, landed on her haunches in the mud. Galina jumped behind her, dragged her half-upright with a crooked arm and began choking her. While I cried out to the treacherous Galina, my mother arched her back and tried to find purchase on the miry earth with her feet. At last she managed it, wriggled out of that vice, the elbow of her old schoolfriend, and staggered away calling my father's name. Galina responded neither to my cry nor to my mother's escape, and collapsed against the hut wall and stared at her bare knees.

It seemed to be soon after that I awoke in the pit with the consoling knowledge that the pit could not hold me. Through the wooden lid high above me I could see the glimmer of an ice-grey morning. I was prodigiously cold and thought in semi-delirium that searchers might be attracted to me by the noise of my organs, above all my heart and brain, creaking under the weight of icy air. I called for help as much to warm myself as in hope. The earthen walls absorbed any cry. My little lumber platform, wedged above the cess, began to shake. I suffered a natural concern as to whether the waste of Frenchmen and Poles and Russian soldiers employed here in the war years would be a foul sea still or would have solidified and become one with the earth itself.

Considering these questions I grew comatose. Once I awoke and knew that it was either dusk or that the steely day had grown unnaturally dim. It was at some stage of that night that I saw the lid removed above me to show stars of savage clarity. A hand reached down to me and I reached up. It was a hand so calloused that I did not need to see the face to know who was rescuer. I concluded, intuitively and at once, that it was the old man I had seen on the corner of Marka and Bryanska Streets on the day Onkel Willi was shot by the partisans. 'Come on, come on,' said a voice in Belorussian. 'We don't die in holes. Not people like us.'

It was all I would hear from him. Gratefully yet shrieking with cold I was lifted out and carried a little distance in a needling north wind and set down in the lee of a pile of lumber.

FIFTY-FOUR

They played the tape in fast motion and then in slow. The images of Delaney's outrage against the integrity of Lynch's jawline appeared on an enormous screen of the type generally found only in clubhouses, in vast areas, amongst bar tables. In the small boardroom, the infamy of that tackle seemed gigantic.

The members of the judiciary board were reduced to stillness by the electronic evidence, the collision between Delaney and Lynch. Even old Bernie Bell's asthma could not be heard.

Now that the board had seen the impact at the speed of the human eye, the official in charge of the video machine let the tape rewind in slow motion. Delaney loped ridiculously backwards into the state of taut innocence which had preceded the tackle. Lynch himself took similarly grotesque backward strides. Yelling, 'Coming through, Baz!' backwards, he got rid of the ball to his five-eighth and disappeared around his flanks. His energy, run in reverse, resembled fear rather than a hard offensive intention. Behind Delaney one of the press men tittered.

Run forward as slowly, however, the event did not look quite so comic. Even to himself Delaney-on-the-screen resembled someone who wanted to punish. His face was set in an aggressive rictus. He seemed to push the slow-footed Yorkshireman, Tancred, out of the way in his rush to launch himself against the developing movement. He looked as though he would come in low, a fine five-eighth tackle. Then he unwisely straightened and drove his forearm against Lynch's jawline.

Behind Delaney someone whispered, 'Jesus!' Nausea overcame him. If I get sick in here, will it do me any good? He remembered the berserk elation he felt as the structures of Lynch's face yielded. Run at normal speed, the tape might support a defence based on reflex action, impulse, lack of malice. Run slow it looked like bloody murder.

Golder had insisted that the club provide him with counsel. The counsel was in this case a young barrister named Vickers, who now asked for an adjournment and led Delaney out of the boardroom and down the corridor into a toilet where hissing urinals provided some cover for private conversation.

'All right,' said Vickers. 'I think now you should be frank with them about Lynch's provocations offered earlier in the game.'

Delaney said he didn't want to do that.

'Come on. Provocation's important! It's all very nice, Terry, to be brave and take your medicine, but we're not schoolboys here. We're talking about a loss of thousands of dollars to you.'

'They won't take provocation as an excuse,' said Delaney. 'They'll say, all right, he gouged you, but you broke his jaw. I don't have a medical certificate for my eyes. He's got a bottler for his jaw!'

'Look, what I'm urging – it'll reduce the period of suspension – if any.'

'If any,' said Delaney. 'This isn't like a court of law. I know these blokes. If I say, "He hit me first, Your Honour," they'll remember that for years to come. They'll despise me. Officials, players – anyone who ever wants to needle me in years to come'll mention it.'

Vickers turned to the urinals as if to seek another human to appeal to. There was no one. He turned back again.

'So your only defence is that it was a reflex action?'

'It *was* a reflex action,' yelled Delaney, and then became ashamed of the noise he'd made. 'Look, Golder doesn't want me to point the finger. It's not the sort of thing you can do to a bloke whose jaw is wired up, even if he is a mongrel. I'm very grateful to you and to him, but I know he doesn't want me to dob Lynch in.'

'Do you ever want to play again?' asked Vickers.

Delaney considered himself in the mirror above the wash-basins.

'I don't think I do,' Delaney said, shocked at the answer. 'If it wasn't for my responsibilities.'

'Same for all of us,' said Vickers. 'I'd rather be windsurfing.'

It was time to go back to the judiciary. Delaney answered the members' questions. It was a reflex action. It was the heat of the event. Lynch had found room up the middle – the forwards just weren't catching him. He had to be stopped by any legal means. 'You notice,' said Delaney, hating the guilty tremor in his voice, 'that I started to go in low and changed my mind. I wanted to stop the pass, not break his jaw.' So he pushed his one defence. 'It's a matter of inches between a good pass-smothering tackle and a broken jaw. I made a mistake. It wasn't a deliberate one.'

Vickers's speech was an eloquent one for a windsurfer. The game by its nature required a certain degree of needle and tiger. It would be possible for members of the judiciary to look at the earlier stages of the particular game in which Lynch had been injured and Delaney sent from the field, and to find instances of Lynch's activities which could credibly be considered incitement. But his client did not want these incidents mentioned. The press, the administration, the coaches, the public admired hard contact, praised needle, welcomed a dash of tiger. Sometimes, said Vickers, turning Delaney's argument metric, the distance between tiger and mayhem was a matter of a few centimetres. There were risks inherent in the nature of the code and it was these inherent risks – rather than an enthusiastic defender named Delaney – which had brought damage to Lynch.

Delaney and Vickers left again and sat in one of the quieter corners of the upstairs bar. The gentlemen of the press stayed over near the Phillip Street windows, drinking light ales and averting their eyes. It was forty minutes before they were all called in to face the judiciary again. Old Bernie Bell's breathing was audible now as he told Delaney that they were suspending him for six months, that the tackle could not be considered on the evidence to be a mere reaction lacking in intent, but that if his demeanour at the hearing had not been so appropriate the period of suspension would have been longer still.

FIFTY-FIVE

The press galloped from the judiciary room to alert their photographers and cameramen downstairs for the prescribed shot
of the guilty player striding abashed down the Phillip Street
steps. Amongst those faces, to whom he was a cipher, a
jaw-breaker, tomorrow's victim of editorial comment, he was
pleased to see that of Steve Mansfield emerging from the back
seat of a taxi. Mansfield yelled, 'Mr Delaney! Your car, sir.'
Inviting the press to bugger off and get stuffed, he dragged
Delaney into the cab. It was full of people. Eric Samuels, best
man from that era when the Delaneys got married, sat in the
front beside the Greek driver. (The Greeks ran the cab business
these days.) In the back were crammed Borissow, Gorrie, and
Steve Mansfield himself.

'Told you,' said the Greek. 'Can't take four in the back.'

'Come on, mate,' said Mansfield. He leant over and stuffed
ten dollars into the pocket of the Greek's shirt. 'We're going to
a funeral.' Steve Mansfield, like the other three, was stuck
uncomfortably between commiseration and bravado.

'Where we going then?' asked the Greek cab driver.

'I told you,' said Mansfield. 'Francesco's at the Cross. One of
those back streets. Forget which one.'

'I know it,' the Greek begrudged them.

In their various ways they consoled Delaney. Leaving the cab
in Bayswater Road, Borissow murmured to Delaney that it was
all a shithouse set-up. Eric Samuels held him back a second as
they were being led to their table. 'What can I say, mate?' he
asked. Later in the evening, halfway through their third bottle
of wine, Gorrie stood at the urinals with him and told him to
keep training, to show the buggers.

'It was a reflex action,' said Delaney.

'Of course it was,' said Gorrie. 'Stands to bloody reason. No player would risk his match payments just for the joy of breaking a bloody jawbone.' When they had their coffee in front of them, their port or cognac on the side, Mansfield announced, 'I know a bordello not so many steps from here. Nice girls. No smack addicts. We'll all pay our own way and cover Terry's costs between us. What about it, eh? Reckon the Pope will let you?'

After the bottle of Hunter Valley white they had treated him to, the idea charmed Delaney. He made a little speech about how no man had better friends. He felt his blood begin to pool deliciously in that reach of his body beneath the table. Wine had made it remoter than Cape York.

'Dear old Gorrie's never been before,' said Mansfield. 'Don't have 'em in Gilgandra. Blokes out there have to use the live-stock!'

Borissow the centre began to give Gorrie the second-rower straight-faced advice. 'Some of these girls do so many blokes a night that their stomach muscles can just suddenly tense up, hard as a vice. I had a cousin it happened to. So tight he couldn't get out. They have to take you to St Vincent's casualty to separate you.'

'Don't tell him that,' said Eric Samuels. Though he too looked alarmed.

Borissow said, 'It's the truth. What my cousin didn't know was that all you have to do to release the muscles is just give the girl a punch in the stomach. She'll thank you for it.'

Everyone began to laugh, except Gorrie and Borissow. Delaney began to wonder whether it wasn't the truth.

'I'm just telling you,' said Borissow.

It was a short walk from Francesco's. Far too short. Delaney felt a rush of panic outside the brothel, a fear that he may not know the etiquette inside and so make a fool of himself. The place was shuttered and painted a trendy brown. Its nature would be a mystery to the passer-by except for the red light above its door. Delaney pulled Samuels aside.

'You know how they run things in these places?'

'No,' confessed Eric. 'Play it by ear, mate.'

They held on to each other on the pavement and trembled with quiet laughter about their innocence.

'Just watch Steve Mansfield,' said Samuels. 'He'll know the drill.'

And so Mansfield did. He knew, for example, that only in movies or in more hidebound cities than Sydney did you have to knock twice and mumble through an eyehole. He opened the door as if he were arriving home, and led the others straight into an orange-lit foyer where a sharp-faced woman in her thirties called them gentlemen and welcomed them with a false enthusiasm which made Eric Samuels continue to shudder with laughter. She motioned them past a barrier of potted palms and told them to take a seat. Three girls could be seen in soft light at the other end of the lounge. They wore party dresses and read magazines – *Woman's Day*, *Cosmopolitan*. They raised their deep mascara-ed eyes from pictures of royal children and questionnaires on the female orgasm to look at what the evening had brought them. One of them was Chinese. 'Who gets the Yellow Peril?' asked Gorrie, sounding awed.

The woman who first greeted them had followed them into the lounge. 'Now, gentlemen,' she said. 'We do not mind greeting guests who have dined well. But I'm sure you understand that we welcome only orderly clients, and that if you wish to be disorderly or loud, then we would be regretfully forced to ask you to go elsewhere.'

The little speech sobered everyone. She had demanded decencies of them, the way they did at school or in the Leagues Club. She introduced them to the three girls at the other end of the room. Karen, Lynette, Suzie. 'All the Yellow Perils call themselves Suzie,' murmured Steve Mansfield. 'You know, after that old movie. Suzie Wong.'

Delaney looked at the one called Karen. Her eyes were bruised with shadow. For the first time in some weeks he felt honest lust. Three of the other girls would be along soon, the sharp-faced woman told them. Then they could make their choice.

A middle-aged waitress appeared and asked them if they would care for a drink. They all ordered, Gorrie mumbling his desire for a Pilsener. 'Geez,' he said when the woman had gone again to fetch their drinks. 'She looks like she could be someone's old mum.'

'Putting her boy through Sydney Uni,' said Steve Mansfield.

Borissow gestured them all to lean in towards him so that he could tell them something that might be to their interest. 'If nobody minds, I don't want the Yellow Peril. They've got bloody fierce muscles in their abdomens.'

'That's jake,' said Mansfield. 'I reckon poor little Gorrie's already carrying a fat for her.'

How will I do it? Delaney was demanding of himself. How, when they all march up, will I be able to say I'll take Karen? What if someone else wants her too? Someone like Eric Samuels. Best man.

Three new girls arrived through a dimly lit door beyond a life-sized glossy statue of a panther. They all carried their handbags with them, as if they could not safely put them down. 'Here we go, boys,' said Mansfield. 'Hang on to your credit cards!' The girls came over and stood in front of the five clients. They said their names were Sally, Jenny, Brook. 'If you'd like to make a choice of companion,' said an angular spokeswoman in a blue dress. Brook.

'Guest of honour first,' said Mansfield, indicating Delaney.

But Delaney said in a panic, 'No, no. You first.'

'Suzie, then,' said Mansfield, slapping his knees and rising. He moved like a habitué behind the swaying Suzie. So much at ease that in the doorway he turned back and said, 'I'll pick up Terry's bill on my Bankcard, and you gentlemen can pay me back later.' And for the information of the girls he pointed at Delaney, who suddenly felt a liquor headache, a seepage of colour from his face, a lack of focus in his eyes. 'It's not that he can't afford it,' Eric Samuels hurried to tell Lynette. 'It's just that it's his, ah, his . . . birthday. You'll read about it in tomorrow's paper.'

Lynette, who may have been twenty, was used to the in-jokes of male clients and did not want any explanations. She did not laugh or speak, yet it was somehow obvious that she – pretty chin, dark eyes and cool agelessness – was the girl Eric wanted.

So it's no contest after all, Delaney realised. It's all done by little signals that everyone else catches on to – your mates, the women. No wonder they call them professional women. Gorrie was already talking to the bony, lean girl called Brook. Discreetly freckled, she was hardcore Australian, a girl from the bush, from some lean-times town like the one Gorrie himself came from. Borissow spoke to a plump blonde, the most expressive of the lot. 'I'll take Karen,' said Delaney, his voice sounding ridiculous to himself, sounding in fact like a mimicry of some marriage ceremony.

Karen, her handbag under her arm, led him at once into a cerise hallway where a refrigerator stood. From it she supplied him with another frosted glass and can of beer. She said she had to arrange with him in front, so that they would not be distracted later, the nature of payment.

'I'm the one my mates are paying for,' he said.

'That's right. Then come with me.'

At the bottom of the stairs she turned and smiled. 'And how are you tonight?'

'I'm fine,' he said. He had been banished from his game. He did not know where his love was. But you could not tell a strange girl these things. 'Never been better.'

'I'm not feeling so well,' Karen said, mounting the stairs before him. It was like the sort of excuse he'd heard sometimes from Gina during their courtship. The intimacy of the confession almost shocked him. 'I went to a curry house,' she continued. 'I've already been sick once this evening.'

'You don't want to do it?' asked Delaney, a sort of hope taking over from desire.

'It's my job. Besides, I like a handsome man of your age. You wouldn't believe how old some of the people are we get in here. Not that I have anything against beer guts.'

Delaney raised the can and the frosted glass. 'I'm working on it,' he said.

'But you're in good condition,' said Karen. 'I like a man in good condition.'

It was a statement. It was not languorously said. 'I'll give you your money's worth,' she said with that same simplicity. 'Even if I've got to stop once or twice. After all, we've got half an hour.'

She led him into a bedroom – mirrors, turquoise paint, a low bedspread with towels. A black-tiled shower cubicle gave off the bedroom with a black toilet bowl and washbasin. First, she said, she would have to inspect him. Would he put on a bathrobe and she would do it now?

He turned his back, undressing as he did in primary school in public baths, crookedly hanging his sports coat and slacks in a cupboard, neatly balling his socks so that she would know that he wasn't slovenly. The way those little nylon and cotton bundles stuck in his brown shoes, like small marsupials emerging from their holes, infected him for some reason with a withering sorrow. He kept his back to Karen who liked tight stomachs and began to shudder, a yelp emerging from his throat, a small supply of tears astringent on his lids.

'Anything the matter?' he heard her call from the bathroom where, still fully dressed, she was cleaning her teeth. He wondered if the sperm of the last stranger was what she was rinsing away.

'Ready?' she asked, through the foam of toothpaste. He came forward dressed in his bathrobe. She took his penis functionally in her hands. She moved the foreskin back and forth across the gland.

Gratefully he felt desire revive. When he asked if she were looking for bugs, she laughed and said no. Lesions, breaks in the skin, rashes, pustules. 'You're fine,' she told him, dropping him and going to the washbasin again to rinse her hands.

It was all a little like a visit to the doctor, he thought.

She sent him to the low bed, where he waited for her. She came from the basin and undressed. He saw the strong young stomach and the elegant legs almost luminous, in the bordello dimness, with shiftworker's pallor. She came across and caressed him – he was willing to let her lead. Straddling him, lowering her body on to his, she felt extraordinarily cool. As Delaney began to arch against her thighs, she turned her head and seemed to retch. 'Pardon me,' she called, vaulting on to the floor and rushing for the black-tiled, black-gulleted water closet.

Of course they have these tricks, Delaney thought. Then they don't have to sit too long on one man after another. He followed her to the bathroom, consumed with a genuine interest in the authenticity or otherwise of her nausea. She heaved into the black bowl. He held her forehead for her as her body was wracked. He saw the sweat bursting out on the back of her neck. 'You really are sick,' he said. 'You poor little bugger!'

Gasping when the spasms ceased, she apologised. 'No, no,' he said. 'There's no need for you to do anything. What if I go down to the front desk and see if they have an aspirin?'

He embraced happily the idea that she *was* an honest woman and now would have been very pleased to play elder brother to her.

'No, no,' she said. 'You've paid.'

She led him back to the low bed and applied her mouth so energetically to him, moistening him with saliva, that he managed to release himself within minutes as a matter of good manners to a girl who was putting herself out of her way. 'Now lie beside me,' he instructed her, 'and have a good rest.' He wished there were tea-making facilities in here.

She was very quickly close to sleep and he forgot her, or she became a token for Danielle. To lie like this at a safe distance, somewhere in Queensland!

The girl was awakened, and he aroused from *that* dream, by a noise from down the corridor. Karen shook herself, found a bathrobe. So too did Delaney. They stepped out into the narrow hallway. Even *its* windows were shuttered, Delaney noticed. Three doors closer to the front of the house, Gorrie was struggling with a large muscular man. Gorrie himself was large and muscular, but this other one was ornately body-built in the manner of a weightlifter, a professional wrestler, of someone who enjoyed throwing weight. From other doors along the corridor strangers and friends appeared. Eric and Mansfield and Borissow, all in the establishment's shaggy bathrobes. Simultaneously, from the stairs, rose the woman who had first greeted them to the place. She seemed pigeon-chested with anger. 'I warned you,' she said. 'We expect *manners* here. You Rugby League crowd never know where to stop!'

Mansfield had begun wrestling loyally with the bouncer, trying to get him to release his hold on Gorrie. 'What happened?' Eric Samuels was asking.

The girl whom Gorrie had chosen, the angular one with the freckles, emerged panting from the door of the room which she had been sharing with Gorrie. 'The bastard started to beat me up,' she said in an aspirated voice, the voice of someone who has been winded.

'Gorrie?' asked Delaney, not believing it.

'I felt her belly clench up,' said Gorrie, out of a throat constricted by the bouncer's forearm.

'I want you all to go,' said the front-of-house woman. 'Unless you'd like a little help from the boys in blue from Darlinghurst.'

'We paid our money,' Steve Mansfield protested.

'I would have thought he-men such as you would have had full value by now,' said the woman from downstairs. The muscular one said nothing but maintained his hold on Gorrie.

'Collect your things, ladies,' the woman instructed the girls. It was like a scene from one of those films, when the headmistress catches the hockey team in the football team's dormitories at schools in England and America as remote as Szechuan from Delaney's comprehension.

'Well,' yelled Mansfield after the madame. 'We'll tell all our mates never to darken your poxy door.'

'I hope you will,' said the front-of-house woman witheringly from halfway down the stairs.

'Sorry, love,' said food-poisoned Karen as she grabbed her handbag and party dress and brushed past Delaney who, for a second, thought he would split with desire. The inarticulate bouncer let the girls pass him, a true eunuch, inadvertent to how well they looked with their glad rags hooked in their elbows and their good legs beneath their bathrobes. When they had all gone by, he released Gorrie and blocked the head of the stairs with his body. Yelling abuse at him, Mansfield and Borissow got dressed in the corridor. Delaney preferred to dress in the dim room where for a short time he had nursed Karen. Her fragrance and that of her colleagues were blended there, not altogether pleasantly, with the tang of a hundred men.

'Come on, Terry,' he heard Eric calling. 'We're off.'

'If King bloody Kong will let us,' Mansfield could be heard screaming.

He led his party downstairs towards the street door, speculating aloud about whether Frankenstein's mother was watching them go on some closed-circuit television set. Before closing the door behind himself and the others, he gestured vastly with his thumb, the old-fashioned profane gesture of their childhood, before Italians and other immigrants had made the middle finger popular in the antipodes.

As they stood in the street, unfulfilled lust and tenderness both souring in Delaney's stomach, he remembered that the first editions of *The Telegraph* and *The Sydney Morning Herald*, detailing his shame, were already printed up. I have no game. I have no love. Employees of the Parramatta lawyer, approached by Margin, had informed their boss, who threatened to have him arrested. In a hearty, corrupt state like New South Wales, it took an idiot like Margin to botch a bribery attempt.

Mansfield had an idea. Why didn't they go up and look at the gay bars in Oxford Street?

'No poofter-bashing,' Eric Samuels stipulated.

'No,' said Mansfield, leading them off. 'Just a visit.'

Everyone told Gorrie what a silly prick he was, except Delaney, who was proveably the silliest prick of the lot. Only loyalty, based on their turning up in Phillip Street earlier in the night, kept him with them at this crack-brained end of the evening.

'These queers are dynamite,' said Mansfield as they began to walk. 'Some of them have five roots a night.'

'That's why they're riddled with disease,' said Gorrie with a sort of bush rectitude.

In Delaney's disordered perception they walked for perpetually dark days. Past car salesrooms on William Street where girls in mini-skirts with pinpoint addicted eyes barely saw them pass. Past little terraces, their doors smack on the street. Delaney would have liked to have gone to sleep, or at least to die for a month or two, on one of those thresholds. After an age they came to Oxford Street and, on a corner, a gay bar called

Cheeks. The very name rocked them with hilarity on the pavement.

The interior of the place was hung with black fabric. A polite and well-built boy in his mid-twenties gave them the sort of lecture the brothel woman had earlier given. They were welcome to have a drink, but would be ejected if they caused trouble. He should also warn them that drinks cost somewhat more than they did in hotels.

'Christ,' said Mansfield. 'You'd think that *we* were the outcasts of bloody society.'

Cheeks was very crowded, even though it was one in the morning. The barman gave a small toss of the head when Mansfield ordered beers. Delaney could see that at remote, dim, candlelit tables Perrier bottles and tall watery drinks were much in evidence. Nearly everyone here wore the loose, voluminous pants which had become fashionable that year, and white shoes with stick-down tabs you didn't have to do up. It's the same everywhere, Delaney recognised, even in the pubs out in Penrith. Everyone has a nightprowling set of gear. Except me, in the sports coat I wore to the judiciary.

They sat at the bar, drinking their beers. Steve Mansfield turned around once or twice, trying to catch an eye, begging trouble.

'Stop begging trouble, Steve,' Delaney warned him.

'How did all this happen?' Mansfield asked the smoky air. 'How did it happen? In the land of the bloody Anzacs?'

None of the others were comfortable. They were bored, they were uneasy. They pecked their beer down into digestions already overloaded. They had come to the wrong place, and there was no time left tonight to find the right one. All of them – except Delaney – had training tomorrow.

'Might be good,' Eric Samuels confided to Delaney, repeating Gorrie's earlier advice, 'if you turned up for training runs. And help on the sideline during games. And when one of us is knocked arse-over-head, run out in a tracksuit with a bucket and a sponge. Might be good to show Golder that the bastards haven't got you down.'

They began to discuss what a good and loyal bloke Golder

was. 'Turning on a lawyer and all. He didn't bloody have to.'

Eric Samuels laughed a little. 'Rough as bloody bags though. His wife's not a bad sort. But a root with him must be like being run down by the Western bloody Pacific.'

Mansfield now grew particularly outraged by the passage to the back of the bar of a boy in a scarlet shirt with spiked carroty hair. 'The things you see when you haven't got a gun!'

But Delaney did not try to follow the boy with his eyes. He was distracted by a familiar voice behind him. It was ordering a reisling and soda, a Campari and soda, a Perrier. As if being suspended for six months were not enough shame, he was about to be discovered in a gay bar by an acquaintance! Then he understood in a sluggish way, all the beer and wine of the evening having spilled to the front of his brain, that the acquaintance was equally vulnerable. He turned. Standing a few paces behind him, in the uniform of Cheeks, the ballooning trousers and the kinky shoes, was Father Doig. What was worse was that Mansfield witnessed the pulse of recognition between Delaney and Doig and began to ask some bumpkin question, 'Hey, aren't you the . . .?'

Doig did not wait to be accused of being anything. He held Delaney's gaze a second, but his face was pale. 'Would you take those over to my table?' he asked the barman. Then he turned and walked out into the street. Delaney left his chair and stumbled after him. Doig was waiting outside.

'Well, Terry,' he said. 'What can I say?'

'Nothing,' Delaney admitted.

'Well, I said it, didn't I? You know – that sexuality could be rationally arranged, that it doesn't have to eat you alive. This is part of my rational arrangement.'

'Are you going to tell your flock about this?' asked Delaney. 'Are you going to explain it away for my old man the way you explain every other bloody thing?'

'I *would* tell them, Terry, if it was within their means to take it in. I should tell you I'm monogamous. A one-man man. I've got a lover who lives out this way, in the eastern suburbs. Without him I would have shot myself.'

Delaney could not sustain the anger as he wanted to. He had

hoped for a while that in Doig he had found the pariah of the evening, but he remained the pariah himself, and in an hour or two people going to work would discover the fact on the back page, Delaney in his best sports jacket and his mute face descending the Phillip Street steps.

'Oh, Jesus, Andrew, you bastard!' said Delaney. The life went from his legs. He sat like a child on the pavement, and for the first time Doig showed old-fashioned embarrassment, or perhaps fear of patrolling police, and tried to drag him upright. Delaney had, however, in a strange self-aware way, lost two-thirds of his consciousness and the control of his limbs.

FIFTY-SIX

By now, on the strength of his ill-starred elevation to the top of the game, Delaney had a telephone in his flat. Gina must have expected as much, have got his number from directory assistance, because one evening she called him. When he heard her he flinched, fearing the tightness of her voice, being intimidated by the correctness with which she offered her sympathies over the matter of his suspension.

As they went on talking, he felt an aggression growing in him. She should be saying, Imagine what we could have done, as a team, with first grade match fees! Imagine what a blow we could have dealt the mortgage! It was unreasonable, Delaney felt, for her not to state that sort of natural regret.

'You probably didn't hear about this,' said Gina. 'It wasn't on television, like poor Brian. A girl had a baby in the fitting room at Fossey's. The one in Main Street. An ambulance man delivered it.' Delaney began to shiver. He could predict the news that was coming. 'It was your friend,' said Gina without any edge, any weight on 'friend'. 'It was Danielle. We were all on the street, watching – thought there'd been a shooting. I saw her carried out on a stretcher. One of those paramedics carried the baby.'

Thanks were not the proper thing. It wasn't right for him, either, to let the phone fall and rush to the district hospital. He asked her how her parents were. Cunning told him that that would quickly end the conversation. As it did. He hung the phone up and spent a little time trembling and distracted, forgetting where his car keys were. Danielle and his child were five minutes down the highway.

The air was full of the sound of protesting babies. The new

generation, Delaney thought, of wronged women and side-stepping five-eighths.

He stopped at the desk by the maternity ward. Still, always, due to Greg's training and his mother's, he was an orderly young man. He could not discover her by bursting through doors. He wanted their reunion to be condoned by the hospital authorities.

He asked for Danielle Kabbel. The woman at the desk tossed sheaths of paper, looking for Danielle's name. This nurse was a pretty woman in perhaps her early thirties, working for the marital mortgage, the first webbings of exhaustion in the corners of her eyes. She couldn't find a Kabbel.

Delaney made a speech about how certain he was she was here, in Penrith District. Unless there were complications. (The idea struck him harder than it did the nurse.) 'But she would have been admitted here,' said Delaney. 'Two days ago.'

The tired mother of two again denied there had been anyone named Kabbel.

'But she gave birth in Main Street, Penrith,' said Delaney. 'It all happened very quickly.'

'Oh, but you mean the Kowolsky child.'

'No. The Kabbel child. Danielle Kabbel gave birth in Fossey's in Main Street.'

'No, not Kabbel. Kowolsky.'

'That's the Polish spelling of their name,' said Delaney with a cleverness he did not know he had. 'I went to school with her, and with her brothers. They grew up in Forth Street, Penrith.'

These homely details captured the nurse. 'That's right. And they live in Kingswood now.'

'Yes,' said Delaney. 'But I don't know the new address.'

'Well, it's that new townhouse set up, isn't it?' said the nurse. 'You know, the one near the Toyota dealership.'

'Oh, yes,' said Delaney.

'Are you *that* five-eighth?'

'That's right,' said Delaney. 'I grew up with the Kabbels – I mean, the Kowolskys.'

At least, amongst all her fatigue and mortgage dedication, the woman knew what a good game of football was. She said, as if it were a service to a team humiliated since the late 1950s, year by year, 'Well, you know the place. Those new townhouses down the highway. Turn left towards the railway line. The Gardens.' She referred to her notes of the recent obstetrical emergency. 'Number 17. But she left within twenty-four hours, you know. A daughter. 3.79 kilos. Tough girl. The brothers and the father wanted to get her home, you know. For once, I pity whoever was the father of the kid.'

'Kowolsky,' said Delaney. He could not believe that a few vowels had defeated him. He muttered his thanks and went off towards the carpark.

The Gardens was one of those small villages of townhouses, well kerbed and guttered, young trees standing along the path-ways. By the time those trees were as large as the one Stanton cut down, Delaney computed, the place would be a slum. For the moment though it had a little style – brick, aluminium windows, shiplap carports. Its internal streets were in the form of a T, and anyone with a child – looking at it and remembering how fast people drove in some suburban streets – would consider it a safe place.

Having spent so long to find the house, Delaney did not now want to approach it too fast. He parked his car in the ill-kerbed and guttered ordinary street which ran past the entrance to the development, and walked in. Number 17 was in the head of the T. It was quiet around the corner. Everyone seemed to be a considerate neighbour. A man of about Delaney's age was kicking a plastic football to his toddling son who – wearing a frown – picked it up slowly with hands splayed from the wrist. At Number 11 a man with slicked hair, wearing both the well-scrubbed after-work look of someone who perhaps laboured in a foundry as well as the prosperous look of someone who cops plenty of overtime, was washing a new Camira. Delaney recognised Rudi Kabbel's Commodore, pride of the fleet of Uncle Security, standing in front of 17. He stood for a while contemplating it, then he turned in past it to the front door and knocked. By his left shoulder were the kitchen windows, but their blinds were pulled down. It was Delaney's intuition that they were down at this hour, when anyone would want them up to catch the last of the afternoon sun, for defensive reasons. The Kabbels were inside, he knew, and they *knew* he could tell it. He did not need to knock again. Someone was sure to answer. Peculiarly, he believed he would only know what to say if it was one of the boys.

It *was* one of the boys. It was Warwick. He opened the door carefully, as if there had been trouble with the hinges. He said hello in his polite, deliberate way. It reminded Delaney of the deliberateness with which the man's son, a few seconds before, had picked up the football.

Delaney asked him how he was. The house had what Delaney thought of as a cold breath, as if the Kabbels had switched off all lights, all radiators, refrigerators, blenders, lest light and warmth and whirring gave Delaney delusions of welcome.

'Warwick,' said Delaney, 'I'd like to see the baby. And I'd like to talk to Danielle too.'

'Well, that's all very well,' said Warwick, frowning. 'Danielle doesn't want to talk to you though.'

'Is Rudi there?'

'Rudi's busy.'

'Look,' said Delaney. He had none of the eloquence he thought he would have when first seeing a Kabbel again. 'Let me see her. And it's my daughter. Not yours. Let me see my daughter.'

'A second,' said Warwick.

He closed the door on Delaney. There would be a Kabbel conference, a busy affair, a hushed one. Delaney stood in the last of the sun and could hear nothing. When Warwick came back, Delaney meant to tell him, 'I hope you gave Danielle a vote. I'm voting for the child.'

Warwick opened the door again. He carried a shotgun in his hands, the breech opened and pointed to Delaney so that he could see both barrels were loaded. With that workmanlike calm of his, Warwick closed the breech and pointed the barrels at Delaney's chest.

'Now listen, Terry,' said Warwick. 'None of us want to see you. We want you to stay away. You know what I'm capable of, eh?'

Even threatened like this, Delaney was still straining to gauge the air of the house, the nuances of scent. Later he would tell himself it was his long experience of teams calloused by defeat which now helped him pick up one of the strains – the acrid musk of lost faith. He remembered now his source at the Newnes pub, the single, never since repeated fully loaded visit of the Kabbels to their canyon.

Without any fear, but out of a conviction that there was a balance inside the house which could easily turn on the baby, Delaney himself reached for the door handle and shut the door on the gun. If the balance was disturbed, armies couldn't save the baby girl. Delaney walked past the carport and out on to the pavement with a confidence that the thing could be done. Warwick's politeness would help do it. Social workers and child-care people could negotiate that politeness.

As he passed the man with the Camira, the well-scrubbed man of Number 11, Delaney saw him wink.

'Come to cut something off, mate?' the man asked him. Delaney did not understand. Because of vibrations in his legs, he would have liked to sit for a while at the man's feet. But a Camira-owner might be appalled by that sort of behaviour.

'They've got nothing left on,' said the man, nodding towards the Kabbels' place. 'Telephone disconnected, electricity. I reckon someone will cut their water off pretty soon.'

Delaney went to turn back to Number 17, to take up this matter with Warwick. The Camira man wanted to be fair though.

'Nice enough people. Dress well. You'd never know there were four people in the place. Five including the baby. And they like the baby OK. Give it a fair bit of sun.'

'But no heat,' said Delaney.

'I suppose they rug up,' said the man.

FIFTY-SEVEN

My sister's letter continues, speaking of happenings inside Michelstadt during my abduction:

> Albert, my sergeant, had an idea of what had happened to you. Not perhaps a concise idea. But he knew it was Belorussian vengeance. All the French guards were in the same position. They knew that it was all beyond the control of Colonel Nouges, that the inmates were dominant, that they might yet have to watch the factional version of gang warfare.
>
> Redich wanted father to find and cough up the Soviet informer. If he could not do that, he would never see you; or perhaps he would see some savaged part of you – a limb or a head. And you still like Belorussians?
>
> Father was of course desperate. On a visit to the family suite of rooms, I heard him tell mother that he had more chance of finding where they had hidden you than of producing a supposed Russian agent. I have heard from old Belorussians here that some time that night Redich and father met, and father put forth an argument he had rehearsed with his – believe me on this point, Radek – inconsolable wife. The argument was this. Suppose there happened to be a Soviet agent or informer but he was in fact a member of the Redich gang. He could well have denounced Gersich as a means of dividing the two factions, of rendering them impotent with mistrust.
>
> Redich would not buy it. He imposed a time limit though. The delinquent had to be surrendered before midnight

the next night. Father and his lieutenants had only some thirty hours in which to find the informer, or if they could not do that, at least deliver to Redich someone they could plausibly call the informer. And father would have found a scapegoat; police work had prepared him for that sort of expedient. Unhappily, he would not have to find any substitute victim. The true victim would present.

Any small intelligence I could extract from Albert and the soldiers, and which I then tried to pass to him later in the night, was spurned. It did not matter anyhow. Amazingly neither the French nor most of the Belorussians knew about the latrines in the old camp. Even if I had known, and had tried to pass him the news, he would have looked upon that as an unwelcome distraction. He had room only for his vanished son. He couldn't deal at the same time with his floozy daughter.

Most of the searches that night were therefore carried on discreetly and within the camp. Father's intelligence set-up told him that none of the Redich lieutenants were outside the wire. That indicated that you also were not outside the wire, but were perhaps trussed and hidden in some ceiling. Although Redich had counselled father not to bother, somehow these little quests were achieved. Or perhaps Redich tolerated them. In any case, you were sought that night not only in ceilings but in broom cupboards, in the lockers where the UNRRA sporting equipment was kept, in the freezers which were America's gift to Michelstadt, in the tool shop and the generator house. The camp doctor had to sedate Tokina, whose recitation of the Rosary for your deliverance had become more and more hysterical.

This woman, my truest friend, had allied herself with father in the idea that somehow my wickedness had brought it all on. Needless to say, if they wanted to drive me into Sergeant Pointeaux's arms they couldn't have done a better job. But I am philosophic about all that now. It's the way families generally operate. It is true though that during those two days I itched not only with panic for you

but with a sort of panic for myself, that my blame would
be demonstrated somehow, by a court of enquiry run by
the French or the Belorussians or both, that everyone
from Tokina to Major Knowles would be summoned as
witnesses.

You remember there was a young policeman called
Kalusich. He was often attached to the guard at our house
in Staroviche. You would certainly remember his child-like
face – the cupid-bow lips and the bland eyes, combined
with a relentless blue shadow of beard. Other members of
the guard teased him about it, sometimes making jokes
that weren't proper and which therefore went through me
like an electric shock, both pleasant and intolerable. I bet
you remember him, because you used to hang around the
kitchen too, being lionised, if you will pardon me for
saying so, after the Onkel Willi affair.

Well, by the noon of the day of grace father had from
Redich, this young naif was being groomed as the 'informer'.
One of father's sergeants of police, who had served with
the Belarus Brigade and survived the rout at Biscencon,
and who now lives in Paris, told me when I visited him in
an old people's home here. For I went through that phase
too – a desire to find out everything that had happened
during those few days, an uneasiness about the accepted
version. The old man told me that it was proposed both to
lie to Kalusich about the other faction's intentions, to
minimise what could happen to him, and at the same time
to threaten him with worse things if he did not allow
himself to be served up to the Papal gang. They were going
to force-feed him his lines. The old man told me that at
the time he didn't think it would fool Redich. But father
was desperate. His judgment had gone.

As for the rest of the incident, and as for what happened
with mother – Pointeaux has always known what
occurred. As I remarked earlier, he is the sort who always
knows what's going on even though intuitions of survival
generally tell him not to put his hand into the machinery.
It was a result of my enquiry amongst old Belorussians

of both factions here in Paris – the Abramtchik crowd are very strong here and some of them work for French intelligence – that Pointeaux decided he had better be the one to inform me. He said that he used to wonder, if I discovered the true story from some old buffer in a hospital, how I would manage to drive home. I have known the facts now for nearly ten years.

You remember how that partisan officer put his head under Onkel Willi's table and said, 'It's the Kabbelski brat,' and didn't do any more. I think father was troubled by that, though not in the same way as if he had lost you. Remember another incident – you may not, in fact. But there was a very fashionable young clerk in Mayor Kuzich's office. Her name was Drusova. She was an agent of the partisans. In the end she vanished in the cellar of the Natural History Museum – remember Bienecke? Hauptsturmführer Bienecke. He was sentenced to eight years by the West Germans – that was in the late '60s. In any case, back to Drusova. She had not been betrayed by anyone – Kuzich had found her stealing documents. The reason you came out of the shambles at Onkel Willi's had much to do with Drusova being caught through her own folly, rather than through the work of an informer.

In saying that I'm temporising. I'll get to the crux. I believe that mother and Drusova had a pact. Mother fed Drusova certain information in return for immunity for her husband and children. Mother was already fed up with Belorussian politics, with flights from Minsk and other places. We knew that very well as children. It is a truism that some people like to pretend the reason that there are more men in politics than women is that women are oppressed. The fact is that women so often have a different kind of politics imposed on them by their biology. Some women anyhow – there is always Rosa Luxemburg and Jeanne d'Arc, and I'm unsure what they do to my proposition.

But the deal between the partisans and Mrs Danielle

Kabbelski was that we had immunity. It is quite possible that
if all the plenteous guards had been withdrawn from around
our house in Staroviche, we would still have lived. Your
experience under the table indicates that.

At nine o'clock on the night of the deadline, father went
to Redich and told him that he hoped within the hour to
be able to produce the culprit. The hatred which ran
between my father and Redich must have been unspeakable,
but Redich would have welcomed that, was the sort of man
to whom politics *was* hatred.

And so, when father came to Redich promising results,
Redich took improper joy in telling father there was no need
to drum up a fake culprit. The true informer had already
turned herself in. She was locked in a storeroom. She
was Danielle Kabbelski. She had given enough detail to
condemn herself, and in that process she had condemned her
friend Galina as well.

Remember Daskovich? He was a promising young civil
administrator they put out in one of the villages in the
hope that he would run it in a model manner. He was
apparently gunned down on the road home after a
conference in town. Well, old-timers who were at the trial
tell me that that was one of the things mother confessed
to – setting Daskovich up for the partisans. She confessed
also that Galina had recruited her to betray Gersich.

Father spent most of her immediate and so-called trial
in a daze. He was shamed, an old man told me, but he
wanted to save her. He objected that Drusova, working in
the mayor's office, would have known about Daskovich's
itinerary without needing to be told by my mother.

Standing before those gangsters, mother expressed no
enmity of Galina. Poor Galina had been blackmailed by
the NKVD, she said. When Galina recruited her, it had
been in a sisterly manner. Galina had said something like:
'I need a few names to keep Sedlov's people happy. It
would be best if they were men with real crimes in their
past. Do it or I might be killed by the NKVD. Do it or the
Soviets might be moved by frustration to unravel the

whole business of forged identities, might come in here and
take everyone.'

Albert, who gave me the crucial news that mother had
not suicided, and all the old men who later confirmed the
story, say – as if it is to be a consolation for me – that she
died well. These bumpkin Belorussians who have all of
them shot Jews and villagers in the neck yet play with the
concept of honourable and dishonourable death! In any
case, she made her contrition, signed a forged suicide note,
and was hanged from the rafters – a degrading business,
a woman hanging in front of men. They all tell me it was
quick, but they would say that anyhow. According to their
vision of what is proper, some say that father and mother
embraced before the hanging, and others that he showed
a proper reserve towards a traitor.

Galina's body was never found. One would not want to
imagine her death. Mother had said at the trial that in a
panic the evening before Galina had tried to strangle her.
I can understand the poor bitch's panic. She was no doubt
carried out of the camp as you were and set upon in the
woods behind the old forced labour camp, then tormented
and murdered. Colonel Nouges would be easily convinced
she had gone missing. That tart was always clearing off to
Stuttgart with her boyfriend.

Immediately after the execution, father was taken out of
the camp to the latrine pits where Redich said you were
hidden. They uncovered the one your abductors pointed to
and found nothing. It was the one, however, since
blankets could be seen down there, and the marks of your
remarkable escape were visible on the edges of the pit.
They followed your tracks and found you behind a pile of
lumber, raving about that Uncle you always spoke of in
your fits, the Uncle I always thought was an extension of
Onkel Willi, someone who was not too busy with
history-making to play a few stupidly wise games with
children. You would of course always maintain that he
had hauled you out of the pit, but poor little sod! You had
hauled yourself out. The state of your fingernails showed

that. You were treated for pneumonia and exposure, told
that mother had suicided, that the uncertainty of her life
had become too much for her.

And father lost his camp leadership and its attendant
privileges, and Tokina let herself waste away and turned her
face to the wall during the following summer, and Albert
was honourably discharged and I went with him – yes, I
even have father's signature on a form. Father had become
a passive man and had lost faith in the whole business. I
knew that if I went wherever he intended to go, it would
be the end of me.

I believe that father emerged from this passivity once in
the ensuing years, in 1955, when Redich fell from a train
in Sydney. If you have ever wondered about this incident,
it is now all explained. Most of the old-time Belorussians
here in Paris take it for granted that Redich was pushed,
and that he deserved to be. You were already in Australia,
studying to become an Australian, when the whole factional
thing came to its head in 1951. Abramtchik's people had
a lot of support from an American secret service
organisation called the Office of Policy Coordination. This
organisation was betting both sides of the factional fence,
and decided to do what the Germans had done before
them, to train both Abramtchik and Ostrowsky people at a
parachute training school in West Germany with the
intention of dropping them into Belorussia and the Ukraine.
The Office of Policy Coordination would spend a fortune
getting these people ready and would drop them 'behind
the lines' – that is how they saw it – and the next time they
would lay eyes on them was when they saw film footage of
their press conferences in Moscow where they would
point to the Western equipment issued to them for their
missions and would beg pardon of the Soviet People. This
happened so much to Abramtchik's people that he began
to lose his hold on the Allies, and Ostrowsky, over in
South River, New Jersey, was the man the Americans in
particular came to trust.

It turned out that both Ostrowsky and Abramtchik came

to believe that the bipartisan blight on their efforts behind the Soviet lines was Redich. Redich had a friend, a spy named Kim Philby, who worked in the Office of Policy Coordination. Philby eventually had to flee to the East. Redich they sent to Australia on a fund-raising expedition. There he could meet the one man they were sure would not let him alight from a train unharmed.

The old-timers here tell me that in those days the doors on trains in Sydney did not pneumatically shut. That did not matter because Australians were innocents and had no ancient grievances against each other. In European cultures they have to be far more careful in such matters.

So Ostrowsky simply sent the news to father, that Redich was – as they say – a mole, that Redich may have been a mole even in Michelstadt and that mother might have died merely to protect his cover. My hope is father gave him a good heave and that he did not die at once.

There it is, Radek. Since it is now late at night and I am exhausted, all I can do is to leave you with the burden of this family news. You must swallow it as I did. You have my affection and best wishes.

Your loving sister,
GENIA

PART THREE

FIFTY-EIGHT

Delaney had put on his best suit for the visit to the Sinclair Funeral Home, an old and gracious farmhouse which the town, in growing westward towards the river, had subsumed. His mind had for the past week been steadied only by his daily call to Penrith detectives to discover when the bodies would be released for burial. Sergeant Dick Webster, an old footballer who – in the time of innocence – had sometimes put a meaty, approving hand on Delaney's shoulder on Leagues Club Sunday nights, had warned him that in view of the wounds there could be no question of open coffins. But it was still worthwhile going to visit the place. Webster had seen enough of the mystery of death and the paradoxes of mourning to know that.

Delaney got there early in the afternoon of a fine day in early May. He shared the waiting room with a slight, frayed blonde woman. The place was well provided with magazines on sailing and photography, as if this were a dentist's surgery. Perhaps whoever Sinclair was saw it in those terms, saw himself as the kindly dispenser of the novocaine of funeral rites.

The blonde woman was trying to read a boating magazine. She had turned the pages back on glossies of twelve-metre yachts, none of which she could ever expect to own. She kept glancing at Delaney.

At last she said, 'My condolences.'

Delaney had to force his vocal chords. 'And mine to you,' he muttered.

'Is it a . . . a parent of yours, perhaps?'

'No, it's a girlfriend.' He began crying, and she came and sat beside him and placed a dry hand on his hand.

'You're here for the Kabbels, aren't you?' she said. 'You know my daughter Danielle.'

The odd use of the present instead of the past was the only betrayal of grief. He looked at her amazed. From this woman came Danielle!

'I'm Mrs Kabbel,' she said. 'I married Rudi in 1955 – we had to put the wedding off because of that other fellow, Redich, falling out of a train at Lidcombe. But, oh yes, I knew that all this was going to happen. I left as if my life depended on it. Soon as Scott was thirteen. Dear God, I can't believe he'd do it, though I knew he would.'

'He?' asked Delaney. 'Which he?'

'All of them,' she said, her eyes unfocused.

It was the right time to state his holy intention. 'I'm going to take the baby. And Danielle, needless to say. The baby's my own.'

'Oh no,' she said, staring at the mid-distance. 'No sense in that. Let them go down with Rudi. Danielle wanted to be some sort of chosen person. Let her go down with damn Rudi. The state runs to not such bad funerals for murder victims who leave a bit of property. Let the state put them all down together. Don't you reckon?'

But he knew the woman was mad. The term 'put them down' – it was a giveaway. As if two Pekingese she owned were pissing on the carpet. 'Put them down!' She wanted the Kabbels and the child disposed of in a lump. For that reason he recognised her at once as an enemy.

'Listen,' he said, finding himself with some surprise on his feet. 'Don't try that! Don't try that on. You're bloody tired of them, eh? I'm not tired of them, you callous bitch. If I could I'd bury them in bloody Northern Queensland.'

The woman rose because she thought he might offer blows. She was angry enough to return them. 'Don't talk to me like that, you damned lout! Because you slept with Danielle a few times doesn't give you any right! I carried the whole mess for years – the voices and the seances and that terrible old father and the talk about Belorussia and people whose names all ended in *chik* and *sky*. I saw Rudi through his fits. So don't call me a bitch or mess up my funeral plans. My husband, my damn children! And I want to be finished with them at one hit!'

Delaney seized her by the upper arms. Full of the ruggedness of a woman who has only to see one simple thing done before she can breathe again, she struck him over the face with her handbag, broke the hold more effortlessly than most professional footballers had in the past two seasons, and fled out into reception. Delaney pursued her. A young man in a suit turned up from the inner chambers of the funeral home, the place where Danielle and Alexandra were lying, inadequately prepared for the earth. The receptionist was standing at her typewriter and telephone, wide-eyed. At a nod from the young man in the suit, she called a number. Delaney was sure that it was Penrith police the girl had called. He had time for his mad plan. He had not been strong enough to hold Rudi Kabbel's wife, yet he believed he might yet carry away Danielle and the child.

He explained the scheme to the young man. The young man said, 'Sir, you should compose yourself. It isn't your place. There was a document the police found with the bodies, I hope you understand that. Requesting a communal grave.'

Delaney decided to fight his way through into the place where the dead were kept, but the young man, a muscular pallbearer beneath his good suit, did his best to block him. And now, Delaney could hear behind him, Mrs Kabbel had found her tears, was loudly keening.

'Cheryl,' the young man groaned, struggling with Delaney, 'tell them to hurry!'

Another man, middle-aged, suntanned from standing beside summer graves and dressed in a more sepulchral suit than the young one, appeared from behind a curtain and helped hold Delaney immobile. This second one was tough. Delaney found himself on the floor, a strong forearm, garbed in black serge, clamped across his chest. Delaney raved and pleaded, but realised that by his craziness he had forfeited the right to be heard. The argument therefore that at least the child should not be buried with its murderers meant nothing to either muscular undertaker.

He heard the sirens drawing close down Main Street, heard the police arrive, heard three sets of boots on the parquetry. He saw old Dick Webster's ageless and ravaged face above him.

'Let go of the man,' Dick Webster told the two undertakers, and only then asked Delaney whether he would do the right thing, if he was going to be sensible.

By now Delaney was beyond sense or resistance. In a short time, without remembering what moves were made to achieve it, he found himself in the back of a patrol car, hunched over his knees, between which he sheltered his hands, and drenching his shirt with tears and saliva.

FIFTY-NINE

'One thing,' said Dick Webster, echoing the wisdom Stanton had once learned from the Serbian husband, 'is that family is very strong. And when a family's got some crazy illusion, that's strongest of all.'

Delaney was very familiar with this small and tired truth. But he loved Webster for going on talking like this – it was exactly the sort of talk Delaney wanted to hear – something that passed for an explanation. Webster had all the marks of the New South Wales walloper – the crenellated face, the brewer's goitre slung over his belt. Once, when he was an unimaginable boy, he had played for Wests, before there was any money in the game. All the marks. Seeing him in his suit, you knew at once he was a detective, a cop badly disguised as a member of society. But what he still had was the ability to be shocked. Delaney could gratefully see that Rudi Kabbel had shocked Webster. Warwick and Scott Kabbel had shocked him. Danielle had shocked him profoundly by being passive. His shock was precious to Delaney, a prodigious comfort. And with it came a willingness to speculate about the Kabbels, and why families should go to hell in a group.

Webster began with his own homely example. 'My wife's family,' he said. 'The thing with them was a disinheritance in the bloody Edwardian era, or maybe early world war one, I'm not interested enough to know the date exactly. My wife's grandfather was cut out of the family wealth because he got into the piss and that crowd were temperance. Quite a pile of money he missed out on. Now my mother-in-law, when I first met her, lived like bloody nobility in exile in a little terrace at Stanmore. She didn't have any sort of life at all – her delusions didn't let her live working class, her poverty wouldn't stretch to anything else. And that's the way *my* wife lived as a girl. It was blokes like me who had to break the news to them, her and her sister, that sorry and all that, but they were just girls from Stanmore.'

'*He* was like that,' said Delaney. 'They all were. Even Danielle. Nobility in bloody exile. He thought he was somewhere else.'

Webster drank reflectively. He's a happy man too, Delaney realised with surprise. Like old Greg. How did they manage it, on a dangerous planet like this?

'You know,' Webster said, 'he was a cluey bastard, Terry. He left a family history, he translated his old man's diary from bloody Belorussian and his sister's letters from French. The state psychiatrist from Long Bay – he's going to give evidence at the inquest – said Kabbel reminds him of that Polish sailor who started writing novels in English. You know, Joseph Conrad.'

Delaney flinched. Danielle had at one time been studying *Heart of Darkness*.

'Talent to burn, poor bloody Rudi Kabbel. But he believed in this voice he heard, this character called Uncle. There are some people of the same nationality have a coffee shop in Parramatta, and Rudi – intelligent Rudi Kabbel – would go round there and talk to these people's old uncle, who could only speak *that* language, and Rudi took everything the poor old bugger said literally. Whereas the old man was senile, the family knew that. He's in Lidcombe geriatric right now, in a coma and on life support.'

'I searched for the old man everywhere,' said Delaney. 'In all the bloody ethnic dives.'

Webster laughed gently and then stifled the laughter. 'It wasn't any Wog cafe the old man came from. It was a place called The Boomerang Milk Bar. Owned by Belorussians sure, but catering to hardcore Aussies.'

Delaney himself began to laugh and Webster joined him uncertainly. What camouflage! The Boomerang Milk Bar!

It was upstairs at the Boomerang, in the flat above the shop, that the old fellow had given the date when civilisation would cease, had slipped the news to Rudi. And on account of that Rudi had bought his farm, stocked it with explosives, had sold his house and let his business go to hell. To keep this holy date, he had taken his family in two cars, towing two trailers, into

Heather's Glen and, nothing happening, had come back down
to the plains again to consult his Belorussian prophet at the
Boomerang Milk Bar. The relatives said there had been a
frightful scene, the old man had grown terrified and yelled, 'His
father killed his mother! His father killed his mother!' He could
just as easily have yelled, 'Fish live underwater!' It was all senile
gibberish. But on hearing it Rudi had suffered a fit and passed
out. Apparently it related to some idea Rudi already harboured
about his father.

'Did you know he had all those weapons?' Dick Webster asked
Delaney. 'Magnum .357s – two of those. Two .22 rifles, three
shotguns, a carbine.'

'Warwick threatened me with a shotgun once.'

'Could've sold them to pay the rent and electricity if that'd
been the point. Warwick – Warwick had a bloody crossbow. All
prepared to shoot wild pigs west of Lithgow when civilisation
ended!'

Civilisation had ended, Delaney came close to telling the
policeman. Mothers died placidly without begging for their
babies' lives.

'And bloody manuals of booby-traps. Would have been damned
difficult to get into the Kabbel property once that tidal wave he
talked about turned up.'

Delaney was pleased to be where they were, in this particular
crowded bar. Webster, after calming him down at the station,
had offered to take him to the Leagues Club, but Delaney
hadn't wanted that, hadn't wanted footballers coming up to
commiserate with him for breaking Lynch's mandible. They had
come to the saloon bar of the Oarsman therefore. Webster
drank scotch for, as he said, the sake of his waterworks, which
must have been extensive in that mass of flesh. Delaney had no
such inhibition. He was young and muscular, had nothing any
more to *do* with his body. He could sin with impunity, if it made
any sense. He drank as quickly as he could, feeling a blunt ache
at the back of his neck, the first sign of the leaden irrational
hope which liquor could generate in him.

Webster asked him, 'Remember that Jonestown thing, few
years ago now. Someone like Rudi took a thousand people into

the South American bush and made a town. Same idea – the world would end and only that little group would come up trumps. Same thing happened, people began to close in, police and politicians. The bloke in charge just like Kabbel, mad as a meat-axe, and suddenly the world isn't going to end for his convenience, isn't going to come his way. So they all drink lime cordial full of cyanide. Some had to be forced, but most were willing. And the thing is, some took it because they still believed in the miracle bloody man, and others took it because they'd lost faith but didn't want to live on without someone divine telling them which way to jump. Same thing here. Same thing exactly.'

He waved to a barmaid who came at once to serve them. He had some pull over her – perhaps once he'd let her off possession of marijuana.

'You don't have to remember any of this,' Webster, draining the watery scotch he still had left, told Delaney. 'I'm the officer assisting the coronial enquiry and I won't forget it for some time yet. But you're under no obligation. Clean slate. Will your missus take you back?'

'She's Italian,' Delaney said, hoping – not for the first time – that that would do as a total explanation. After giving it, he found himself weeping against his best will not to. He was shamed because Webster might think it was merely marital remorse, doubt about whether his Italian wife might forgive him.

'OK, son,' Webster murmured. 'It's been fucking horrifying, I know.' The mountainous detective took him at once by the elbow and helped him out of the saloon. It might have looked a bit comic, Delaney understood without caring a damn. It might have looked halfway between arrest and protective custody. No one in the saloon took any notice except an idiot by the door looking up from the afternoon *Sun*, the sort of fool who bought the paper not to find out if the geriatric President intended to fry us all in our tracks, but to play the Bingo card thrown in with each copy. 'Did a Rabbitoh hit 'im back?' the man asked Webster.

'Watch your bloody mouth,' said Webster.

There were thunderclouds over the mountains, a sheet of falling water over Brian Stanton's way. Stanton waited on bail, under that torrent, for his case to come up. If he did something irrational, fled to the Northern Territory, say, it would break Delaney for life.

Webster propped him against the boot of his Holden and asked him how he was.

'I know,' said Webster, repeating his original thesis. 'You thought you could lever her out of that mob. We all have ourselves on about that. But it's their hutch, you know, their original nest, that's what counts with them. While they're becoming the very woman their old woman was, they keep on being the girl they were there, you know, in a home you know bugger-all about, a foreign country. I mean if you don't believe me, I'll give you a loan of some of the stuff Kabbel wrote.'

Choking on the words, Delaney said, 'I'd like to read that stuff.'

'No you wouldn't. Besides, it's really not available until after the inquest. Look, I've got to go, taking the missus to Parramatta for dinner. Forget it, eh? Give yourself a chance. And don't fight the burial arrangements. The message they left was in favour of the present set-up. They want to be interred together. Wouldn't surprise me if they all bloody expect to rise again.'

'They didn't ask the child for its opinion. All right for them to bloody lie together!'

Webster said, 'Oh Jesus!' and kicked one of the front tyres of Delaney's car. 'Listen, the people next door heard Danielle talking at the back of the house that morning. They heard her say to her father, "Don't be cruel!" She wasn't shouting, just conversational. "Don't be cruel." Did I mention that to you?'

'No.'

Delaney could hear her, the sentence was palpable. It was the dominant aspect of the earth. It hung over the parking area, the automobile-crazed highway, the hacking voices of men on their way to drink. Delaney saw Webster anxious all at once that he had made a mistake, that he had given a further argument for the rescue of Danielle's body and the child's from the Kabbel shambles. And that Delaney would use the news rashly, build it into a system of faith that would cause him mischief in the end.

'And I'll tell you something else,' said the detective quickly. 'You can't look at her as a victim in the normal sense of the word. She lay on the bed, Terry, and pulled a pillow over her head and waited for Warwick to finish her. It was a calm death. Believe me, I've seen all the variations.'

After Webster had gone to take his wife to dinner, Delaney sat on in his car. His hands were slung over the steering wheel, but the clammy tedium of the thing, manufactured of something chemical which mimicked both cloth and steel, revolted him at last and made him drop his hands into his lap. The rain made marks like tiny fractures on his windscreen and then fell without stint.

'Don't be cruel,' said a voice to his left.

Author's Note

In a suburb of Sydney, Australia, in July 1984, a family of five willingly ended their lives. Their consent to their own destruction had its roots in events which occurred during world war two, in voices heard and insupportable fears endured in that era.

Apart from this broad similarity with real events, the chief figures of *A Family Madness* are not meant to resemble anyone alive now or in the past, even though some of the minor characters bear the names and traits of historical figures.

The author would like to thank NEC Australia for their assistance with computer services during the writing of this novel. He would also wish to acknowledge the invaluable Belorussia information contained in *The Belarus Secret* by John Loftus.

THOMAS KENEALLY

SCHINDLER'S ARK

Winner of the 1982 Booker McConnel Prize

In the shadow of Auschwitz, a flamboyant German industrialist grew into a living legend to the Jews of Cracow. He was a womanizer, a heavy drinker and a bon viveur but to them, he was a saviour.

This is the story of Oskar Schindler who risked his life to protect the beleagured Jews in Nazi-occupied Poland, who continually defied the SS, and who was transformed by the war into a man with a mission, a compassionate angel of mercy.

'An extraordinary achievement'
Graham Greene

'Brilliantly detailed, moving, powerful and gripping'
The Times

'A magnificent book, powerful, harrowing and beautifully written'
Sunday Express

'Thomas Keneally has done marvellous justice to a marvellous story'
Sunday Times

'Keneally is a superb storyteller. With SCHINDLER'S ARK he has given us his best book yet, a magnificent novel which held me from the first page to the last'
Alan Sillitoe